HOW TO UNDRESS A MARQUESS

LAUREN ROYAL

March 2021 Edition
FORMERLY TITLED "EMERALD"

HOW TO UNDRESS A MARQUESS by Lauren Royal

Formerly titled EMERALD
Originally published in paperback by Penguin Putnam Inc.

Published by Novelty Books, a division of Novelty Publishers, LLC, 205 Avenida Del Mar #275, San Clemente, CA 92674

March 2021 Edition

Cover Art Illustration by The Midnight Muse

Learn more about the author and her books at www.LaurenRoyal.com.

ISBN: 978-1-63469-151-2

MORE CHASE FAMILY BOOKS

❧

For my mother,
Joan Falbaum Royal,
who taught me how to read and write

and

For my father,
Herbert Charfess Royal,
who taught me to appreciate and
respect all genres of literature

With my everlasting love to you both

ONE

Chichester, England
August 1, 1667

"*J*ASON, YOU cannot mean to kill him."

Jason Chase stopped short and wrenched from the grasp his brother Ford had on his upper arm. "By God, no. But I'll learn why he did this and bring him to justice if it's the last thing I do."

"I've never seen you like this—"

"Because *I've* never seen anything like sweet little Mary lying still as death. Or her mother's torn clothes and bruised face as she chanted Geoffrey Gothard's name over and over." Trembling with rage, Jason's hand came up to worry his narrow black mustache. "My villagers." He met Ford's gaze with his own. "My responsibility."

"You've plastered the kingdom with broadsides." Ford's blue eyes looked puzzled, as though he were unsure how to take this new side of his oldest sibling. "The reward will bring him in."

"I'm bloody well satisfied to bring him in myself."

Jason turned and continued down East Street to where Chichester's vaulted Market Cross sat in the center of the Roman-walled town. Carved from limestone, it was arguably the most elaborate structure in all of England...but the beauty of its intricate tracery was at odds with the evil that lurked inside.

An evil that Jason intended to deal with.

Scattered businessmen, exchanging mail and news beneath the dome, paused to glance his way. He recognized the Gothard brothers from the descriptions his villagers had given him: Geoffrey, tall and slim with a stance that bordered on elegant; Walter, shorter and rawboned.

Jason's footsteps echoed as he strode through the open arches, his own brother following behind. In their wake, people seemed to stream from all four corners of town, rushing to catch the show.

Walter Gothard scurried back like a frightened rabbit.

With a click of his spurred heels, Jason came to a halt and drew an uneven breath. He pinned Geoffrey Gothard with a furious gaze. "You'll come with me to the magistrate," he snapped out, surprising even himself at the commanding tone of his voice.

Gothard merely stared at him. For a fleeting moment Ford seemed dumbfounded, then he stepped away and motioned back the crowd.

Jason's hand went to the hilt of his sword. "Now, Gothard."

The other man's gaze held hard and unwavering. "My nearest and dearest enemy," he drawled in an insolent tone.

A line Jason recognized from Shakespeare. The man wasn't uneducated, then—indeed, his bearing was aristocratic, and his clothes, though rumpled from days of wear, were of good quality and cut.

Confusion churned with the anger in Jason's stomach. "Why should you call me your enemy?"

Gothard's gaze roamed Jason from head to toe. "The Marquess of Cainewood, are you not?"

"I am," Jason said through gritted teeth. He wanted nothing more than to go home to his calm routine, back to his estate, his life. But he could think only of little golden-haired Mary following him around the village, begging him for a sweetmeat, her blue eyes dancing with mischief and radiating trust.

Blue eyes that might never open again.

And there stood the man who had battered her, shaded by the Gothic structure overhead.

"I've done nothing to draw your ire—we've never met." Jason

squinted at the man in the shadows. Gothard and his brother were pale, with the type of skin that burned and peeled with any exposure to the sun—and it looked as though they'd seen much exposure of late. "Stand down and consign yourself to my arrest."

The man's blue eyes went stony with resentment. Jason blinked. He seemed to know those eyes.

Maybe they *had* crossed paths.

"To the devil with you, Cainewood."

Jason squared his shoulders, reminding himself why he was here. For justice. Honor. The questions could wait—for now.

He slowly counted to ten, focusing on the fat needle of a spire that topped the old Norman cathedral across the green. As responsibility weighed heavily on his mind, his hand tightened on the hilt of his sword.

Father would have expected this of him. To defend what was his, stand up for what was right—no matter the personal cost.

Deliberately he drew the rapier from its scabbard.

"Damn you to bloody hell." Gothard pulled his own sword with a quick *screak* that snapped the expectant silence. "We'll settle this here and now."

Jason advanced a step closer, slowly circled the tip of his rapier, then sliced it hissing through the air in a swift move that brought a collective gasp from the crowd. The blade's thin shadow flickered across the paving stones.

His free hand trembled at his side.

With a roar, Gothard lunged, and the first clash of steel on steel rang through the still summer air.

The vibrations shimmied up Jason's arm. Muscles tense, he twisted and parried, danced in to attack, then out of harm's way. His heart pounded; blood pumped furiously through his veins.

Like most men of his class, he'd been trained and spent countless hours in swordplay—but this was no game. And his opponent was skillful as well.

Two blades clanked with deadly intent in the shadow of the Market Cross.

TWO

*A*DAM LESLIE dipped his quill in the inkwell and carefully added "My" in front of "Dear Sister," frowned, then squeezed in "est" in the middle. *My Dearest Sister.* There now, surely Caithren wouldn't be miffed at his news after such an affectionate greeting.

Gazing up at the paneled walls of the Royal Arms, he flipped his straight dark blond hair—so like his sister's—over his shoulder. That he wouldn't be home soon shouldn't come as a surprise to her —it wasn't as though he'd spent more than a few weeks total at home these five years past. But it wouldn't hurt to be loving when he imparted the news...he did love her. And he knew that she loved him as well, even if he was rarely home.

Och, Scotland was boring. He was happy to leave the running of the Leslie lands to Cait and their father. He chuckled to himself, imagining Da's latest ineffective efforts to marry her off.

"Are you not finished yet, Leslie?"

He glanced over and smiled at his friends, the Earl of Balmforth and Viscount Grinstead. Dandies, they were, dressed in brightly colored satin festooned with jewels and looped ribbons. Though he kept himself decked out in similar style, he considered himself lucky they let him keep their company, untitled as he was —at least until his very healthy father died sometime in the distant future.

Da was naught but a minor baronet, so Adam wasn't entitled to call himself anything but Mister until he inherited.

"Leslie?"

"Almost done," Adam muttered, pushing back the voluminous lace at his cuffs before signing his name to the bottom of the letter. He sprinkled sand on the parchment to blot the ink, then brushed it off and folded the missive.

"An ale for my friend!" Balmforth called.

Adam nodded. This was thirsty work. Hell, any work was thirsty work.

He preferred not to work at all.

He flipped the letter over and scrawled *Miss Caithren Leslie, Leslie by Insch, Scotland* on the back. After dusting the address with sand as well, he rose and crossed the taproom to the innkeeper's desk, pinching the serving maid on her behind as she sauntered by with his tankard of ale.

She giggled.

"Have you any wax?" Adam dropped his letter on the scarred wooden counter and dug in his pouch for a few coins. "And you'll post this for me, aye?"

The innkeeper blinked his rheumy eyes. "Certainly, sir."

"Leslie, come along!" Grinstead shouted. "We're fair dying of thirst."

Laughing, Adam pressed his signet ring into the warm wax, then went to join his companions. He lifted his ale and leaned across the table. Their three pewter mugs met with a resounding *clank*.

"To freedom!" Grinstead said, shaking off some foam that had sloshed onto his hand.

"To freedom!" Adam echoed. "Till Hogmanay!"

Grinstead gasped. "You told her you'd be gone till the new year?"

"At the least." Adam swallowed a gulp and swiped one hand across his mouth before the froth dripped onto his expensive satin surcoat. "We've the week hunting in West Riding, then Lord Darnley's wedding in London come the end of the month. Wouldn't care to miss Guy Fawkes Day in the City. Then I might as well stay through the Christmas balls, aye?" The taproom's door banged open. "No sense in going home, then leaving again straightaway."

"No sense at all," Balmforth agreed, staring toward the entrance.

"Will you look at what just walked in? Do you think she might be that MacCallum woman everyone's talking about?"

Their gazes swung to the tall lass and followed her progress as she sat herself at another table.

"Nary a chance." Adam contemplated the contents of his tankard for a moment, then tossed back the rest of the ale and signaled the serving wench for another. "Emerald MacCallum dresses like a man."

"She's carrying a knife," Balmforth argued in a loud whisper. "And she looks hard. Like the sort of woman who'd track outlaws with a price on their heads."

Grinstead let loose a loud guffaw. "You're in your cups, Balmforth. Emerald MacCallum carries a sword and a pistol."

"The MacCallum wench would kick your sorry arses." Adam tugged on the lacy white cravat at his neck. "And mine, too, I expect."

They all burst out laughing, until another bang of the door caught their attention.

An excited old-timer stood in the opening. "Duel at the Market Cross!"

THREE

*A*S HE AND Gothard both fought for better footing, Jason hurried out of his midnight blue surcoat and tossed it to his brother, his gaze never leaving that of his foe. Gothard smirked as he lunged once again, barely giving Jason time to adjust.

Gothard was fleet, but Jason was faster. They scrambled down the steps, and the crowd scurried back. Gothard was cornered, but Jason was incensed. He edged Gothard back beneath the dome, skirting the circular stone bench that sat in its center as they battled their way to the other side of the octagonal structure. Gothard took sudden advantage, and Jason found himself retreating as their blades tangled, slid, and broke free with a metallic twang.

His arm ached to the very bone. Perspiration dripped slick from his forehead, stinging his eyes. But the other man's breath came ragged and labored.

All at once, a vicious swipe of Jason's sword sent Gothard's clanging to the stones and skittering down to the cobbled street, far from his reach.

Jason's teeth bit into his own lower lip. "I didn't come to kill today, Gothard. I merely want to see justice done." He sucked in air, smelled the other man's desperation. "Are you ready to come peacefully?"

Sweat beading on his sunburned brow, Gothard stepped back until his calves hit the round stone bench. Frantically he scanned the mass of people still pouring from the surrounding establishments. Three more men stumbled out of a taproom and crossed the dusty street to the dome, the bright rainbow colors of their clothing marking them aristocrats.

Their leader wove through the crowd, clearing a path for his two companions. "Come along, Grinstead!" he yelled as they pushed their way to the front.

Gothard's eyes narrowed. In a flash of movement, one of his arms snaked toward the newcomers, the other down to the wide cuff of his boot, where the curved handle of a pistol peeked out.

Jason's jaw tensed; his knees locked. Time appeared to slow. His surroundings seemed impressed on his senses: the heated babble and musky scent of the excited onlookers, the cool dimness in the shaded dome, the bright green grass and streaky sunlight beyond.

As Gothard rose from his crouch, Jason rushed headlong, his sword arm rigid.

Gothard jerked one of the men in front of him as a shield. Jason tried to check his momentum, but his blade forged ahead, piercing satin and flesh with an ease that came as a shock to a man unused to killing. As long as he lived, he would never forget the astonished look in the man's hazel eyes.

The sword pulled free with a gruesome sucking sound that brought bile into Jason's throat. The man collapsed, his eyes going dull as his bright blood spurted in a grotesque fountain that soaked Jason's shirt and choked his nostrils with a salty, metallic stench.

Stunned, he watched the blood pump hard then slow to a trickle —a spreading red puddle that seeped into the cracks between the stones. The dead man's face drained of color, to match the white lace at his throat.

Geoffrey Gothard raised his arm, cocked his flintlock, and pulled the trigger.

The explosion rocked the Market Cross, momentarily startling everyone into silence. "I'll see you at the gates of hell," Gothard muttered into the void. Then he turned and pushed through the crowd, signaling his younger brother to follow.

Ford Chase rushed forward when his own brother, the thirty-two-year-old Marquess of Cainewood, clutched his chest and crumpled to the ground.

FOUR

$\mathcal{S}$URELY HE WAS in hell.

   Crackling sounds slowly filtered through his conscious-
ness. A grunt. A dull thud.

His eyes slit open, and his head split in two. Or it felt like it.

Hell.

Wincing at the brightness, Jason forced his eyes open wider.
Shiny dark red curls swam through his vision as his sister Kendra
moved to toss another log on the already blazing fire. Another thud,
and waves of heat washed over him.

Hell. It was hot as hell in here.

He blinked once, then again. "Where—where am I?" he stammered out.

Kendra whirled. "At Cainewood, Jason. Home." She rushed to
his bedside and swabbed his brow with a warm, damp cloth. Her
familiar lavender scent wafted around him. Her light green eyes
were filled with concern.

Kendra, his sweet, exasperating sister Kendra, so full of life—but
her expression worried him. And the heat.

"Damn, I'm hot." He pushed at the covers—two thick quilts and
a velvet counterpane—and tried to sit up. Pain knifed through his
body. He fell back, touching his shoulder and chest gingerly. Thick
bandaging. "What happened?"

A quick frown marred her wholesome features, then was gone. "Don't you remember? You were shot."

It all came screaming back: the limestone Market Cross, the weight of the rapier in his hand, the shock as it sank into flesh. Gothard, that whoreson, pulling a man from the crowd to use as a shield.

"Holy heaven," Jason whispered.

He'd killed an innocent man.

"You're going to be fine," Kendra rushed to reassure him. "It was naught but a shoulder wound, and the ball came clean. The surgeon said you'll be fine."

No, he wouldn't. He'd never be fine again.

Jason shut his eyes and turned his head to hide the hot, unmanly tears that threatened. He was always so level-headed; whatever had possessed him to take the law into his own hands?

Rage, that was what. Black, unreasoning rage. The sight of Clarice Bradford's ghost-white face and her motionless, bruised young daughter. Just remembering made his blood seethe anew.

"Mary?" he croaked.

"She still lives. But she's no better." Kendra smoothed her lemon-yellow skirts, a cheery color that seemed to clash with the sadness clouding her face. She put a hand to his forehead. "You don't feel hot. You're not feverish." She swiped at her own damp brow. "How are you feeling?"

"Like hell. It's hot as hell in here."

"The surgeon said to keep you warm."

"Surely you took him too literally."

She bit her lip in a rare show of uncertainty. "I'll go get Ford." Giving his hand a quick squeeze, she sighed, then hurried from the room to fetch her twin.

Jason lay still, staring at the familiar stone walls of his ancestral home. Colorful tapestries lent the cavernous chamber an intimate feel and kept the drafts to a minimum. Cainewood Castle had always made him feel safe, peaceful.

But not today.

Pangs of guilt swept him in waves, only to be swamped by anger at Geoffrey Gothard's actions. This was no longer just about Jason's villagers—the coward had used a blameless man as a shield. A man who would live today if Jason had chosen to wait for the authorities.

But damn it, he hadn't gone there to kill Gothard, let alone an innocent bystander. He'd intended to see Gothard detained, brought to justice…

The pain in his head intensified.

He knew also the Gothard brothers would have been long gone had he not acted immediately upon hearing word of their whereabouts. Law enforcement in these parts was sorely lacking.

He raised a hand to his aching head. Why the devil did Gothard consider him an enemy?

Ford sauntered in at Kendra's heels, flashing a hopeful smile. "How do you feel?"

"Like hell," Jason and Kendra said together, way too loudly.

Wincing, Jason pushed the long black hair from his eyes.

"It's the laudanum." Ford stated the facts like the analyst he was. "The surgeon gave you enough to fell a middling-sized horse. Said you'd need it to survive the trip home, but that it may well give you a headache."

"He may well have been right." Jason closed his eyes and sucked in a steadying breath before opening them again. The candlelight seemed brighter than usual. Too bright. He blinked at the cobalt blue canopy overhead. "What day is it?"

"Friday. Evening." Ford cleared his throat and leaned against one carved, twisted bedpost. "You were out over twenty-four hours. Damn, it's hot in here."

Kendra glared at her twin. "I'll open a window."

"The door as well. And for heaven's sake, bank that fire." Ford turned to Jason, smiling at their sister's overzealousness. Then his expression sobered. "I believe Gothard thinks you're dead. You were covered in blood—"

"That of the man I killed." Jason's chest constricted painfully. "Who was he?"

Ford blinked. "I don't know. I rushed to care for you, and when I looked up, he was gone."

"He was with two other men. They must have taken him. We'll have to make inquiries—"

"In due time." One hand on her hip, Kendra frantically fanned the door open and closed. "Cooler now?"

Her face was flushed to match her dark red hair. Jason smiled, though even that movement hurt his head. "Sit down, Kendra."

The bed ropes creaked as she sat gingerly on the mattress. "I rode into the village this morning." One of her fingers traced idle circles on the blue velvet counterpane. "I talked to Clarice."

"She's talking?" He struggled up on his elbows, ignoring the pain in his shoulder, the throbbing in his head. After the incident, Clarice had uttered nothing but Gothard's name. He had to go to her, see if he could do anything for her daughter, get the answers to his questions—

"Take it easy," Ford warned.

Ignoring his brother's advice, Jason tried to swing his legs off the bed, then stopped with a defeated groan. "I'm not going anywhere," he muttered, his head dropping back to the pillow. "What have you learned?" He looked to Kendra. "How did Clarice know Gothard?"

"She'd seen him around the village."

"He made no attempt to hide his identity while he was here," Ford added.

"True." Frowning, Jason steepled his fingers atop the counterpane. "The brothers registered at the inn. They talked to people; I was able to get descriptions for the broadsides and the sketch from Martinson." The blacksmith was known for his clever characterizations.

Ford paced the carpeted floor. "It's clear the Gothards didn't come here intending to do this."

Kendra nodded. "Clarice told me that when all was said and done, they were each furious with the other. And frightened at the consequences. That's why they ran before finishing the..."

"Rape," Jason ground out. "You can say it, Kendra. Thank God at least Clarice was spared that." She'd been badly hurt, though, and his hands clenched as he vowed no one would ever hurt another woman like that while she was under his protection. "But why? Why did they do it?"

Kendra's gaze dropped to her folded hands. "Clarice said he told her..."

"If he couldn't have your castle, instead he'd have your woman," Ford finished for her.

"My woman?" Jason's head felt blank, until suddenly it dawned on him. "My mistress?" he said incredulously. "He thought Clarice was my mistress? A villager?"

"She's pretty enough." Ford shrugged. "He saw you hugging

Mary and handing her to Clarice. He believed she was your daughter."

"My daughter?" Marriage and family were so far off in Jason's plans, his mind boggled at the mere thought. "How...what happened...with Mary?"

"She wouldn't stay quiet." Kendra's eyes turned misty. "Geoffrey threw her against the wall to shut her up. Forever, it seems. The doctor says she'll never wake."

"Holy heaven." He could picture her, the sweet little girl he'd come to know, limp and motionless, slipping into death.

And somehow, he was responsible.

FIVE

Leslie, Scotland

"**MARRIED?** I haven't any plans to get married!"

The last strains of the funeral bagpipes were still echoing in Caithren Leslie's ears when she found herself facing the family lawyer across her father's desk.

As though it weren't enough she had to bury Da today, now this. Unbelievable. "Have I misheard you?"

Lachlan MacLeod sighed and ran a hand through his grizzled hair. "There's nothing wrong with your hearing, Miss Leslie. All of Leslie is Adam's...that is, unless you see fit to wed within the year. Then the larger portion that came through your mother will revert to you and your husband. In which case you'll provide for your brother, of course. The minor lands entailed with the baronetcy aren't sufficient to support a man."

"At least not in the style to which Adam is accustomed," Cait's cousin Cameron put in dryly.

"Heaven forbid my brother should put Leslie before pursuing his own pleasure," Cait said, pensively twirling one of her dark-blond plaits. "It's been five years since he's been home for more than a visit." She closed her eyes momentarily, then focused on the lawyer. "Crivvens, this cannot be."

"It can be, Miss Leslie, I assure you." MacLeod's arthritic hands stacked the papers on the desk. "While it's rare for a daughter to hold title, it isn't unprecedented. Your father's wishes will stand against a challenge."

"Nay, that wasn't what I meant." Caithren stared at her father's desktop. It had always been littered with papers, reflecting the goings-ons at busy Leslie. Now it was neat. Too neat. Her heart ached at the sight. "Da told me that if Adam didn't mend his ways, one day Leslie would be mine. That part isn't surprising." She looked toward Cameron for strength, feeling a bit better when their hazel eyes met. He'd always been there to lean on. "It's the marriage requirement that makes no sense."

Taking her by the shoulders, Cam gently pushed her across the flagstone floor and into a brown leather chair. He perched his tall form on the arm and looked toward the lawyer expectantly. "Maybe if you read that wee portion of the will again. I don't think Cait quite heard it."

MacLeod shuffled pages, then cleared his throat. "'I am sorely sorry for this requirement, dear daughter, but it is my hope that you will grow to understand my position. As you're twenty-one already—'" The lawyer broke off and tugged at one pendulous earlobe. "He wrote this last year, you understand, before he—"

"Aye, while I was naught but a bairn." Caithren crossed her arms and legs. Beneath her unadorned black skirts, the leg on top swung wildly up and down as she talked. "Now, having attained the advanced age of twenty-two, I imagine I'm a confirmed spinster—"

"'As you're twenty-one already,'" MacLeod rushed to continue, "'I find myself concerned for your future. In addition, I promised dear Maisie on her deathbed that I would see you safely wed. Since you're hearing these words, it's apparent I failed to live long enough to do so. Caithren, my love, you cannot but admit to a certain streak of stubbornness and inde-pendence, and bearing such, have left me no other avenue to make certain your dear mother's wishes are granted. I know you'll do right by your mother, myself, and your own life, rather than see Leslie fall into your brother's incompetent hands. Please forgive me my duplicity and know it's for your own good.'"

Silence enveloped the small study, the pitter-patter of the rain unnaturally loud against the window. Caithren stared up at the timber-beamed ceiling.

Cameron's hand brushed her arm. "It's sorry I am for you, sweet. This is a hard day for you, I know."

"Da suffered. It's a blessing he's gone. Didn't everyone tell me that today?"

But despite having decided she was done crying, her throat seemed to close painfully, and something in her eyes was blurring her vision.

She blinked hard. "I have no intention of marrying."

Rising to tower over her, Cameron wiped his palms against the dark blue and green Leslie kilt he'd worn for the funeral. "Never?"

"Ever." Cait tightened her arms around her laced bodice, hugging herself.

"But—but so many have courted you," Cam sputtered, running a hand back through his straight, wheaten hair. "Surely there must be one man..." He blinked, then focused. "Duncan. Maybe you'd consider Duncan? He has land of his own, and the village maidens are forever tittering over his good looks—"

"He's a fool." When Caithren stood, Cam stepped back in self-defense. "He'd be no better for Leslie than Adam. And he'd never let me have a hand in running things, or you, for that matter."

Cameron blinked. "James, then. James is no fool."

"Aye, you've the right of it there. But James isn't one for the land. He keeps his nose in a book all the day. He'd be no better than Adam, either."

Cam walked to the window and gazed out at the pouring rain. "Surely there must be someone." His voice bounced muffled off the uneven glass. "What sort of life would you live, then? Your folks were so happy...don't you want as much for yourself?"

She joined him there and watched familiar gray clouds glide slowly over the green rolling hills where her family had lived for generations. Beyond a stone wall, the ponies she and Cameron were breeding fed in a nearby field, swishing their long tails. Tenant farmers worked in the distance—people she knew as well as her own kin.

She'd lived her entire life in this fortified house that looked like a wee, turreted castle. Da had built it for her mother—he'd always treated Mam like a queen. *Love owercomes the reasons o' mind*, Mam used to murmur when she walked up the path to her home; *the heart always rules the head.* But she'd said it with a laugh and a blush of pleasure.

Aye, Mam had been loved. But she'd still been the property of a man.

"For all Da loved her, Mam had nothing to call her own. I want to be independent, free to run Leslie—with you, Cam, the way we've been doing it since Da fell ill. Together. Any husband of mine would inherit my property upon marriage, and no man would allow you an equal partnership." One of her fingers traced the crooked line of a raindrop as it trailed down the pane. "We'd never realize our grand plans. Even my own dear father plotted to manipulate me from the grave. All men are the same."

"Not all men, Cait."

When she turned to him, Cam's eyes held a challenge.

"Maybe not all," she conceded. "Not you." Turning back to the window, she traced another raindrop...two...three.

Then hope leapt in her breast as it occurred to her. "You!" She whirled to face him. "I shall marry you! Leslie should be yours in any case—how many times have I said it?"

Cameron stared, incredulous. "Me? Are you daft? We're kin."

"First cousins." MacLeod's voice came stern across the room. Caithren had forgotten all about him. "I've heard it said that such inbreeding can result in diseased children."

"Inbreeding?" Cam was still sputtering beside her. "Cait, I...I love you, but not that way. More like a sister."

"I knew as much." She paused for a breath. "And my love for you is much the same. I never expected to wed at all, much less for romantic love." She felt a lump rise in her throat as her excitement gave way to defeat. "It's hopeless."

Her fingers went absently to play with her laces as she wandered back to MacLeod, tears swimming in her eyes. "Is there no other way? Must I wed or see it all go to Adam?"

"Well..." The family lawyer met her gaze, then looked away.

"Aye? What are you thinking?" Slapping her palms onto the desk, she leaned toward him. "You've an idea, don't you?"

MacLeod glanced heavenward. "May your father forgive me for circumventing his plans." He straightened his fine wool doublet. "If you could persuade your brother to sign over his rights—"

Caithren's heart galloped in her chest. "That would work? Such a paper would be legally binding?"

"I cannot see why not. It wouldn't be signed under duress, and who would there be to challenge? I assume, in exchange for a generous allowance for his keeping, that Adam would jump at the chance to relinquish his responsibilities. If I know your brother at all—"

"Aye, you do," Cameron said in wry confirmation. He walked closer to Cait. "And he'd still have the title. Sir Adam Leslie, Baronet. Not that he deserves it."

"I don't care about that, but it's all *he* cares about, which is why this should work." Caithren turned around to think. "I must go to Adam." She spun back to her cousin. "My letters never seem to reach him, and he may be off to India soon."

"India?" Cameron frowned. "Do you know where he is now?"

"A letter came just yesterday." She hurried to the desk and pulled out a sheet of parchment. "He mailed it the first of August, from Chichester." She scanned the single page. "He said he was in the company of two friends on their way to West Riding near Ponte-fract, where Lord Scarborough had invited them hunting. Then to London for Lord Darnley's wedding on the thirtieth. And he hopes to make it home for Hogmanay, but there's talk of a voyage to India." She looked up. "He should still be at Scarborough's. Ponte-fract is about halfway to London, isn't it? Not so far."

"I'll go."

"Nay, Cam. I must ask this of Adam myself."

"You don't trust me to ask him to sign a piece of paper?"

Caithren winced at the hurt look on her cousin's face. "It wouldn't be the same request, coming from you." Setting the letter aside, she put a hand on his arm. "I do love him, you know, but I also see him for what he is."

Cam's hand covered hers and squeezed. "Then I'll accompany you—"

"Nay, it's here you're needed. The harvest approaches." She raised a palm to stem his next protest. "You may see me to Edin-burgh and put me on the public coach, but then it's back to Leslie where you belong. I can deal with Adam."

"I don't like to think of you traveling alone."

The thought of a solo journey did make a wee tingle of fear

flutter in her stomach. But she pushed it away. "We can hire a chaperone in Edinburgh. You may choose her personally, if that will make you feel better."

When Cam's shoulders slumped, she sensed her victory. He took her chin in one hand and tilted her face up. "There's no arguing with you, is there, sweet Cait?"

"Nay, and there never was." She rose to her toes to kiss him on the cheek. "I'm thinking it's about time you learnt it, cousin."

He gave a wry shake of his head, followed by a speculative smile. "Do you know, I reckon you may be right."

"Aye?"

"There may be no man willing to take you to bride, you stubborn lass."

"Crivvens! Be off with you!" She swatted at him playfully. "You know what Mam used to say."

"I cannot wait to hear this one."

"Ha freens and ha life."

"Good friends make a full life," Cameron murmured.

She locked her gaze on his. All she had left to love were Cameron and Leslie.

She would not lose either.

"You're a fine friend, Cam. The best. Leslie will fare well in our hands."

SIX

*H*URRYING INTO the Edinburgh room she and Cameron had taken overnight, Caithren opened her satchel to add the ribbons she'd just bought.

Mrs. Dochart, the chaperone Cam had chosen, clucked her tongue. Her three chins wobbled, and one foot tapped against the bare, wood-planked floor. "What took you so long, lass?"

"I'd wager you five to one she got lost on her way back," Cam told the woman with a grin. "What happened, Cait? Did you go to Whiteford House instead of White Horse Close?"

"Worse," she muttered. She tied two black ribbons on the ends of her plaits, then slipped the rest into the satchel. "I was wandering around Brown's Close. I remembered it was a color, but forgot which one." She fished out her money pouch and added the coins she'd received as change. "And I set down my hat, then couldn't find it."

Cam laughed. "How is it that anyone as efficient as you can be constantly misplacing her hat?"

She sent him a scathing look. "They're just hats, not all that important. I usually have much more pressing matters to worry about. The Widow MacKenzie's health, or the proper time to shear the sheep."

"We shall have to advance our schedule by half an hour from here on out." Mrs. Dochart brushed at the mustard-colored cloth that laced over her pillowish bosom. "One cannot be late when the public coach is running." Her beady black eyes honed in on Caithren's open satchel. "What have we here, lass? Men's clothing?"

When Cait went to shut the bag, Cameron nudged her hands aside and pulled out a couple of garments. "Breeches? A shirt?"

"I may ride a horse at Scarborough's. Adam went there for hunting, aye?" She pushed him away and stuffed the clothes back inside. "I'm not used to riding in skirts."

The chaperone pursed her lips. "You're off to England, lass. Not the wilds of Scotland." She bundled up in an ugly mud-colored cloak that reached to the floor, covering her uglier calico skirt. Caithren thought she looked like a lumpy brown mountain. "Women in England ride sidesaddle, garbed in riding habits."

Cam snatched his woolen plaid off a hook on the plastered wall, wrapped himself in it, and jammed his hat on his head. "Mrs. Dochart's right, sweet. You won't be on your own land where you may act as you choose and none will say nay. Those Sassenachs are *civilized*." He pronounced the word with more than a modicum of distaste. "I'll tote the breeches back home for you."

"I want to take them." Cait took tiny framed paintings of Da and Adam off the table and snuggled them on top of the clothing. She shrugged as she fastened the closure. "Whether I'll wear them or not remains to be seen."

While she donned her own tartan wrap, Cam hefted the satchel. "Take what you wish. You're the one who has to carry it all." He handed her the bag, failing to hide his amusement when she strained under its weight.

Squaring her shoulders, Caithren followed Mrs. Dochart from the room and down two of the five narrow flights of stairs before Cameron caught up and took the satchel from her. "I'll miss you, Cait."

She managed a brave smile. No matter what she'd said last week in Da's study, it was a scary thing to be going to England alone. "I'll miss you, too. But I won't be staying in Pontefract long, not with Adam off to London for that wedding. I cannot believe I had to wait a whole day just to leave here."

Cameron laughed. "My impatient Cait. The coach runs naught but once a fortnight." He pushed open the inn's door. "You were lucky, sweet."

Caithren touched the old emerald amulet she wore on a chain about her neck—her good-luck charm. She sighed as she stepped into the gray Edinburgh day. A persistent drizzle kept the cobblestones wet and shining. Canongate teemed with coaches, horses, and humanity, and Holyroodhouse loomed in the background, tall and imposing.

It was as different from peaceful Leslie as she could possibly imagine.

She drew her blue and green plaid tighter around her shoulders. "I can only hope there are no more delays, or I'll miss Adam for certain. Then I'll have to go all the way to London." She paused for a breath. "I'd prefer not to even consider that possibility."

"Me, neither." Cam chuckled as he handed her satchel to an outrider and watched him heave it onto the coach's roof. "I cannot imagine you making it all that way without getting lost."

Mrs. Dochart paused on the coach steps. "Worry not on that account, lad. I'm goin' all the way to London, and if need be I'll make it my business to see she gets there on time and in one piece. That's what you hired me for, after all."

Cait watched the woman's ample rear disappear into the coach. "God alone knows how I'll survive the eight days to Pontefract with that old bawface, let alone nine more to London if need be. Already I cannot abide her, and I only met her this morning."

"She's exactly what you need, sweet cousin. I hired well." Cameron carefully counted eight pounds to pay the two women's fares. "I can only pray Adam will do as well finding a chaperone for you on the other end." He glanced at the slate sky, then drew off his hat and settled it over her plaits. "Here, I don't want to see you go hatless."

She looked up at the plain brown rim, then grinned. "Do you think I look bonnie?"

"Oh, aye." His eyes lit with humor. "A man's hat suits you." His expression sobered as he rooted beneath his plaid, then pressed a pistol into her hands. "And I want you to take this as well."

"Da's gun?" It felt heavy and vaguely menacing, the dull metal pitted, the wooden grip worn smooth from years of use. "But why?"

"I don't trust the English. Short of accompanying you myself, I'd at least send you with some protection."

"But I don't know how to use it."

He handed her a heavy little pouch and a flask of gunpowder. "Pour a wee smidge of powder into the muzzle, then wrap a cloth patch around a ball, ram it—S"

"Nay, that wasn't what I meant. I've seen Da load this pistol hundreds of times. But I've never shot at anything, Cam."

"Damn, I wish I'd known that. I would've practiced with you." He took back the pouch and flask, hesitated, then reached beneath her plaid and stuffed them into her skirt's deep pocket. "Take it anyway. You're a bright lass, Cait. If need be, you'll figure out how to use it."

Slowly she slid the pistol into her other pocket. The weight of it did make her feel somewhat safer. And she'd seen Da shoot it often enough; she reckoned she could do it if she had to.

"Take care of yourself, Cait." Cameron leaned to kiss her cheek.

She blinked back the tears that threatened, lest her cousin see them. Thankfully he couldn't see her heart racing in her chest, or tell that her stomach rebelled at the mere thought of traveling so far with naught but a stranger for company.

She forced a smile. "I'd better go before the old bawface starts yelling at me."

With a laugh, Cam helped her up the coach steps.

SEVEN

"*D*AMN, IT WILL take three days to cover Cainewood in this bloody creeping carriage. Pass me that journal, will you?"

"Clever change of subject." Kendra handed Jason the leather book and one of the pencils made from the graphite mined on the property. She hitched herself forward, frowning at him seated across from her in the carriage. "You're not well enough to go. It's been barely more than two weeks."

"I'm not waiting much longer." He flipped open the estate journal and made a note to have the Johnsons' roof rethatched. "The reward I posted isn't bringing in Gothard. I've killed an innocent man, thanks to him."

"Thanks to Gothard? It's yourself you're blaming." As usual, Kendra was too observant for his comfort. "Someone else is hurt, and naturally, it's all your fault."

Ignoring her sarcasm, he scribbled reminders to buy another bull and see that Mistress Randall's spinning wheel was repaired. "Not hurt, Kendra—killed. And poor Mary fares no better. It's a wonder she still breathes." The attack on Clarice and Mary might not have been premeditated, but the episode at the Market Cross proved the brothers were cornered. Dangerous. He rolled the pencil between his hands. "I'd have left already if only I had some clue to the Gothards' whereabouts. They seem to have disappeared."

"They'll resurface. And the reward you've posted will ensure you'll hear of it."

"When?" He banged the journal closed and slammed it onto the seat. "When will I find the whoreson who made me kill an innocent man? How many others will die before he's caught?" His fists bunched between his spread knees. "And who died at my hands? The least I can do is send condolences to his family, make some reparations. Where the hell is Ford?"

Kendra stared at him. "He's working on it," she said carefully.

Her pale green eyes looked so troubled. He consciously relaxed his jaw and, with a sigh, reached to put a hand on her shoulder. "I'm sorry. I don't know what's come over me." He glanced out the window at the peaceful fields of Cainewood, struggling for the calm that usually came to him so easily. "I feel so damned powerless."

Kendra's gaze followed his and caught what he'd missed in his blind fury. "Look, he's back." She leaned to watch her twin gallop up the lane.

Jason knocked on the roof to stop the carriage and threw open the door. "News from Chichester?" he asked. "Do we know who I killed?"

"No." Breathless, Ford shook his head. "Whoever he was, his companions bore him away without so much as reporting his identity. That's not what I rode out to tell you, though." He swept off his hat, dragged a hand through his wavy brown hair. "There's a stableman waiting to see you. At home. Two of your horses have been stolen."

A hard ball of anxiety hit Jason in the stomach. "Not Chiron?"

"No. Pegasus and Thunder."

"Thank God for small favors."

Although he was relieved his favorite mount had been spared, Jason still cursed the slow carriage a hundred times before it finally rolled over the drawbridge and through the barbican into Cainewood's grassy quadrangle. A man waited on the wide steps that led to the castle doors, cap in hand and a crude blood-stained bandage tied around his head.

With an agility that wrenched his shoulder and made him wince, Jason leapt from the carriage and made for the double oak doors. "Porter, come in, will you?" He gestured the stableman into the entry.

The man frowned and touched his fingertips to his forehead.

"Come in," Jason repeated. "You're no longer bleeding. And these floors have seen their share of blood through the years, in any case."

With obvious reluctance the man climbed the steps after Kendra and Ford. Staring up at the slim pillars that supported the stone hall's vaulted ceiling, he seated himself gingerly—not in one of the carved walnut chairs that Jason indicated, but on one of the iron treasure chests instead, probably figuring it would be easier to clean.

Jason followed Porter's awed gaze as it swept the entry, taking in the intricate stone staircase, crowned at intervals with impressive heraldic beasts. "Who?" he asked impatiently. "Who has stolen my horses?"

The man dragged his gaze back to Jason's. "Those men, my lord. The brothers. The ones on the broadsides."

"The Gothard brothers? In stark daylight?" Jason's jaw dropped open in astonishment. "Right from under our noses?"

"They knocked me out." Slowly Porter shook his injured head. "I'm sorry, my lord. I didn't hear much, and I couldn't seem to move."

"What *did* you hear?" Jason crouched at the man's feet and peered into his apprehensive eyes. "Anything. Anything you can remember, I want to hear it."

The groom fiddled with the cap in his hands. "The one was saying he didn't want to take the horses." He set the cap in his lap. "I couldn't hear what the other said."

Reeling with confusion and frustration, Jason touched the stableman on the knee. "Anything else?"

"They did mention another man's name. They were headed to Lord Scar—" He stopped and squeezed his eyes shut for a moment. "I cannot remember," he said at last. "Lord Scar-something. He said his brother was entitled to whatever this other lord has. And they were going to take the horses and go get it."

"Gothard." Jason stood and cursed under his breath. "Cuthbert Gothard, the Earl of Scarborough. Why didn't I think of that connection?"

"It's a common name," Ford said. "You had no reason to think the Gothard brothers were connected to Lord Scarborough."

But he should have. It was his job to eliminate any threat to his village. "I could have sent a letter of inquiry to Scarborough, asking if they were relations and what he knew of their whereabouts." He paced the three-story chamber, his footsteps echoing off the vaulted stone ceiling. "Now it's too late—the brothers are on their way already." He paused midstep. "If I hurry, maybe I can reach Pontefract before they do and give Scarborough fair warning. Then lie in wait."

"Lie is right." Kendra slanted him a look of utter disbelief. "You'll end up lying in the road somewhere. You'll never catch them if you're riding in a carriage, with them on the backs of your fine horses. And you cannot ride Chiron such a distance in your condition."

Hadn't his father told him to stand up for what he believed in? Even without his personal responsibilities, common decency would demand he warn the earl.

"I can ride Chiron, and I will." He turned to Porter. "I thank you for a job well done. They'll doctor you in the kitchen. Tell Ollerton I said you may have the day off."

"Thank you, my lord." Porter stood and bowed, but Jason's attention was already elsewhere.

"Ford, ask Claxton to bring a portmanteau to my chamber. I'm off for West Riding."

"No, you're not!" Kendra ran after him up the wide stairway and jumped ahead of him as he entered his chamber. "You were shot two weeks ago, for heaven's sake!"

Shouldering her out of the way, Jason strode to his chest of clothes to choose a few of his plainest shirts. "It's not serious; the surgeon said so himself. The first days found me groggy from the laudanum, and I've let you coddle and care for me since. But now the bastards have stolen my horses, and I've a lead where they're headed. Nothing you say will keep me here. Lives may be at stake, and apparently, for reasons I cannot fathom, I am involved."

Ford came in with Claxton, who had brought the portmanteau and moved to pack it. "This is no ordinary journey," Jason told him. "I'd best choose my wardrobe myself."

His manservant blinked. "Then I shall go ready myself for travel."

Jason shook his head. "I go with no valet, but alone, dressed as a commoner. If Gothard thinks I'm dead, it makes no sense to call attention to myself."

"Alone, Jason?" Kendra railed as Claxton left the chamber. "Who will care for you?"

He walked to the bed, opened one of the two leather bags, and tossed in the shirts. "The shoulder doesn't pain me much," he said, stretching the truth, "and there's no sign of infection." That at least was fact.

And if his siblings were looking at him as though he'd gone around the bend, so be it. He would do what was expected of him. What he expected of himself.

Kendra pulled the shirts back out and folded them neatly. "You should have let Claxton pack."

"I may be surrounded by servants, but I'm capable of caring for myself." Bending over his chest, he selected two fine lawn shirts and a snowy cravat, depositing them into his sister's outstretched hands. He threw open his tall, carved clothes press and took a dark blue velvet suit from a hook. Three pairs of his plainest breeches and a couple more workaday shirts found their way into his bag. The boots on his feet would do.

"Geoffrey Gothard must be stopped." Jason paused in his packing to gaze out the diamond-paned window. In the sunshine beyond lay his land, his people. "I cannot face my own villagers until it's done."

"You sent broadsides near and far," Kendra argued. "It's common knowledge Gothard is a wanted outlaw. For the hundred pounds you've offered—"

"—that MacCallum woman will see it done," Ford finished for her.

"Emerald MacCallum? That fabled Scot who wears men's clothing and carries a pistol?" Jason blinked and dragged his gaze from his land back to the dim room. "Don't tell me you've fallen for that claptrap. A woman tracking outlaws for the reward—why, you'd have to be maggot-brained to believe such fancies—"

"Then someone else will see it done." Kendra crossed her arms.

Jason could feel his face heating. Part of him agreed with her, but the expectations he'd been raised with overrode her cool logic. "I cannot wait for *someone* to see it done. Since King Charles abolished Cromwell's Major General districts, there's no central authority of any kind." His sturdiest stockings joined the pile of clothing. "For heaven's sake, didn't you see it with what happened in Chichester? A man was killed, and no one even knows who he was."

"Charles did well to abolish the districts," Ford protested. "Their main activity was to tax us Royalists." He raised a finger to make another point, then shook his head as though realizing this was not the time for their old argument. "Jason, think about what you're doing."

"I've thought of little else. England has never seen such lawlessness." Jason paced the red and blue carpet, snatching up an ivory comb and his shaving kit as he moved past his dressing table. "There's no provision for passing vital information from one county to another. Depending on a reward offer—someone's greed—in order to see this man put away...no, I cannot do so."

He dropped to sit on the bed, fighting to marshal his temper. "I killed an innocent man. I won't able to live with myself until Gothard is behind bars, never to murder again. And I'll hear from him just what he thinks my part is in this debacle."

Kendra came to stand before him. "I've checked the church's birth records, and, contrary to popular belief, your middle name is not 'Responsible.'" She smiled, a gentle smile that tugged at his heart. "Gothard is gone from this area—you can be sure of it. You're injured. You have people here, people who need you. And family. Jason—"

"That's enough, Kendra." He couldn't let her sway him. Rising from the bed, he grabbed a ball of hard-milled soap from his washstand, threw it into the portmanteau, flipped the bags closed, and secured the latches. "No more arguments." He went to his sister and gave her a hard hug, ignoring the jolt to his shoulder. "They've singled me out—how can I turn away? What kind of man would that make me?"

Kendra opened her mouth, but Jason cut her off. "You cannot stop me, sweetheart." He smoothed her dark red curls. "Just wish me Godspeed."

"If you won't wait to heal, then at least wait an hour or two for Ford and me to get ready. You've never gone off without us. I can care for your wound—"

"This isn't a holiday, Kendra. You would slow me down."

He saw her take a deep breath before the fight drained out of her.

When she nodded up at him, he turned to Ford. "Find out who I killed, will you? Ask around again in Chichester. *Someone* must know the identity of his two acquaintances. Then locate them, follow up. Send word to Pontefract if you hear anything."

"Jason, it wasn't your fault."

"Do it," he ordered. He jammed his sword into his belt, tucked a small pistol into his boot top, lifted the portmanteau. "Watch over Cainewood for me. God willing, I won't be long."

"And then we can lay this nightmare to rest?" Kendra asked.

He stared at her a long time while the chamber filled with an oppressive silence. Then, unable to make that promise, he kissed her cheek and strode from the room.

"Godspeed," she whispered after him.

EIGHT

*H*ER BACK TO the other passengers straggling in and queuing to get rooms, Caithren stared at the innkeeper in disbelief. "Are you telling me there are no horses for hire in this town?"

He rubbed a hand over his bald head. "That's what I'm telling you, madam."

Mrs. Dochart took Cait by the arm. "Come along, lass. Maybe the situation will change on the morrow." With her other hand she set down her valise and dug inside for coins. "We'll take a room upstairs, Mr. Brown."

Caithren shook off the woman's hand and leaned farther over the innkeeper's desk. "Are there no hackney cabs, either?"

"No hackney cabs."

"But Pontefract is a stage stop!"

"We've extra horses for the public coach, naturally. But not for hire."

Behind her, Caithren heard feet shuffling impatiently on the gritty wood floor. "Hurry up, there," someone grumbled.

"Hold your tongue," Cait shot over her shoulder. "I've spent eight days shut up in a hot coach"—with a crotchety, meddling old woman, she added silently—"just to get here and visit with my brother at the Scarborough estate in West Riding."

Rubbing his thin, reddish nose, the innkeeper slanted her a dubious look. "The *Earl* of Scarborough's estate?"

"Aye, the same."

He shrugged. "You can walk. It's nice enough weather and naught but a mile or so." The man opened a drawer and pulled out a thick, leather-bound registration book. "Out there, then head east. The road will take you straight past the Scarborough place. You'll find it set back on the right side, perhaps a quarter mile from the road. An enormous stone mansion—you cannot miss it." With a dismissive thump, he set the book on the desk and opened it to a page marked with a ribbon. "You may leave your satchel if you wish. Should Scarborough invite you to stay"—his tone conveyed what he thought were the chances of *that* happening—"I reckon he'll send a footman to fetch it."

He waved her aside and the next person forward.

"Come along, lass. We'll be losing the light soon." Mrs. Dochart set her own bag alongside Cait's behind the desk. "Unless you'd prefer to wait for the morn?" she added hopefully.

Cait reached up a finger to twirl one of her plaits. "Nay, I wish to go immediately." *Without* a chaperone. "But I'm...I mean to say... well, I expected we'd part company here. Not that I haven't enjoyed yours," she rushed to add, waiting for a lightning bolt to strike with that lie.

She couldn't remember ever uttering a more blatant falsehood.

The old bawface looked dubious. "Your cousin hired me to look after you, lass, and—"

"Only so far as Pontefract. He was well aware I was getting off here, aye? My brother will hire a chaperone for the return journey."

Though Mrs. Dochart sniffed, it was clear she had no wish to tramp over the countryside. "If you're certain, then—"

"I'm certain." For want of another way to end their association, Caithren executed a little curtsy. "It's pleased I am to have met you, Mrs. Dochart, and I thank you for keeping me company."

That lie might have topped the first one; Cait wasn't sure. Feeling a great burden had been lifted from her shoulders, she crossed the inn's taproom and headed out into the waning sunshine and down the road.

She hadn't progressed ten feet when the woman's voice shrilled into the quiet street. "Ah, Caithren, lass!"

With a sigh, Cait composed her face and turned back to the inn. "Aye, Mrs. Dochart?" The bawface stood framed in the doorway. A cracked wooden sign swung in the light wind, creaking over her head. "I told you I shall be fine."

"But the innkeeper said east. It's west you're walking."

"Oh!" Her cheeks heated. "Right."

"Nay, left."

"Right. I mean to say, aye. Left, east."

Reversing her direction, Cait hurried past, murmuring "Thank you" over her shoulder. She heard the woman mutter under her breath and was soon relieved to be out of earshot.

The evening was warm, and the slight breeze felt wonderful after the stuffy, confining coach. It was passably pretty country, the land green and flatter than at home. She much preferred the harsh contours of Scotland—the beautiful glens, the blues and purples of the wooded mountains, the little lochs and streams and waterfalls everywhere. But she didn't have to live here, after all. She could enjoy the land for what beauty could be found.

Her heart sang to be free at last, on her way to meet Adam and perhaps rest a few days, depending on the returning public coach's schedule. In two weeks' time she'd be back at Leslie, signed papers in hand, giving Cameron the tongue-lashing he deserved for saddling her with that irritating old woman.

Glancing down, she spotted the distinctive red-green leaves of meadow rue poking from the edge of a ditch. With a gasp of delight, she knelt to pick some, wrinkling her nose at the strong, unpleasant scent. Bruised and applied, it was good to heal sores and difficult to find near home. Pleased, she tucked it into her pocket and continued on her way.

She rubbed a hand across her forehead and tried not to think about how tired she was. Instead she focused on the hours ahead. Following what promised to be her first decent meal in weeks, tonight she'd luxuriate in a big tub of clean, steaming water. She couldn't wait to wash off the dust of the road. And she couldn't wait until tomorrow morn, when she'd be snug in a soft feather bed at Scarborough's, imagining the public coach rattling down the road toward London with that bawface tucked inside.

The thought was so vivid and appealing, she nearly missed the gravel drive that led to a yellowish stone mansion in the distance.

The building threw a long shadow. The sun was setting. She tucked her plaid tighter around her black bodice and skirt. When Adam saw her dressed in mourning, he'd understand right off how completely he'd neglected his family and home. It would be a simple matter to persuade him to sign the papers MacLeod had drawn up.

In the fading light she hurried along the path, marveling at the way the gravel was so raked and pristine. Scarborough must employ an army of servants. But they weren't here now, she realized as she drew close.

The mansion was shut up tight as a jar of Aunt Moira's preserves!

The sun sank over the horizon as Caithren stared at the heavy, bolted oak door. Hearing the call of a single hawk overhead, apparently the only living creature in the vicinity, she stifled a sob.

So much for her happy daydreams. She would have to stay the night in Pontefract, steel herself to climb back on the coach in the morning, then somehow survive the nine days it would take to reach London.

She counted on her fingers. She should arrive on the day of Lord Darnley's wedding, just in time to present herself as an uninvited guest. It was the only place she knew for certain she'd be able to find Adam.

Touching her amulet, she prayed there'd be no summer storm or anything else to delay the coach, because God only knew where Adam would be headed the morning of August thirty-first.

A scuffling sound on the roof made her glance up. Probably some sort of wee animal. Or rats.

Cait shuddered. "Set a stout heart to a steep hillside," she said aloud, imagining her mother saying the words. She squared her shoulders and was turning back toward the road when there came the snort of a horse and an answering neigh.

Horses meant people. Her spirits lifted. Maybe Adam and his friends were here after all, and they'd just been out hunting. And even if it were strangers, maybe they could spare her the long walk—

She heard a muted *thump* and the crunch of gravel, as someone apparently dropped from the roof. Then another *thump*.

"Sealed up. Cannot even get inside and snatch a few trinkets to pay our way. Damn it to bloody hell." Coming from around the side of the mansion, the man's voice sounded cultured. But he was cursing a string of oaths the likes of which Cait had never heard.

She scooted into the archway that housed the front door and pressed herself against the cold stone wall.

"I'm glad it's sealed up." The second man's voice was whiny. "I don't fancy taking things, Geoffrey."

"Everything here is ours, Wat. Or should be. You crackbrain."

The man called Wat didn't respond to the insult. "But Cainewood's horses? What about those?"

"The horses are rightly mine." The first man kicked at the ground, or at least Caithren thought he did. It was difficult to tell from around the corner. "We had to take them. We were low on funds with no way to get here. Can't you get that through your thick skull? Did you want to walk? Sleep in the open and beg for our supper?"

"We could have found work."

"Work? When hens make holy water. Should we stoop to chopping wood for a living? Baking bread? Shoeing horses?"

"Geoff—"

"Enough!"

Caithren heard the crunch of gravel beneath someone's shuffling feet. "So. Lucas is gone. What now, Geoffrey?"

"He'll be at the London town house, I reckon."

Cait heard the sound of pacing. Then a prolonged silence, followed by a low whistle.

"What are you thinking?" Wat sounded wary. "I don't care for the look in your eyes."

"We'll go to London." Next came a significant pause. "And we'll get what belongs to us."

A chill shot through Caithren, though the night was still warm. Apparently Wat felt the same way. "You cannot mean to hurt him?"

"Whatever it takes. He's got it coming, and you're next in line. When you're the earl, we'll be sitting pretty."

"When *I'm* the earl?" Cait could hear her heart pounding while Wat mulled that over. "Geoffrey," he said slowly, "you're not... you're not talking...murder?"

"Maybe I am."

They were planning to *murder* someone? Cait's breath seemed stuck in her chest.

"You would kill him?" Wat squeaked.

"I don't believe it will come to that. But it would be his fault for kicking us out. Just as it's his fault we're in this trouble. And his money we'll be using to get out of it."

Wat had nothing to say to that.

Or maybe he was shocked speechless.

"With Cainewood's death on our hands, we've nothing to lose," Geoffrey added gruffly. "Come along."

As she listened to them mount their horses, Cait began to tremble. It wasn't long before they rode around the corner of the mansion at a slow walk, heading straight past the front door where she hid. She scurried into a corner of the arched entry.

"I cannot do it." Even through Cait's fear, Wat's whine was grating on her. It was a wonder Geoffrey didn't put killing him next on his list of misdeeds.

But evidently Geoffrey chose not to listen, because he ignored the protest. "We have enough coin left to pay for a night at the inn. We'll let everyone see us."

"See us?"

"We'll leave for London come morning. People will remember us here, and if we ride like the dickens, no one will believe we could have arrived there in time. We won't be suspected of hurting our dear brother."

"But Geoffrey..." Wat's voice was so drawn out and plaintive, Caithren almost felt sorry for him. As they rode before her and then past, she risked inching forward to get a look at them.

Two men, both rumpled and sunburned. They spoke like quality, and looked it, too—overly proud, even if their clothes could use a washing. But they were robbing, murdering scum. English scum.

Cameron had been right about Englishmen.

"Now let's find some women." As they moved down the drive, the last of Geoffrey's words drifted back, faint but intelligible. "The last kitchen maid the housekeeper hired on before we left—she was a comely one, wasn't she? If she's not visiting her mama while Lucas is gone, she must be staying in Pontefract."

Women. The scum were in search of women. Caithren hugged

the tops of her crossed arms in a futile attempt to stop herself from shaking.

England was as evil a place as she'd always heard. What was she doing here all alone? She should have let Mrs. Dochart accompany her out here to Scarborough's. Or Cameron—she should have let Cameron make the journey. This certainly had been an ill-conceived undertaking.

Though she couldn't hear another word the men said, she was still shaking when they disappeared from view, still shaking when she started the long, lonely walk back in the dark. Still shaking after she'd reclaimed her satchel, paid for a room at the inn and extra for a bath, and trudged upstairs to wash off the dust of a week's travel.

She slipped into her plain room, shut the door and leaned back against it, a palm pressed to her racing heart. She had to get herself in hand.

Nothing—leastwise a couple of scummy Englishmen—was going to stop her from finding her brother.

NINE

*J*ASON SLOWLY slid off Chiron, feeling stiff as a day-old corpse. It seemed the ache in his shoulder had extended to every bone in his body. He detached his portmanteau and set it on the stable's dirt floor, then stretched toward the rough-beamed ceiling, a delicious pull of his abused muscles.

"Will you be stayin' at the inn, sir?"

His arms dropped, and he looked down into the lined face of a gnarled old stableman. "Only long enough to eat and wash. Then I'm headed to the Scarborough estate in West Riding. I understand it's nearby?"

"Aye, but no one's there." The little man's face split in the involuntary grin of someone imparting bad news. "Scarborough shut the house and made off for London two days ago."

Jason could barely keep himself from groaning aloud. After six days of hard riding, had he arrived only to leave again?

He forked some hay beneath Chiron's nose. Perhaps the man was misinformed. "How come you to know this?"

The smile turned self-satisfied. "Cousin Ethel's worked there thirty-odd years. She's staying hereabouts while the lord is gone—likes to stop by to pass the day." He puffed out his scrawny chest. "Servants, we know everything."

Jason rubbed his stubbled jaw. "Then old Cuthbert is gone?"

The stableman blinked. "Old Cuthbert is dead."

"Dead?" *Dead?* At the hands of his relatives, the Gothard brothers?

"A month past. He and Lady Scarborough—they died crossing the channel. Young Lucas is the new earl. 'Course he's not so young, exceptin' compared to me." He eyed Jason up and down. "About your age, I suspect."

He bent to unbuckle Chiron's saddle. "Things over there be different now. Took the new earl no more 'n a week to toss his brothers out on their ears, with nothing but the clothes on their backs and some pocket change." With a little grunt, he lifted the saddle and hung it on a hook. "Deserved it, they did. Cousin Ethel tells stories…that Geoffrey tormented Lord Scarborough—the new one—from the day he was born. Geoffrey hated Lucas, he did, because Geoffrey was older but couldn't inherit."

Interesting. The little man was a fountain of information, if only Jason could keep it flowing. He reached for a currycomb and ran it through Chiron's glossy silver coat. "Why was that?"

"Rumor has it he be Lady Scarborough's son from another marriage, you see." When the stableman filled the trough, Chiron drank greedily. "That Geoffrey, he had it in for Lord Scarborough— the new one—before the lad was walkin'."

"And the younger son?" Jason probed. "Walter, is it?"

"Wat? Dumber than a box of hair. Geoffrey led him around by the nose since he teethed his first tooth. Two against one it was, and Lord Scarborough—the new one—just waitin' till the day came he could toss the two of them out. 'Course it's sad that was sooner rather than later."

"Does everyone in the village know all this?"

"All I know is what Cousin Ethel's told me." The man looked up from where he was crouched, cleaning Chiron's hooves. "But I know how to keep my own mouth shut. You can lay odds on that."

"Be an interesting wager." Despite his disappointment, Jason's lips twitched beneath his mustache. "Geoffrey and Walter, they're in the area?"

"Nah." He dropped a hoof and moved around to lift another. "Disappeared the day after the funeral. I've yet to set eyes on 'em since."

If anybody would know the brothers had returned, it would be this man. Some of the stiffness left Jason's shoulder. "I think they may have found trouble," he said carefully. "Talk has it there's been a reward posted for Geoffrey."

"That so?" The man's eyes lit up. "Well, then, I'm hopin' he'll come back and that Emerald MacCallum woman after 'im. A Scottish lass taking our own son, born and bred. Now that'd be a sight to see, here in little old Pontefract. We'd be talkin' about it for years."

"I imagine you would."

If the rumors of Emerald MacCallum were any more than fanciful nonsense.

Jason leaned to hand the groom the comb. "I reckon I'll be staying the night here, after all." Fetching his pouch from his coat pocket, he pressed a silver coin into the man's age-spotted hand and patted the horse's flank. "Keep an eye on him for me, will you? His name's Chiron. Appreciate the chat."

He lifted the portmanteau and headed from the stables. Now he knew why the Gothards had it in for their brother.

But what they had against *him* remained a mystery.

TEN

*I*T SURELY FELT good to be clean, Caithren thought. Even if she'd had to fold her knees up to her chin to fit into the inn's small wooden tub.

She tipped the wee bottle of oil she'd pressed from Leslie's flowers, pouring a few more precious drops into the bath. Scooping a palmful of the lukewarm scented water, she smoothed it over her shoulders.

It smelled like Scotland. Like home.

When the water grew cold, she donned the clothes she'd brought for riding: soft brown breeches and a coarse white shirt, castoffs outgrown by Da's stable lad. After plaiting her dark-blond hair, she piled it atop her head and jammed Cameron's hat on top.

There was no mirror in her room, but she hoped she looked enough like a lad that the men downstairs would leave her alone. She'd had her fill of English men tonight. Just her luck, the scum brothers would be staying at this inn. And in search of women.

She ducked out the door, then turned and went back in to paw through her satchel and find her father's pistol. It was an ugly thing of cold, mottled steel, made for naught but utility. It felt heavy in her hands—heavy and surprisingly reassuring. Bless Cameron for making her take it; how had he known how alone and out of place she'd feel so far from home?

Remembering how Da had done so, she made sure the pistol

was loaded, then half-cocked it and stuck it in the back of her breeches.

She dug her plaid out of the satchel to cover it. Unlike the English cloaks, a plaid was neither masculine nor feminine; Cam's looked exactly the same as hers. With any luck, she might pass.

As an afterthought, she tucked both the miniature of Adam and his letter into her breeches pocket, then headed downstairs to the taproom, doing her best to swagger like a man.

The paneled room was lit by oil lamps burning cheerfully on each of the round wooden tables. Pewter spoons clinked on pewter plates, and the buzz of leisurely conversation filled her ears. Homey scents of meat pie, fresh-baked bread, and brewed ale hung in the air. Her stomach growled.

She made her way to the taproom's bar. "Mr. Brown?"

"Yes?" The innkeeper looked up from wiping the counter. His brow creased, as though he were wondering how she knew his name. So he didn't recognize her; her disguise must be working.

She felt better already. "I'm looking—" She cleared her throat and deepened her voice. "I'm looking for my brother, an Adam Leslie. He was staying with Scarborough this week past."

"Adam Leslie?" The man set down his fistful of rags and wiped his hands on the front of his breeches. "I don't recall a man by that name."

Caithren's heart sank. Adam was fond of frequenting public taprooms, so she'd been hoping the innkeeper would know where he'd gone, what route he might have taken. Maybe she wouldn't need to travel all the way to London.

The man ran a hand across his bald head. "What does he look like?"

"Tall, fair, longish blond hair..." She dug in her pocket and brought out the portrait. "Here," she said, holding forth the wee oval painting. "I'm wondering if he told anyone where he was headed next."

Brown took it and considered, frowning. "I'm sorry, but I recall no man named Adam Leslie, nor anyone who looks like this picture." He handed it back. "Is it a decent likeness?"

She nodded.

"I have a good head for people, sir...er, madam?"

"Aye." Caithren sighed. Her disguise wasn't working after all.

Mr. Brown piled some discarded trenchers on a tray and lifted it to his shoulder. "I'm sure I would have remembered your brother had I seen him."

Blast it, another lump was rising in her throat. She'd never been a crybaby, and she didn't intend to take up the practice now. She pulled the letter from her pocket and unfolded it, scanning the worn page. "He was traveling with two other gentlemen, Lords Grinstead and Balmforth. Might you have seen them?"

"I'm afraid their names aren't familiar, either."

"Oh." A burst of laughter in the background seemed to mock Caithren's distress. Her hunger had faded…although she could very much use a mug of ale.

"I'm sorry," he repeated.

"It's no fault of yours." Slipping the letter and painting back into her pocket, she glanced about. She couldn't face the other travelers eating and socializing in this room—she'd spent the best part of a week with some of them already, with more forced togetherness promised to come.

And what if Mrs. Dochart came downstairs? The old bawface didn't know she was back yet—with a quick escape and any luck at all, she could spend one night alone in her peaceful, solitary room.

She turned back to the innkeeper. "Might you have some supper sent up? Room three."

"Certainly, Miss…Leslie, is it not?"

"Aye. Thank you."

"No trouble a'tall." With another appraising glance, he disappeared into the kitchen, and she decided to order an ale before heading upstairs.

ELEVEN

"THANK YOU kindly." Jason pressed a coin into the serving maid's hand and settled back with his ale. Taking a swallow, he watched her sway from his shadowed corner into the lamplit center of the taproom. A nice sway she had, too, but he had neither the stamina nor inclination to pursue her right now.

He rubbed his tired eyes. God knew he wasn't good for much more than people-watching this evening.

He downed a second gulp as a boy, tall for his age, turned dejectedly from the taproom's bar and made his way to the stairs. The lad was overly pretty, way too thin, and young—not even shaving yet. Strange to find him in a taproom alone, but perhaps his folks were waiting upstairs. Jason hoped so—he knew what it was like to be young and alone, and he wouldn't wish it on anybody.

Massaging his sore shoulder, he took another sip. It was aggravating to find himself so worn out, weeks after the injury. But having pushed himself to the limit to beat the Gothard brothers here, he was relieved to find he'd managed it.

Obviously they weren't overworking his horses. When they arrived, tomorrow or the next day, they'd be in for a rude surprise. He'd get the answers to his questions, and this chapter in his life would be closed.

Or almost. No word had come from Ford as to the identity of the man he'd killed.

He took another sip of his ale, watching the boy start up the bare wooden steps, a mug of ale in one hand. Two men came down and met the lad halfway, blocking his progress on the staircase's tiny landing.

Geoffrey and Walter Gothard.

Jason bolted up, his heart beating a wild tattoo.

The poor lad began visibly shaking. He tightened the blue and green shawl he had wrapped about his shoulders, squaring his slender frame. "I know who you are," he told the brothers bravely in a distinct Scots accent, his voice high as a girl's with tension. "You won't get away with your wicked plans."

The wean sounded like he meant it. Halfway there to intervene —not to mention capture Geoffrey Gothard once and for all—Jason froze. Was the boy after Gothard as well? There was, after all, the hundred-pound reward he'd offered—an absolutely vast sum to someone like this lad.

The boy took a step back down the stairs, then suddenly dropped the ale. It spilled down the stairs as he reached beneath the plaid wool and pulled something out, brandishing it daringly.

The soft glow of metal spurred Jason into action. No matter how bone-weary he was, there was no way he could allow a lad to become Gothard's next victim. A wild bellow rose from his throat as he drew his rapier and reached the stairs in four running strides. No doubt drawn by the racket, Geoffrey's eyes met his and went wide with recognition. The bastard turned and bolted up the steps.

Shouldering the boy aside, Jason yelled, "Send for the authorities!" and reached to snag Gothard by the arm. He whipped him back around, then deliberately dropped his sword—another death was not the way to end this. Instead, his fingers closed around Geoffrey's neck as the sword slid clattering down the stairs. Walter tried to sidle past, but Jason shot out a foot and tripped the younger Gothard, who thumped down, whining loudly.

Still holding Geoffrey by the throat, Jason held Walter hostage with a boot pressed into his gut. A sickening crunch and a short, sharp cry of pain drew his attention to the bottom of the stairs. He looked down, startled to see the boy had fallen sometime during the scuffle. Even worse, Jason's rapier lay dangerously nearby, and a bright splotch of blood stained the lad's shirt.

He lay still as death, face up amidst the tangle of his unwrapped plaid shawl. His hat had fallen off...

No, *her* hat.

Hell and furies, it was a woman! A woman with long, tawny plaits. When Jason half-turned to get a better look, his fingers loosened.

Walter squirmed from beneath his foot and stumbled down the stairs. "It's the ghost of Cainewood!" he yelled as he reached the bottom and ran for the door.

"Dunderhead!" Geoffrey rasped, one hand flying up to cradle his abused throat. Murder in his eyes, he dealt Jason a mighty shove that sent him to his knees and clunking down two steps. While Geoffrey pushed past to follow his brother to freedom, Jason righted himself and made his way down the stairs after them.

But at the bottom of the steps, the woman moaned softly at his feet. With a regretful glance at the door, he knelt by her side. Blood still trickled from the cut on her shoulder—a cut from his sword that had tumbled downstairs in her wake.

A negligible injury, but his fault nonetheless.

"Wake up!" Jason shook the woman's other shoulder, but her eyes failed to open.

He couldn't help but gape at her. How on earth had he ever thought she was a boy? She was a woman, full grown, with a woman's bosom that heaved beneath her man's shirt. Smallish, perhaps, but a definite bosom nonetheless.

He rubbed the back of his neck. Why, that sorry excuse for a disguise wouldn't fool a living soul...well, perhaps only someone as single-minded as he'd been these days past. The lingering pain from the pistol wound must be muddling his brain.

He rose, shoved the rapier back into his belt, and bent to try to rouse her once again. No luck.

A pair of dusty shoes strolled into his vision and stopped by the woman's head. Jason straightened. "Did you send someone to fetch the authorities?"

"The magistrate's in Lancashire. Visiting his ill mother."

Typical, Jason thought in disgust.

The innkeeper, a wiry, balding man, rubbed his nose. He eyed the woman with sympathy. "She's staying in room three. If you wouldn't mind taking her up?"

"I expect I owe her that, at least," Jason agreed gruffly.

He grabbed the woman's pistol off the floor—the oldest, ugliest gun he'd ever seen—and lifted her into his arms. A limp bundle she was: slim, soft, and smelling of flowers. Feminine.

So why the boy's clothing?

It hit him like a bolt of summer lightning: she was after the reward.

He stared at her, picturing Geoffrey Gothard already miles down the road.

Damnation.

The whoreson had eluded him again, and all because of an incompetent Scottish reward hunter who would certainly bungle the capture—if she didn't get herself killed outright.

Jason had laughed at the ridiculous rumors, but the joke was on him…because here was Emerald MacCallum, right in his arms.

TWELVE

$\mathcal{W}$ ITH A GRUNT, Jason laid Emerald on the bed, then lit a candle and set it on the plain wooden table beside her. Rubbing his aching shoulder, he stood staring at her chalk-white face.

The flickering flame cast a sense of movement he knew was only an illusion. He lifted one slim wrist and let it drop back to the bed. Limp and deathly still.

Just like little Mary.

A strange hollowness opened in his gut. He reached to feel for the pulse at her throat, relieved to find it warm and steady beneath his fingers. After drawing a restorative breath, he untangled the plaid shawl. As he tossed it over the spartan room's only chair, the woman's soft floral scent wafted to his nose.

Though he was no stranger to undressing ladies, he couldn't remember ever stripping one he'd never laid eyes on before. The room seemed suddenly short of air. He drew off her shoes and dropped them on the planked wood floor, then rolled her stockings down shapely calves and off her small, arched feet.

He'd never noticed a female's feet.

Clearly it had been far too long since he'd had a woman. Of late, his responsibilities to the estate and as a father figure to his siblings allowed precious little time for pursuing personal pleasures.

Ignoring the unwelcome twinge of desire, he hurried to find the damage from his sword. He loosened the laces of her shirt, eased it down, and brought the candle close to her shoulder. The cut was small and shallow, the blood already clotted against her creamy skin.

His heart calmed somewhat, then raced again as he caught himself studying her half-exposed breasts—silky, bare breasts that looked as though they were made to fit in the palms of his hands. With a muttered oath, he set down the candle and tugged the shirt back into place, noticing a pendant nestled in her cleavage.

He lifted her head and drew off the necklace. Warm from the heat of her body, a rectangular green stone shone in an ornate gold setting. The simple link chain had seen much wear. Candlelight glinted off the stone's smooth, rubbed surface.

An emerald. Emerald MacCallum.

He set the pendant on the bedside table with a little *click* that seemed to reverberate in the quiet room. A soft moan from the woman lifted his hopes and drew his gaze back to her.

Emerald looked sweet and unspoiled. Like a dairymaid, truth be told, since she'd plaited her hair to conceal it beneath her hat. She wasn't at all like he'd pictured the fabled Emerald MacCallum, but then, it weren't as though anyone knew what she looked like. Drawings on broadsides were of the outlaws, not their pursuers.

But the thought of a petite woman like this capturing outlaws was laughable. The breeches left little to the imagination, and he couldn't help but notice she was thinner than the current fashionable ideal. Someone needed to feed this woman. Guilt lodged in his stomach as he rubbed a thumb along her cheek, glancing at her long, full lashes and wondering what color her eyes were.

Her wide mouth looked kissable.

With a huff of impatience, he jerked his hand away and rolled her onto her stomach, then wrestled the thin quilt from beneath her and settled it over her back. Gingerly he explored her head for the lump he knew must be there, given that she'd been knocked unconscious. He winced when he found it, hard and large and warm to the touch. The tight plait on that side couldn't be comfortable.

He set to undoing it to relieve the pressure. Long and shimmering, hair every hue of blond and brown slid between his hands. When the first side was loose, his fingers lingered at the place where her straight, white part ended at the nape of her neck. Baby fine hairs glimmered gold in that spot.

No matter that the woman was Emerald MacCallum, the downy little hollow looked innocent and vulnerable. Anger fired up. At himself, at the world.

He'd thrown down his sword to avoid bloodshed, and now someone else was hurt.

His fingers absently loosed the second plait while he seethed at the whole situation. Though he tried to block a vision of poor little Mary, the effort only led him to picture Emerald in the same condition. The thought made him shake.

And those bastards had slipped away. Again. He rose and paced around the room, lighting more candles and cursing himself.

He should have gone in with loaded pistols and blade at the ready, prepared to handle the brothers once and for all, with no thought to fairness or avoiding violence. Father would have done it that way.

"Father would have handled it," he muttered in self-disgust and walked across to the window.

THIRTEEN

*H*EARING A voice, Caithren shifted on the bed, her head in a painful fog.

The voice had been a dark, harsh whisper. She wasn't sure whether she'd actually heard it or if it had been part of her disturbing dream. She tried to move, but her head hurt. She moaned, struggling against the nausea.

Swift footsteps approached. "You're awake, then?" It was the same man's voice, but rich, comforting, and laced with relief.

Cait tried to roll closer to the sound.

He held her in place with a large, warm hand. "For heaven's sake, be still." Tinged with worry, his voice wasn't quite as nice. "You bumped your head but good."

She was lying facedown with her nose mashed into the pillow. She couldn't breathe properly.

The man's hands gripped her shoulders, gently helping her turn. "Are you dizzy?" he asked, moving to arrange her aching head on the pillow.

She intended to say aye, but when he came into view, her answer got lost somewhere between her mind and her mouth. Clear green eyes—too beautiful for a man—were studying her. His shadowed jaw and fine tanned features were framed by glorious, long raven hair that was wavy and prettier than her own. Bent over her as he was, the ends threatened to tickle her cheeks.

He looked frustrated and concerned. And she had no idea who he was.

"Can you talk? Emerald, are you all right?"

"Emerald?" she echoed. She supposed she was all right, if she didn't take her aching head into account. Her gaze was riveted to a faint dimple in the stranger's chin. There was only one thing she was certain of in that moment. "I-I'm not Emerald," she managed.

"Oh?" Beneath a narrow black mustache, his chiseled lips curved, but not in humor. "You're Scottish," he said, as though that explained everything.

"You're English," she countered, batting his hair from her face. He straightened, and his spicy scent wafted away, leaving her head a little clearer.

The room swam into view. She lay beneath not the dusky rose canopy of her bed at home, but a utilitarian beamed ceiling, the plaster cracked and at least a century older than Leslie Castle.

She was somewhere in England, and Da was dead.

Disoriented, she raised herself to her elbows, then flopped back to the pillow. A fresh burst of pain detonated inside her head, forcing a moan out through her lips.

"I told you to keep still." With a gentle hand, the man swept her hair off her face.

She pushed his hand away and fingered the ends of her hair, confused. He'd unraveled her plaits. Her other hand drifted up to touch the side of her head where the pain was the sharpest. "I'm not Emerald."

"You're Scottish"—he held up a palm to stop her words from tumbling out—"you're wearing men's clothes, you're carrying a pistol, and you're after a wanted outlaw. Now tell me you're not Emerald MacCallum."

"I'm not Emerald MacCallum."

His mouth curved as though he were amused. "Did the knock on your head damage your memory?"

"My memory is intact, thank you. But my name isn't Emerald." Despite her denial, her brain seemed impossibly muddled by the throbbing pain. "It's Caithren," she managed finally. "Caithren Leslie. Not Emerald."

"Hmm…" The man raised one black brow. "If you're not Emerald, then can you explain what you're doing here?"

Her brain might be muddled, but she knew an accusation when she heard one. "Why shouldn't I be here?" she asked on a huff. "Is there some law against my visiting your country? England and Scotland share a king, last I heard. Though not for long, I'm hoping."

Looking less than satisfied, he crossed his arms while one booted foot tapped against the wooden floor. Obviously he was waiting for her to explain herself.

Arrogant cur.

She wouldn't look at him, then. Her gaze swept the room, taking in the plain whitewashed walls, a simple wood cabinet, a utilitarian washstand, a small tub full of dirty bathwater that should have been carried away.

Pontefract. She was in her room at the inn in Pontefract. She was here in Pontefract...

She squeezed her eyes shut tight, blocking out the man so she could concentrate. "I've come to find my brother," she said at last, opening them in relief.

"Hmm, is that so?" he challenged in a calm voice laced with a touch of irony. "Then I suppose you can explain to me how you know Gothard."

She stared at him blankly. "Gothard?"

"Geoffrey Gothard. The man you tried to shoot in order to collect the reward. I'm not a half-wit, Emerald."

"I'm not Emerald. And I'm not a half-wit, either, but you're certainly making me feel so, since I haven't the slightest notion what you're blethering about."

He sat at the edge of the bed and studied her for a while, as though trying to gauge her sincerity. The mattress sagged beneath his weight, rolling her too close to him for her comfort. The queasiness clawed at her stomach again.

She was alone with a strange man. A strange *English* man. Her mouth went dry, and she licked her lips.

His eyes darkened, making her nervous. With a sigh, she reached up to fiddle with a plait, then remembered her hair was loose. She fisted her hands atop the bedcovers. "It's God's own truth I'm telling you, Mr...."

His mouth twisted up in a hint of a smile. "Chase. But you may call me Jason."

"I may, may I?" Stuffy, these English. Well, it wasn't as though

Cameron hadn't warned her. She took a deep breath and decided to try again. "Do you believe me?"

"I think not." His sarcastic tone grated on her. "What is your brother's name?"

She struggled against the pain in her head. "…Adam."

"And why do you have cause to think he'd be here?"

"He was invited by…"

As she strained to come up with the name, he shook his head, sending the glorious hair swinging. "You'll have to invent these lies more quickly if you expect them to sound believable."

"Scarborough," she gritted out.

"The *Earl* of Scarborough?" A sparkle came into his eyes, as though he were entertained by the thought of someone related to her being invited anywhere by an earl.

Just like the innkeeper downstairs.

Did she look that provincial? Her clothes were in decent condition. Her father had been a baronet.

"I'm surprised at you, Emerald." His mocking voice interrupted her musings. "You've a reputation for being the cunning sort. Surely you can come up with a better story than that. It must be the knock on the head."

How this man could think she was someone else was beyond her. Exasperated, she slammed her hand against the mattress, wincing when it jarred her. "Bile yer heid."

"Pardon?" Clearly amused, he raised a brow. "Are you suggesting I boil my head?"

Clenching her teeth, she looked away. Her plaid was tossed over a chair, her shoes and stockings on the floor. Alarm shot through her. "Did you undress me as well, then?" She thrust her hands beneath the bedclothes to see what else he might have taken off of her.

That brow went up again. "I reckon you'll find you're still decent. Bloody hell, woman, what do you take me for?"

"An Englishman." Her clothing was all in place, although the laces on her shirt had been loosened. She gave them a vicious tug, then looked down and gasped. "There's blood on my shirt." She felt for the source, though it didn't really hurt much.

"You were cut. Nothing serious."

Slackening the laces, she peeked beneath. He was right. The meadow rue she'd picked would heal it in no time.

"That's why your shirt was unlaced," he continued. "I...checked."

When she looked up, his face was red. A proper gentleman he was, then, but he was still an Englishman. And he was staring at her. Caithren bit her lip and felt for her good-luck charm.

Her hands closed on air.

"Where's my amulet?" she squeaked in a panic. She struggled up on her elbows again and felt the dizziness rush back.

"I have it right here." He reached to the bedside table, lifted the amulet, and dangled it over her head by its chain. The emerald swung in a hypnotizing pattern. "I'm hardly in the habit of stealing from unconscious women."

"Well, I don't know you, do I?" She snatched it to her chest.

"But you know Geoffrey Gothard, don't you?"

Crivvens, the man was persistent. She shot him a peeved look and slipped the chain back over her head, feeling better when the amulet was settled in place. She wrapped a hand around it.

That Geoffrey he was talking about, she remembered who he was now—the murdering cur she'd overheard at Scarborough's and met again on the inn's staircase. That terrible, horrible man and his scum of a brother.

Englishmen.

She shivered and tugged up on the thin quilt. Here she was, alone with another Englishman, a strange man in a strange country. Well, at least this one Englishman was looking out for her, even if she didn't care for him badgering her with questions. And though he was plainly annoyed, he'd yet to raise his voice to her.

"Thank you for your help," she said softly by way of apology.

When she tried to smile, his eyes softened. He leaned closer and brushed the hair from her face. One warm finger trailed her cheek.

He was staring at her mouth, looking as though he wanted to kiss her, like that bampot Duncan had looked at the village dance last month.

What a daft thought. The Englishman, kiss her? He didn't even believe who she was.

The knock on her head must have been harder than she'd supposed for her to think something like that. And he was vexed with her, although she'd done nothing to warrant it. Nothing she could recall, anyway.

She squinted up at him. "Why are you so vexed?"

"I had a job to do, Emerald," he said with a sigh that, if she didn't know better, she might take to be apologetic. "And you got in the way. No fault of yours." He waved a dismissive hand. "Stay away from Geoffrey Gothard. He's a dangerous man."

Despite his annoying use of the wrong name, Caithren's heart melted a little. He'd rescued her downstairs, and now he was warning her, trying to protect her. "I saw that for myself," she said, seeking to reassure him. "But he's unlikely to be a danger to me, seeing as he's on his way to London."

"London?" She saw his body tense. "How come you to know this?"

"I...overheard him and—his brother, aye? When I went out to Scarborough's to find Adam." Because he seemed concerned for her welfare, she added, "They didn't see me."

The Englishman's beautiful green eyes narrowed on hers suspiciously. "Why are you telling me this? To send me off in the wrong direction?"

"Pardon me?"

He stood abruptly. "Just stay away from Gothard. Find yourself another reward to collect." The candle flames flickered as he strode to the door, disturbing the room's musty air. His gaze settled on her emerald amulet for a moment before he pierced her with those incredible eyes. "I admire your persistence—it puts me in mind of my family—but I cannot see why you refuse to own up to who you are."

"You know what my mam would have said?" Caithren crossed her arms beneath the quilt. "Telling it true, pits ain in a stew."

He paused with his hand on the latch. "I cannot understand you."

"Then permit me to translate. Telling the truth confuses your enemies."

"I'm not your enemy." He blinked several times. "Why of a sudden does everyone think me his enemy?"

He said it to no one in particular, his gaze aimed toward the blackened beamed ceiling, as though he were looking for the heavens to send down an answer.

"I should be on the road after Gothard," he mused to himself. Then he sighed and looked back to her. "But damn if I don't feel responsible for you."

"Well, you needn't be," Cait said. "I can take care of myself."

"Not from what I've seen. And now, thanks to me, you're even less equipped physically to deal with men like the Gothards."

"What do you mean, thanks to you?"

He frowned. "Surely you realize you fell down the stairs as a result of my intervention? And it was my sword that cut you. Accidentally—I wasn't even holding it—but it's my responsibility nonetheless." She heard a click when he pushed down on the latch. "I insist you accept my help."

"I'd say you've helped me quite enough already." This man was out of his mind. "Your kind of help I don't need."

He didn't seem to hear her, or else he simply dismissed her opinion. "Get some sleep," he said, "but make sure you awaken. The last thing I need is another Mary."

Mary? Who the devil was Mary?

He opened the door. "I'll check on you in the morning. If your head still aches, we'll have a doctor in to examine it."

Caithren was so confused and frustrated that if she'd had the energy, she'd have kicked the door shut behind him. As it was, it closed softly.

Did he think she was there for his bidding?

I'll check on you in the morning.

Not if she had anything to say about it.

FOURTEEN

*T*HE SILVER *blade flashed, vibrations sang up his arm, and the man before him crumpled to the ground. Blood pumped, sickeningly slick and bright—*

His heart racing, Jason sat straight up in bed, sweat breaking out to coat his clammy skin. His breath came in short, hard pants.

Who was this man he'd killed? Had he been a husband, a father? Certainly he'd been a son.

How many lives had Jason ruined with that fateful thrust of his sword?

Hopefully not as many as when his own parents had been slain on the field of battle. Heaven forbid he should put another family through a hell like that. Not even, as his parents had, for honor.

Senseless honor. They'd died fighting for the king, yet Cromwell had prevailed.

He raked a hand through his hair and swung his shaky legs off the bed. Dust motes floated in the brightness that streamed through the crooked shutters. Sunshine. Daylight. He'd overslept. Another restless, too-short night, like they all seemed to be since he was shot.

He stumbled to his clothing, pulled out his pocket watch, and flipped open the sapphire-adorned lid. Almost noon. Damn, Gothard would be long down the road by now.

And Emerald after him. Cunning Emerald, the woman Jason had

found himself absurdly tempted to kiss. He was the one who ought to have his head examined.

He threw on a shirt and breeches, then padded across the corridor to knock on her door. Silence. He tried the latch, and the door swung wide to reveal an empty room.

Cursing at himself, he returned to his own room and pulled on his boots. His family had been right—he had no business going after Geoffrey Gothard. But it had nothing to do with the state of his health. The fact was, he belonged behind a desk or riding his land. He'd always valued peace and tranquility; he didn't know how to do this. He was botching it good and proper.

Downstairs in the taproom, the early dinner crowd was much too cheerful for Jason's mood. A quick glance failed to reveal Emerald among the diners. The harried innkeeper was rolling a fresh barrel of ale into place behind the counter. When he paused to mop his red face, Jason jumped behind to help him upend it. It settled into place with a *thump*, displacing more than its share of dust.

Jason coughed. "Do you know where I might find the woman who was injured last night?"

The man wiped his shiny brow with a handkerchief. "She left this morning. On the public coach."

"The coach? Not a horse?"

"No horses available in Pontefract. Told her that yesterday when she wanted to hire one."

"She had no horse of her own?"

The innkeeper shrugged. "She arrived on the coach."

Jason rubbed his aching shoulder. One didn't use public transportation to track outlaws. If Emerald had arrived here looking for a horse, something must have happened to hers. She must be on her way to the next town to find herself another.

His hand dropped. "The coach towards where?"

"London."

"London?" Surely she'd gone in another direction; she'd only said London to confuse him, hadn't she? "Are you certain?"

But the moment the question was out of his mouth, he knew the innkeeper was right. The old stableman had told him Scarborough was in London. If the Gothards had come to West Riding to speak with their brother—to get something from their brother—it made sense that now they'd head to see him in London instead. And of course Emerald would go after them.

The man dabbed at his dripping nose. "London, yes. It's Thursday, no? The coach leaves for London at eight every Thursday."

"Eight. Damn." She had a four-hour lead. But the public coach was slow as a condemned man mounting Tyburn gallows, and Chiron, Jason's silver gelding, had won his last three races in Sussex. If Emerald hadn't found a horse yet, he might be able to catch up to her. "How much do I owe for the room?"

He slapped coins on the counter and ran upstairs to fetch his belongings, then headed back down to the stables. Blasted woman thought she could fool him, did she? The Gothard brothers were riding for London, and here she was, going after them at her first chance.

She was Emerald MacCallum, all right, no matter the lies that tumbled from her enticing lips. And he had to keep an eye on her, lest she get to Geoffrey first—because she was bound to get herself killed in the process.

She might have a reputation for tracking men—indeed, she'd done a credible job of it so far, tracing the brothers to here—but she'd never come up against the likes of Gothard before. The man was evil.

And now she was injured, thanks to Jason. He owed it to her to follow her, watch over her. Protect her.

Luckily, they seemed to be heading in the same direction.

It would be no trouble.

FIFTEEN

$\mathcal{J}$ASON CAUGHT up to Emerald's coach—at least he hoped it was her coach—in Doncaster. Passengers had disembarked. A few walked along Church Street or Greyfriars Road, stretching their legs while the horses were changed.

Emerald was nowhere in sight.

He tethered Chiron and poked his head into the coach's cabin, finding it empty. Neither was she inside the Greyfriars Inn, where other passengers were taking refreshment.

Bloody hell, she must have hired a horse and left already.

Frustrated, he paid for an ale and paced Church Street while drinking it. He decided he should be relieved—it would have been hell following a public coach. Too damned slow. Once he found her —assuming he could—it would be much better with her on horse-back. He could follow surreptitiously and keep her safe, without worrying about the brothers getting too far ahead.

Yes, it really was quite a relief. Anxious to get on the road after Emerald, he tilted his head back and drained the rest of the ale. And looked back down to see a woman across the street.

A woman who looked rather like Emerald MacCallum.

Instead of breeches, the woman wore a dark green skirt over a long-sleeved, high-necked shift, topped by a brown laced bodice that looked like it belonged in the previous century. She rounded a corner of the Church of St. George, disappearing from Jason's view. He took off after her.

He hadn't caught sight of her face. But the sun had glinted off dark-blond hair woven into two plaits. He'd thought Emerald had plaited her hair last night only to hide it under her hat, but he could have been wrong in that assumption.

Absurd hairstyle for a grown woman.

There she was, standing by the double doors of the majestic medieval building. Stopping in a graveyard a safe distance away, he concealed himself behind a monument and watched.

It was quite definitely Emerald. Evidently she only dressed like a man when her quarry was in range. Or maybe she hadn't found time yet to wash the blood off her shirt and mend the slash from his blade.

Gazing up at the massive planked doors, she reached a finger to trace a section of their scrolled ironwork before her hand closed over the latch. But she stopped short of opening it. Instead she heaved a visible sigh and began wandering around the church, toward another graveyard that looked ancient compared to the one where Jason hid. Idly she bent down to pluck off part of a small plant and slipped it into her pocket. Strange woman.

It hit him then. As in Pontefract, there must have been no horses available here in Doncaster. She was only biding her time until the coach was ready to leave.

Damnation. He would have to follow the coach after all, until Emerald managed to find herself a horse. And thereby risk Gothard getting to London ahead of him, potentially endangering other people there and along the way.

Setting the empty tankard atop a gravestone, he groaned aloud at the thought. But he had no choice.

Or did he?

SIXTEEN

*T*ILTED, MOSSY stone markers were spaced unevenly on the grass. Caithren strolled the crooked rows, touching one here and there. The same names appeared over and over through the centuries. Mowbray, Southwell, Hodgkinson.

She shivered as she touched the rough headstone of two Southwell bairns. They'd been dead more than two hundred years, one at the age of four, the other listed simply as "Infant Daughter." Cait's throat tightened at the thought of losing family. The recent loss of Da still hurt.

"Boarding!"

Startled, she glanced around the kirk toward the Greyfriars Inn. She'd enjoyed her solitude till the last possible moment, but now the coach had pulled up before the rounded corner of the red-brick building, fresh horses in place, and the first passengers were climbing aboard, that old bawface Mrs. Dochart among them. With a sigh, she kissed her fingertips and touched them to the sisters' gravestone, then turned to make her way back to the inn.

The sun disappeared behind a cloud. Suddenly the cemetery seemed eerie and forbidding. A soft wheezy sound set her heart to pounding. Was she hearing muffled footsteps?

Spooked, she froze in her tracks.

It's the wind, she told herself. The wind whistling through the old kirk. Cameron always said she had too active an imagination. But her fingers flew to her amulet as her body tensed, ready to run.

A louder footstep sounded behind her, and a hand clamped on her shoulder. Whirling, she shrieked.

"Whoa, there." Beneath his wide-brimmed hat, the man looked puzzled and apologetic. "You look like you saw a ghost."

The face registered, and Caithren's jaw dropped open. Her hands went to her heaving chest. It took a moment to find her tongue, but when she did, she let loose.

"You!" The Englishman had said he felt responsible, but she hadn't figured he was insane enough to follow her. "You scared me half to death."

"I'm sorry. I didn't mean to frighten you, only—"

"What the devil are you doing here?" Still trembling, she leaned on a gravestone. "Did you follow me? I told you I don't want your help."

He shrugged in answer as he gazed around the cemetery. "You're shaking. I suppose you believe in ghosts?"

"I've yet to meet a Scot who doesn't," she said shortly.

His lips curved as though he found that amusing. He motioned his head toward the gray stone kirk. "Why didn't you go inside?"

She glanced from him to the building, then back. "You were watching me?"

The thought was disturbing. She'd wanted to explore the elaborate medieval kirk, not to mention pray there for the stamina to put up with Mrs. Dochart for eight and a half more days. Lord knew she needed some help. But she'd been afraid the coach would leave without her, so she'd stayed outdoors instead.

And he'd been watching her. A vague sense of unease stole over her. Her hand went into her pocket, feeling for the familiar comfort of Adam's portrait she'd put there to remind her of her goal.

"I-I must go. Please, just leave me alone."

"It's a beautiful building." He gestured at the bell tower, where no less than sixteen pinnacles crowned the battlement. "You really should have a look inside."

The sun came back out, dispelling her nervousness. He was only a man, albeit a misguided one. "I don't have time to go inside. The coach is leaving."

He nodded. "I'll walk you through."

"There's a door on the other side?" She frowned but followed him, dimly wondering why she was cooperating with an Englishman. But she supposed he was trying to help.

Inside, it was cool and deathly quiet. Deserted as well, at two o'clock on a Thursday afternoon. The flames of votive candles made shadows dance in the dim light that filtered through the kirk's beautiful stained-glass windows. She paused to silently admire the ancient grandeur, loath to disturb the utter peacefulness with unnecessary words.

With a tug on her hand, he urged her down a side aisle.

"Last call!" The driver's voice managed to pierce the thick stone walls. Looking up, Cait could see that some of the colorful windows were old and broken, no doubt letting in the sound, as well as the wind that had frightened her in the graveyard.

"Let go of me," she whispered, trying to pull from the Englishman's grasp. He had no business touching her. "I must go."

He held tight and continued doggedly toward a small private chapel that projected outside the main wall. It would be near Church Street and the inn. That must be where the door was.

But when they stepped through an archway and inside, a scan of the wee chapel revealed only a single wooden bench and a simple altar with three small burning candles. Afternoon sun shone through a cracked window, projecting brilliant colored patches on the stone floor.

Alarm skittered through her. "There's no door."

"I never said there was a door."

She stifled her urge to yell—she couldn't be making a racket in the kirk. "I must *go*."

"I think not."

He wanted to *keep* her here? She moved for the main sanctuary and front door, but he was faster and blocked her path. Losing patience, she shoved at his arm. "Please move out of my way."

"I'm not going to hurt you." He wedged himself into the archway, spreading his feet at the bottom and his hands at the top. "I want only to protect you."

Protect her? The man was daft. She beat both fists against his chest, and he yelped. But he was solid and immovable.

Through a high cracked window, she heard the call of her name. Panic welled in her throat. She needed to be on the coach. Her future depended on finding her brother. She didn't have time for this stranger and his accusations and claims of responsibility.

She gave him another shove and kicked at his shins, but he stood firm, his mouth a straight line beneath his thin mustache. She heard her name called again and wished she hadn't left Da's pistol in her satchel on the coach.

When she heard the creak and groan of the coach departing, her panic blended with white-hot anger. Frantically she tried to duck under his arms, through his legs, and finally turned her back, sputtering incoherently. Only when the sound of the wheels faded into the distance did he step from the archway.

No matter they were in a kirk—she whirled and slapped him hard across the face.

"Holy heaven!" His hand came up to cover his cheek where her finger-shaped imprints were already making a blotchy, red presence. "You've got a hell of an arm."

"Don't you blaspheme in the kirk!" she yelled, bringing her hand up again.

Neatly he caught her by the wrist. "Once, you're quick. Twice, I'm stupid," he said drolly.

"You're stupid, all right! I missed my coach!" She wrenched free and shrank away from him, back into the wee chapel.

"There's nowhere for you to go," he said calmly. "I won't hurt you."

"Why should I believe you?" But she did, though it made no sense. "How am I going to get to London?"

"There will be another coach."

"In three days! And I must be in London by next week!"

He rubbed his injured cheek. Absurdly, she noticed he hadn't shaved. He must have been in a hurry this morning.

"Next week," he mused, as though to himself. "What for?" He came close, his hand dropping from his face to clamp her shoulder, holding her from bolting. As if she had anywhere to go. "Why do you need to be in London? Think fast—I'm sure you can come up with a good one."

"My brother is expected there." She twisted from his grip. "I told you I'm looking for him. I need him to sign some papers."

"That story's getting old, Emerald."

"It's God's truth!" Tears threatened, but she blinked them back.

She didn't know whether she was more enraged that he'd detained her or that he insisted on calling her Emerald. Both made her spitting mad. "If I miss him in London, he might go to India. And how will I find him then, I ask you? What will I do then?"

"India? Your creativity knows no bounds." Wincing, he bent to rub one of his shins, and she was gratified to think she'd damaged him. "India," he muttered, his voice unmistakably disgusted.

The tears did fall then, fast and furious. All she'd wanted was to find Adam. It had seemed such a simple matter to go to him and have him sign the papers. Now everything had gone awry.

"I must get to London!" The Englishman's face looked all blurry through her tears. "Why did you keep me here?" she wailed. "Whatever for?"

He opened his mouth, then closed it. Then opened it again. "I told you last night. I feel responsible—"

"I'm not your responsibility!"

"—for seeing to your safety," he continued unperturbed. "I only hoped to delay you a few days, to allow me to deal with Geoffrey Gothard before he can do you harm."

"Gothard again?" She stamped her foot, hard. It seemed the candle flames wavered, but the Englishman didn't budge. "I hate you!"

"You're not my favorite person, either. I'm only trying to help you." He shook his head. "India." The sigh that escaped his lips was so elaborate it ruffled his long black hair.

She sat down on the single bench and dashed impatiently at the wetness on her cheeks. Wheesht! She rarely cried at home, but here she was a veritable fountain.

England was a very nasty place. Cameron didn't know the half of it.

"What am I supposed to do now?" Her shoulders trembled. "Will you take me back to the coach?"

"Forward to the coach. And the answer is no." His black boots shuffled on the stone floor. He plopped to sit beside her. "Please don't cry."

His voice sounded miserable. He hated tears, did he? Good. She let loose a particularly pathetic wail.

He scooted to the far end of the bench. She angled toward him so he could see the tears run down her face. He rose and walked away, pacing the breadth of the wee chapel and back again. When he came to stand before her, arms crossed, she dropped her head into her hands and sobbed uncontrollably.

Or at least she hoped he thought so. She had to convince him to take her to the coach.

"I'll take you to London," he muttered.

Tears forgotten, she looked up. "If you think I'd go with—"

"Look, I must go to London regardless." He frowned at her puzzled glare. "To find Gothard. I can protect you this way. I don't suppose it will be too much trouble to take you along."

She stood and rose on her toes before him, so she could stick her face near his. "Oh, aye?" He flinched, but she only pushed her nose even closer. "Thanks to you, I don't have any clothes or money—it's all on the coach. I don't even have a hat! I expect you'll be sorry before this is over."

His face turning red, he swept off his hat and stuck it on her head. "I'm sorry already."

"Good," she said through clenched teeth. Because it *was* good. He was unhappy and he was getting her out of here: both good things, in her estimation.

She tipped the hat's brim and swiped the tears from her cheeks.

As soon as they caught up with the coach, she'd be off, and best of luck to him in foiling her plans again. Fool her once, he was quick. Twice, she was stupid.

And Caithren Leslie was far from stupid.

SEVENTEEN

$\mathcal{J}$ ASON SAT Emerald before him on his horse. Not ten
minutes later, he knew it was a mistake. Damn woman
kept wiggling against him, which made him uncomfortable in more than one way.

He hadn't considered how the two of them would get to London
on one horse. Truth be told, he hadn't considered much of anything
before coming up with this harebrained scheme to detain her—to
ensure she didn't do anything foolish that might get her killed.

Before they left Bawtry tomorrow, he'd have to buy another
horse. He hoped mightily he'd have better luck finding one than
she'd had.

They rode two long hours before she said a word. As he guided
Chiron through a stand of trees and turned back onto the Great
North Road, she finally uttered a sentence. Grudgingly.

"Don't think I haven't noticed you took the long way round to
avoid the coach."

He snorted. "To the contrary, Emerald, I'm quite certain you
notice everything."

She leaned back to glare up at him, bumping her head on his
sore shoulder. "I'm *Caithren*."

He grunted and scooted back in the saddle, but only momentarily. Holy heaven, the wench smelled good. Like a heady mix of wild-

flowers. His arm tightened around her waist, even though the close contact made his aches and pains more achy and painful.

Bloody hell, was there anyplace she hadn't kicked or hit him?

"How did you find me?" she asked in a peevish tone.

It had been blind luck, but in his present mood he couldn't resist needling her anyway. "For a tracker, you're not very good at covering your own."

"I'm no tracker, whatever that might be."

"You trail outlaws and bring them in to collect the rewards." His gaze kept returning to that vulnerable little hollow at the nape of her neck. "Perhaps the Scots have a different word for it, but we call that tracking."

"Do you mean to say you think I do this regularly? Not just for this Gothard fellow, but for others?"

"It's exactly what you do, and we both know it. See here, Emerald, you're becoming legend. There are few hereabouts who don't know what you do, and I won't have you telling me you're one of them."

She huffed and jerked on the reins, jarring his bruised body and causing Chiron to shy. The end of one of her plaits flew back on the breeze, tickling his face. His stomach growled.

"Hungry, are you?"

"It's long past time for dinner." He didn't know which hurt worse: his poor abused body or his empty belly. "And I left without breakfast this morning, thanks to you."

"Thanks to me? This wasn't *my* idea."

He didn't rise to that bait, and they rode for a while more in uneasy silence. He wondered if he should give in and return her to the coach. But then he noticed her fingering her amulet.

Emerald.

Remembering her nick from the scuffle with the Gothards, he stiffened his resolve. She could get herself killed out there alone.

"You'll thank me for protecting you later," he murmured under his breath.

"You're not doing this out of responsibility and kindness." Emerald's smug words held a challenge. "Did you really think I'd fall for such an unbelievably noble excuse? You want to kill this man Gothard, and you're afraid I'll get to him before you do and steal your reward out from under you." Evidently proud of her powers of deduction, she leaned back with a grunt of satisfaction, jabbing her shoulder into his wound.

He opened his mouth to argue, then thought better of it. Let her believe that nonsense, if it pleased her. Though she could hardly have accused him of a motive that was more out of character, it wasn't surprising a woman like Emerald would find such a rationale acceptable. Telling the truth, that he was concerned for her life, must have insulted her independent nature.

Her explanation suited his purposes perfectly.

For the first time in days, he found himself pleased by a turn of events.

EIGHTEEN

*T*HAT EVENING, the clink of cutlery on pewter and the buzz of ale-lubricated conversation filled Caithren's ears as her gaze wandered the well-lit taproom of the Crown Hotel in Bawtry.

She inhaled deeply of a steaming chunk of meat pie before popping it into her mouth. "Not bad for English food," she admitted around the bite. "Hunger is the best kitchen."

Mr. Chase set down his tankard and steepled his fingers. "Translate?"

"Food tastes better when you're hungry. English food, at any rate."

Ignoring the barb, the Englishman lifted his spoon. She watched him, remembering when she'd first set eyes on him and thought he was so handsome. Now he just looked stubborn and irritating. Imagine finding oneself attracted to a man who had the gall to keep her off a public coach.

She deliberately looked away, out one of the Crown Hotel's large, fine glass windows. Across the street and to the right, candles glinted through the mottled windows of a nice, small plastered inn called the Turnpike. Down on the left sat the Granby Inn, a squat, square building that looked perfectly acceptable.

The Englishman had certainly chosen an enormous, expensive hotel. She wondered if he had money. He didn't look it. But she felt like she was staying in a private mansion. There were *marble* pillars in the entrance hall. And the hotel had fifty-seven rooms. Fifty-seven!

She wiggled on her chair, which was plush and upholstered and felt luxurious. At home they had only plain wooden chairs around their table. After spending half the day on horseback, the padding was welcome.

"You'll reach London much faster on horseback than by coach," the Englishman said, interrupting her musings. "This arrangement will work to your benefit."

"Aye?" She touched her emerald amulet. If all went as planned, *this arrangement* would end come midnight or so.

"We'll make it there in five or six days instead of nine. Long before the coach. And I hope before Gothard."

She took a dainty bite of her pie. "Gothard?" she echoed, unable to resist baiting him.

"Geoffrey Gothard," he clarified and stabbed his spoon into his own pie.

"Oh, him." On impulse, she reached across the table to touch the Englishman on the arm—then yanked her hand back. What was she doing? "You'd best go faster if you're planning to catch him. He was fixing to 'ride like the dickens,' whatever that means."

"It means like the devil." He polished off the last of his bread, studying her with a calculating green gaze. "How is it you know this?"

Cait sighed. "I *told* you I heard Geoffrey and Wat talking, when I was looking for my brother at Scarborough's place."

"Well, we made decent time today." He flexed his shoulder, a pained look coming over his face. "We shall ride like the dickens, then, and God willing I'll find the bastard right off."

"God willing, is it?" Toying with the handle of her dull pewter tankard, she drew a deep breath. "You can assist God by looking for Gothard at the home of someone named Lucas."

He stopped mid-chew. "Pardon?"

She took time for a sip of ale, half-hoping he would choke from curiosity. "The Gothards are going to London to get something from this man Lucas." She sipped again. "If he fails to give them what they want, they plan to murder him."

"Lucas Gothard? They plan to *kill* the Earl of Scarborough?"

Caithren shrugged. "Is that Scarborough's given name? Adam didn't say."

"What else did they say?"

"You cannot expect me to remember an entire conversation."

He said nothing, but she saw a muscle twitch in his jaw. Uncomfortable under his gaze, she reached into her skirt pocket to touch the miniature portrait of Adam. Her one memento of home—and the only thing she had to her name right now, save the clothes on her back.

The Englishman was studying her, his eyes narrowed. "Why did you let the Gothards get away?"

"I told you—"

"Yes, and it's a nice story. Very well done of you. But for you to know this much, well, it's perfectly clear you're none other than Emerald MacCallum, and there isn't a chance you'll convince me otherwise. Are you going to eat that?" He indicated her bread.

"Help yourself."

As she watched him reach across and break off a piece, Cait struggled for calm. She'd punished him with silence earlier, but it had been at least as hard on her as it had on him. No sense continuing the unpleasantness when she'd never see him again after tonight. Although if he called her Emerald one more time, a swift kick where it hurt might be in order.

He washed down a second piece of her bread with his ale. "Tell me why you're looking for your brother."

His tone implied he was trying to pacify her. That would annoy her if she let it, but she wouldn't.

Maybe if she told him more of her story, he would come to believe her.

"According to my father's will, Adam will inherit all of Leslie unless I marry within the year."

Plates rattled and diners chattered in the background. "And…?"

"Marriage is out of the question." She flashed him a bright, facetious grin. "Men are too demanding and controlling."

He appeared to be coughing up his ale.

"Is something amiss?"

"No." He thumped himself on the chest, then winced. "Continue."

"Well, Adam isn't fit to run Leslie. A restless sort, Adam is. And since I don't plan to marry, I need his signature on some papers relinquishing his rights to the property in exchange for a generous allowance." She fixed him with her best accusing glare. "The papers are in my satchel on the coach."

"I'll have another set drawn up in London." He blotted his mouth with his napkin. "At my expense."

"Your generosity knows no bounds."

Ignoring her sarcasm, the Englishman gazed at her supper. "Are you going to finish that?"

She shoved her half-eaten pie in his direction. "By all the saints, you're a bottomless pit. It's a wonder you're not fat as old King Henry."

"Runs in the family." With a scrape, he pulled it closer.

"As the sow fills, the draff sours."

"Pardon?"

She watched the pie methodically disappear. "The more you eat, the less you enjoy your food."

"Another of your mother's pearls of wisdom?"

"Aye, her words were wise."

"In this case, her words were wrong." He washed down the last of her supper with the last of her ale, then stood. "It was quite enjoyable. Now I must dash off a note and post it to Scarborough, to warn him of his brothers' intentions. And another note to my family. They'll be wondering where I am." He rooted in his pocket and pulled out a key. "Would you like to go up? The innkeeper had naught but a single room, but I'm certain we'll fare well together."

"You are, are you?"

"Yes," he said, so tolerantly she gritted her teeth. "Room twenty-six, upstairs and to the left. I'll meet you there in a few minutes."

Handing her the key, he started out of the taproom, then turned back.

"I can trust you to wait?"

The key's hard metal edges bit into her clenched fist. "I'm not going anywhere," she assured him blithely.

Not yet, anyway.

NINETEEN

CAITHREN HEADED up the fancy wrought-iron staircase, fuming as she looked for number twenty-six.

It was clear the Englishman didn't like her, yet he expected her to share his chamber tonight. Fifty-seven rooms and only one available? She didn't believe him for a moment. He planned on keeping his eye on her.

She was glad she'd be rid of him soon. She'd never figure him out. Most especially, she'd never figure out what it was about him that made her want to goad him. Or what is was about him that made her want to touch him.

If she were to be honest, that was the most puzzling thing of all.

Reaching the end of the corridor, she turned in disgust. She must have gone right, not left.

The Englishman was standing at the other end, watching her. "Are you lost?" he called.

"Nay." She hurried toward him. "I only wanted to have a wee look around."

Raising a brow, he took the key from her hand and fitted it into number twenty-six's lock.

When the door swung open, she gasped and shot him an accusatory glare. "There's only one bed."

"I told you there was only one room. It's no fault of mine it has only one bed." He walked in and set his portmanteau on the bed in question. "We'll manage."

She stood on the threshold, eyeing the room with trepidation.

"Come in, will you? I may be an Englishman," he added dryly, "but I'm not in the habit of forcing myself on unwilling women."

"I didn't think you would." With a start, Caithren realized it was true. As infuriating as he was, she felt safe in his presence. It made no sense. She knew it made no sense, which was she was nervous.

Since she couldn't just stand there, she entered but left the door open. He removed his surcoat and tossed it over the back of a lovely carved chair, then went around the room lighting candles.

She wandered over and fingered the fabric of the brown coat. Fine stuff, although plain. Stitching neat enough to rival her mother's. "Mam always despaired of my sewing," she blurted.

What an inane thing to say. As though he cared. But she'd never been good at controlling her mouth when she was jumpy like this.

He shut the door, blocking out the noises of other people in the corridor and downstairs. "Did she, now?"

"Aye, she claimed I'd never make a proper wife. Never mind that I'm capable of seeing to the health and provisioning of every soul at Leslie."

He moved an extra candle to the dressing table. "At Leslie, huh?" From his leather bags came two shirts and a pair of breeches, which he left in an untidy heap on the bed, then an ivory comb, a razor, and a ball of soap. "If you can do all that, I cannot see whereas sewing would make a difference one way or the other."

"Don't you need a wife who can sew?" She hadn't finished saying it before heat rushed to her cheeks. Crivvens, she couldn't stop blethering.

"I don't need a wife at all." He set the implements on the dressing table and examined himself in its fine mirror. "My sister, Kendra, takes care of running my household."

"How about after she marries?"

His eyes met Cait's in the silvery surface. "Not bloody likely. Anytime soon, at least."

His gaze held hers for a moment. Her stomach fluttered. Perhaps she wasn't as safe with him as she'd thought.

He stroked his mustache, then sighed and set to work with the brush and soap, making a fine lather. When he started brushing it onto his face, Caithren felt she shouldn't watch. It seemed too inti-mate. Instead she walked to the window and drew aside the drapes.

It was pitch black behind the hotel, and she couldn't see a thing. With a sigh, she let the curtain drop and ran a hand down the wall beside the window. It had wallpaper—thick sheets nailed to the wall, with flock printing. The paper's pattern felt velvety under her fingers. She'd heard of wallpaper, but she'd never actually seen any before.

The blade made a small scraping noise that sounded loud in the silence. Despite herself, she sneaked a glance in the mirror. She hadn't seen him clean-shaven, and devil take it if her fingers didn't itch to touch the newly exposed smooth skin. Looking away, she went to the bed and started folding the clothes he'd left there.

But her gaze kept wandering to the emerging planes of his face.

He dipped the brush again, rubbed white foam in a wide arc beneath his nose, caught his upper lip with his teeth—

"What are you doing?" she burst out.

"Removing my mustache." Calmly—as he did everything else—he drew the razor over a section, rinsed it in the washbowl, shaved the next patch. And on, until many black hairs floated on top of the water, and the space above his lip was bare and paler than the rest of his face.

He rubbed it ruefully. "Feels odd."

He flashed her a grin full of straight, white teeth she hadn't noticed before. And those chiseled lips. Such a beautiful mouth. Her own mouth gaped open as she laid the second shirt on the bed and sat herself at the edge, her hands clenched in her lap.

"What do you think?" he asked.

She finally found her tongue. "You look young."

He laughed. "And just how old did you think I was?"

"I don't know," she hedged, mentally kicking herself for making such a brainless comment in the first place. "Thirty, maybe?"

"I'm thirty-two." He looked back in the mirror, turning his head this way and that.

"Thirty-two? But you look—"

"I know. That's why I grew it sixteen years ago. I was handed a lot of responsibility at an early age, and I thought if I looked older..." His fingers moved to stroke the absent whiskers, then jerked away. "I miss it already."

"I thought you wore it in imitation of the king." She gestured at the gorgeous long hair that reached to the middle of his chest. "You look like a Cavalier."

"My family did support Charles in the war," he said distractedly. One hand went up to stroke the wavy mass. "Well, there's nothing for it," he announced in resigned tones.

Puzzled, she cocked her head. "Nothing for it?"

"The hair." He reached for his knife. "It must come off as well."

She leapt from the bed, reaching to still his hand. "Why?" she breathed.

In response to her horror, his eyes crinkled with humor. "Same reason I shaved the mustache. Gothard knows I'm alive now. I don't want him to notice me following him. I'll look different, yes?"

"Well, aye." Suddenly she realized she was touching his hand voluntarily. She pulled back. "But you look different already."

He glanced in the looking glass again. "Not different enough." Holding a hank of the beautiful black silk, he measured it against his shoulder and hacked off a hunk. Crookedly.

She winced. "You're going to look like a wallydraigle."

His expression went from pained concentration to obvious amusement. "A what?"

"A most slovenly creature." She moved closer. "I'll cut it for you," she said, "if you'll go down to the kitchen and ask to borrow a pair of scissors."

Relief relaxed his features. "Done."

He left the room before she quite digested the offer she'd made. Cut the man's hair? She wanted nothing to do with him. What had she been thinking?

She paced around the large chamber. The carved oak furniture all matched, and the counterpane and bedhangings looked to be of silk. Once again, she wondered how he could afford such a place. But apparently he'd been thinking ahead. He'd needed a mirror to accomplish this transformation, and not many small inns would provide one.

She jumped when he barged back in, holding forth the scissors. "Did you think I was a ghost again?"

"Nothing that benign." She dragged a chair over to face the mirror and waved him into it.

He sat and grinned at her reflection in the glass, handing her the scissors over one shoulder. "Go ahead," he urged.

The black waves felt soft in her hands. With a wince, she measured and cut, measured and cut, a wee bit at a time. Soon she was engrossed in the careful work, but not so much that she didn't steal glances at him in the mirror.

His striking features looked even more arresting without the mustache. She hadn't noticed the long black lashes that crowned his clear, leaf-green eyes. A spicy masculine scent permeated his hair and skin.

With her hands on him like this, he didn't seem so irritating and dangerous. As his dark locks slipped through her fingers, it seemed as though a different man were emerging. Surely not, but she felt differently toward him all the same. And chided herself for it.

He studied her in the mirror as well. "What color are your eyes?" he asked.

"My eyes?" She clipped, then glanced up. "Hazel. Why?"

"They looked green earlier today, but now they look blue."

She frowned. "Well, they're hazel." Placing the last silky sheared hank on the dressing table, she stepped away to assess her handiwork. His hair now neatly skimmed his shoulders.

"Thank you," he said softly. "It's a much better job than I would have done."

She glanced at his knife on the table's marble surface. "I expect so," she said, a wry smile teasing at her lips.

Despite all her reservations, she was feeling rather kindly toward him—until he stood, stretched, then unlaced the top of his shirt and pulled it free from his breeches.

"What are you doing now?" she burst out.

He sat back on the chair to pull off his boots. "Getting comfortable for bed. We've a long day ahead of us tomorrow. We're planning to 'ride like the dickens,' if you remember."

"I remember," she said. "But—"

"Are you not going to take off your outerclothes?" His second boot fell to the floor with a loud *plop*. "I'm not planning to attack you."

"I have nothing else to wear, thanks to you. My nightgown is in my satchel. In the—"

"—public coach." He peeled off a stocking. "I know. That thing beneath your bodice, the garment that looks like a blouse? I'm no expert on women's clothing, but it's quite long, is it not? A shift, is it called?"

"Aye, it's a shift." She plucked distractedly at its sleeves. "Not that it's any of your concern."

She stalked to the bed and tucked the shirts and breeches she'd folded back into his portmanteau, then moved it to a table. Pulling back the lovely counterpane, she found a thick quilt resting beneath. She lifted one corner and climbed into bed.

"Sleep well," she said, in a tone meant to speak of finality.

He rose and moved to look down on her. "You're going to suffocate," he predicted. "At least loosen your bodice."

When she made no move to do so, he threw back the quilt, leaned over her, and made quick work of untying the bow at the top of her laces.

"Unhand me!" she squeaked in disbelief. Before she collected her wits enough to bat his hands away, he began tugging at the laces. "I-I cannot believe what you're doing! No other man has ever loosened my clothing, yet this is the second time you—"

"A pity, sweetheart," he interjected smoothly while finishing the job he'd started. "Though I find that difficult to believe." One long fingertip trailed softly alongside her face. "Don't you fret, pretty thing—I may be the first to loosen your clothing, but I'm certain I won't be the last."

She felt a flush crawl up her neck, heating her cheeks. She opened her mouth to say something, but nothing coherent came to mind.

"There they go again," he said. "Your eyes were just green, and now they've turned blue." He reached for her amulet.

"This stays," she said firmly, finding her tongue. "I never take it off."

He shrugged, moving to the foot of the bed to pull off her shoes. "Now you'll rest easier." Caithren was still sputtering when he flipped the quilt back to cover her.

Glaring at him, she lay silent as he walked around the room snuffing the candles. In increments, the chamber descended into darkness. He slid in on the other side of the bed, his substantial weight depressing the feather mattress, making her nearly roll into him. She gripped the quilt in tense fists, holding herself in place.

"Sleep well, now," he called in a voice that was annoyingly unperturbed. Apparently giving him the evil eye had had no effect on him at all. "We've a long journey ahead of us."

When he leaned to blow out the candle on the small table by the bed, Caithren raised herself to an elbow to do the same on her side. Her heart pounded hard in her chest as she lay back down and stared into the darkness. It didn't seem as though he planned to attack her, and yet...

She realized suddenly that her pulse wasn't racing from fear, but from something else.

Da had fed and clothed her, Cameron had offered protection and companionship, and more than one suitor had connived to press his lips to hers. But no man had ever made it his business to care for her in a physical sense. The Englishman's hands on her had felt different than Da's or Cam's or those fumbling courting lads'.

She wasn't at all sure whether she cared for the feeling. And why did it matter, aye? Her hand went up and wrapped around her amulet. She'd be rid of him after tonight.

Rigid, she lay beside him, willing herself to stay awake while her eyes adjusted to the darkness. Had they crossed their arms over their chests, she imagined she and the Englishman would resemble one of the marble effigies in her village kirk, a lord and lady frozen together in time. But she was no titled lady, and the Englishman was certainly no lord.

He wasn't even a gentleman.

She had to get away from him. Back to the coach, where she hoped and prayed they were still carrying her belongings. It would be a miracle to find her money there as well, but she couldn't worry about that now.

It seemed like forever before his breathing evened out in sleep. She waited a few minutes until she was sure, then jogged his shoulder to double-check. He groaned as though in pain, then settled down with a soft snore. She leaned over him, remembering other moments he'd seemed to be hurting. Suddenly she wondered if *he* could have been injured last night as well. Helping her.

Rising, she swept her shoes off the floor, then caught herself looking back to him. But even if he'd been hurt, it was no fault of hers. She couldn't let herself be swayed. Her decision had already been made.

Slowly she backed away, then turned and opened the door. With one last glance over her shoulder, she slipped into the corridor and eased the door closed behind her.

Leaning against the wall, she calmed her pounding heart while she straightened her bodice and relaced it snugly. Then she slid into her shoes, marched downstairs, through the taproom, and out into the night, trying her best to look as though she hadn't a care in the world.

It was chilly and drizzling. She had no money to hire a horse, no alternative other than to start walking. But the coach would have stopped in one of the towns they'd passed, so if she followed the road, she'd be sure to get back to it by morning.

She set off into the long night that loomed ahead.

TWENTY

"MAMA, MUST you go? You've been home nary a month."

"I must, wee Alison." Flora MacCallum moved to her youngest's bed and bent to kiss her little forehead. She smoothed the fine, chestnut hair from her daughter's face. "Maybe, with any luck, this time will be the last."

Malcolm crawled over his sister and down to the floor to hug his mother around the knees. "Are you going to be Emerald again?"

"Aye. I'm going to be Emerald one more time."

"But it's the middle of the night."

"Nay, dawn approaches. And others are doubtless on the Gothards' trail already." She knelt to give her bonnie lad a fierce hug, breathing in his scent to sustain her through the days and weeks ahead. Soap and milk, underscored by a faint trace of the dirt she could never quite get out from under his fingernails. She wished she could bottle the aroma and take it with her.

Unwinding his small arms from around her neck, she stood to shrug into a man's surcoat.

"It's lucky you two were of a height." Hearing her mother's voice, Flora turned to see her leaning against the doorway that separated the two rooms of their cottage. "Not many women can wear their husband's clothes."

"Aye?" A strand of long gray hair had escaped her mother's

plait; Flora walked over and pushed it behind her ear. "It was the only lucky thing between us."

"Now, Flora—"

"Don't go defending him, Mama." Though her words were firm, she pressed a kiss to the top of her tiny mother's head. All of Flora's height—and she was the tallest woman in Galloway—had come from her father. "I'll never forgive my husband for pledging our home in a game of dice and then getting himself killed in that border raid. Damned halliracket."

"Wheesht! The bairns are listenin'."

"And right they should be." Flora twisted her unruly red hair and piled it on her head, then jammed her deceased husband's hat on top. "It's fair they know why I have to leave them."

"Flora—"

"Just give me peace till this is finished, Mama. One last time. With the reward posted for Gothard, I can pay off Kincaid and then some. We'll be able to breathe. Give the farm our attention. Maybe even get wee Alison her own bed. Won't that be nice?"

"Nice, Mama!" Alison repeated.

Flora's mother bent to sweep a length of broken reed off the floor. The roof needed replacing as well. "Damn your daftie of a father for ever takin' you tracking," she muttered. "Thought you were the son he never had."

"Neither of us chose our men well." Flora stuck a pistol into her boot top and snatched up the sword that was propped in the corner. "Still and on, if Da hadn't taken me, I wouldn't be able to get us out of the mess we're in today." She kissed her mother's parchment cheek. "Take care of the bairns, Mama. God willing, I'll be back to stay."

Hard kisses for Alison and Malcolm, and she was off to do what needed to be done.

Once and for all.

~

*J*ASON JERKED awake. Emerald was gone. Again.

Dawn's hazy gray light seeped through the window. He slept soundly these days, the bone-deep weariness of a healing body coupled with hard hours on the road. But still...how was it that a woman could rise, dress herself, and leave without waking him?

Cursing himself—which was getting to be quite a habit—he pulled on his boots and went downstairs, hoping she'd only gone in search of something to break her fast. But the Crown's cheerful taproom was eerily empty. Too early yet for guests to be up and about.

And Emerald was gone, really gone.

He winced at the thought of her out there alone. But there was nothing for it. He could ill afford to waste precious time searching for her, even supposing it were possible he'd be successful. It had been a different matter when she was on a lumbering coach taking a specific route. She could be anywhere by now, and he didn't know the first thing about tracking a body—that was her skill, not his.

He would simply have to make it his business to get to London first. How long was her head start? Had she found a horse? With no money, she'd have a hard time of it—

Panicking, he pulled out his coin pouch and spilled the contents into his hand.

Nothing was missing.

Idiot woman.

Slipping the pouch back into his pocket, he tramped out into the gray morning and went to wake the stable boy.

TWENTY-ONE

*F*OUR HOURS had passed since Caithren had seen a soul. Soaked to the skin, she shivered with a bone-deep cold. She'd passed through three wee villages—if one could even call them that—but only one had boasted an inn, and no coach had been parked in its courtyard.

It felt as though she'd descended into an evil land where no one existed save herself.

As dawn approached, a talkative family rumbled by in an ox-drawn cart. She would have loved to beg a ride, but they were going the opposite direction. Regardless, just the sight of them brought a tiny smile of relief.

Walking backward, she watched them fade into the distance, their cheerful voices becoming fainter and fainter until all was quiet, save for the steady beat of the rain. A lonely sound.

Summoning her last reserves of energy, Cait turned and walked faster. She had to be near the coach by now. Squinting her eyes, she thought she could see a village ahead, a silhouetted irregular line of rooftops. A church spire, or maybe it was only more trees. She couldn't be sure, and rain suddenly pelted from the sky, obliterating the hazy view and making her shiver even more.

Water sluiced down the gently sloping road, hiding the deep, slushy ruts. She tripped into one of them and fell to her knees in the mud, wrenching a foot as she went. The tears that had been threatening all the long night pricked hot behind her eyelids.

No, not the tears. Not again. She blinked hard and took a deep breath, then dragged herself up.

Though she'd twisted only her ankle, her whole leg throbbed. Her teeth were chattering, and the hand clenching her amulet was shaking and white-knuckled with strain. When she heard a horse approaching from behind, she couldn't find the strength to turn around and see who it was. Why did it matter, really? Maybe the traveler would help her. More likely he'd simply ignore her.

But just in case, she pulled the amulet off over her head and shoved it up her soggy sleeve.

Not a second too soon. The heavy thud of someone dropping from a horse made her force herself to turn and look.

Leading an obviously ill-treated nag by the reins, a man was trudging toward her, his boots squishing in the mud. Black eyes leered wildly from his rough-hewn face, which was dark with unshaven stubble that didn't look anywhere near as bonnie as it had on the Englishman.

"What have we here?" he asked.

Caithren backed up. "I-I have no money," she managed to stutter out. To demonstrate, she turned her pockets inside out, revealing naught but the miniature portrait of Adam, which she hastily shoved back inside.

Undaunted, the man dropped his mount's reins and stepped closer. The horse looked too worn out to bother going anywhere. Even through the scents of rain and mud, the man's stale, liquor-tinged breath choked Cait as he came near and peered into her face.

"P-please, sir. I haven't anything you'd want."

"We'll see about that." With a lunge, he plunged one grimy hand down her bodice, rooting around.

Horrified, she twisted in his grip. "I have nothing! Unhand me!" Bile rose in her throat as panic tightened her chest. "Stop! Unhand me! Now!"

"No money in here?" The rough fingers shifted and clawed one breast in a painful squeeze. "Ah, but I wouldn't say you have nothing."

Anger and indignation boiled up. Cait's hands clenched round his thick neck, but though her vision blurred with the effort, he didn't seem to notice. She yelled, kicking at his shins, but her injured ankle threw her off balance, and he was managing to back her up into the trees at the edge of the road.

His other hand reached down, hiking her skirt as they stumbled together in the mud, a writhing mass of combat. Gathering her wits, she brought one knee up—hard. With a stunned grunt, the man pulled away and hunched over. But she knew he'd be after her again. She'd never outrun him with her hurt ankle.

If only she could get to his horse.

She sprang for the animal, but the man reached to snag her by the wrist. Still crouched, he managed to whip her back around. Thinking quickly, she gritted her teeth and reached her free hand to pat his body, searching for a gun, a blade—

Beneath his soggy, smelly coat, her fingers closed on the grip of a knife. As she tugged it from its sheath, the man growled in rage and wrenched himself upright.

"Keep back!" Bravely, she brandished the knife in his face.

And a gunshot rang out.

The sheer shock of it forced her backward into the mud. As her bottom met the ground, her breath expelled in a rush and the knife dropped from her hand.

But the bullet hadn't hit her. It had come from another direction.

The man turned and bolted for his horse. Hammering hoofbeats were drawing near—indeed, were it not for the pounding rain and the veil of her own fear, Cait knew she'd have heard the sound earlier.

Her attacker was mounted and moving before her rescuer arrived and reached a hand to help her rise.

She looked up into the face of the Englishman.

She stared at him in disbelief. No matter where she went, he insisted on showing up. But she found herself absurdly grateful he'd shown up now. While she didn't understand him, at least he'd never tried to take advantage.

Her hands splayed on her chest, trying to erase the feel of the monstrous man who was riding away. With a lingering glance at the man's retreating back, the Englishman slid from the saddle and gathered her into his arms.

"Are you hurt?"

Shuddering, she shook her head. It was the only answer she

could manage. But she took comfort from his nearness, his warm body against hers.

"I can scarcely credit how much trouble you are," he muttered, the words laced with a quiet fury.

She'd have felt better if he'd have just yelled at her. "What did you say?"

"I said, are you hurt?"

That wasn't what he'd said. Certain they both knew it, she lifted her chin. "Nay, only shaken a bit," she said in a voice that indeed sounded shaken. She wished she could say it more bravely. Though she wanted nothing more than to stand on her own, her hands gripped his shoulders convulsively.

Her manhandled breasts burned beneath her bodice, and her ankle shot fire if she put any weight on it. But she wouldn't cry. He'd already said she was trouble, and she knew he hated her tears almost as much as she did.

After giving her a few awkward pats on the back, he set her away. She blinked in dismay at his face: the clenched, chiseled jaw; the hard, accusing eyes.

Predictably, his voice was as calm as ever. Calm and berating. "What the hell did you think you were doing wandering alone in the middle of the night?"

He had the nerve to be outraged on her behalf? Protective? The cur. Anger coursed through her anew. "I was going back to the coach! To get my things and complete my journey! I was almost there, too. Just leave me be!"

He stared at her, his mouth working as though he wanted to say something but couldn't think how to word it.

"I don't need your help," she added, though she wasn't at all sure what would have happened if he hadn't charged in on his silver horse. "I was taking care of myself just fine. I had a knife."

"I could see that." He eyed the dull gray blade in the mud. "And I saw you, um…with your knee…"

"Um-hmm." She gave him a smug smile.

"But I'd expect that from Emerald MacCallum."

"Very well, then," she forced through gritted teeth. "I appreciate your gallant rescue, but now I'll be on my way."

Gathering what little was left of her composure, she swiveled, hobbled over to fetch the knife, and started limping down the road.

She could feel his eyes on her back. One, two, three steps…four, five, six…

"Emerald." His voice wasn't reproving any longer—instead it sounded mocking. "Oh, Emerald…"

She didn't stop. Her name wasn't Emerald. Nine, ten, eleven, twelve…

"You're walking in the wrong direction."

She dropped the knife back to the mud. He was behind her in a flash, his hands large and heavy on her suddenly trembling shoulders. "That's London ahead. We passed the coach. Most likely it stopped in Rossington, north of where we slept."

"I knew that." Staring into the distance, she fished the amulet out of her sleeve and slipped the chain back over her head. She rubbed a wet finger over the smooth rectangular stone. "I wasn't walking north?"

"No." He came around to face her, his expression softening. "You've been walking south."

Tears welled in her eyes; she couldn't seem to stop them. She hoped they were disguised by the rain.

His hand went up to stroke his missing mustache, then dropped and curled into a fist. "Didn't you notice the landscape was different?"

"Different?" Her voice went higher than she would have liked. She struggled to control herself as she scanned the drenched countryside. "It's flat, just the same as yesterday. All England is flat and ugly."

He shook his head and gestured at the gently rolling land. "Between Doncaster and Bawtry, it's flat planted fields, bordered with trees. Here, there are hills used for grazing."

"Hills, hah!" she said, even though he was right. Oh, why did she suffer from such a terrible sense of direction? Why couldn't she have normal faults, like normal folk? A lisp, or blotchy skin.

"Where I come from, this is flat." She sniffed back the tears, determined not to let them fall. "W-will you take me there, then? To Rossington, where the coach is?"

She hated herself for the wobble in her voice.

"No."

She hated *him* for being so disagreeable.

"Why not? What do you want from me?"

"I don't have time to backtrack. And I want to keep an eye on you." Rain dripped off his wide-brimmed hat, but he didn't look nearly as miserable as she felt. "I cannot allow you to face Gothard alone."

"Gothard!" The name was the last straw, the end of her hopeless struggle. The tears overflowed and ran down her cheeks. "I don't want this man Gothard," she wailed. "I want my brother, Adam! I want my bed at Leslie, and my cousin, Cameron. I want something —one thing!—to go right for a change! And my name is Caithren!"

Her chest heaved with a sudden sob, and the Englishman reacted immediately, wrapping her into his arms.

"I hate you!" Reaching up, she pounded on his shoulders.

With a grunt, he shoved her away. "Bloody hell, will you stop beating up on me?" he said much more calmly than the words would imply. "I told you I'd take you to London. I'll replace your clothes and your precious satchel and whatever else was inside. I'll repay your money, and should it turn out you really do have a brother"—his face showed what he thought were the chances of *that* —"I'll hire a solicitor to draw up your bloody papers. Just stop hitting me, damn it."

He paused for breath, and his voice dropped, almost to a whisper. "I'm not out to hurt you. I want only to get to Gothard first. I cannot get on with my life—whatever is left of it—until I do so." The eyes that bore into hers were filled with pain. "Can you not try to understand that?"

Despite herself, she nodded, hot tears trailing down her face to mix with the cold rain. When she swayed, he gathered her close once again.

She melted against him willingly, her tears flowing faster. What would she have done if he hadn't come after her? She was so far ahead of the coach now—far too far to go back. It made much more sense to head for London. But with no coin, she had no way to get there by herself, even if she managed to keep going the right direction. She couldn't walk there in time, and horses and food and beds all cost money.

But she hated the fact that she needed him, especially because his arms felt so reassuring around her. He was a scoundrel who wouldn't believe her story. A scoundrel who'd kept her off the

HOW TO UNDRESS A MARQUESS | 93

public coach, endangering her plans to meet Adam and stranding her with nothing. A scoundrel who kept calling her Emerald.

And still, she felt safe in the circle of his arms. Beneath his chilly, wet cloak, his spicy male scent warmed her nostrils while rain pattered all around them.

"Have we a bargain?" he asked quietly.

She nodded against his chest.

He stepped back and reached out a finger, lifting her chin. "Was that a yes?"

"Aye, it was." She drew a shaky breath.

"And you won't disappear on me again?"

"I won't try to escape you."

"And you won't hit me again?"

A tiny smile threatened to burst free. "That I cannot promise."

He heaved an elaborate sigh. "I suppose I will have to take what I can get, then."

"I suppose you will." Despite her best efforts, her lips curved, after all. She simply couldn't help herself.

He was staring at her mouth. He moved close and placed his hands on her shoulders...and still, he was staring at her mouth.

"Shall we seal this agreement?" he asked softly.

"What?" Was he fixing to kiss her? Nay, that couldn't be. She backed away. "I said we have a bargain, Mr. Chase."

He blinked. "Mr. Chase? Didn't I tell you to call me Jason?"

"I haven't been calling you anything. I've been trying my best to ignore you, if you hadn't noticed. Out loud, that is. In my head, I've been calling you all sorts of things."

"I'll bet you have." He bent down and fished the knife from the mud, pulled out a handkerchief, and wiped the blade. "I'm thinking you should have leave to call me Jason."

"Oh, aye?"

A gleam came into his eyes. "After all, we have slept together."

Her cheeks flushed hot. "Not exactly. *You* slept." Looking down, she readjusted the soggy bow at the top of her laces. "I was taught to address my elders with respect."

"Your *elders*? Do you think me so old and decrepit?"

He sounded so disconcerted, Cait's gaze shot up to his face. It took all she had not to laugh. She wished she had the talent to paint;

if she could capture his expression on canvas, she could laugh at it forever.

"Very well, then," she said, keeping her voice businesslike. "Since I've no other means to get to London—thanks to you—I will stay with you willingly. As your equal." He opened his mouth, but she rushed on. "And as such, I will call you Jason. Out loud. I cannot promise what I'll call you in my head."

Frustration and amusement mingled on his face as he shoved the knife into his belt. "Here," he said gruffly, shrugging out of his cloak and settling it over her shoulders.

"You'll get wet," she protested even as she snuggled into it. It felt heavy and blessedly warm from the heat of his body. But his brown surcoat was becoming peppered with the dark splotches of raindrops. "I'm already soaked. It will do me no good."

"You're shivering. It will cut the cold." He removed his hat and plopped it on her head. "I won't have you catching a chill."

He'd tied his hair back with a ribbon, making a short, neat tail at the nape of his neck. She watched as it became soaked, too. "Now we'll both be miserable," she said. "But I thank you for your gallantry. Why you deserve thanks is beyond me, but Mam always said 'guid manners suffer bad yins.'"

Thin rivulets of water ran down his blank face and dripped off the end of his nose. She saw a muscle twitch in his jaw while she waited for him to ask for a translation.

"Courtesy outshines poor manners," she finally said.

His eyes narrowed but he said nothing, only swung her up into his arms. Before she could protest, he marched to his horse and deposited her on the saddle with a bit more force than was necessary.

She let out a little grunt.

"I'm sorry," he mumbled. "Are you all right?"

"I reckon I'll live."

He reached up to wipe a tear from her cheek, a futile gesture considering the continual rain. "Why didn't you pull your gun on that bastard?"

"It's in my satchel, in—"

"—the coach." He sighed. "I know. My fault. I'm sorry." He reached down to draw a pistol from his boot. The smallest one she'd ever seen, much fancier than Da's, with a brass barrel and a mother-of-pearl grip inlaid with brass wire scrollwork. "Here, take this one," he offered.

It looked very expensive. "Nay, I—"

"Take it. You should have something to protect yourself." When she didn't move to claim it, he reached beneath the cloak and stuffed it into her skirt pocket.

"Thank you," she said stiffly, clutching the cloak closed in front with two cold fists. "It may be that I'll need it; there seem to be a high proportion of unscrupulous men about England."

He fixed her with an assessing green gaze, then mounted behind her. His arms came around her waist, altogether more comforting than she expected, and they took off at a decent clip down the muddy road.

"You seem to paint all Englishmen with the same brush," he said presently. "Tell me, Emerald, are there not bad people in Scotland as well?"

"My name is Caithren," she snapped. "And we save our aggression for the English."

It wasn't even close to the truth, but it sounded good.

TWENTY-TWO

*S*EATED BEHIND Emerald in the saddle, Jason watched her head bob as she drifted in and out of sleep. He found himself leaning close, hoping for a whiff of the flowery scent he'd already come to think of as hers. Whatever it had been—bath oil, perfume, or the like; he was certainly no expert on women's toiletries—the rain had washed away every trace.

But plain Emerald smelled almost as good.

He glanced at the sky, happy that the rain had let up. The road in this area was clay, normally stiff and easy to travel, but the miserable wet had made it into a path of mud. On both sides of the slushy mess, barley fields glistened green in the dwindling drizzle.

When he stood in the stirrups to relieve his stiffness, Emerald came awake with a start. He grabbed her to keep her from falling. She yawned into a small, feminine hand.

It certainly wasn't a hand that looked accustomed to holding a pistol, but he supposed that was to her advantage. The less she looked like a threat, the more likely outlaws wouldn't notice her coming after them.

"Tired, are you?" he drawled, resettling both her and himself and adjusting again to Chiron's rhythmic sway.

"I didn't sleep, if you'll remember."

"What I remember is waking up alone, wondering where you were and if you were safe."

"You mean wondering if I'd managed to get to Gothard before you could."

"I didn't say that, Emerald."

"How many times must I tell you I'm not Emerald MacCallum?" She twisted around to see him. "Why won't you believe my story?"

"You do a pretty job of telling it, but it doesn't wash. For one thing, it hinges on you or your brother inheriting some land. Besides the fact that I cannot imagine you as a landowner"—that earned him a glare before she turned away, her chin tilting up—"you're from Scotland. Land there isn't owned by individuals," he said smugly. "It's owned by the clans."

"A fat lot you know." Her voice was unmistakably scornful. "I'm from the east, not the northern Highlands. Can you not tell from my accent?"

That lilting accent was muddling his brain. "You sound like a Scot to me." He guided Chiron back to the center of the road, away from the dangerous bogs that plagued the edges. "Scots are Scots."

Before him, her back went stiff. "Curious," she said softly. "You don't strike an initial impression of an uneducated man, but you seem to be unaccountably lacking in knowledge."

"And I suppose *you've* been to university?" The fact that he hadn't had always rankled him. Following the Civil War, he'd spent his early adulthood in exile with the king. Of all the Chases, only the youngest brother, Ford, had received a formal education.

"Close enough," she said. "I read all of Adam's books after he was booted out. Didn't want to see them go to waste."

"Don't tell me they believe women should be educated in that wilderness you call a country."

Though he'd said the words in all good humor—he'd seen to it that his sister Kendra was educated—an outraged squeal came from before him. Emerald bounced, her elbow unintentionally lodging in his gut.

At least he thought it was unintentional. "Ouch!" He rubbed his ribs. "Sit still, will you?"

"Well," she said with a huff, "I'm thinking you should buy another horse. Then you wouldn't care how I sit. And we could go faster. The Gothard brothers are on two horses."

"Don't I know it," he grumbled. *His* two horses.

She had a point. But though yesterday he'd planned to buy

another horse, today he was having second thoughts. With another horse, Emerald would have the means to run off on her own.

Besides, his complaining aside, he rather liked having her sitting in front of him.

"This horse is faster," he said. "Even with us riding double."

"How can—"

"Take my word for it." He knew those horses; they were decent stock, but not in Chiron's class. The brothers had started well ahead of him toward Pontefract, yet he'd beaten them there traveling wounded.

"I'm sure they're not riding any more hours than we are," he said, anticipating her next protest. "This road is plagued by highwaymen at night, not at all safe to travel. And their horses need the rest; they've been riding them for weeks."

"They said they would ride like the dickens," she reminded him. "They could be changing horses."

"I've no fear of that. They haven't the money to be changing horses."

Beneath her borrowed hat, her plaits swished as she shook her head. "If *you* haven't the money for another horse," she said in a patronizing tone, "you can just say so. It's nothing to be ashamed of."

She truly had no idea who he was. He smiled to himself, glad to see his cover of a commoner was convincing. It was safer that way for them both.

"Speaking of money," he said, "why didn't you take some when you tried to leave? How did you expect to fend for yourself with no silver to pay your way?"

She was silent a moment. "Are you saying I should have *stolen* from you?"

"Some folks wouldn't look at it as stealing." When Chiron started up a hill, she slid back against him. Too close. "As you miss no chance to point out, it's my fault you have no coin. It's a dangerous world; you really need to look out for yourself."

The road flattened, giving him relief when she drew herself straight. "Two wrongs don't make a right."

"Does your mother say that, too?"

"Everyone says that. You must have heard it before?"

"I've heard it." Spotting a bridge up ahead, he tensed. "I just don't think it applies in this case." Deliberately he drew his gaze from the bridge. "Have you ever considered there might be such a thing as being too honest?"

"Wheesht! You actually sound angry I didn't take your money."

"Not angry. Only concerned for you, with your habit of chasing all over England." The sun peeked through the clouds just as the road fed onto Bridgegate. "I won't always be here to protect you."

"My *habit* of chasing all over England? I've never been here before. And it will be a long time before I'm tempted to come back. *And* I can take care of myself."

He'd seen no evidence that was true, but he was wise enough not to argue. Stopping at the bridge's end to wait for a cart and two mounted riders coming from the other direction, he wondered how she managed on her own. As unpleasant as this association had been, he felt he'd be signing her death warrant if he allowed her to go it alone. His father would never have left a woman to cope by herself.

Just then, the sun came out. The River Idle sparkled in the new, bright light, and a brilliant rainbow arched from its center.

"Oh, the colors are lovely!" Some damp strands had escaped Emerald's plaits, and she pushed them off the side of her face. "But rainbows mean bad luck, aye?"

"You think so?" he asked, amused.

She nodded. "I know a verse against it."

A carriage lumbered toward them across the bridge. "By all means, chant it if it would make you feel better."

Her chin went up. "Are you mocking me?"

"Never." At the driver's wave, he smiled and inclined his head. "I'm waiting to hear it."

She cleared her throat.

"Rainbow, rainbow, haud away hame
A' your bairns are dead but ane
And it lies sick at yon gray stane
And will be dead ere you win hame

Gang owre the Drumaw and yont the lea
And down by the side o' yonder sea
Your bairn lies greetin' like to die

And the big tear-drop is in his eye."

Finished, she waited expectantly.

"What a long, bothersome charm that is," he said. Not to mention he'd understood but half the words. "Can't you just cross the rainbow out?"

"Cross it out?" When Chiron shifted, she knotted her fingers into his mane. "What do you mean by that?"

"Hereabouts, folk place a couple of twigs on the ground in the form of a cross and lay four pebbles at the ends."

"I've never heard of such a thing." She cocked her head. "Will you be doing it, then?"

"Hell, no. I don't fancy myself superstitious." Another rider was crossing the river. "Would you like to get down and do it?"

"Nay. The verse will do well enough."

Chiron snorted and gave an impatient toss of his head, making Emerald sway. Jason steadied her.

"Shall we cross already?" she asked.

A father and two sons were on the bridge. "I just…" There was no way to hide it—they'd be crossing many rivers. He took a deep breath. "I prefer to ride down the center of bridges."

"Down the center?" He could hear the smile in her voice. "And you say you're not superstitious."

"The bridge is clear now," he muttered and started across.

"Down the center," she repeated with a giggle. "I'd never have thought you'd keep a ritual like that. A man who scoffs at ghosts and superstitions."

He kept his eyes trained on the far side of the river. "I'm pleased to entertain you."

Though her shoulders shook with mirth, she kept her counsel as they rode through the town to the square.

The marketplace bustled with commerce. Sellers hawked wheels of yellow and white cheeses while buyers haggled over fresh produce. Cattle for sale crowded a smelly pen, and farm laborers stood around, waiting to be hired. Noticing a booth filled with a mishmash of household goods, Jason thought he spotted a few garments in the mix. With any luck, a new skirt for Emerald.

Perched along one edge of the square, Ye Olde Sun Inn was a timber-framed building with a central chimney and a narrow upper story beneath a steeply sloping roof. "Olde," indeed. But delicious scents wafted out the open door.

"Damnation, I'm hungry," he said.

"When are you not?"

"Since I met you? Never. You've a disconcerting habit of keeping me from my breakfast." As she drew breath to protest, he added, "I'll buy us a meal and take a room for a couple of hours. You can wash off the mud and then sleep while I find you dry clothes."

"Sleep," she breathed, apparently placated for the moment. "Oh, a wee sleep sounds heavenly."

TWENTY-THREE

"*E*MERALD. IT'S nearly noon. Time to wake up."

"I'm not Emerald," Caithren moaned, batting Jason's hand from her shoulder. Her nap had been entirely too short—after walking all night, she could have slept the day away and then some. But there was no time to waste. No matter how tired she was, she needed to get moving in order to find Adam.

She forced her eyes open.

Dressed in clean, dry breeches and a fresh white shirt, Jason leaned over her, too close for her comfort. His broad shoulders blocked her view of the room, and suddenly she felt frightened, alone with this stranger. It had been different last night when she was planning to leave. Now she would have to forge some sort of relationship with him. Sharing a room at an inn was an intimidating way to start.

Even groggy, she was utterly aware that, because her clothes were all wet, she was naked beneath the sheets. And one of her breasts was already bruised with the marks of an Englishman's fingers. But she remembered Jason's pistol tucked beneath her pillow. Proof that he wouldn't be taking advantage of her, because surely he wouldn't have given her the means to defend herself.

She drew a shaky breath.

"Emerald?" He leaned closer yet, unsettling her even more. "I brought you something from the marketplace."

Yawning, she struggled to sit up while self-consciously clutching the quilt beneath her chin. "What is it?"

"A Shropshire cake." He held out a flat yellow pastry with a diamond pattern scored into the top. "Try it."

She stared at his hand, transfixed by the sheer size of it—the sheer size of *him*—until a delicious scent drifted to her nose, shifting her gaze to the cake. "Very thoughtful," she allowed. She leaned forward to have a bite. "Mmm. It tastes like shortbread."

"Well, take it."

Not wanting to disappoint, she bravely risked releasing a hand from the quilt to hold it and eat more. "*Scottish* shortbread," she said around a mouthful.

He smiled. "I'm glad you like it. I bought four."

The buttery pastry seemed to melt on her tongue. "Where are the other three cakes, then?"

With a sheepish grin, he pointed to his stomach.

"I see." She took another bite. "It's honored I am that you saved me one."

"It was a sacrifice," he said solemnly. "And a peace offering."

"For what?" The last morsel went into her mouth, and she licked her fingers. "I thought we already had a truce."

"For this." From behind his back, he produced a large, soft packet and set it on her lap.

Slanting him a sidewise glance, she used the same hand to slowly unfold the paper. When it lay open across the quilt, she could only stare. "You don't expect me to *wear* this, do you?"

This was a bright red gown, complete with an indecently sheer chemise and an embroidered stomacher—a long triangular contraption worn on the front of the dress to cover the laces. Cait looked wistfully at her shift, skirt, and bodice where they hung on three wall pegs drying. Or rather, no longer dripping. They were far from dry.

"It was all I could find," he said apologetically. He swept the gown from the bed, shook it out, and held it up. "It's not all that bad." He frowned at what was surely a look of pained disbelief on her face. "Is it?"

"It's fit for an English doxy."

Despite what looked like a heroic effort to control himself, his lips twitched. "If you think that, I'm forced to conclude you've never *seen* an English doxy."

Cait closed her eyes and touched her fingertips to her forehead. "It will have to do, I suppose. Temporarily."

"I'll leave you to get dressed." Quickly he stepped outside, closing the door behind him.

Resigned, she rose from the bed, wincing as she put weight on her ankle. When she slipped the chemise over her head, it slithered down her body, feeling like less than nothing. The gown went on next. She tightened the laces, then stared down at her cleavage exposed in the deep, curved neckline. The chemise's lace trim barely peeked out over the edge. Unlike her shift, it was mere decoration, apparently not meant to preserve the wearer's modesty.

No chance was she going into public with half her bosom hanging out. She loosened the dress and wiggled out of it, then took her shift off the wall and wrung it out mercilessly.

Jason's voice came muffled through the door. "Are you decent yet?"

"Just give me peace till I tell you I'm ready," she called impatiently. She shook out the shift, wishing she had an iron. It was more wrinkled than old Widow MacKenzie's haggard face.

Well, there was nothing for it. She pulled it on, shivering at the clammy dampness. Though she usually wore it open at the neck, she tightened and tied the ribbon so the collar was snug around her throat. After donning the dress, she lifted the matching stomacher and stared at it stupidly.

With a huff, she limped to open the door. "I cannot figure how to attach this."

Jason stood on the threshold with his mouth open.

"I know the dress is too big," she added, although she knew he hadn't noticed the loose waist. He was too busy gawking up higher, where her rumpled shift filled in the gown's plunging neckline. "Don't you dare laugh."

"I wouldn't think of it," he fairly choked out, reaching for the stomacher. He came into the room and shut the door without a single snort, which she imagined was some feat.

"Hold it here," he instructed, plastering the stomacher against her front. "And then you attach the tabs, like this—"

"I cannot breathe." The stiff stomacher flattened her belly and breasts, pushing the latter up higher, which made her even happier for the cover of her shift. Experimentally she leaned forward, grunting when the pointed bottom dug into her lower abdomen. "What's in this thing?" she asked. "Wood?"

"Yes. Or bone."

Though she'd been half-fooling, Jason sounded serious. She watched his long fingers work. "You appear quite the expert at this."

"You think? I never expected to be dressing a woman." Finished, he looked up and grinned. "I have more practice taking these off."

"I'll wager you do." Recalling him loosening her clothes last night, she blushed at the thought. Embarrassed, she lowered her gaze. "I don't suppose you brought me dry stockings?"

"Stockings. Oh, hell, I—"

"No matter," she said quickly, preferring not to discuss intimate clothing. "Mine are almost dry."

While he made their damp garments into a bundle he could hang from his portmanteau, she pulled on the stockings and her garters, lifting her skirt as little as possible. It was no easy task since the stomacher prevented bending over. "How is one supposed to sit a horse while wearing this contraption?"

"Ladies generally ride sidesaddle—"

"Balanced precariously for miles and miles?" Finished, she stood straight and arched her back, her body already protesting the antici-pated hours on horseback. "Not a chance. I'll manage."

Closing the portmanteau, he slanted her an assessing glance. "Achy, are you?"

"Nay, only practical." She stepped into her still-wet shoes.

He nodded thoughtfully. "Emerald MacCallum would be practical."

"Caithren Leslie is practical." She dug beneath the pillow and slipped his pistol and Adam's portrait into the gown's pockets. "Shall we go?"

TWENTY-FOUR

*T*HREE TEDIOUS hours later, Emerald tugged up on the stomacher for the dozenth time. "All England is not flat fields," she admitted wonderingly. "We're actually riding through a forest."

The shadows of leaves overhead made pleasing patterns of light and dark on the road. "Sherwood Forest," Jason told her.

"Oh!" Her cry of discovery delighted him. "Robin Hood rode here, didn't he? I'd like to stop and have a wee look around Robin's forest."

He sighed. "Your nap this morning cost us hours. We haven't even made it to Tuxford. There's no time for wee looks."

"By all the saints! First you keep me off my coach, leaving me with no money or belongings so I'm stuck with the likes of you." She twisted to shoot him a glare. "Now you reckon you can make all the decisions?"

Bloody hell, she made him sound—and feel—like a tyrant. He pushed on her shoulder to face her forward again. "We cannot afford to let Gothard get too far ahead."

"I wish to go into the woods." With a huff, she leaned back against him as she had for much of the ride, supposedly to ease the discomfort of the foreign stomacher. "I hope to find plants I may be needing. My box of herbs was left in my satchel—"

"On the coach. I know," he said irritably. His body was reacting to her close proximity. "Is that why you plucked leaves off a plant by the church yesterday?"

"Aye. Featherfew, for the headache. I believe I feel one coming on." She made a great show of rubbing her forehead, and the movement ran through him like a tremor. "Ten minutes. If I haven't found what I need by then, we'll be on our way. I wish to find something to relieve the swelling of my ankle. And something to heal wounds."

He scooted back in the saddle, but it didn't help. "Wounds?"

"Like the one I have," she pointed out, "thanks to your sword."

"Very well, then," he muttered, annoyed. She was entirely too talented at triggering his guilt, not to mention his physical responses. "Ten minutes."

He guided Chiron off the road and dismounted, tethering him to a tree. Then he reached to help her down.

She pushed his hands away. "I can do it." But after a few clumsy attempts, she folded her arms over her well-covered chest, looking even more annoyed than he was. "Nay, I cannot. How am I supposed to move with this board strapped to my middle?"

Hiding a smile, he reached for her again, catching a whiff of her rain-washed scent. As soon as her feet hit the ground he released her, grateful to break the contact.

She flexed her knees, stroking Chiron's silvery mane. "What do you call him?"

"Who?" he asked, distracted.

"Your horse." She slanted him a look, took a few tentative steps, then headed off into the woods.

Her limp did nothing to alleviate his guilt. "Chiron," he said, following her. "I call him Chiron."

A giggle floated back through the trees. "Think yourself the Greek hero, do you?"

"A hero?" His answering laugh was humorless. "Not a chance."

"Jason, the Greek hero." She knelt to inspect some small plants by the base of a tree, allowing him to catch up to her. "One-blade," she murmured, sounding pleased. "The Greek Jason's guardian was the centaur Chiron, aye?"

"Aye. I mean, yes. My sister loves the legends; it was she who named my horse." Leaning against the tree, he frowned at the top of her head as he watched her pick a few blue-green leaves. She seemed surprisingly knowledgeable about plants. Knowledgeable about lots of things. "How is it you know that tale? A Greek myth. And the English tales of Robin."

Slipping the leaves into her pocket, she rose and wandered off, her gaze trained on the moist, dark earth. "You think I'm an ignorant fool then, do you?"

"No." That wasn't what he'd been thinking at all. Far from a fool, she was quick and creative—at least when it came to inventing lies. "I don't know what to think of you," he said honestly, following her again. "Or what to do with you, for that matter."

She whirled so fast he nearly ran into her. The dress she detested swirled around her legs. "What do you mean, what to do with me? You promised you'd take me to London."

"And I will—"

"This arrangement wasn't *my* choice." She appraised him for a few heartbeats before crouching to inspect another bit of greenery. "But I don't mean to be trouble."

Despite himself, his gaze was drawn to the nape of her long, slim neck. "Of course you're trouble." He shrugged uncomfortably, grateful her eyes were on the plant. He didn't want to know what color the hazel had turned to now. "But it's no fault of yours. All women are trouble."

She straightened to face him. "All women?" The two words were laced with challenge.

He took a defensive step back. "Are you not going to take any of that plant?"

"It's useless. I was hoping it was moonwort, but of course it's too late in the year." With a look that said the conversation was far from over, she meandered along and knelt by another plant. "Surely your mother wasn't trouble?"

"Her above all." He sighed, his mind far in the past—a past he preferred to forget. "She abandoned four children, effectively leaving me, as the eldest, to raise the rest."

She glanced up. "Abandoned you?" she asked softly.

He surveyed the fragrant forest, the cloudy sky, anything to avoid the pity in her gaze.

The last thing he wanted was this woman's sympathy.

"Well, she died, which amounted to the same thing. She insisted on following my father into battle against Cromwell. Not a woman's place, but—"

"Not a woman's place?" Shading her eyes with a hand, she sent him a glare clearly meant to intimidate. "Who are you to tell women where their places are, Jason Chase?"

He blinked. "I imagine I should expect such an attitude from a woman who does a man's job."

"If running Leslie is a man's job, then aye, I do one." Fallen leaves crunched beneath her as she rose. "Given your attitude toward women, I expect your three siblings are sisters?"

"Only one." Thinking of his sister prompted a smile. "But Kendra was enough trouble for three. And still trouble—she refuses to get married, at least to anyone remotely suitable."

"Poor, poor Jason." Her commiserating noises were clearly less than sincere. "Imagine a woman wanting to choose her own husband." She came near, her skirts swishing again, drawing his attention to the curves underneath. "Imagine a woman wanting a husband at all. They're all like you, thinking they can keep their women in place."

Those changeable eyes looked green now. He backed up until he bumped smack against a tree and could go no farther—at least not without looking like more of a fool than he already felt.

She moved closer again. Too close. "It's sorry I am if your mam was a halliracket, but—"

"A what?"

"An irresponsible person." She fixed her gaze on his. "But *my* mam would say a scabbit sheep canna smit a hail herself."

He crossed his arms and stared back at her, his mind a complete blank when confronted with such gibberish.

"One evil person cannot infect the whole. You cannot judge all women by your own isolated experiences."

He cleared his throat. "I suppose your mother is an angel on earth?"

Shrugging, she lowered herself to inspect another plant. After a moment, her voice drifted up, quiet and subdued. "She's an angel in heaven. Mam died when I was but twelve." Slowly she tilted her face until her gaze was locked on his. "And my Da died a few weeks ago."

A faint glaze of tears seemed to brighten her eyes. Though he didn't know how much of her story he believed, he found himself drowning in those eyes, wanting to reach for her and offer comfort.

He blew out a breath. "I'm sorry."

Thankfully, she focused back down, fingering a small whitish leaf. "It was a blessing." He watched her pluck it, her fingers both graceful and deft. "He had a fit last spring and couldn't move but to blink his eyes and swallow." She looked up again. "I wouldn't care to live like that."

"Nor I," he assured her, not knowing what else to say.

"Now my family is only Adam."

"Yes, you told me about him." A few too many times. "Adam MacCallum."

"Adam Leslie." With a huff, she stood. "By all the saints, you have got to be the stubbornest man I've ever met."

"Runs in the family," he said dryly, watching her pull her amulet from under her shift and fold one hand around it. It looked ancient. He wondered how many Emeralds had worn it over the years. "Have you no other family at all?"

"A cousin, Cameron." The necklace fell from her fingers. "Leslie," she added before he could suggest otherwise.

He was beginning to think he'd never trip her up; she was a bright one, all right. And she asked way too many questions. Personal questions. "What is that?" he asked, indicating the leaf in her other hand.

"Bifoil." She added it to her pocket. "Good for wounds."

He bent and touched the plant's second leaf. "Why didn't you take this one?"

"I must leave some to grow and flourish for the next person who needs it. Removing too much is rude. We must respect Mother Earth if we wish her to provide."

She ambled off again, her gait made awkward by more than a twisted ankle. It was clear she was suffering from the long ride. Though he'd felt the same his first few days on the road, he wouldn't tell her that, any more than she'd admit to her pain.

It struck him that in some ways they were all too similar. Not particularly good ways, either.

She paused by a tall plant with a spiky bush of pale flowers, but left the blossoms alone, instead plucking off their ash-colored leaves. "Snakewood," she told him, the word trailing off into a yawn.

That reminded him she'd had no sleep in two days, other than the one short nap. He could see the weariness etched in her face, the dark circles under her eyes. Responsibility weighed heavy on his conscience, mingling with that tender feeling he found so confusing and disturbing.

His stomach rumbled, and he remembered they were almost to Tuxford. "Your ten minutes are up. Are you hungry?"

When she shook her head, his gaze raked her slim frame.

"You need to eat more."

"The gown is too big."

Her pert nose went into the air, a gesture so amusing it dispelled his strange mood.

"It's no fault of mine if you're no judge of women's sizes." She hugged herself around her loose waistline and started back toward Chiron. "You shall have to find me some decent clothes, Jase."

"Don't call me that," he said, following her. "Jase Chase. It rhymes. It's disgusting. What were my parents thinking when they named me?"

The question was rhetorical, but she responded anyway. "Evidently they weren't thinking at all." She turned and walked backward, watching him avidly, her grin too fetching for his comfort. "Or maybe they had a ripe sense of humor, Jase."

He growled deep in his throat. "Nobody calls me Jase."

At that, she turned back around. "I do," she called over her shoulder, sounding altogether more cheerful than she had since they'd met. "So long as you call me Emerald."

TWENTY-FIVE

"**W**HAT ARE THEY gawking at?" Caithren said irritably a few hours later.

Waiting at the end of the bridge into Newark-on-Trent, she yanked up on both the stomacher and her shift, giving the evil eye to the two shabby men who were crossing. "I'm not wearing this doxy's dress again."

She smiled to herself when Jason guided Chiron down the exact center of the bridge. "Careful, you're going towards the right—I mean, left. You wouldn't want to risk something bad happening should you veer from the middle."

"Very funny." His tone was dry, but she thought she could feel him laughing behind her. "It's clouding up again, so I think we'll stop here and try to make up the time tomorrow."

"Are you sure?" she asked. "It isn't dark yet. Though the thought of a bed is very appealing." And in the last twelve miles she'd learned the folly of turning down dinner in Tuxford. It felt as though a hole sat in the place where her stomach was supposed to be.

The sky did look menacing. After the soft, rain-soaked road, Chiron's hooves sounded loud on the town's cobblestones as he carried them down Beast Market Hill and onto Castlegate. "If we're going to stop, then I see just where to stay," Cait teased. On their right, the street's namesake loomed over the riverbank. "Since you seem wont to choose the most impressive place."

Now he laughed aloud. "It's Newark Castle, and after the war, Cromwell ordered it demolished. Fortunately, the people refused to complete the job, so the face of the castle remains. But behind it, nothing. I expect you wouldn't be comfortable."

"It's a beautiful facade." She mourned the loss. "We've many large castles in Scotland."

They jostled their way through Chain Lane, a narrow alley of a street lined with tiny shops of all sorts, and on into the marketplace. Jason rode through an archway beside a large inn called the Saracen's Head.

When Caithren slid to the cobblestones, her knees threatened to buckle. She sternly forced them to comply. Jason wouldn't see any weakness on her part—not if she had any say in the matter.

The Saracen's Head boasted fine stables. A liveried ostler came forward to take Chiron in hand, and Cait and Jason hurried toward the inn just as the first raindrops were falling.

Spotting bright yellow by the windows, she paused to snap off a couple of marigolds. Jason frowned. "I don't expect the proprietor will appreciate that."

"Earth's bounty is for all to share," she argued. "This is just what I need for my ankle. I'll ask for some vinegar to mix with the juice, and by morning I'll be right as rain."

"We'll both be *soaked* with rain if we don't get inside." When she would have reached for another flower, he took her by the hand and dragged her through the door and to the innkeeper's desk.

Jason set his portmanteau and their bundle of damp clothing on the floor. "One room," he told the seated man, a large fellow with a huge smile and a pockmarked face. "If you please, Mr. . . . ?"

"Twentyman," the man said.

"Two rooms," Caithren corrected.

"One," Jason repeated.

With a huff of disgust, she decided he could handle this alone and wandered off to the taproom. Something smelled wonderful, and her poor belly was just begging to be filled.

"Good eve," a jolly, rotund woman greeted her. She had round red cheeks and a round brown bun that shone in the well-lit room. "We've a lovely mushroom pie this evening."

Caithren glanced toward the lobby. The way she saw it, Jason owed her whatever she wanted to eat. And then some. "I'll try it, then," she said happily. "And a sallet. And..."

"Spice cake?" the woman suggested.

"Aye. And a tankard of ale. I thank you."

"I thank *you*, milady," the woman said. "Seat yourself, if you please."

Milady. Though Caithren wasn't a lady, it was nice to be mistaken for one. Especially after the treatment she'd received thus far in this country. Smiling at the woman, she seated herself at a fine, polished table. When Jason came in and asked what she wanted, she was pleased to tell him she'd taken care of herself already.

He might think he was calling all the shots, but she would prove otherwise.

He ordered for himself and joined her at the table.

"Twentyman," she mused. "Where does one get a name like that?"

"That's a story," the jolly woman said, coming up from behind Cait to set two ales before them. "My husband's family was originally called Lydell. It's said that one of the Lydells pole-axed twenty men, hence the name Twentyman."

She walked away.

"You English are strange," Cait said flatly.

Jason just threw back his beautiful dark head and laughed.

Though Mrs. Twentyman had three serving maids to help her, she made it a point to bring Jason and Caithren's supper herself. The pie smelled divine. Its flaky crust was filled with gingery mushrooms and melted cheese, and Cait was in heaven with the first bite.

"Delicious," Jason told their hostess. "Newark was Royalist during the war, was it not?"

Mrs. Twentyman took that as an invitation to seat herself. "Aye, we were. Hull, Coventry, and Nottingham turned against King Charles in the troubles, but Newark was a loyalist stronghold." Warming to her subject, she hitched herself forward. "In 1642 the king paid a visit here, and the whole town turned out to greet him. There are secret underground passages where the wealthy people deposited their deeds, jewelry, and valuables during the war for safekeeping. One leads from our cellar," she confided.

"Secret passages?" Her curiosity piqued, Cait focused on Mrs. Twentyman while she stabbed blindly at her lettuce. "Where do they lead to?"

"They crisscross beneath the marketplace, connecting in various spots. Besides stashing their treasures there, some Royalists used them to hide."

Cait took a sip of her ale. "Were they in danger?"

Mrs. Twentyman glanced around, making sure her serving maids were doing their jobs. "Most certainly they were in danger. As long as I live, I shall never forget one morning when their worst fears were confirmed. A party of Roundheads were spotted on Beacon Hill, waiting to attack."

Caithren toyed with her cake. "What happened?"

"My husband's grandmother brought an old army drum out of her house. It needed repair, but it could still make a racket. Her young grandson, my husband's cousin, sounded the alarm, boldly striding through the town, beating the drum loudly, shouting, 'Who will stand up for King Charles?'"

"And they did," Jason told Cait. "They supported him courageously."

"Yes, indeed. They had few guns but put on a brave show with their pitchforks and staves and whatever they could find. That day their luck was in. The Roundheads took one look at the mob and made a hasty retreat. Thanks to the loyal citizens and their little Twentyman drummer boy, Newark was still free."

"Sadly, only for a while," Jason put in.

"We withstood three sieges," Mrs. Twentyman said proudly. "Of course, I was but a babe at the time."

Feeling full after half her pie, Cait leaned back in her chair, lulled by the storytelling lilt of their hostess's voice and the quiet roar of the other guests eating and conversing around them. She yawned behind her hand.

Mrs. Twentyman began to rise. "Poor dear, you're sleepy. And here I am yapping away."

Cait shook her head. "Your stories are wonderful, really." When another yawn forced her mouth open, she blushed. "But I *am* tired." She glanced at Jason, then back to the nice woman. "Do you think you might spare a little vinegar?"

"Vinegar, milady?"

"To mix with the nectar from these." Caithren pulled the marigolds out of her pocket. "My ankle is a wee bit swollen, and it will help."

"Will it, now?"

"Aye."

When Mrs. Twentyman began stacking the plates, Cait noticed something on her hand. She reached across the table and touched the woman's thumb. "And if you squeeze a wee smidge of juice from a dandelion stalk on this wart, it will clear up in no time."

A little gasp came from Jason at her forwardness, but the innkeeper's wife looked pleased. "I will try that, milady. First thing tomorrow."

Cait smiled. "I would love a bath." She looked to Jason. "Assuming you can afford it?"

The minute the words were out of her mouth, she regretted them. Mrs. Twentyman had been treating them like husband and wife. She was mortified, thinking now the woman might realize they were sharing a room but not married.

Jason exchanged an embarrassed glance with their hostess. "I think I can manage that," he said carefully.

"And I shall be needing some decent clothes."

She wasn't surprised when Jason didn't argue. "I'll do my best to find some while you bathe. Let me just see you up to the room."

"You'll be needing clothes?" Mrs. Twentyman asked.

"Aye. And a nightgown. Mine went...missing," Cait explained feebly.

Mrs. Twentyman looked between them, obviously curious. "I can lend you one of my sleeping gowns," she said generously.

When Jason eyed Mrs. Twentyman's ample form, Cait kicked him under the table. "I'd surely appreciate it," she said.

"Then I'll fetch one and send it up along with a bath and the vinegar." With one last puzzled glance, the woman smiled and took herself off.

Jason leaned to rub his ankle, eyeing Cait's half-eaten pie. "Are you going to finish that?"

She shoved it toward him wordlessly. He ate three bites, then looked up with a question in his gaze, and she passed him her leftover sallet as well. She sipped at the last of her ale while she watched him make her food disappear.

"If you're wanting to go upstairs," he said, "I'll be needing to keep the key." He eyed the remnants of her cake, then shook his head and sat back. "In case you fall asleep before I return."

The thought of sharing his room made her nervous, but she knew she had no choice. Her gaze wandered to the door in the corner. She was exhausted, aye, but not quite ready to go upstairs and face the night.

"Do you think that door leads to the cellar?"

"Probably." His brow furrowed. "Why?"

"I've a hankering to check out those tunnels." She rose and started toward it.

"Wait." Leaping from his chair, he caught her by the wrist. "I thought you were tired."

She shrugged. "I'm curious. Maybe we'll find some treasure."

"I don't think the Twentymans would appreciate—"

"Wheesht!" When she tried to pull away, she only succeeded in pulling him along with her. Other supper guests turned to watch. She lowered her voice. "Don't you have any sense of adventure?"

Without waiting for any reply, she tugged open the door and started down the cellar steps. She heard him mutter to himself as he grabbed a candle off an empty table and followed.

The door above them shut, and the flame pierced the sudden darkness. At the bottom of the stairs, she swiveled to face him. "Do you always do what you're supposed to?"

"Pretty much."

"Boring," she pronounced. With a swish of her English skirts, she turned and looked around. The cellar's walls were lined with provisions, the air chilly. A shiver rippled through her, born of the cold or a tiny frisson of fear; she wasn't sure which. But it felt a wee bit forbidden and exhilarating to be down here.

Jason looked annoyed and tense. And darkly handsome in the cellar's shadows, if she were to be honest. "Has anyone ever told you you're impulsive?" he asked.

"Cameron. Every day. He finds it endearing."

Jason's response was a muted snort.

A narrow wooden door was set into one corner.

"That must be it." Her voice trembled a little.

He moved between her and the door and folded his arms across his chest, looking much like the man who had kept her from the coach. "I really think we should go back upstairs."

"You don't want to see the tunnels? There could be treasure—jewelry or money left since the war."

He widened his stance. "It wouldn't belong to you if you found any."

"Of course it wouldn't. I wasn't planning to keep it. But it would be exciting to discover, all the same. Aren't you intrigued?"

"No."

With a small huff, she skirted around him. "Then I'll meet you upstairs. Which room number?"

"Four. But—"

She pushed open the door.

A musty smell came from the cramped, dark passage beyond. A rush of excitement made her knees weak and forced a giddy chuckle through her throat as she stepped inside.

Jason slipped past her and held the candle high. "Come along, then," he muttered.

Smiling to herself, she followed him along the dank, earthen tunnel. The curved walls oozed with moisture, and the place had a mildewy odor that spoke of long disuse. Something scurried across her path, and she jumped and let out a squeak, reaching for Jason's arm.

Bobbling the candle, he turned to her and cupped the flame to prevent it from blowing out. "It's only a mouse." His smile was disarming. "Ready to turn back?"

"Nay. I wasn't afraid, only startled."

"Very well." He cleared his throat and looked pointedly down at where her fingers were still clamped on his arm.

When she snatched her hand back, he proceeded.

His footsteps sounded loud on the deserted pathway. After a few yards, he stopped and glanced over his shoulder. "See any treasure yet?"

"Nay."

He walked twenty more feet. "Any treasure now?"

In answer, she blew out an amused breath.

Ten more feet. "Now?"

She half-groaned, half-laughed. The candlelight disappeared as he took a sharp turn. She followed him around the corner.

And caught sight of something over his shoulder that made her stop short.

TWENTY-SIX

A SOLEMN MAN in a hooded robe stared at Cait, his eyes unbearably sad and hollow.

He floated four feet off the ground.

Even as a shocked gasp escaped her, he faded.

"What is it?" Jason whirled toward her, his eyes wide with alarm.

Shaking, she put a hand on his shoulder to steady herself. "Didn't you see him?"

"See what?" He turned to look, but the passageway was empty.

"He was there. I saw him, I swear."

"What?"

"A ghost! A man dressed in robes. But his feet didn't touch the ground. And then—then he just faded away. Into nothingness."

"Calm yourself." He switched the candle to his other hand and curved an arm around her shoulders. "There's no such thing as ghosts. It's spooky down here. You imagined it."

"I did not!"

"Very well, then, you saw something. But there must be a logical explanation."

"I want to go back."

"Fine." Brushing by her, he started down the passage. "I never wanted to come down here in the first place."

She hurried to catch up and grasped his hand, not caring what he thought. As she ran to keep up with his long strides, she threw anxious glances over her shoulder.

The ghost didn't reappear, but she shivered anyway. "Do you smell something?" Somehow, speaking aloud was reassuring. It blocked the echo of their footsteps and the eerie sounds that seemed to bounce off the walls. "The atmosphere down here is strange."

Jason's hand tightened on hers, making her already high-strung nerves tauten a bit more. "We're almost there." He turned and walked backward, peering through the semidarkness to see her face. "Are you all right?"

Before she could answer, a blast of frigid air whooshed down the corridor and snuffed the candle, plunging them into darkness.

Caithren screamed long and loud, ceasing only when Jason pulled her into his arms and her mouth was muffled against his warm chest.

"Hush." He rubbed her back in a circular motion. "It was only a draft."

The tunnel was black as the Widow MacKenzie's ancient kettle. She heard the squeak of a mouse, a slow drip somewhere, the rapid beat of her own heart, the slower beat of Jason's. "I don't like it down here."

"The door isn't far." His words were measured and patient. "We'll just feel along the wall."

Gingerly she reached out, her fingers meeting grainy, clammy dirt. She jerked back.

"*I'll* feel along the wall," he amended, turning within her grasp. "Just hold onto my waist, and I'll have you out of here in no time."

They progressed a few feet, then stopped cold when light suddenly flooded the passage.

"I heard a scream." Mrs. Twentyman stood in the open doorway, one hand to her ample chest and a lit lantern in the other. "Oh, it's you two."

Cait hurried past her and into the cellar, dropping to sit on a sack of flour. She crossed her arms and hugged herself in an attempt to stop the trembling. "I saw a ghost down there."

"No, she—" Jason started.

But Mrs. Twentyman interrupted. "Gilbert," she said matter-offactly. "Our resident ghostly monk. One of the passageways leads to the old friary."

Caithren looked at Jason, still standing in the open doorway. "I told you he was wearing robes."

"Gray, with a hood?" The woman nodded sagely. "That's Gilbert, all right. But don't you worry, dearie, he's never hurt anyone. Though he does sometimes move bottles around in here—the serving maids dislike coming down to the cellar alone."

Jason shut the door to the tunnel, and Cait released a shaky breath. He came over and helped her stand, wrapping an arm around her shoulders. "I apologize," he said to Mrs. Twentyman, "for trespassing. She was curious—"

"Bosh. Think nothing of it. You're not the first guests to take it in your heads to go exploring, and I'd wager you won't be the last." She winked at Jason. "And quite certainly not the first man to lure a woman down here and scare her into his arms."

Embarrassed, Cait jumped away from Jason just as he quickly dropped his arm. What must the Twentymans think of them? And her wearing an English doxy's dress.

The kindly woman turned to Caithren. "Your bath is likely getting cold, though, so you'd best run along."

She needed no more of an invitation to bolt up the stairs.

By the time she reached the taproom, Jason caught up to her. He reached for her hand, clasping it as he had in the tunnel. "I'm sorry she thinks that of us. I know it disturbs you."

Low and tender, his voice made her remember the heat of his body embracing her protectively. His hand felt warm and sent tingles up her arm. She wished he would hold her again...when she wasn't frightened of a ghost. Just thinking that made the blood rush to her face, and she brought her free hand to her cheek.

"Are you sure you're all right?"

"I'm fine." Falling in behind him on their way up the narrow staircase, she slipped her hand into the gown's pocket to touch Adam's picture. She needed to shake these ridiculous thoughts. "You still don't believe it, do you?"

"That you saw a ghost? No," he said flatly. "I reckon someone was down there, same as we were. Perhaps taking a shortcut or searching for forgotten valuables."

"He was *floating*. If you'd seen him, you'd believe."

"But I didn't." Jason reached the landing, turned, and shrugged. "Can we agree to disagree? Though I fought going down there, I thank you for coaxing me. It was fun."

"*Fun?*"

He grinned. "I haven't done anything impulsive in a long while. Maybe ever, it seems." His mouth reversed into a frown. "Other than taking you with me, that is."

"And you're not sorry for that either, are you?"

"I cannot say that I am." He guided her down a short corridor. "Here we are. Room four." Releasing her hand, he unlocked the door and waved her inside. "I'll leave you to your privacy."

"And my bath." She clenched her other hand around the one he'd dropped, but it didn't feel anything like when he'd held it. "I can still smell the mustiness from the tunnels. It will feel good to be clean."

"Oh," he said. "I almost forgot. I have something for you. From the marketplace this morning." He dropped the key back into his pouch and withdrew a tiny, corked ceramic bottle.

Puzzled, she took it from him.

"Smell it," he urged.

She pulled out the cork and waved the bottle under her nose, drawing a deep whiff of the fragrant scent.

"Flowers of Scotland," Jason said proudly. "Or so the woman at the marketplace told me."

Caithren was stunned. "It-it's lovely," she stuttered.

"It's the oil you use in your bath, no? And to wash your hair?"

"Well, I press my own myself. But aye, from Scottish flowers. Flowers of Scotland." What a sweet gesture. From a man who had as good as abducted her.

It was confusing, to say the least.

"It's lovely," she repeated.

"I'll replace whatever else you lost as well." He backed up, easing the door closed. "I never meant to cost you your belongings."

She gazed at him mutely, then nodded.

"I'm glad you understand, Emerald."

But she didn't. She didn't understand anything. Least of all why she found herself starting to like him when he was still calling her Emerald.

And he was staring at her amulet. He found a green stone more convincing than all her protests.

"I understand," she said, although she was more confused than ever. With a small smile, she added, "Jase," and then shut the door in his face.

TWENTY-SEVEN

"MARY! NO!"

At the sound of a muffled yell, Caithren startled awake. Wide awake. She sat upright, her gaze frantically searching the room.

Across the chamber, Jason jerked and twitched. The fire had burned so low she had difficulty seeing him, but his face looked slick with sweat although it wasn't overly warm. The room had two beds, and she'd awakened in hers alone—but she felt disoriented and dismayed to find herself in a dark room with a man.

"No..." The single word was forced through a mouth contorted in pain. "No, no..."

Her stomach knotting with compassion, she rushed over, tripping on the hem of Mrs. Twentyman's much-too-long nightgown and stopping her fall with his bed.

"Jason, wake up." She put a hand to his shoulder, jiggling it a little. When he only moaned, she shook him hard...harder. "Oh, please wake up!"

He half-rose and threw his arms around her. Her legs tangling in the nightgown again, she tumbled on top of his long, hard body.

She lay upon him in shock, both of them trembling.

The thick white nightgown had a high ruffle around the throat, full sleeves to her wrists, and enough fabric to wrap around her three times. But she could still feel Jason through the voluminous garment. His size, his warmth. His spicy male scent overwhelmed her.

She felt dizzy, like when she'd awakened in Pontefract. But she hadn't been hit on the head this time.

"Wake up," she repeated, her voice muffled against his chest.

Muttering an unintelligible response, he tightened his arms around her. Her heart lurched madly, and she sank into the embrace, molding herself against him, reveling in the feel of his hard planes against her softer curves.

"Good heavens, you feel good." He buried his nose in her hair. "Smell good."

His mouth trailed from her hair across her cheek, settling soft and warm on her lips.

The kiss was a sensuous, persuasive caress, nothing like the unschooled pecks she'd received from village lads. When his tongue sneaked out to trace her bottom lip, she gasped.

He bolted upright, and she flailed back, landing on the floor in a twist of nightgown and limbs.

Above her, he blinked himself awake and stared at her on the floor, his eyes glazed with confusion. "I'm sorry." He ran a hand through his hair, staring at his fingers when it apparently ended way before he thought it should. "Bloody hell, I...did I wake you? I'm sorry. I...what did I say? Did I knock you over?"

She struggled to her feet. "Never mind."

"I was dreaming."

"I certainly hope so," she said with a huff, sitting primly on the edge of the bed. Though she was feeling anything but prim right now. It took everything she had to stiffen her spine. She felt boneless. "What were you dreaming about?"

His heavy sigh pierced the darkness. He lay silent a moment before words tumbled out, soft and rushed.

"It's always the same. I see Mary, little Mary, dying, lying still as stone. And then the scene changes, and I'm fighting. A duel, to the death. I run a man through with my sword. Not my enemy, but an innocent man. Accidentally. He dies." His voice hitched and dropped to a whisper. "I don't know who he is."

She yearned to touch him, but instead clasped her hands together in a death grip. "How perfectly dreadful," she whispered back, all but reeling from the pain that radiated from him.

"All the more dreadful because it's true." He reached a hand to pry hers apart and laced their fingers together on the coverlet. "In pursuing Geoffrey Gothard, I did kill an innocent man. Gothard is to blame, and the reason I cannot rest until justice is served." His eyes searched hers in the dim reddish light given off by the dying fire. "Would a woman like you fault me, Emerald MacCallum?"

Her heart squeezed in sympathy. He was needing forgiveness— from himself, not her—but she couldn't resist the pleading in those sleep-heavy eyes.

"Nay, a woman like Emerald wouldn't fault you," she whispered. "And neither would a woman like Cait."

His fingers gave hers a wee squeeze. Some of the tension drained from his body, and he rolled to his side, his eyes sliding shut. "We should sleep," he murmured. "The sun will be waking us soon. Between the rain and your nap, we lost time yesterday—we must make it up in the morning."

When his hand slid from hers, she felt a little pang of loss. He could be disagreeable and overbearing, but his was a tortured soul, and he could be kind, too. He'd been a rock of security down in the tunnel.

Perhaps she should give him the benefit of the doubt and start over in the morning. She'd let him call her whatever he wanted. She was stuck with him, and she had to get to London; she might as well make the best of it.

Besides, she couldn't remember ever before feeling quite like she had when Jason held her in his arms.

Her lips still burning from his kiss, she crawled into her bed and sank back into exhausted sleep.

TWENTY-EIGHT

*D*OWNSTAIRS THE next morning, Jason looked up from the news sheet he'd spread on the polished wooden table. "Coffee," he told Mrs. Twentyman. "And…"

He hesitated.

Emerald was still upstairs getting dressed. Though his sister drank chocolate with breakfast, a woman like Emerald might prefer coffee instead. But maybe…

"Chocolate for the lady," he decided. As Mrs. Twentyman nodded and hurried off, he looked back down to the news sheet and began to scan the articles.

England was receiving New Netherlands in North America in return for sugar-rich Surinam in South America, under terms reached at Breda. Remembering his brother Colin's secret participation in that treaty with the Dutch, Jason smiled to himself.

A man named Jean Baptiste Denis had succeeded in transferring blood from a lamb into the vein of a boy. Amazing.

And Christopher Wren had—

He looked up when two men sat down at the adjacent table, already deep in conversation.

The ruddy fellow leaned across the table conspiratorially. "Me cousin wrote from Cumberland to say that none other than the celebrated Emerald MacCallum is in the vicinity."

She's not in Cumberland anymore, Jason thought with a smug smile.

"Damn me, but how does your cousin know that?" The man's companion, a thin, pale fellow, shook his head. "This Emerald MacCallum is naught but a fetching rumor, to my mind."

Just what Jason had once thought. He opened his mouth to clear up the confusion, but then thought better of it. No sense making it known he had Emerald in tow, he decided as a serving maid arrived with two steaming tankards.

A woman like Emerald might be liable to attract an unwanted entourage.

The first man hitched forward. "Me cousin talked to her."

"Surely you jest."

"God's own truth. He asked her why she does what she does." He ran a hand back through reddish-blond hair. "Woman's got two little children to feed, a boy and a girl, and her husband died, leaving her with a mountain of debt."

"Emerald MacCallum is a mother?" the thin man mused.

Emerald MacCallum is a mother? Jason mentally repeated, stunned.

Could that be true? It might explain why she seemed sweeter and more nurturing than he'd expected of a woman who made her living tracking.

But a *mother*?

"He also said the woman's over six feet tall. Imagine that."

Imagine that, Jason echoed in his head, stifling a laugh. Here she came now, meandering down the stairs, all five-feet-four-inches of her.

Unless, as she kept claiming, she wasn't Emerald.

His breath caught.

But that was impossible. He'd found her, a Scottish woman dressed in men's clothing, holding a pistol on a wanted outlaw.

As she came closer, the sight of her emerald amulet reassured him. Emerald was fast becoming legend, he decided, and folk always exaggerated legend. Look what they said about William Wallace...seven feet tall, indeed! As absurd as Emerald's being six feet, and likely off by a similar measure.

"Me cousin said she was kind," the ruddy fellow added. "He

was sufferin' from the sore throat, and she gave him some strange Scottish herbs and told him to boil them in wine and drink the lot down."

Now, *that* sounded like the Emerald Jason knew. As she slid into the chair across from him, he resumed breathing.

TWENTY-NINE

"*H*UNGRY?" JASON ASKED, sliding a tankard in front of Caithren. "I can reorder if you'd like, but I reckoned you'd fancy chocolate over coffee."

She breathed deep of the sweet steam. "You reckoned well."

"How is your ankle this morning?"

"Much better." Cupping the warm drink in both hands, she sipped. "I borrowed your comb. I hope you don't mind."

"Not at all." He raised his own tankard. "I paid Mrs. Twentyman for the nightgown. Did you pack it like I told you to?"

"Aye. Thank you for that. And for having my clothes laundered and pressed." She smoothed her hunter green skirt and grinned. "Even if they were tossed over that chair rather haphazardly."

"My pleasure." His eyes danced with good humor. "It was the least I could do since I couldn't find you new ones." Sobering, he took a sip of Mrs. Twentyman's strong brew. "We can reach London in four days if we hurry. I've a mind to make it to Stamford by nightfall, but it won't be easy." He measured her thoughtfully for a moment. "I want to thank you."

"For what?" Caithren couldn't imagine. So far as she could remember, she'd done little but complain.

His lazy smile made her stomach do a flip-flop. "Last night, when I—well...I didn't mean to wake you with my nightmare, but it was nice to have you there."

She couldn't think of anything to say to that. It wasn't as though she'd had a choice. And it had been nice for her as well…if one could call those feelings *nice*.

She wasn't sure how to describe them.

Her tankard made a swishing noise when she twisted it back and forth. "Who's Mary?"

"Mary?" He busied himself swallowing his coffee and folding the news sheet.

"You spoke of a Mary in the night."

"Ah." An enigmatic glint came into his eyes. "A girl I love."

"Oh." She studied her chocolate.

"A young girl, all of five years."

"Oh!" The rush of relief took her by surprise. "What happened to her in your dream?"

"It's what happened to her in real life that signifies. Geoffrey Gothard was intent on taking pleasure of her mother, and Mary got in the way. She still breathed when I left, but she hadn't awakened. The surgeon said she wouldn't last the week."

"By all the saints."

"Mary was an orphan, abandoned in London's Great Fire. My brother rescued her, and I found her a home in my village. With the childless Widow Bradford—her husband had died in a mill accident. No fault of mine, but I felt responsible."

"Why?"

"It was my mill," he said lightly.

His mill? Jason was a miller? She wouldn't have thought so, but then she hadn't thought at all of how he might earn a living. She'd been too busy being furious with him.

Or, since the wee hours of last night, wishing he'd kiss her again.

To hide her suddenly burning face, she sipped.

"Mary was bright-eyed and intelligent," Jason continued. "She loved to laugh. She used to follow me around the village, and sometimes I'd stop by the Bradford house and play with her—"

Cait's tankard clunked to the table. "Play?" She tried to picture Jason on his knees with a small child.

"Yes, play. Backgammon and the like. She's remarkably good with numbers."

"You play backgammon?"

"Why does that surprise you?"

She shrugged. "I cannot picture you playing anything."

"My family plays lots of games. The man you've seen...he's not me at all." He rubbed his smooth upper lip. "When Gothard came into my life—destroyed people I cared for..."

"What of the mother?" She ran a fingertip around the rim of her tankard. "Do you love her, as well?"

He drank leisurely, delaying his answer. "No, but I feel responsible for her." He lowered the tankard, then steepled his fingers and studied her across them. "Why do you care?"

"I'm stuck with you, Jase. I'm trying to puzzle you out."

A slow smile dawned on his face, and he hadn't winced at the nickname.

She decided to push her luck a little. "Who *do* you love? Besides Mary?"

"What I'd love right now is breakfast," he said cagily. "And here it comes."

And that was that for now, she supposed as Mrs. Twentyman set a plate before each of them. But he wouldn't keep her in the dark now that she'd put her mind to figuring him out. He might think he understood women, but he'd never met the likes of her.

With a secretive smile, she watched him begin to eat.

He did love to eat.

Now she just had to figure out the rest.

THIRTY

"TELL ME another," Jason said later, after they'd been on the road for hours—miles and miles of flat road that snaked through rich but unchanging farmland. It made a monotonous view that begged for a diversion. Lucky for him, Emerald had proved quite diverting indeed, regaling him with Scottish tales all morning.

"Can we not stop for a while?" She flexed her shoulders uncomfortably. "Is it far still to Grantham?"

"Not too far. One more story." He tugged playfully on one of her plaits. "In the sea fairy story you mentioned mermaids. Do you know a mermaid's tale?"

She thought for a moment. "Aye. But it's a sad one."

"Tell me. By the time you finish we'll be there and stop for dinner."

"Very well." She sighed and shifted on the saddle, a diversion in itself. "In the Land-under-Waves live the mermaids, which we call Maids-of-the-Wave. They are lovely to look at, and their voices are sweet and melodic. Their lower bodies are shaped like the fishes and glitter like salmon in the sun. They have long, coppery hair, and on beautiful days they sit on the rocks and comb it." She paused. "Unlike me, they have combs."

Jason laughed. "I'll buy you a comb before the day is out, I promise. And a Chase promise is not given lightly."

"I shall hold you to that."

He didn't doubt it.

"On moonlit nights," she continued, "the Maids-of-the-Wave sometimes take off their tails and don pale blue gowns. They can walk on the land then, and they're fairer than any land-dweller woman."

"Not fairer than you," Jason protested.

She shook her head. "If you're attempting to flatter me, I warn it will get you nowhere."

"You cannot fault me for trying."

"Do you want to hear the story?"

"Did I interrupt?" Behind her back, he grinned. "Pray, do go on."

She cleared her throat. "One moonlit night, a handsome young farmer was walking along the cliffs when he heard the most beautiful voices raised in song. He looked down to see a company of fair women, all dressed in pale blue, dancing in a circle around one who was the fairest of the fair. Then he noticed nearby a pile of scaled tails, still wet and glistening in the moonlight. He crept down the rocks, took one, and ran home with it."

Absently, Jason trailed a finger along the part in Emerald's hair.

She looked up and back, bumping her head on his chin in the process. "What do you think you're doing?"

"Did I do something?" Whatever had possessed him to do that, anyway? Irritated, he clenched his fist. "What happened next?"

Sending one more puzzled look over her shoulder, she faced forward. "When the mermaids saw the man stealing away, they screamed and ran for their tails. Hurriedly they put them on and jumped into the sea. All except one, the fairest of the fair. Her tail was missing."

"This *is* sad," Jason remarked, failing to hide the smile in his voice.

"Hold your tongue," she admonished. "Now, the farmer locked the tail in a box and hid the key. Before long, someone came to his door and knocked on it. He opened it to find the most beautiful woman in the land. Tears were pouring from her big blue eyes—"

Interrupting herself, she looked up. "That's the tallest spire I've ever seen," she said, sounding awed.

"St. Wulfram's," he told her.

A sight to see, the church seemed a combination of every period of Gothic architecture mixed with traces of Norman and possibly

Saxon work. She gawked until he turned onto Grantham's busy High Street, a distinguished row of modern gray stone buildings interspersed with the occasional old, half-timbered Tudor.

"Now, to find a place to eat," Jason said. "In the meantime, please do continue your tale. You cannot leave me hanging on the precipice of such tragedy."

"Very amusing. Now, where was I?" She fussed at her skirts. "Oooh, look at that angel."

The carved stone angel was brightly gilded, giving it the look of solid gold. It perched over the gateway of an inn called—appropriately enough—The Angel.

"Whose heads are those?" she asked.

Jason halted and squinted up at the corbel above the winged cherub. "King Edward the third," he decided. "So that must be his queen, Philippa of Hainault."

She nodded thoughtfully. "I see you're not completely uneducated." Before he could protest that thinly disguised insult, she added, "Edward was brutal to the Scots."

"Everyone was brutal in those days," he pointed out. "Edward was after revenge for Bannockburn."

"He got it," she said dryly.

"So this is what comes of educating women," Jason mused as he guided Chiron through the archway and into the courtyard at the rear.

He helped her down and led her inside. The Angel's taproom had a fine timbered ceiling and an enormous stone hearth, but no fire this summer day. Since the weather was warm, Jason opted for a cold dinner of bread, cheese, and small pickled onions. He carried it to where Emerald had seated herself by a stone vaulted window.

"There are so many people," she marveled, watching them pass by on horses, in carriages, and on foot.

"Wait till you see London." He sliced the thick slab of cheddar. "So, what happened after the woman showed up?"

"Pardon?" She dragged her gaze from the window.

He handed her a piece of bread topped with cheese. "The mermaid."

"Oh. The Maid-of-the Wave." She took a bite. "Well, when we left her she was standing there in her blue dress, greeting. I mean, crying."

"Greet means to cry?"

"Aye. And she said, 'Won't you have pity and return my tail, so I can go home to the Land-under-Waves?'"

"Let me guess." He popped an onion into his mouth. "He couldn't stand to see the woman cry, so he returned her tail."

"Nay." Her eyes danced, looking turquoise today. "Maybe that's what you would do. But not this young farmer. He thought she was so gentle and beautiful that he couldn't bear to let her go. He told her, 'What I have I will keep. But shed no tears, fairest of the fair, for you may stay with me and become my bride.'"

She paused for a sip of The Angel's strong ale.

"Did she marry him?" Jason asked.

Cocking her head, she studied him. "Would *you* marry someone who kept you forcibly?"

He nearly choked on his own ale. An uneasy silence stretched between them until he wiped his mouth and said, "So, what happened?"

"She was a daftie—a fool. She walked away and returned to the sea, but without her tail she couldn't join her people. Instead of standing up for herself, in the morning she went back and agreed to be the man's bride. She begged him to be kind and never tell anyone who she was or how she came to be there, and he promised."

"And they lived happily ever after?"

"Nay. I told you it was a sad story." A faraway look in her eyes, she touched her emerald. "All the people of the village loved the Maid-of-the-Wave, but the man kept his promise and didn't tell them where she came from. They believed she was a princess, brought to them by the fairies."

"Half-witted fools," he said and ate another onion.

A frown appeared on her forehead. "You don't believe in fairies, either?"

"Hell, no."

"Well, then, that makes two of us," she said with a grin.

He laughed. "So were they happy together?"

"Oh, aye, for a spell. They lived in peace for seven years and had two bairns, a lad and a lassie. The Maid-of-the-Wave loved them dearly. Then came a time the farmer went to town to trade. It was a long journey, and he was gone several days. The mermaid was lonely without him, so she wandered the seashore with her little ones. As she sang to her wee lass, she remembered her people who lived in the Land-under-Waves."

"Very sad. Are you going to finish that?"

With a roll of her eyes, she handed him the rest of her bread. "One evening her son came to her and said, 'I found a key. It opens Father's box, and I looked inside. There's a tail in there, a big, shiny, beautiful tail that looks like a salmon's.' She gasped with shock and excitement and asked for the key."

"And he gave it to her?"

"Of course. She was his mother. After supper she put her children to bed and sang them to sleep. Then she opened the box and took out her tail. She sat by the fire for a long, long time, for she wanted so badly to go home to her people, but she didn't want to leave her bairns." She paused for a heavy sigh. "But then she heard the sound of singing coming from the sea. Her sister mermaids were calling to her. She kissed her two children and wept—"

"Greeted."

She smiled, though her eyes looked sad. "—greeted over them until their precious faces were wet with her tears. And still she heard the songs from the sea. With a heavy heart, she took her tail and hurried to the Land-under-Waves."

"Abandoning her children," Jason put in with no small measure of disgust.

"Aye," she said and nodded. "When the farmer returned the next morning, the sounds of joy and laughter floated to him from the sea. In his cottage, his children were fast asleep. But the box was open and empty. He sat down and wept, because he knew that the Maid-of-the-Wave had gone."

She released a shaky breath, tearing at Jason's heart. Without thinking, he leaned to cover her hand with his. "You must miss your own children."

A puzzled look came over her face. "What do you mean?"

"Your children. Your...bairns. A lad and a lassie, like the mermaid's, yes?"

"You think I have children?" She tugged back her hand. "Me? I've never even—"

"Never mind."

He hated the feelings of doubt that had been niggling at him ever since he'd overheard the men at breakfast. But his gaze strayed to her amulet. A ray of sunshine through the window made the old stone glint green. Emerald green.

Of course she was Emerald. Emerald would deny this, like everything else.

He damned the aggravating niggle and drained the rest of his ale. "Did the mermaid ever come back?"

One finger traced her crisscrossing laces while she studied him a moment. He shifted uneasily. He didn't want to be studied.

"Nay," she said at last. "But it's told that she often returned in the night to peek through the cottage windows at her bairns as they slept. She left trout and salmon outside the door. The farmer told his children that their mother was far away but would never forget them. When her son grew up, he sailed the seas, and no harm ever came to him, even in the fiercest storms, for the Maid-of-the-Wave followed his ship and protected him."

"That's not quite so sad, then."

A wan smile emerged. "Nay, I suppose it isn't. She had to go back to her place, didn't she? Her home, where she belonged." A muddy green now, her eyes met his. "Even though they'd never see her again."

Like Emerald would go back to Scotland. Her home, where she belonged. "Yes, she had to go," he agreed, though damned if the thought of never seeing her again didn't seem somehow incomprehensible.

THIRTY-ONE

*T*HE ROAD FROM Grantham was hilly with lots of trees and sheep, a welcome change after traveling through flat land all the day.

At Stoke Rochford they took a wee bridge over a wee river—Jason didn't even hesitate—and rode up to the Church of St. Mary, which was perched on high land with a spectacular view. The village had no inns or taverns, though—no excuse for Cait to get off the horse and ease her aching legs and bottom. Her teeth were aching as well, from gritting them against the pain. But she wouldn't admit that to Jason.

Stretton had enormous trees and a lovely field of yellow wildflowers, but nothing else of note. They plodded on. A sleepy stone village called Casterton boasted a pretty Norman kirk, but Jason didn't suggest they stop and have a look.

After hours in the saddle, Caithren thought she would scream if she didn't get some relief. The sun was on its downward slide when she spotted a jumble of stone and patted Jason's knee.

"Do you think I might stretch my legs?"

"Why?" he asked, sounding amused. "Is something wrong with them?"

"Nay." She set her jaw. "It's only that I've a mind to explore that ruin over there."

"Oh. I see." By his tone, she guessed he saw all too much. "I suppose we could do that," he said, steering Chiron off the road and up the grassy rise that led to the crumbling castle. "We've made excellent time today. And I could do with a bite."

"I thought I heard your stomach rumbling," she said as he dismounted. "Are you always hungry, then?"

He spanned her waist with his big hands to swing her down. "Seems so," he said with a grin.

While he tethered Chiron to a tree, she flexed her knees and looked around. The remnants of the castle's walls meandered up and down gentle, grassy slopes, loosely connected by steps that seemed to lead nowhere. It struck her as both sad and terribly romantic.

From a corner of the site rose the keep, a square tower that was tall but open to the sky.

Rather than sharing her enchantment, Jason was digging in the portmanteau for the chicken, bread, and cheese he'd bought before leaving Grantham.

"Come up the keep," she said. "I'd wager there's a lovely view."

"Go ahead." He pulled a flask from one leather bag. "I'll arrange our supper."

With a shrug, she started up the winding stone steps. Though in better shape than the rest of the castle, the keep was far from habitable. The floors were half gone, and big chunks of the walls were missing. The narrow stairs bore deep depressions from centuries of feet, and there was no rail, but the steps themselves felt solid and safe.

She trudged up painfully, wondering if this was really a good idea after so many hours in the saddle. When she finally reached the top, puffing from exertion, she leaned on the crenelated wall and gazed out over the countryside.

"Oh, it's glorious!" The land rolled away in all directions, dotted with trees and houses, divided by glistening ribbons of rivers and streams. "You can see from here like a bird in the sky. You must come up!"

"Take your time," he called to her. "I'll wait for you here."

"Nay, come join me!" She rushed to the other side, saw the endless, brown swath of the road, steeples of churches, a working mill. "You can see a mill from up here, Jase! It's running. The top of a mill—wouldn't that be interesting?"

He was a miller, after all.

But his chuckle floated up the ancient stone walls. "I've no need to see a mill. I have one of my own."

"I knew that. But there's a big river too, and"—she worked her way around the perimeter—"a town, Jase! A bonnie large town!"

"Stamford," he told her. "We're nearly there." From her high perch, he looked small as he walked around to her side. The sun glinted off his hair. "I can see the town from here," he called up. "The keep is built on a hill. They usually are, you know. A motte, the hill is called."

"You cannot see it as well as I can," she argued. "It's a lovely town. With wee toy carriages going all over it."

Laughing, he seated himself on what was left of a crumbling stone wall. "Enjoy. Come down when you've seen enough."

"Please come up," she begged. She wanted to share this with someone. The beauty, the wonder. "Please."

He stared up at her for a minute. She wished she could see his expression better, especially when he released a long-suffering sigh. Finally he said, "Has anyone ever told you you're stubborn?"

Without waiting for an answer, he stood and brushed off his breeches, then disappeared around the other side of the keep.

A few footsteps echoed up the stairwell, slow and measured. Then…faltering? There was silence for a minute before the footfalls resumed, then stopped again. More silence, followed by the padding sound of walking on grass.

Then the sun was glinting off his hair again. He was standing below her, outside the keep.

"I changed my mind," he called up.

Awareness slowly dawned.

How very wrong she'd been. Ashamed, she slowly made her way down the tower. He met her at the bottom of the steps with a shrug and a self-deprecating grin.

"You've a fear of heights," she said softly. "That's why you won't ride at the edge of a high bridge, isn't it?"

Warm color flooded his cheeks. "Well, I did tell you I'm not superstitious."

It was just like a man not to come out and say it. "You should have told me the truth. I wouldn't have teased you so."

"You'd pass up that opportunity?" He rubbed the back of his neck. "It's hardly a manly admission."

"But I understand. Though it's not exactly the same, my mother feared small spaces."

"Did she, now?" He raised a brow. "And I imagine she quoted you wisdom for this sort of thing?"

Caithren smiled. "A common blot is nae stain."

"Come again?" He started toward where he'd left Chiron and their food.

She trailed after him. "Don't fret about small faults that are common to everyone."

"I see." Handing her a round of bread, he took the chicken and cheese and seated himself on a broken stone wall. "Well, I thank you for not laughing. I've never admitted this particular fault to anyone."

An unexpected warmth spread out from her heart, that he would choose her in which to confide. Never mind that it was so obvious he'd have looked the fool for denying it—it was a rare man who would own up to such an affliction.

She dropped to sit cross-legged on the grass, arranging her skirt to preserve her modesty.

"Miss your breeches, do you?" he asked, ripping a healthy portion from a chicken leg.

Composing herself, she tore off a hunk of the bread. "When I'm riding, aye. Maybe you should buy me a pair."

He only grinned, but the brilliant slash of white made her breath catch. Up here on this hill, she felt close to this man. Closer than she'd ever felt to any man before.

It made no sense. He'd kept her off the coach. He refused to believe a word she said. He was an Englishman.

She ate in silence for a while, watching the comings and goings of people passing under the medieval gateway at the bottom of the hill.

"It's a pretty town, all stone," she remarked.

"A rich town. The wool trade has made their fortune." He took a swig from his flask of water, then passed it to her. "They've a fine marketplace. There, see? And it looks as though they've a fair in full swing this eve."

She squinted into the distance. "Oh, just look how busy. So many booths!"

"Would you like to go?"

"Oh, aye!" But London was beckoning. Gothard was on the loose. She needed to find Adam. "We haven't the time," she said with a sigh.

"We couldn't possibly make it to another sizable town by nightfall." He gestured toward the sun, low in the western sky. "We'll be staying the night in Stamford regardless."

She considered. "There will be things to buy at a fair, aye?"

One eyebrow arched. "What, have I not bought you enough?"

"One gown! One half a gown, truth be told." Her hand fluttered up to cover the top of her chest, although she was wearing her own laced bodice and modest shift.

Jason's laugh boomed over the hillside. "I was fooling, sweet." Her heart turned over at the careless endearment, even though she knew it meant nothing. "I'll buy you a comb. And some clothes, if they've any ready made," he added before she could ask. "And we can eat."

"Are you not eating already?" She aimed a pointed glance at the bare drumstick in his hand.

"Fairgoing victuals," he explained, grinning as he chose another. "One cannot attend a fair without eating. Fair food doesn't count as real food."

It sounded too good to be true, an evening of frivolous entertainment in the midst of their urgent journey. But they had covered quite a distance today, and it would serve a purpose as well. Jason did owe her replacements for her belongings.

And she still hadn't recovered from him calling her a pet name, never mind that he hadn't seemed to notice.

Confused, Cait stood and walked over to a pile of rubble, then climbed over it into an enclosure. "When was this built, do you think?" She gestured at the remnants of walls that marked what used to be chambers, now carpeted with soft grass instead of fragrant rushes. "It looks to be very old."

"Norman, I believe," he said with a nod that drew her attention to his arresting features.

My, but he was a beautiful man. *Sweet*, he'd called her, and it had sounded entirely different from when Cameron called her sweet.

Awareness flooding her being, she deliberately looked away from him. "Can you picture this castle all solid, with banners and tapestries on the walls? And knights battling. Over there, maybe." Feeling giddy, she whirled in a wide-armed circle. "Oh, I expect it was glorious!"

She stilled and turned to see him shrug. "I expect it was cold and rather crude."

Compelled by some pull beyond her control, she moved toward him. His hair shone blue-black in the deepening shadows, and his chiseled features looked sculpted in stark relief.

A curious quiver of wanting ran through her. "Do you not like castles?" she asked softly.

"I like them well enough." He made himself busy gathering the remains of their supper.

She stepped over the rubble and knelt to help him. "I live in a castle."

He looked up sharply, assessingly. "Do you?"

"Aye, but it's not quite a real one, you see. I mean, it's not ancient." Once again her nerves had her blethering, but she couldn't seem to stop herself. "Da built it for my mother on the land that she brought to their union. He always called her his queen. It's fortified, but just a house for all that...fifteen rooms."

"The castle at home—Cainewood—has stood five hundred years. It has maybe a hundred rooms."

"A hundred rooms? Are you sure?" Looking up at him, she reached blindly, encountering his hand instead of the napkin she was aiming for.

His fingers gripped hers. "I said maybe," he said with a grin. "I don't know if anyone has ever bothered to count." He swiped up the napkin and stood, pulling her to her feet with him.

"How can they not have counted?" Marveling, Caithren followed him back to Chiron. "Is that castle in ruins, then, like this one?"

"Oh, no. Though Cromwell did his best to flatten it, it still stands. I—people live in it."

"Is it very grand?"

He shrugged. "It's home. A home, I mean."

"Have you been inside?"

An enigmatic look crossed his face. "As a child, I used to play in the keep. That part is in ruins, though not as far gone as this. Of course, I never went up to the top," he added with a wry smile.

"As a child," she mused. "I cannot picture you as a child. What was your childhood like?"

"Happy. Until the war." He opened the portmanteau and started stuffing everything inside. "My parents were staunch Royalists. Father deposited us with friends and went off to defend the king, taking my mother with him. They both died in the Battle of Worcester. I was the eldest, at sixteen."

He was making a mess of packing the two bags, but she was afraid to interrupt to help. She sensed this was part of the puzzle. "You did what you thought your father would have wanted. Kept the family together."

He closed the first latch. "I was a man by then—"

"You were sixteen."

"He was a war hero." The second latch snapped into place. "Honorable, brave, self-sacrificing. I've never been able to live up to him."

She moved closer. "You make him sound like a god. He couldn't have been."

"You didn't know him."

Her stomach felt odd. She moved closer still.

His eyes darkened, and he cleared his throat. "How is your shoulder?"

"My shoulder?"

"Where it was nicked by my sword. Would you mind if I looked?"

She blinked, feeling heat stain her cheeks. "All right." Slowly she loosened the laces of her bodice and pulled it and her shift off the shoulder, feeling terribly naked beneath his gaze.

Nothing marked the skin but a tiny dark scab.

He bent close, nodding. "Looks good." His voice sounded husky by her ear, and her skin tingled at his nearness. Beneath the sleeves of her shift, the little hairs stood up on her arms.

"I-I thank you for taking care of me." Her fingers fumbling, she shrugged back into her clothes and tightened her laces. Tying the bow, she swayed forward involuntarily, peering up at him. "For caring."

His gaze locked on hers. Her heart skipped a beat. His knuckles came up and brushed her cheek.

She looked from his compelling green eyes to the lips that had touched hers last night…

He sucked in a breath. "The fair will close at nightfall," he said, pulling back. "We'd best be moving."

THIRTY-TWO

CAITHREN DODGED a couple of dogs that were chasing each other near the entrance to the fair. "It's delightful!"

"It stinks," Jason countered.

She wrinkled her nose against the ripe smells of cattle and fish. But the odors didn't dim her enthusiasm. "Aye, but it's exciting, don't you think? We've nothing like this near Leslie."

She pushed into the noisy crowd, heading straight toward the area where vendors displayed an amazing array of merchandise. She passed stands piled with soap and candles, sugar and spices, making a beeline for a table strewn with a hodgepodge of gloves, ribbons, and lace.

"The blue suits you." Jason lifted a spool of ribbon and held it up to her hair. "Would you like a length?"

Her smile was quick, but she couldn't ask for luxuries—at least until Jason collected the reward he'd been blethering about. She opened her mouth to say nay, but he was already handing the ribbon to the vendor.

"A yard, if you please. And some of the red as well." He glanced at her skirt. "No, make that the green."

"Jason—"

"You'd prefer the red? I thought you'd rather not wear that dress."

"Nay, it's only—"

"All three, then." He dug in his pouch for a coin. "Do you know where we might find a comb for sale?"

"To the left, sir," the merchant said as he handed Jason his change.

Jason stuffed the coins and ribbons into his pouch. "Come along, Emerald." He took off in the direction the vendor had indicated, leaving her to follow.

Too excited to be irritated at the name, she found her attention pulled in all directions at once. A stall selling eggs, milk, and butter sat beside one offering fat brown sausages. The rich aroma of coffee beans competed with the scents of tobacco and cocoa.

She looked up, and Jason was gone. Craning her neck, she spotted his raven-topped head above the crowd and hurried to join him.

"Do you fancy this one?" The comb he held was made of the finest ivory, like his own, the creamy white polished to a high sheen.

"One of those will do." She indicated a comb of brown, mottled tortoiseshell. "Or this one." She picked up a plain wooden comb.

Jason plucked it from her hand and set it down. Experimentally he lifted one of her plaits and ran the ivory comb through its tail, then dug once more in his pouch. "We'll take it," he said, and that was that.

Caithren blinked in astonishment. She'd never seen anyone make such quick decisions.

Exchanging coin for the comb, he handed it to her. "Will this fit in your pocket?"

She nodded and slipped it inside, beside his pistol she still carried.

"Good. Now, for a gown…"

"I don't think we'll find a gown here, Jase. The fabric, aye, but—"

"Come along—we'll look."

He dragged her up one row and down another, past bolts of silks and muslin and calico. But as she'd said, no ready-made garments were for sale. She found it difficult to keep up with his purposeful strides, so she was happy for a chance to catch her breath when he paused before a gingerbread cart.

"I'm hungry again." He grinned at her sound of disbelief. "Would you like some as well?"

She shook her head, watching while the baker dusted a wooden board with ground ginger and cinnamon. He scooped a hunk of hot brown dough from a pot and rolled it out, then cut it into small discs. Without further cooking, he piled several on a piece of paper.

When Jason paid the man and had a warm little circle of cake in his hand, the savory scent was too tempting. Her fingers crept toward the treat to break off a bit, and he laughed and handed it to her, taking another round for himself.

The gingerbread was spicy but not very sweet, and the doughy texture was unusual but not unpleasing.

A small hand tugged on Jason's breeches, and they both looked down to see a wee lad's grubby face.

"What, you too?" With another laugh, Jason handed a piece to the child.

When the boy stuffed it into his mouth and swallowed convulsively, Jason sobered. "So that's the way of it, is it?" Returning to the cart to purchase another serving, he handed it to the lad, along with the coins he'd received as change. "Run along, now, and buy yourself some milk."

The child's eyes widened in his dirty face. The coins disappeared into a fist gripped so tight the poor lad's knuckles turned white. Without so much as a thank you, he took off running.

Caithren lifted a turquoise plume from a nearby stand and waved it through the air thoughtfully. "That was nice, Jase."

He shrugged and pinkened beneath his tan. "It was nothing. Do you want that?"

"Nay!" She dropped it back to the table as though it had burned her fingers.

Was he intent on buying her everything she so much as looked at? Maybe it was a sign he was softening toward her, and that was a pleasing thought…or maybe he was only feeling guilty she'd lost her belongings on his account. Either way, she didn't want him spending his money unnecessarily, so she'd best keep her hands to herself.

A wild burst of laughter drew her attention from the merchandise. With Jason in tow this time, she fought her way into a crowd that circled a troupe of ropedancers. "Look, Jase!"

Indeed, she didn't know where to look first. One man was performing on a low rope, another on a slack rope that looked mighty dangerous, and a third was scaling a daunting slope. A fourth man danced upon a rope with a wheelbarrow in front of him, two children and a dog perched inside. A duck on his head was singing to the crowd and causing much of the laughter.

At the absurd sight, Caithren joined in, laughing even harder when the man executed a silly little bow, nearly tumbling from his rope in the process. The duck squawked in alarm, but of course it was all just a part of the show.

"I never thought to hear you laugh," Jason said wonderingly beside her.

She turned to see an unfathomable look in his eyes. A look that, if she hadn't known better, she might interpret to mean he liked her.

"I've had nothing to laugh at lately," she said gravely, the moment of light, unburdened hilarity lost.

"No, you haven't," he agreed. "Let's see what else I can find to amuse you."

With a light touch on the small of her back, he guided her through the throng and across a trampled field. Ahead loomed another enthralled crowd. "Ah, a mountebank," he said.

"A what?"

"A man who calls himself a doctor."

"Calls himself? Is he a doctor, or nay?"

He looked down at her, flashing an enigmatic grin. "You decide." And he pulled her into the cluster of onlookers.

"Is that the mountebank?" she asked, indicating a rather rumpled looking fellow in a velvet suit that looked much too hot for the summer afternoon.

"Hush," Jason said. "Listen."

"Ladies and gentlemen," the man called out, "do ever you suffer from distempers and ails of the digestion? Why suffer when you can take Dr. Miracle's Universal Healing Potion? My tonic is made from a secret recipe sent down through the ages from the sages of Rome. Along with healing herbs, it contains miraculous powdered bones from the relics of the saints."

"Powdered bones won't cure anybody," Caithren scoffed under her breath.

"Rubbish!" bellowed a stout gentleman standing beside her.

"Ah! We've a disbeliever here, ladies and gentleman. Well, sir, what must I do to prove my miracle cure?" The mountebank put one dirty finger to his chin and tapped it three times. Then his eyes lit up. "Aha! I shall poison someone, then cure him!" With a smarmy smile, he reached into a black bag at his feet and pulled out a squirming green creature that croaked. Cait jumped.

Chuckling, Jason put a reassuring hand on her shoulder.

Dr. Miracle raised the small, warty thing for all to see. "I have here a toad, the most poisonous creature known to mankind." His calculating eyes scanned the gathering. "If a fellow swallowed this animal, it would lead to almost certain death, would it not?"

The crowd murmured its agreement.

"But!" He raised a grimy hand. "I will have it be known that my Universal Healing Potion will cure even this toad's mighty poison. Now..." He paced in a slow circle. "Who will volunteer to swallow this creature? Who among you be brave enough?"

Around and around the mountebank went, while the crowd backed away, until suddenly he stopped right before the man who had shouted "Rubbish!" He strode forward and thrust the toad in the man's face, which was too close to her own for Cait's comfort. She leapt back, right into Jason's solid form.

His warm arms came around to steady her. "Watch," he whispered in her ear.

"Are you brave enough, my man?" the mountebank asked. "Will you swallow the toad and take the cure?"

With a huff, the man turned and elbowed his way out through the crowd.

Dr. Miracle smirked as the mass of people parted, then closed in where the man had been. "Very well, then, I shall pay someone six pence if he will offer to swallow this poisonous toad, then be cured by my tonic." He walked slowly around the interior of the circle. "Will no one volunteer? Ten pence, anyone?" The toad sat docilely on his open palm, though Caithren could see its fat little sides heaving. "Hmm...I'll make that a whole shilling and include a free bottle of Dr. Miracle's Universal Healing Potion, worth another shilling. Now, who will volunteer?"

"I'll swallow it for a shilling." A ragged young man stepped into the open. He looked like he could use a shilling.

The mountebank puffed out his chest. "Ladies and gentleman, may we have a round of applause for this brave fellow?"

Everyone clapped, and some hollered and whistled. More fairgoers came to see what the commotion was about, pressing Cait closer to the center of the circle.

Dr. Miracle handed the young man the toad, then reached into his black bag and drew forth a dusty brown bottle. He tugged out the stopper. "Worry not," he assured the man. "My healing tonic will revive you—even should you be dead."

The volunteer looked alarmed at that pronouncement. He swallowed hard and gripped the toad harder. It croaked in protest.

"A whole shilling," the mountebank reminded the man. "Just for swallowing this fat little creature."

The young man scrunched up his face and squeezed his eyes tight before opening his mouth and stuffing the toad inside. With a gulp that could be heard to the back of the circle, he swallowed. Gasps and muttering ran through the crowd as they waited for something to happen.

After a tense minute, the man doubled over and let loose a pathetic moan. His head went back, and his eyes rolled up in his skull. "Cure me now!" He fell to his knees. "I'm dying!"

Dr. Miracle raised the brown bottle high into the air. He turned in an agonizingly slow circle, hampered by the suffering man, who was clutching at his ankles.

"Shall I administer the cure?" he bellowed at the crowd.

"Save him!" a woman screamed.

"Let him die," a man yelled. "Serves him right for being such a gull."

"No, cure him!"

The young man collapsed on the ground and curled up in a ball.

"Give him the cure!" someone hollered.

Several joined in the chant. "Cure him! For heaven's sake, give him the cure!"

Caithren twisted to see Jason's face, but he didn't look alarmed. His arms tightened around her as he watched over her head. She turned back to the toad-eater, who was now rolling on the grass in screaming agony.

"Cure him! Cure him! Cure him!"

The mountebank knelt slowly and cradled the young man's head in one dirty hand. He shoved the bottle between his lips, encouraging the man to drink. Two swallows later, the man's body relaxed and stilled on the ground.

In silence, the crowd waited. And waited.

The man drew a sudden breath, and his eyes popped open. His hands went to his stomach and felt around. He raised his head, then sat up, then stood up and did a little jig.

"It's a miracle!" he cried. "The miracle cure works!" He skipped around the circle, snatched the bottle, and took another swig. "Give me no shilling," he told the doctor, "but an extra bottle of this Universal Healing Potion." When Dr. Miracle handed him a second bottle, he clutched them both to his chest as though they were made of diamonds, not glass.

The mountebank pulled more bottles from the bag. "Who else would like a bottle? Only one shilling for my miracle cure!"

As people jostled to buy, Jason pulled Caithren from the crowd. "What do you think?"

"Very entertaining," she declared with a smile.

"Entertaining?"

His look of confusion didn't fool her. "The toad is in that young man's pocket," she said. "I wonder how much the mountebank pays him for each bottle sold?"

"I wonder how else I've underestimated you," Jason returned. But he didn't look displeased. "Should we buy tomorrow's breakfast and dinner now?" Low in the sky, the sun streaked the wispy clouds with shades of pink and red. "It's getting late, and we'd best make an early start if we want to outpace Gothard."

And the fun was over, Caithren supposed with an inward sigh. She needed to find her brother and go home.

Before she could even nod her assent, Jason went into action. He purchased a burlap sack from one vendor, then wove through the market filling it with selections from others: bright yellow cheese, tart pickles wrapped in parchment, and small round loaves of bread. From a produce stand he chose apples and costly oranges while Caithren amused herself watching two lambs in a pen, gamboling after their mother. She didn't like to think they might be someone's supper tonight.

Across from the fruits and vegetables sat a table laden with leather goods. Belts were arranged in neat rows, alongside coin pouches, scabbards, and luggage.

And by itself to the side sat one magnificent backgammon board.

It was a sight to behold. Black leather pips alternated with gray, the whole embellished with scrolling designs stamped in gold leaf. Two dice, fashioned of the blackest jet, lay as though just spilled from their matching leather cup. The markers were carved of jet and ivory.

Caithren smiled to herself, remembering hours on end spent playing with Cameron on Da's scarred wooden set. Jason wandered to her side, his burlap sack bulging with what she reckoned must be food enough for a week. "Do you know how to play?" he asked.

"I do." She squinted up at him. "I wager I could beat you."

"Do you, now?" He studied her, his features schooled into serious lines. But his green eyes danced. "And what might you be willing to wager?"

She blushed furiously at the tone of his voice. "I haven't any money—"

"—thanks to me," he finished for her in a singsong manner. "Well, I expect we'll come up with something." Once again, he spilled coins from his pouch and motioned the vendor over.

She'd meant to have a match then and there, not for him to buy the board. She should have known better than to even look at it. Though she gasped at the price, he didn't react. After closing the deal, he presented her with the set, picked up his sack, and announced that he was thirsty.

She carried the board across her forearms, like it was a king's scepter.

Without asking if she wanted any, Jason bought white foamy drinks for them both. "Syllabub," he said, leading her to a bench.

She frowned into her goblet, then sipped. "Oooh," she breathed, sipping again. It was the lightest, creamiest, sweetest thing she'd ever tasted. "It would set the heather alight!" she exclaimed. "It's wonderful!"

Laughing, he reached to wipe a foam mustache from atop her lip. Heat rushed to her face, and she turned away. Sipping their refreshments, they watched silently as other fairgoers paraded past. Cait balanced the backgammon set on her lap, careful not to let any syllabub drip on the fine leather. She still couldn't believe he'd bought it.

The sun was setting, casting the horizon in brilliant colors. As it sank below, a brief green flash lit the sky.

Part of her wishing the evening would never end, Caithren sighed. "Tomorrow will be a clear day."

He sipped from his drink. "And how do you know this?"

"Didn't you see the green ray? They say it portends of fair weather. Have you never heard the verse?" She drank, then licked her lips. "Glimpse ye e'er the green ray," she quoted, "Count the morrow a fine day."

"Is that so?"

"Aye." She touched her amulet. "And it's said that to see the green is to gain powers of seeing into the feelings of your heart, and thus not to be deceived in matters of love."

"Hmm. Sounds like yet another superstition."

She shrugged. "I didn't say I believed it."

He took a long swallow, then rubbed his bare upper lip with a finger. "I'm sorry there were no gowns here today."

"English gowns, pah! My own clothes will do if I wash them." She reached over the backgammon set to brush some dust off her forest green skirt, then toyed with an ivory marker, sliding it back and forth across the board. "It's decent clothes I was wearing when you—"

"Helped you off the coach?"

In the midst of a sip, she nearly snorted syllabub out her nose. "Aye, you might put it that way…if you were a candidate for the asylum."

Jason let loose with a loud peal of laughter, accompanied by the first genuine, unaffected grin she'd seen from him.

It lit up his face, and a place in her heart.

She smiled in return, lifting her goblet to hide the blush that threatened.

"Wait." He set his goblet on the bench between them. "Just wait right here."

At a loss, she sat and watched him take off, threading his lean form through the teeming crowd. Not a minute later he was walking toward her with his hands behind his back. He stepped up close, so close their knees almost touched, and leaned to tuck a small bunch of violets behind her ear.

"Ah, lovely," he said. "Of a sudden, I thought that would complete the picture."

"Picture?" Now she really blushed.

What was happening to them?

"When you smiled, it was like a...oh, never mind." He looked away.

"Thank you," she said, drawing his gaze back to her. She reached up to touch the soft, fragrant petals. "I do love violets."

Behind them, wives haggled over herrings, oysters, and mackerel. Across the way, feathers flew as a hundred chickens squawked their protest at being crammed in a wooden pen. But when Jason took the game off her lap and held her hands to pull her to stand before him, it was as though they were the only two beings there.

Her breath caught, and she'd swear her heart stopped for a moment, then pounded so hard she wondered if he could hear it.

His eyes burned into hers. Slowly he ran his hands up her arms to her shoulders, squeezed, then trailed back down to lace their fingers together. When he lowered his head, her lips parted in anticipation.

But he only kissed her on the forehead.

Her heart plummeted. The gesture was warm and sweet, but she'd yearned for more.

"We'd best be going," he said. "It's almost dark, and with the fair in town, I expect the inns will fill up early around here."

THIRTY-THREE

*C*AITHREN POPPED an orange section into her mouth and licked her sticky fingers before rolling the dice.

"Double sixes!" she crowed. Removing four white markers from the backgammon board, she added them to her stack with a gleeful *clink.*

Looking wary and distracted, Jason shook the dice as he scanned the large, plush common room at the George of Stamford.

Cait separated another section of the orange. "What are you looking for?"

"Not what. Who." The leather dice cup stilled in his hand. "The Gothard brothers."

"You think they're here in Stamford?" She hoped not. "Have you seen any sign of them?"

"No." He rubbed the back of his neck, still glancing around. "It's just a feeling. I know they could be far ahead or behind us, but something tells me they're near."

She made her own survey, seeing nothing alarming. People conversed in pairs and groups. They went in and out of the taproom or through the double doors into the more formal dining room. Two men played cards in one corner. A couple made their way up the stairs, laughing, their arms full of purchases from the fair.

"Well," she said, "I'm thinking those brothers cannot afford a coaching inn as nice as this one. Or any of the other inns you've chosen along the way." The patrons in the common room looked well-heeled and groomed, not rumpled like she remembered the Gothards. "Is that why you've been choosing as you have? In order to avoid them?"

A ghost of a smile curved his lips as he rattled the dice. After a moment it became obvious he wasn't going to answer. But she'd bet he was attempting to steer clear of them.

To keep her from getting the reward?

She'd never understand him.

He rolled a one and a two. With an exaggerated groan, he advanced one of his black markers a paltry three pips. "Why did I buy this backgammon set?"

"I don't know, but I'm glad you did. Though Lord knows how we'll manage to carry it."

She rolled again, a three and a five. Two more white markers came off her side. She held out a piece of orange. "Would you like some?"

He tossed the section into his mouth and rolled the dice. Double fours, and he was finally able to remove three of his black markers. But three rolls later the orange was finished and the match was over.

Two up on him now, Caithren celebrated her victory with naught more than a yawn. "What time is it?" she asked sleepily.

The watch he dug from his coat pocket brought her wide awake. The mere sight of it made her jaw drop. Solid gold, the thing was, with blue jewels stuck on the lid.

"Eight o'clock," he said and snapped it shut.

"May I see?"

"I know it's early." He handed the pocket watch over. "But if you're wanting that bath I promised, you'd best head up and take it now. We'll have to get an early start tomorrow if we want to be sure of catching the Gothards."

She stared at the watch, turning it gingerly in her hands, then flipped it open. "Eight o'clock," she murmured. That wasn't why she'd asked to see it—she'd believed it was eight o'clock. She'd just wanted to feel it, to touch such a wonderfully beautiful thing.

Maybe there was no cause for concern on Jason's behalf. Maybe he had more money than she'd imagined.

But he was a miller.

"Where did you get this?" she couldn't help asking.

Taking the watch from her, he pocketed it with a smile. "It was a gift from a lovely woman."

"Oh." A gift from a lovely woman. Why should that matter to her? Three days from now they'd reach London, and then they'd part company. It was what she'd wanted all along, wasn't it?

"My sister-in-law," he added.

"Pardon?"

His grin widened. "The watch. It was a gift from my sister-in-law. You do know what a sister-in-law is? The woman who married my brother."

"I know what a sister-in-law is, Jase." She rose and snatched up the backgammon set. "I simply cannot imagine you having one, let alone her being fond enough of you to gift you with a watch like that."

"Oh?"

"Oh, yes," she said, heading for the stairs. "You're too ornery by half."

His laughter followed her up all the way up.

THIRTY-FOUR

*A*N HOUR LATER, Jason knocked on the door and entered to find Emerald sitting by the fire, swishing her new comb through her long, silky, bath-damp hair.

He'd never seen anything quite like Emerald's hair. The women in Cainewood's village always bound up their hair or hid it beneath a cap. And the court ladies of his acquaintance were always fussing with theirs, cutting it and curling it and crimping it and twisting it into all sorts of unnatural creations.

But Emerald's hair was straight and thick and shining. *Swish.* The ivory comb he'd bought her ran along its gleaming length. *Swish. Swish.*

Her eyes were downcast, but he remembered them lighting up at each of the small things he'd bought her. He pictured them sparkling with delight when she tasted the syllabub, crinkling when she laughed at the ropedancers, and flashing when she tsked at the mountebank.

Swish.

Jason didn't think he could stand it a moment longer. His fingers itched to bury themselves in that silk. He wanted to wrap the strands around his hands, pull her head back, and expose her creamy throat for his lips to plunder.

Bloody hell, he wanted to kiss her until she was breathless.

He'd dreamt of kissing her and hadn't wanted to wake. The real experience couldn't possibly be as good as the dream, but damn if he wasn't tempted to find out.

Stiffly he crossed the chamber and began loosening his cuffs. It didn't help that, thanks to the many bookings by fairgoers, the only room he could get had naught but one bed. Neither did it help that Emerald wore nothing but Mrs. Twentyman's nightgown. Her old clothes and the red gown were wet, draped over the backs of two chairs to dry.

At last she stood and set the comb on a bedside table, beside the violets he'd given her, which she'd stuck into a pewter cup filled with water. The sight of them, bedraggled but saved, made his heart turn over.

He turned away and sat on the bed to pull off his boots, chucking them across the floor.

Her hair waterfalled when she bent to retrieve them and set them side by side against the wall. "You really should learn to be neater."

He loosened his shirt and lay back, crossing his hands behind his head and staring up at the beamed ceiling.

Her head swam into view. "May I have one of the ribbons?"

"Of course. Bring me my pouch."

She fetched the brown leather pouch and brought it over. Holy heaven, she looked beautiful standing above him, her thick hair bunched in one hand, the firelight revealing hints of her slender form beneath the white nightgown. He could barely tear his gaze away long enough to fish in the pouch and pull out the blue ribbon.

It was much too long to simply tie back her hair, but she used it anyway, leaving the long ends to dangle down her back. He'd been right: the blue suited her perfectly.

He swallowed hard and closed his eyes, listening to the little sounds of Emerald readying herself for sleep.

When she crawled into bed next to him, he made no move to get under the covers. His blood was too hot; he couldn't trust himself to keep his hands off her. The dream had done that to him.

The dream and the woman beside him.

Whenever she looked at him, whether outdoors by that ruined castle or over a backgammon board, it was with eyes that pleaded, a mouth that begged to be kissed.

He wouldn't allow himself.

He *couldn't* allow himself. Emerald MacCallum was not the sort of woman he was looking for—not that he was looking at all.

Emerald was a liar and she was Scottish. Scottish, of all things! It didn't matter that she felt soft and smelled sweet. That was only part of the deception.

His eyes flew open when she turned to him and levered up on an elbow. A true hazel now, her gaze was riveted to where his shirt lay open across his chest, revealing the angry puckered scar. "Does it still hurt?" she asked softly.

"Sometimes," he admitted. "But it's healing. It's been more than three weeks."

"I should make a poultice for you." She reached out, making his breath catch, but then her hand dropped away. "What happened?"

He couldn't tear his gaze from her concerned face. And that luscious wide mouth. He was sure it was soft. It had been soft in his dream.

"Geoffrey Gothard shot me."

"He shot you?" She sat up in bed and shook her head violently. The dark blond tail of her hair shimmered as it swished back and forth. "You said he hurt, perhaps killed a wee lass. And nearly raped—"

"That he did—all of that. And when I went after him to take him to the authorities, he shot me."

Twisting to face him, she moved his shirt aside with gentle fingers and touched the pink, ridged tissue lightly.

Something melted in his gut.

"It was dangerously close to your heart," she said seriously.

A choked laugh escaped his lips. "No, it's only my shoulder. But I was already covered in another man's blood, so Gothard figured he'd hit his mark."

"It's no wonder you're after killing him, then." Her fingers exploring, she leaned closer. Her hair fell forward, and the ends of the ribbon tickled his chest.

"No, I..." He couldn't seem to think. "I'm after him because he killed a little girl, and he'll kill others if he isn't stopped." Absently he pulled one end of the blue ribbon until the bow came untied. Her eyes widened, but she didn't back away. "And—bloody hell, I know this is weak of me—but I cannot forgive him for causing me to kill a man. It's a burden I'll carry the rest of my life. But that he shot me…

no. *That* I blame on my own carelessness. I wasn't fast enough; I was stunned." His fingers combed through her hair as the words tumbled out. "And perhaps I shouldn't have been taking the law into my own hands to begin with. It's not...not the sort of man I am. Though you've seen no other, so I cannot fault you for believing so."

"Nay, I believe you. I've seen the man you are, Jason Chase." Her fingertips brushed his jaw. "I've seen a man of honor and compassion, and sometimes, when you let it slip, even a wee bit of charm."

Reversing their positions, he came up on an elbow and hovered over her. She fell back to the pillow, and her lips curved into the sweetest smile, her eyes filled with blue light. Free from her customary plaits, her hair was a mass of colors shimmering against the sheets. She trembled beneath him, and his name escaped her lips in a breathy murmur.

Of its own volition, it seemed, his hand moved to cup her face. His mouth descended toward hers. "Emerald..."

The light in her eyes died, and she jerked her head away.

Unsure what had happened, he gazed at her a moment longer, then flipped onto his back and stared at the ceiling, saying nothing. There was nothing he could possibly say. He had no business kissing her in the first place, so he could hardly fault her for disallowing it.

Not that he was worried for her reputation. She was no chaste virgin, but a woman of...a woman of...

What was she, exactly?

A Scot, a mother, a daughter, and a sister—if he could believe her. A...businesswoman? What did one call a female who made her living tracking outlaws?

Well, whatever she was, he needn't worry about ruining her. Whether husband or lover, someone else had got there first. But that didn't mean it was all right to kiss her. It was very much not all right. Beyond her sensibilities, he had reasons of his own to keep his distance.

If only he could be a greater distance from her now.

He swore he could feel her warmth penetrating the bedclothes. With a muttered curse, he took the top quilt and slid off the bed. It wouldn't be the first time he'd slept on the floor.

Assuming he could sleep at all.

THIRTY-FIVE

"*T*HE BIRDS ARE singing," Caithren said the next morning when they were back on the road.

Since their almost-kiss last night, Jason had said hardly a word. While she didn't know how she felt about him, she did know she didn't care for the awkward silence. "Isn't it a beautiful day?"

"It's hot," he complained.

"It's warm and clear, just as the green flash portended. Will you open your eyes? The clouds look like wool before spinning."

She felt him shrug behind her. "They look like clouds to me."

"Is everything so black and white for you, then?" One of her hands went into her pocket to feel for Adam's miniature. For all his faults, Adam had an imagination. Too much of one, maybe; he couldn't be less like Jason. "Do you never see gray sometimes? Or purple?"

"Black is black, and white is white. I see no reason to call them otherwise."

"You're grumpy this morning." He was cross with her for rejecting his kiss. Well, she was cross with herself as well. She sighed and tried to put a note of compassion into her voice. "Did you suffer the bad dream again last night?"

"I wish I could have." With his free hand, he rooted in his coat pocket for his water flask. "It was rather impossible to dream given that I didn't sleep."

"Well, nobody said you had to sleep on the floor. I shared a bed with you the first night, and you didn't hear me complaining."

"Is that so?" He brought the flask before her so he could use both hands to pull out the cork. "Maybe that's because you didn't stay long enough in it—"

"Wheesht." She cupped an ear. "Do you hear water?"

He shook the flask. "No. It's empty." Disgruntled, he corked it and shoved it back into his pocket. "Are you thirsty?"

"Aye. And I hear a burn. Running water. There, to the right—I mean the left."

Following where she indicated, he guided Chiron off the road and along a small path that had been trodden through the trees.

Dismounting, she sighed in pleasure at the sight before her. The stream babbled through a sparse emerald forest, its banks studded with multi-colored pebbles that looked like so many wet jewels.

"Oh, it's lovely!" She sat upon a log to remove her shoes and stockings.

Jason turned from where he was tethering Chiron. "What on earth do you think you're doing?"

"I wish to take a stroll in the water. Does it bother you, then?"

He shrugged. "I suppose not."

"You said it was hot. A wee wade would help you cool off." While Jason didn't strike her as a man to doff his stockings and wade in a burn, it was worth a try to get him out of his dour mood. "Come along," she cajoled. "Be impulsive. Isn't that what you called it when we went down into the tunnel? And you said it was fun."

His eyes locked with hers for a long moment, clear and unfathomable. "Very well," he said at last. "Get started." He waved her along the bank. "Let me fill the flask and check the map, and I'll follow along in a bit."

The stream felt lusciously cold on her bare toes. Raising her skirt, she inched in until the water lapped at her feet and then her ankles. She wandered along for a few minutes, keeping a hopeful eye out for the dark green notched leaves of water betony as she skipped stones across to the other bank. The burn smelled fresh and enticing. Bunching her skirt in one hand, she bent to scoop a palmful of water with the other and took a deep, refreshing drink.

When she looked up, it was into the beady black eyes of a wild boar.

Caithren's heart paused, then skittered before beating again. The beast stood a goodly distance away, perhaps twenty or thirty feet, eyeing her malevolently. She took a step back, pitched forward and had to catch herself from tumbling. The bottom of the stream wasn't the smooth slope she'd been expecting. It dropped off toward the center.

The boar took a step forward.

"J-Jason?" she stuttered ineffectively, afraid to yell and provoke the animal. She stepped back again, more gingerly this time. The hem of her skirt dipped into the water, and she hiked it higher and tucked it into her waistband.

Her hand went up to grasp her amulet. The smooth, polished emerald felt solid and reassuring in her clenched fingers. But the stone's protective powers didn't seem to be in force. Staring at her unblinkingly, the boar came two steps closer.

Her heart pounding, she reached her other hand into her pocket, her fingers closing on the grip of Jason's little pistol. Slowly she pulled it out and cocked the flintlock.

At the distinctive click, the boar moved again. She would swear his eyes narrowed.

"Jason? Are you nearby?" Her hand shook as she raised the barrel. "S-stay back," she ordered in the most demanding voice she could muster.

Ignoring her command, the boar came closer.

"Jason!" she wailed.

Her breath was coming in panicky gasps. The boar took another step. "Stay back!" she screamed. "Keep away from me, you mawkit beast!"

But it wouldn't listen, and Jason wasn't coming to her rescue. When the boar came yet closer, she closed her eyes and squeezed the trigger.

The resulting *bang!* left her heart in her mouth. The pistol's kick sent her sprawling on her bottom in the cold burn, and the boar charged splashing into the water, straight at her. She scrambled to get up, but her feet skidded on the muddy streambed, and the pistol slipped out of her grasp, plunging to the bottom.

Just as she was sure she was about to die, the animal collapsed.

The silvery blade of a sword flashed in the sun, jammed between its shoulder blades.

Shuddering in both horror and relief, Caithren sat in the water, feeling a sudden warmth as the beast's blood spread in red ribbons beneath the surface. Her gaze was riveted to the motionless boar where its hairy back made a hump in the shallow stream.

Jason waded to her side and reached a hand to pull her up. She stood there, dripping, her hands clenching her crossed arms in a futile attempt to control the shaking.

"It wouldn't have attacked you if you hadn't shot," he said calmly.

"B-but he wouldn't stop." Her teeth chattered, although the day was no less hot than before. "He was coming towards me."

"At a walk, no? He was only curious." He rubbed the back of his neck. "Boars don't attack people unless they're provoked."

"H-how was I supposed to know that?" Her sodden skirt had come untucked and floated about her knees. Her bodice and shift were plastered to her skin. The pale ivory sleeves were streaked a sickening shade of pink.

She stared at the fallen animal until Jason took her by the hand and tugged her upstream. His fingers felt warm and reassuring.

"Submerge yourself," he urged. He waded back to the boar, lifting his boots high, heavy with water. "Go ahead," he called back. "The blood will wash out."

Numbly she obeyed, watching him tug the sword free and rinse the blade. He slid it back into his belt, then plunged his arm into the water and came up with his pistol.

For a long moment he held it dripping above the surface, looking from it to Caithren and back again. He cocked a brow. "I reckon it's best I keep this, no?" Tucking it into his boot top, he splashed his way back to her.

She plucked her soaked bodice away from her body, trying to gather her wits. "It's sorry I am that your boots are ruined."

"They'll dry." He shrugged, then his forehead furrowed. "You're a lousy shot, Emerald."

"I'm not Emerald." Irritated, she waded out of the water at full speed. "I've never shot a gun before. I didn't like it much."

He emerged from the burn and sat on a stump, shading his eyes with a hand as he gazed up at her. "You were carrying a pistol when I found you."

"Found me? Tricked me into staying with you is more like it."

His hand dropped. "I can do without the wordplay." He yanked off a boot and spilled out a gush of water. "What were you doing carrying a pistol if you don't know how to use it?" His stocking came off next. He wrung it in his hands. Absurdly, she thought he had nice toes. "Well?" he barked.

Her head jerked up. "It was Da's. Cameron made me take it. To protect myself from Englishmen like you."

A look of uncertainty seemed to cross his face, but he regained his normal implacable expression while he poured slowly from his second boot. "You're certainly one for the stories. Quick thinker, too." He peeled off his other stocking. "It's a good thing the outlaws don't know you cannot shoot—that could put a damper on your business, I expect."

She glared at him in disbelief, then turned and stalked upriver, back to where she'd left her things. "You've an aggravating master," she informed Chiron. Plopping down upon a log, she spread her skirts around her, hoping they might dry a wee bit in the sun while she pulled on her stockings and shoes.

Her eyes were still trained downward when Jason's nice toes marched into her field of vision. She squinted up at him. "Where is the food you bought yesterday? I'll be wanting a chitterin' bite."

"A what?"

"A chitterin' bite. Do you not eat something after a swim, to keep from catching cold?"

"No." He stared at her as though she'd left her head in the water. "Is that another of your Scottish superstitions?"

"It's not a superstition—it's a health precaution. And I don't care for the way you say *Scottish*."

He raised a brow. "Will an orange do?"

"Aye. Sweet is preferable to savory."

"I will file that information." He fetched an orange from the portmanteau and handed it to her. "You'll have to wear the red dress," he said, pulling it out as well. He draped it over the log, a jarring splash of crimson against the green of their forest surroundings.

"Nay." Ignoring it, she bit into the bitter skin of the orange and started peeling. "I won't wear that dress again."

Ignoring her in turn, he shrugged out of his surcoat and took dry breeches from one of the leather bags.

"Crivvens!" She jumped up, scattering orange peel all over the ground. "You're not going to undress right here, are you?"

"Nobody is around. What would you have me do?" In one single lithe motion, he pulled his shirt free from his waistband and off over his head. "I'd as soon not ride about the countryside soaking wet."

Cait knew how bairns were made. She was certainly familiar with breeding animals, and, as her best friend, Cameron had always answered her questions. She'd even seen Cam without his shirt. But never a stranger.

Her gaze was riveted to Jason's chest. Lightly defined muscles rippled beneath a sprinkling of silky black hair.

When he began unlacing his breeches, she gave an outraged huff. "I'd rather not have to watch." Despite the calm words, her heart beat much too fast. "Indulge me in my false pretense of innocence," she said sarcastically, then whirled to walk away.

His laughter followed her. "Come back and take the red dress. I won't have your skirt drenching my nice dry clothes as we ride."

The skirt in question was dripping on her nice dry shoes and stockings. In disgust she turned back and snatched the red gown from the log.

"Here," he said, digging in the portmanteau. "You'll be needing this as well." He held out the sheer chemise that had come with the dress.

Instead of arguing, she took it, though she had no intention of wearing it. Carefully she set the half-peeled orange on the log and made her way through the trees, far enough that she was sure he couldn't see her. She checked thoroughly for boars before unlacing her soggy bodice.

Goose bumps sprang up on her skin as she undressed. From cold, or confusion? This vexatious and misguided man kept insisting on calling her Emerald...but he never hesitated to come to her rescue. He was exasperating and rigid...yet oddly compassionate and honorable in his way. And though she'd never been as cross with anyone in her life—he'd completely ruined all her plans! —his slightest touch sent her heart to racing.

That last point didn't bear thinking about. She didn't want to be with any man. She wanted to find Adam and get back to Leslie where she belonged.

He was right, blast it—her shift was entirely too soaked to wear beneath the dress this time. Disgusted, she dropped the chemise over her head and wiggled it into place. The gossamer fabric might as well be air for all the concealment it offered. She stepped into the gown, laced it up, and attached the stomacher with fumbling fingers. Covering her exposed bosom with both hands, she made her way back to the streambank.

She was sure her face was as red as the gown.

Thankfully, Jason was decently clothed. But when his gaze trailed from her burning face to her hands splayed on her chest, he burst out laughing.

"Sorry," he mumbled, digging in his pocket and pulling out a handkerchief. "Here."

She cocked her head.

"To fill in the neckline."

"Oh. I thank you." She shoved it down the front of the dress and tucked it in as best she could before reaching for the orange. "You should have a chitterin' bite as well," she told him.

"Why? So I won't catch cold?"

"Aye." She sat on the log and divided the fruit, handing him half. "So you won't catch cold."

He stuffed a section into his mouth and dug out some fresh stockings before joining her on the log. "I thank you for your concern," he said. "I was under the impression you'd just as soon I caught consumption and died."

Her mouth hung open. What a thing for him to say.

Why had she ever thought she might like him?

"Not until you get me to London," she snapped.

THIRTY-SIX

$\mathcal{A}$N HOUR LATER, Caithren dismounted at the Haycock Hotel and followed Jason into a charming courtyard with stone archways and mullioned windows. "A hat?"

"Yes, a hat. While you were busy provoking the boar, I checked on the map, and this is the only sizable village between here and Stilton. Should we ride all that way on a day like today with but a single hat between us, one of us will end up sunburned and suffering." He nodded at his hat, which was perched atop her plaits. "I'd as soon it not be me, though common decency dictates it will be."

"Oh." She slowly drew off the hat and held it out to him.

He took it from her and set it back on her head. "The shops are closed on a Sunday, but I'm hoping to persuade someone here to part with a hat in exchange for a generous payment." They both scanned the patrons in the inn's sunny courtyard, well-off ladies and gentlemen sharing conversation or lingering over news sheets. "Perhaps a more feminine design would suit you?" he added, tilting the hat's brim up with a finger.

Since his comment by the burn, she'd acted cold as a Scottish winter—and he repaid her by being thoughtful. Flustered, she tucked his handkerchief deeper into her neckline. "Sometimes you're too nice."

"I'm not nice." He drew back his shoulders. "I'm doing what I have to do. No more, no less. I'm responsible for you, and for every-thing you lost due to my actions."

"For my things, yes. But how many times do I have to tell you you're not responsible for *me*? I can take care of myself."

His mouth opened, closed, then he turned on a heel and strode into the cool, shadowed lobby to make inquiries at the desk.

Cait trailed behind him and stared at his back while he explained his problem to the innkeeper. Her legs were aching again, and her brain felt muddled.

She went closer and tapped Jason on the shoulder. "I'm away for a wee dander."

He stopped mid-sentence and turned. "A wee what?"

"A walk." She gestured toward the door. "Down the street a bit, to stretch my legs."

"Stay on the High Street," he told her.

Wansford boasted *only* the High Street, so far as she could tell. She wandered down it, enjoying the sunshine and the solitude she'd lacked the past few days. Her irritation with Jason melted away as her feet put distance between them.

Charming stone cottages with tiny gardens lined the road, bees buzzing around carefully tended flowers. There was one other inn, the small Cross Keys. Farther down the street, a little kirk sat with its door open.

A service was in progress. Cait sidled closer to listen. The drone of the vicar's sermon sounded peaceful and familiar. It was comforting to find that Sunday rituals, at least, were the same here as in Scotland. She slipped inside and into the back pew, feeling at home for the first time since she'd stepped onto the coach in Edinburgh.

THIRTY-SEVEN

*A*T THE END of a frantic search, Jason found Emerald in the church. Dozing.

Taking her by the arm, he pulled her up and out the door. "I was worried sick," he told her in hushed tones, tugging her away from the building. Once out of earshot, he turned her to face him. "I couldn't find you."

"Your face is red," she said, wrenching her arm from his grasp. "You're cross."

"Damn right I'm cross."

"But you're not yelling."

One of the two of them belonged in Bedlam. "What does that have to do with anything?"

"You should just show it. Why don't you show it?" She grasped her emerald necklace like it would save her from his nonexistent wrath. "And you're cross because you thought I'd escaped and gone after Gothard on my own."

Amazing how she clung to that image of him. He took a calming breath. "Stay with me from now on, will you? I don't want you out of my sight." He swept his hat from her head and drew one with a white feather from behind his back, setting it atop her plaits. "There. Now we'd best get back on the road."

"I've never owned a hat with a feather." Hurrying down the

street beside him, Emerald pulled off the hat and turned it in her hands. "It's bonnie. I thank you."

He donned his own hat. "Don't lose it."

"Have I lost anything yet? Without your help?"

"No." He looked down at her and, despite himself, grinned. "I've been a great help in that area."

With a reluctant smile, she jammed the hat back on her head. "The Gothard brothers were sunburned."

Baffled, he slanted her a glance. "And you're saying that why?"

"You were talking about getting sunburned."

"An hour ago." He would never understand how women's minds worked.

"Well, they were both sunburned." They turned a corner and continued toward the stable yard. "Do you think the Gothards cannot even afford two hats?"

"From what I understand of their circumstances, I wouldn't be surprised." Chiron was brought forward, and he handed the groom a coin.

"Then they really wouldn't be able to change horses," she mused as he hoisted her up and mounted behind her. "And he's a blockhead."

"Who's a blockhead?"

"Geoffrey Gothard. We were talking about him, aye?"

"Were we?" He tapped her on the shoulder. "Gothard is not as stupid as you think. You'd best keep that in mind."

"I didn't mean to say he was stupid. I meant he is *literally* a blockhead. He has a square head."

He squinted, trying to picture the man, and decided she was right. Delighted, he laughed and squeezed her around the middle, and then, without conscious thought, tilted her hat forward and pressed his lips to that enticing spot on the nape of her neck.

"What was that?" she squeaked.

He asked himself the same question.

Why the devil did he find her so alluring?

She was everything he wasn't. Superstitious. She believed in ghosts. She wanted his king out of her country. And though it was clear she was educated, half of what she said was lost on him between her accent and all those unintelligible words.

A Royalist and a Cavalier born and bred, he couldn't imagine why he was drawn to someone so provincial and...well, Scottish.

"I don't know," he said at last, meaning it.

THIRTY-EIGHT

*A*FTER WHAT seemed an interminable day, Caithren and Jason finally arrived at the Bell Inn in Stilton. Leaving him to settle Chiron in the stables, Cait wandered into the inn's courtyard.

A black cat ambled over and wove through her legs, making her smile. The pretty inn's walls were enlivened by fragrant flowering plants and a vined trellis. She knelt, absently petting the cat as she read the words engraved in stone above the courtyard's arched entry.

To Buckden 14 Miles, Huntingdon 12, London 74.

Still such a long way to go, she thought with a sigh.

Spotting a well in the corner, she approached it from the east on the southern side, lest she risk bad luck. At least, she *hoped* she'd come from the east. In silence she drank three handfuls of water and closed her eyes to make a wish.

Please let me find Adam. And...

She squeezed her eyes shut tighter.

. . . let Jason kiss me again.

Her eyes flew open. What an utterly improper wish! Never had she thought she'd ache for a man's kiss. She hadn't believed she had it in her.

Lifting the hem of the red gown, she raised the chemise to her teeth to rip off a narrow strip and turned to find Jason's gaze on her from just inside the open stable doors. Heat flooded her cheeks, but that didn't stop her from tying the scrap to the branch of a nearby tree.

The ritual complete, she seated herself on the lip of the well facing Jason. He kept glancing in her direction, a puzzled look in his eyes. A blackbird watched her from the tree, cocking its head as though it were puzzled as well. The cat meandered over and leapt onto her lap.

When Jason finally joined her, the look on his face told her he thought her more than a wee bit daft.

Not that *that* was anything new.

"Whatever were you doing?" he asked.

She stroked the cat, feeling it purr beneath her hand. "This is a clootie well, isn't it?"

"It's a Roman well, I believe." He placed his portmanteau and the backgammon set, which he'd carried in the burlap bag, atop the well's ledge. Leaning over, he looked inside. "What the hell is a clootie well?" he asked twice as his voice echoed back up.

"It's a well where you make a wish."

"Oh, a wishing well. But then you tear your clothes? What was *that* about? Or is it only that you hate the dress?"

"When you make a wish at a clootie well, your troubles are transferred to the cloth. Then you tie it to a tree and leave the troubles there."

"You believe this?" he asked, clearly incredulous.

"Of course I don't. But it doesn't hurt to do it anyway. It's a tradition."

"Ruining your clothes is a Scottish tradition?"

She laughed and shook her head. "Normally you'd tear a handkerchief or a rag. Ruining these clothes was an extra bonus."

A brief, amused smile curved his lips—until he tensed and shot a quick look over his shoulder.

"Do you see something?" she asked.

"No. I don't think so. But for a moment I thought I did." He blinked and cocked his head like the blackbird. "So...what did you wish?"

If only he knew! She blushed to think of it. "My wish won't come true if I tell," she said, then held up a hand. "Nay, I don't really believe that, either. But I'll hold to it all the same."

"Hush a moment." He turned in a slow circle, his gaze sweeping the grounds. "I have a strange feeling," he said low.

She set down the cat and watched it scamper away. "What do you mean?"

"I'm not sure." He grabbed the bags. "Let's go inside."

She'd given up hoping for her own room, but she was pleased to see two beds when Jason opened the door to their chamber. Kisses were one thing; sharing a bed, quite another.

She unpacked their wet clothes and smoothed them on the bare wooden floor, hoping they would dry by morning. Her task complete, she turned to him. "Let me guess. You're hungry."

"Actually, I'm not. I know you're shocked," he teased, "but don't faint on me, now." To her complete surprise, he followed up with a lunge to catch her in the imaginary faint.

She giggled, feeling overly warm where his hands gripped her upper arms. If he could loosen up and become more playful, so could she. "Emerald MacCallum would never faint."

"No, she wouldn't," he agreed slowly. His hands dropped from her arms, and he backed away, watching her.

"It was a jest," she said. When he didn't respond, her voice dropped to a whisper. "I'm not Emerald, but I cannot find the words to convince you."

He said nothing, only ran a hand back through his hair. Her own hands moved to play with her laces but met the embroidered stomacher instead. Feeling a tightness in her chest that had nothing to do with its stiffness, she tucked his handkerchief more securely into her neckline.

"I'm going for a walk," he said abruptly.

"All right," she said with no small measure of relief. The time alone would be welcome. Time to think about how she was changing. How *they* were changing, together.

He turned toward the door, hesitated, and turned back. "I think you must come along."

She groaned. "We've only just arrived. I'd rather stay here and have a wee rest."

Taking her by the hand, he pulled her toward the door. "I don't want to leave you alone."

She tugged her hand from his. "I'm not looking to escape you."

"I'm not concerned you'll escape. I trust you." He paused as though he couldn't believe those words had passed his lips. "But something has me uneasy. We both go, or we both stay here."

The four walls of the small room seemed to be closing in on her. With him in his present mood, the thought of spending all evening in here was daunting. With a sigh, she followed him.

A coach was departing as they went downstairs, its squeaky springs audible through the lobby's open front door. As they approached the innkeeper's desk for Jason to leave the key, another coach pulled up. Neither of them were Cait's coach, though. In truth, she'd given up looking. She knew it had to be days behind them by now.

"Busy place," Jason remarked to the clerk.

"A mail-posting station." The pale man shrugged. "The postmaster makes no wage—he paid forty pounds to obtain the position. Keeps the inn full." He nodded toward the door, where three more guests were straggling in.

In order to avoid all the activity in the front, they went out the back way and into the courtyard again. Once more Caithren's gaze was drawn to the engraved archway. LONDON 74.

"How many more days?" she asked.

Jason's gaze followed hers. "Two, I'm hoping." Propping one booted foot on a bench, he glanced around distractedly.

"You're worried the Gothards'll get there before you?"

"Pardon?" He looked back to her. "No, not really. I sent Scarborough a letter. Even should he not have received it, I think we'll have ample time to warn him. The brothers might beat us there by half a day, but I doubt they'll ride straight to his home and shoot him." He plucked a large leaf off the climbing vine overhead. "They'll want to plan first."

"It sounds like you're more concerned about saving Scarborough than finding the brothers."

"Scarborough's life is at immediate risk." As though he were uncomfortable, he rolled his shoulders, then winced and put a hand to where she knew the wound was hidden beneath his clothes. "The rest can wait. But not too long...the Gothards have gone too far already. God alone knows what they'll plan next."

Cait nodded. "I'm thinking we should rise early tomorrow and try harder to outpace them."

"I won't complain about leaving this place at first dawn." His fingers worried the leaf as he scanned the courtyard. "There's something eerie here."

She grinned, trying to lighten his mood. "Are you sensing a ghost, Jase?"

With a thud, he brought his foot down from the bench. "How many times must I tell you—"

"—there's no such thing as ghosts," she finished for him and laughed. "Is this where you wanted to walk?"

He tossed the shredded leaf to the gravel. "We'll walk around to the High Street."

They strolled out of the courtyard and around the corner. As they crossed the street, Cait glanced back at the Bell. It was a long range of stone-built bays and gables, with two massive chimney stacks and an impressive coach entrance. An ornate wrought-iron bracket supported a heavy copper-plate sign, painted with a large red bell.

There was nothing sinister about the place. But her hand went to her amulet, just in case.

Another mail coach pulled away as they started down the bustling road. There were fourteen public houses and inns along the High Street, and sounds of laughter and frivolity drifted out as they walked past. Beyond the candlelit windows, Caithren could see people eating, conversing, conducting business. Living their lives. Unlike her, none of them seemed to be questioning the very foundations of their plans.

This night she hardly recognized herself and her feelings.

Jason's boots slapped the packed dirt road; her own shoes made a softer, shuffling sound. Had he really kissed the back of her neck? She couldn't be sure. It had all happened so quickly.

Past the Talbot, the street became residential and quiet, two neat rows of stone cottages with carefully tended gardens. Beyond that, nothing but the dusty Great North Road, stretching all the way to Scotland.

Caithren was so far from home. Her hand slipped into her pocket, feeling for Adam's portrait. She wondered what Cameron was doing right now. Dusk was falling, casting shadows along the street; Cam was probably having supper. He'd want to find his bed soon, to get an early start and take advantage of the long summer day. There would be a lot to do, with her not home to help him.

"What are you thinking?" Jason asked.

"Of home." The black cat from the inn came strolling up beside her. She reached down and picked it up.

"You sound melancholy." His tone was apologetic. "We'll be in London soon. Once I've...done away with Gothard"—he shrugged uncomfortably—"I'll give you the reward. For all your assistance. I don't need it." He stopped walking and turned to her. "That's why you're doing this, isn't it? For the money? I assume glory isn't nearly as important?"

When her fingers tightened in the cat's fur, it squealed and jumped from her arms. "How much did you say the reward is?"

"It said on the broadsides." He shot her a sharp glance. "A hundred pounds."

"And you're not needing that kind of money?"

He shook his head.

"Very prosperous mill you have there, Jase."

Mill? Jason thought. What did his mill have to do with this? For the life of him, he couldn't think of a response.

They'd reached the end of the village now, and he led her across the road. In silence, they headed back toward the Bell. Another coach creaked by, this time from the north. The sun was setting, and he saw her shiver at a sudden chill in the air. Their footsteps sounded loud in this sparse end of the village. She crossed her arms, uncrossed them, reached up to twirl a plait.

The faint sound of plodding hoofbeats followed the coach. Two horses. Feeling the hair prickle on his neck, Jason turned and walked backward to have a look. Two men. Too distant to see their faces, but they were hatless, and damn if one of them didn't have a square head.

Although somehow he'd known all afternoon, he gaped in disbelief.

A cold knot formed in his stomach. His thoughts only of Emerald, he swiveled and grabbed her arm, dragging her between two houses.

"What are you doing?"

"Hush," he whispered. "We're being followed." His hands went to her shoulders, and he backed her against the side of the nearer house. "Hold still."

As they waited, he felt her pulse speed beneath his fingers. One of his hands went to the hilt of his rapier, the other itched to reach for the pistol he'd hidden in his wide-topped boot.

But if he confronted Geoffrey Gothard here and now, what would become of Emerald? Torn in two directions, his thoughts raced incoherently. What would his father do? Protect the woman or stand up to the brothers like a man?

The hoofbeats came closer.

Panic.

Releasing his grip on the sword, he angled her away from the street, tilted her face up, and crushed his mouth to hers.

THIRTY-NINE

STARTLED, Caithren pushed weakly against Jason's chest with both hands.

"Kiss me, will you?" His lips brushed hers as he spoke. "They mustn't see our faces."

"Who?" she asked, but the question was smothered against his mouth, and her thoughts whirled and skidded when he gathered her into his arms. Maybe to shield them from view, but the truth was, she couldn't have cared less.

Improper or not, she was getting her wish, and she meant to make the most of it.

Her arms came up; her fingers wound themselves in his silky, blunt-cut hair. His mouth caressed hers, clever and persuasive. Heat sprinted along her veins. This kiss wasn't like that bampot Duncan's, or like anyone else's at Leslie. As the laird's daughter, all the kisses she'd received had been chaste and respectful.

Jason's was anything but.

A little moan rose from her throat, and he coaxed her lips apart with his own. Her bones seemed to melt when his tongue invaded her mouth, soft and warm and more exciting than she ever could have imagined. She'd never tasted a man before, and this one tasted divine.

Just when she thought she could never get enough, he stilled. "I think they're gone," he whispered against her mouth.

She pressed closer, wanting more. "Are you sure?"

"Mmm." Another light kiss sent her heart to racing. "Pretty sure."

He pulled back, and she slumped against the wall.

He stepped out into the street for a moment. "They're gone," he said as he returned.

"Who?" Her voice came out thin and reedy.

He drew a deep breath. "The Gothards."

"The Gothards?" She struggled to pull herself together. "Why didn't you just shoot them?"

"I...it...didn't feel like the right time." He looked into the street, down at his feet, everywhere but her eyes.

She gave a violent shake to her head, and it cleared with a rush of shock and outrage. "I heard no footsteps following us! You only...you used that as an excuse to ravish me!"

"Ravish you?" He appeared to choke back laughter. "I think not. When I've ravished you, sweetheart, you'll know it." His hand went up to stroke his missing mustache, then fisted and dropped to his side. "Besides, I didn't hear you take exception. You kissed me back. I'm not the one who put your arms around my neck."

"You claimed we were being followed! I wanted to make it look good."

"Hmm, is that so?" He didn't look convinced.

He didn't look at all spooked anymore, either.

"You set this whole thing up," she accused him. "From the outset this eve, you've been telling me something was wrong. All so you could kiss me."

Now he did laugh. "That hard up I'm not. I needn't make up stories to get women to kiss me. For example..."

He pulled her away from the wall, bent her backward, and ravished—there was no other word for it—*ravished* her mouth with his. Any protest died on her lips as tendrils of sensation stole along her nerves. His tongue traced the line where her lips met, and she opened her mouth, and he nibbled on her bottom lip. His spicy, warm scent flooded her senses.

When he set her away, carefully standing her straight, she just stood there, trying to catch her breath. No words came to her stunned mind.

He had plenty of words for them both, though. "So, you see, I've no reason to make excuses. If I'd wanted to have you, I've had ample opportunity. You wouldn't have stopped me, as our little demonstration just proved."

"Oh," she breathed, shaken and embarrassed. Her knees trembling, she walked to the edge of the houses and looked out into the street. Although dark was encroaching, the little village was still busy. People drifted in and out of taverns and rode the street on horseback. She didn't recognize anyone, but they were all far away and hard to see in the failing light.

She turned back, not quite sure if she believed him or not. While he was kissing her, a coach-and-eight could have thundered by and she wouldn't have heard it with the blood rushing in her ears. She glanced up at the hard line of his mouth. If she questioned his intentions again, he'd surely argue, and she didn't want to argue with him.

She wanted him to kiss her again.

Her legs felt wobbly, and her heart was still racing.

He looked down at her. "As you saw for yourself, they're definitely gone."

His voice was gentler—not that it had been terribly harsh in the first place. His innate calmness unnerved her. When a man was upset, he ought to show it.

He tucked a stray strand of hair behind her ear. "Don't be frightened."

She wasn't frightened; if she looked peaked, it was because she still hadn't recovered from his sensual assault. When she failed to respond, he took her hand. Even his fingers felt warm and exciting. Though she'd rather he held her hand because he wanted to, for him to hold it out of gallantry was almost as good.

"Come along," he said. "We'll get you some supper, and you'll feel better."

That prompted a smile. "Is food your solution for everything, then?"

"Pretty much." He grinned, then led her back to the street. As they walked along, she shifted her fingers so they laced with his. That felt even better.

In tacit silence they made their way back to the Bell, their footsteps echoing in the dark. Jason seemed to be on the alert, leaving Caithren to her own thoughts.

After supper, Jason would leave her in their room for a while to give her privacy while she changed into Mrs. Twentyman's nightgown. He'd return, remove his surcoat, loosen his clothes. She'd unplait and comb her hair, then reweave it into a single plait down her back. They'd climb into their separate beds. So it had gone almost every night.

But tonight felt different. Just thinking about sharing Jason's room tonight made her knees feel weak. Remembering the touch of his lips, feeling his hand in hers, her whole body seemed afire.

She wanted him to kiss her again.

"Let's go into the stables," he said, interrupting her thoughts.

"Why?" As they turned off the High Street alongside the inn, her mind raced with possibilities—mostly ones that made her blush. Some stables had nice lofts. "Are you worried for Chiron?"

"No. I want to make sure the Gothards aren't staying here."

"Oh." When disappointment flitted through her, she told herself she was being ridiculous. Of course his mind wasn't on kissing her —he'd convinced himself they were being followed.

He drew her into the Bell's stables and quickly paced the length, looking into every stall.

Pulled along by the hand, Caithren hurried to keep up. "Do you reckon the brothers are so poor they'll be sleeping in stables?"

"Not exactly." Reaching the end, he visibly relaxed and dropped her hand, leaning to take a fistful of carrots from an open wooden box. "I was looking for their horses. They're not here, though, so I assume they're staying somewhere else."

Cait followed him to where his own horse was stabled. Chiron munched contentedly while Jason resettled the thin night blanket over his back. She moved closer and smoothed a corner of the cloth. "You would recognize their horses?"

He gazed down at her, his eyes dark and unfathomable. Her heart skittering, she tilted her face up, hoping for a kiss.

He blinked. "I believe so," he said and turned to leave the stall.

With a warm hand at the small of her back, he drew her outdoors. Their footsteps crunched on the gravel in the courtyard. When his fingers meshed with hers, she inhaled sharply at the contact.

Something drew her to this man, though she couldn't figure why. She didn't want to ever marry, to share Leslie with anyone but

Cameron. But the feelings Jason kindled in her were fascinating. She'd never thought much of the marriage bed or what she would miss, but surely she couldn't want that with him. Just another kiss. He wasn't immune to her charms—she was sure of it. There must be a way she could coax a kiss.

One more kiss.

As they headed to the taproom for supper, she came up with a plan. Now she just had to find the nerve to carry it out.

FORTY

"**N**AY, PLEASE don't leave."

The door to their room halfway open, Jason turned to look at Emerald. She'd finished unplaiting her hair and was slowly dragging her fingers through the crimped, dark golden mass.

"Pardon?" he said.

"Will you remove this stomacher for me?" She licked her lips, her hands moving to fumble with the tabs. "I've got it knotted. I'm not very good at it."

For a moment he could only stare. "You removed it yourself in Newark-on-Trent."

"It was a struggle." She sighed prettily, her eyes a soft blue. "You should have been there."

He raised a brow. "Amusing, was it?"

"Nay. I mean you *literally* should have been there." She came closer, reaching past him to shut the door. "Please?" With a coquettish flourish, she whisked his handkerchief out of her neckline and tossed it onto the nearest bed. "You said you had a lot of experience taking these off," she said huskily, leaning into him.

What was going on here? What had got into her? Where was her usual willful independence?

Flowers of Scotland were muddling his brain.

"Very well," he said, since she wasn't giving him much of a choice. "I'll help just this once." Easing her back into the room, he began detaching the tabs. "This really is quite simple, though. Watch."

She looked down, her warm breath fanning over his fingers. "I'm watching," she all but purred, sounding nothing like the Emerald he'd come to know. "Oooh, Jason, you really are quite good at this."

She shot him a provocative glance, as though...she couldn't be trying to *seduce* him, could she? Emerald? Blushing, straightforward *Emerald?* What a contradiction she was!

With a nervous laugh, he set the stomacher on the bed. "There."

"Thank you," she whispered, leaning close again. She raised her face, all but begging for a kiss, just like she had in the stables.

But he couldn't kiss her, not in the stables and not now. Though he'd honestly begun kissing her to hide her from the Gothards, the kiss hadn't ended that way. Bloody hell, the reality of kissing Emerald had proved ten times better than the damned dream. Kissing her again would surely lead where neither of them should go.

But as he made to turn away, her eyes seemed to spark with something akin to desperation. Her fingers went to the gown's laces, loosening them, spreading the bodice wide, wider—wide enough that he could see the rosy tips of her breasts beneath the sheer chemise under the dress.

He watched, stupefied. This was *so* unlike her. "What the devil are you about?"

"I'm g-getting comfortable for bed," she stammered. "Like you keep telling me to." Her breasts rose and fell when she took a huge breath. "Mrs. Twentyman's nightgown, well, it's really too big and cumbersome."

He struggled to keep his face impassive. When she swayed closer, he stepped back.

Her eyes going hard with determination, she pulled out the lacing completely, tossed it on the bed, and began wiggling the dress down her body. The candlelit room was rather dim, but not so dim he couldn't tell she wore nothing beneath the thin chemise.

He swallowed hard. "Um...Emerald? Just how, um...*comfortable* are you planning to get?"

The gown dropped to the floor, puddling around her feet. She bit her lip and stepped shakily from the folds. "This ought to do it," she said in a soft, trembling voice.

It did it, all right. His gaze raked her all the way down to the torn hem of the chemise. He wondered if she knew her entire form was silhouetted beneath the off-white cambric. Her nipples were hard points against the front of the filmy garment. And it wasn't cold.

Feeling overly warm himself, he removed his coat and loosened the laces on his shirt.

She walked up to him. *Right* up to him. Her scent surrounded her like a cloud. A soft, dizzying cloud. Flowers of Scotland again.

Her hands came up to rest lightly on his shoulders. He stood, speechless, while she went on tiptoe and pressed her lips to his.

Warm lips. His body responded immediately, and her lips parted, inviting him to explore the sweet cave of her mouth. Ignoring a painful wrench in his shoulder, his arms went around her to press her close, and then closer—close enough to feel the hard rectangle of her emerald between them. Her almost-bare back felt small and vulnerable against his hands.

Vulnerable? Emerald MacCallum, vulnerable?

He pulled away. Of course she was vulnerable, or he wouldn't be bound on protecting her. He would have gone after Geoffrey Gothard tonight, instead of worrying for her safety and deciding to wait until she was settled somewhere safe—very safe.

But she was still Emerald MacCallum. A woman with whom he had no interest in becoming entangled. No interest whatsoever, at least in his mind.

He wished he could convince his body of that.

She was gazing at him, her eyes now darkened to a deep, hazy blue. Her tongue came out to moisten her lips, leaving a delicious sheen that he ached to kiss away. Deliberately he lifted her hands from his shoulders and moved to get into his bed.

She followed him, sat herself on the edge of the mattress, and leaned close, silently begging him to kiss her again.

Damn if some part of him didn't want to. The nonthinking part.

He forced a laugh instead. "Your bed is over there, Emerald."

She straightened, and one hand went up to draw her thick hair over her shoulder. Twirling it slowly, she looked nervous and innocent. It must be his imagination—either that, or she was quite the actress. There wasn't a chance she could actually be innocent. Not a mother. Not an independent, free-thinking woman like Emerald MacCallum.

"Are you sure?" she asked.

Forcing another laugh, he looked pointedly toward the second bed.

Her lower lip trembled. "I know there are two beds in this room, Jase. You don't have to laugh at me." Averting her gaze, she rose and walked slowly to the other bed, lowering herself to it as though she might break. "So my efforts to allure you are humorous, are they?"

He would swear he'd heard tears in her voice, making him feel like a sorry excuse for a man. "It's not that. It's—" he started, then stopped.

He didn't know what to say, couldn't find the words to explain. He didn't want to hurt her, but he couldn't have her thinking he wanted her—no matter that he did.

He couldn't act on his dishonorable urges, couldn't take her for all the wrong reasons. No responsible man would.

"Go to sleep, Emerald," he said through clenched teeth.

FORTY-ONE

CAITHREN SET down the candle and shook Jason's shoulder. "Wake up."

"What?" He struggled up, then fell back to the pillows. "It's the middle of the night," he complained, blinking in the near-darkness. "The birds haven't even started their chorus yet." He rubbed his eyes, then focused on her. "You're already dressed?"

"You said you wanted to leave at first dawn." She turned away and reached for her shoes, mostly so she wouldn't have to look at him. After what had happened last night, she couldn't bear to see the rejection in his eyes.

She could hardly live with herself, let alone what Jason must think of her. She'd made such a fool of herself—he must think she was a wanton. In her quest for a kiss, she'd all but begged him to bed her—and the worst of it was that, in the heat of that moment, she might actually have gone through with it had he given her the opportunity.

Cameron's teasing had proved right on the mark. Impulsive, that's what she was. She had to learn some self-control.

She wanted to be outdoors, in front of Jason on his horse, where he wouldn't be able to see her face and she wouldn't be able to see his. She wished more than ever that he'd obtained a second horse, because she suspected sitting so close to him would be almost as much torment as looking at him.

He was falling back asleep.

She shook him again. "You said this town made you uneasy." Thank God she had a viable excuse to wake him and leave while it was still dark. "Do you wish to overtake the Gothard brothers, or nay? We haven't any time to waste."

"All right. Give me a minute." With a groan, he rose from the bed and changed his shirt, tightened its laces and those of his breeches. Her eyes averted, she parted her hair and hurried it into two plaits, tying the ends with the green ribbon he'd bought her at the fair. Thankful that her own clothes were dry, she folded the red dress and chemise and packed them away.

"Hurry up," she said.

"What's going on here?" he muttered, tugging on his second boot.

He was going to keep at her unless she managed to put this behind her. She gathered herself together. "About last evening," she said to the floor, "do you reckon we can just forget it happened?"

"Nothing happened." He shoved yesterday's shirt into his portmanteau.

She pulled it back out to fold it. "Jase—"

"I've forgotten it already. I lack the sleep to think straight, in any case. It's a wonder I remember my name, let alone events from yesterday." Taking the shirt from her hands, he stuck it into the portmanteau and opened the door. She followed him out and downstairs.

On the way from the inn he peeked wistfully into the dining room, but it was unattended and pitch-black. "The minute the sun comes up, we're stopping for food."

"Far be it for me to deny your stomach."

He handed her the room key, dug in his pouch for some coins, and slapped them into her hand. "Leave these on the counter, will you? I'll ready Chiron. No sense ruining the stable lad's sleep, too."

With a theatric sigh, he headed for the stables.

FORTY-TWO

HE **BIRDS WERE** singing by the time they reached Sawtry. A small, sleepy town, its few public buildings bordered one side of the village green, the other three sides lined with thatched-roof houses. There was naught but one tavern, a rectangular stone building called Greystones.

Jason chuckled when he saw the sign.

"Whatever do you find so amusing?" Cait asked.

"My brother—um, he…lives in a place called Greystone."

"So?"

"It just struck me as funny, is all." He swung himself down to the street. "We'll stop here for breakfast."

"Why don't we eat it on the road?" she suggested, looking at the square, at the sky, at anything but him. "I'll wait here with Chiron while you go inside and get something."

"The Gothard brothers were in Stilton, which means they're not making better time than we are. I'm certain they're fast asleep. We have time to stop and eat."

"I'd rather not, if you wouldn't mind." She didn't want to face him across a table. "I'll stretch my legs while you fetch the food."

Without agreeing, he helped her dismount. She took his horse by the reins. "I'll just walk Chiron over there"—she indicated the village green and a post with a sign in its center—"and wait for you."

"I'd rather you come inside. After yesterday—"

"You said the brothers will still be sleeping. How unsafe could it be? You can watch me from the window."

He fixed her with a penetrating gaze that made her quickly look elsewhere. "Very well," he said at last. "But stay in sight."

The grass was soft and springy, and it felt good to walk after more than an hour in the saddle. She was delighted to discover that she wasn't really sore anymore. After four days on horseback, her body was finally adjusting.

She tethered Chiron to the signpost, which was topped by a fancy wrought-iron affair with letters spelling not only SAWTRY, but also SALTREIAM, the village's name from Roman times.

Doffing her shoes and stockings, she wiggled her toes in the grass and wondered what Jason was thinking of her after last night. He was acting normal. Probably because he didn't want her, so her behavior hadn't mattered to him.

A depressing thought.

In an effort to cheer herself, she rolled her shoulders, reached for the sky, then bent to touch her feet, coming face to face with a fresh, white daisy. She plucked it from the grass and brought it to her nose, smiling at the sweet, familiar scent. Sprinkled liberally throughout the green, the flowers reminded her of a childhood pastime, and she picked a handful, tucking up her skirt to collect them.

Jason found her sitting cross-legged and working industriously. "Is that what I think it is?" he asked, amusement lacing his voice. "A daisy chain?"

She slit the last stem and slipped the first daisy through it, completing the circle. Then she looked up into his smiling eyes, finding it easier than she'd expected.

"For you," she said, rising. "A peace offering." Standing on tiptoe, she crowned him with it. "A daisy chain is supposed to protect you from the fairies."

Instead of teasing her about another superstition, he turned pink beneath his tan, revealing freckles she hadn't noticed before. "We've found peace between us already," he said. "Have we not?" With a sheepish smile, he removed the daisy chain and put it on her own, smaller head.

It slipped right down and around her neck. He leaned closer, settling it into a gentle curve atop the swell of her bodice, his fingers lingering there longer than was necessary.

A frisson of confusion ran through her. She licked her lips and looked down, then reached to grasp the amulet that lay framed within the flowers. Something solid and familiar to cling to in the midst of all this foreignness.

When she glanced up, he was contemplating her bare feet. He bent to pluck another daisy and tucked it into the plait behind one ear. Stepping back, he grinned.

"You look very Scottish," he said.

"Do I, now?" She met his gaze, surprised to find she was able to do so and smile. "Well, *you* look very English."

"Hmm..." he said in a thoughtful tone. "Both of us managed to say that without sounding insulting." He turned to untie Chiron. "Imagine that."

"Imagine that," she echoed.

Imagine that, indeed.

FORTY-THREE

WHITE AND yellow wildflowers dotted the gently rolling land on either side of the narrow lane leaving Sawtry. As they rode, Jason could see Emerald lazily fingering the daisy chain around her neck, silent as the peaceful landscape. But for once it wasn't an adversarial silence, merely the silence born of exhaustion, the comfortable silence that comes to pass when two people coexist without the need to fill it with senseless chatter.

Indeed, the only sounds were those of Chiron's hooves on the rutted road and the occasional travelers who passed. Until there came a wild yell, and three young bareback riders came racing down the road right at them, all but forcing Chiron into the stream that ran alongside.

"Gypsy lads!" Emerald came alive. "They pass through Leslie every year, and oh, they play the most lovely music." She cocked her head. "Can you hear a lute?"

"Easy, boy." Jason reined in. "I can hear nothing except—damn, here they come again."

From the other direction, they thundered past.

"Follow them," she urged. "They must be encamped nearby."

Sure enough, over the next hill came the delicate notes of the lute she'd heard. The lively tune grew more distinct as they turned off the road and followed the trail of clumps kicked up by the racing horses.

The Gypsy boys halted and slid from their mounts beside a makeshift community of people milling among tents, carts, and pack animals. Smoke rose into the air above the encampment. The lads bent over in laughter, pointing at Jason and Emerald.

An old woman motioned them closer, flashing a gap-toothed grin.

Emerald turned and tilted her head back, one hand on her hat to secure it. "Have we time to stop? Just for a minute?"

He'd never seen her so excited—he couldn't deny her dancing turquoise eyes. "Ten minutes."

Emerald was already waving to the short, round-faced woman. "Hallo!" she called as they pulled close.

"Hallo, me lady," the Gypsy woman returned. She wore a long, many-layered skirt in a myriad of bright colors and a head scarf of another color altogether. Thick gold loops hung from her ears. "Will you buy?"

"I could have told you that's what she wanted," Jason muttered.

"Wheesht!" Emerald admonished. She slid from Chiron. "I haven't any money."

The woman patted Chiron's flank. "A beauty." She pulled an apple from her pocket and held it out for the horse to munch. "How much?"

Jason dismounted and held the reins possessively. "He's not for sale."

"Pity." She sighed. "Trade?" With an expansive gesture, she offered several horses grazing nearby. "Two for one?"

Jason laughed. "No trade, either."

"Pity." Giving a dismissive wave, the woman turned and walked into the tent village.

Emerald shrugged. "Come, let's find the music. They don't usually mind visitors."

He lifted Chiron's reins. "Is it safe to leave him here?"

"They won't be stealing him, if that's what you mean."

It felt deucedly strange to be asking Emerald for advice, but the truth was, he felt completely out of his element. As a young man in exile he'd lived all over the Continent, but he'd never felt as much at odds with his environment as he did in this little pocket of foreignness here in his native land.

He tethered the horse, then followed her into the encampment.

They wove between tents made from fresh-cut hazel pushed into the ground and bent over, which formed a resilient frame the Gypsies covered with colorful blankets. Delicious smells came from a huge iron kettle suspended over a stick fire. Women sat on stools around it, weaving lace and chattering in the Romani language, guarded by soft-eyed lurcher dogs.

As they walked by, a woman rose to stir the soup. When she set down the wooden spoon, a dog came up to lick it. "Bah!" she said, throwing the spoon into the fire.

At Jason's sound of surprise, Emerald turned to face him, walking backward. "It's *mockadi*," she explained. His face must have registered his confusion, because her laugh rang out over the lute's music. "Dogs and cats are unclean," she clarified.

"Cats make my sister sneeze," he told her, feeling bemused.

"You really are a *gaujo*, aye?" She cocked her head at him and laughed again. "A house-dweller."

"The woman fed Chiron by hand," he said. "Horses are not mock"—he frowned as he searched unsuccessfully for the word—"unclean?"

"Nay. Horses are revered. And they're not *mockadi* because—" She stopped walking backward, and when he almost ran into her, she put a hand to his chest and raised on tiptoe to whisper in his ear. "They cannot lick their own backsides."

He laughed so loudly they attracted several stares. A tall, gaunt man with a wide mustache ducked out of a tent. He wore ordinary breeches and a shirt topped by a colorful vest. His black eyes fastened on the sword hanging at Jason's side. "Sharpen it, milord?"

"No, thank—" Jason started.

"Oh, for certain it should be razor sharp, *my lord*." The sparkle in Emerald's eyes revealed her amusement at the thought of him bearing such a title.

If only she knew.

"You must let him do it." Reaching for the hilt, she pulled the rapier from his belt. "Since you'll be wanting to"—she cleared her throat conspicuously—"take care of Gothard with it."

It was plain she still thought he was out to kill, but Jason didn't argue. He let her hand the sword to the fellow, though he had no intention of killing anyone with that blade ever again. One innocent man was more than enough life lost at his hands.

The man sat at a portable whetstone and began grinding. Over the sound of the wheel, the delicate notes of the lute were joined by other instruments: a guitar, a violin, drums, maybe something else. The music rose, becoming even livelier. After Jason retrieved his sword and handed the man a coin, Emerald took off in search of the musicians, leaving him to follow.

In a small clearing, dancers swirled, a wild mass of colors. Emerald turned to him, an avid look on her face. "Shall we dance?" She took both his hands, held them up between them, and pulled him toward the clearing.

He took several tentative steps, then stopped. "This isn't the minuet, nor even a country dance."

She giggled up at him. "Nay, it's not. Can you feel the music?" Indeed, it seemed to vibrate from the grass beneath their feet. "Cameron and I dance with them every year. Doesn't the music make you want to move like they do?"

They were whirling in circles, stomping their feet, clapping their hands, snapping their fingers. "No, it doesn't," he said honestly.

"Come, try it!" She tugged his hands harder, until he stumbled into the midst of the dancers. But his feet refused to move like theirs, no matter how hard he tried. After a few halting steps, he pulled his hands from hers and backed away with a small bow and a sheepish smile of apology.

And he watched. Watched her swirling and dipping, swaying to the music that quite clearly spoke to her soul. Others watched as well, their own feet slowing as they watched hers fly.

Her hat flew off, and he ducked into the fray to retrieve it, then hurried back out. Her plaits whipped around, shimmering in the summer sunshine. The daisy chain about her neck whirled in her breeze, swooping up and down and around with her.

Murmured conversations sprang up all around him. Though he didn't know a word of Romani, he did know admiration when he heard it. Emerald was a—*gaujo*, had she called the house-dwellers? —becoming one with their Gypsy music.

He shifted on his feet, his eyes riveted to her lithe body, a blur against the backdrop of colorful clothing, tents, and trees. She'd come alive, an effervescence he'd been unaware of spilling out...and lodging somewhere in his heart.

Here was a small piece of England where she was more comfortable than he. What a difference it made. And, in contrast, how difficult it apparently was for her to operate in *his* world.

When the music ended and she stopped, the Gypsies burst into wild applause. Her cheeks reddened, she made her way over to him, stumbling and laughing at her dizziness. Another tune took up where the last one had left off, and she swayed to the beat.

"It's like a fair, isn't it?" she said breathlessly. "Except we're the only ones in attendance." She twirled in an exuberant circle, her arms wide, the daisy chain flying again. When she stopped, her eyes sparkled to rival the sunshine. "Imagine living like this every day."

He moved closer to resettle the ring of flowers around her neck. "It would be exhausting."

A frown flitted across her features. "There you go again, seeing the world in black and white."

"Right here I see it as most colorful." He tugged on one of her plaits, then set the hat back on her head. "And quite lovely."

She blushed prettily. Why had he never noticed before how very pretty Emerald was? The milkmaid had bloomed before his eyes.

"I've never seen anyone dance quite like that," he said, struggling for the words to describe it. To describe *her*. "So...free."

"The dancing brings the freedom, aye? While I'm dancing, I don't care."

"About what?"

"About anything."

Their eyes locked, and a moment of silence stretched between them. The Gypsy music pumped in the background. Slowly he nodded, and she smiled, then sighed. "I suppose we must get back on the road. It's been more than ten minutes."

"Wait, me lady." The old woman came out of nowhere and plucked Emerald on the sleeve. "You buy first."

"I told you I have no money," Emerald said firmly.

Jason laid a hand on her arm. "I have money."

The woman's lips curved up in her gap-toothed grin. She led them to an area between the tents, where carts were piled with goods. "Basket, me lady?"

"We cannot carry that," Emerald told her. "We're on horseback the next few days."

The woman frowned. "Livin' like you are, you got no need for a broom or a rake, then."

Emerald smiled. "Nay."

"Cooking utensils?" the woman asked hopefully. "Nails? Tools?"

Now Emerald laughed. "No nails or tools, either."

A foot tapped the grass beneath the woman's colorful skirt. "Me lady like silver?" Her gaze fastened on Emerald's amulet. "Or gold?"

Emerald grasped the green pendant. "Nay."

Not for a moment did Jason believe her. "Show me what you have," he told the Gypsy.

The woman ducked into a tent and came out with a handful of black velvet. She pulled up a stool and sat, opening the fabric in her lap to reveal a heap of gold trinkets.

Leaning over, Jason stirred the pile with a fingertip. The jewelry gleamed in the sunshine. Every piece was embossed or engraved with elaborate designs, and some of them were set with gemstones besides. "They are lovely, madam."

"You buy one?"

He selected a flat engraved band embedded with tiny, bright green emeralds. Turning to Emerald, he took one of her hands and slipped it onto the fourth finger. It fit perfectly.

Her pretty mouth hung slack for a moment. Her eyes turned a cloudy blue, and a frown appeared between them. "I cannot take this."

"Of course you can. Keep it as a memory of this day."

"I'll remember without it."

"Then as a token of thanks. From me. I enjoyed watching you dance."

Her cheeks flamed hot. She twisted the band around her finger. Another Gypsy tune was playing in the background, but she didn't move to the music. "I...I cannot take it," she said again.

"Go away, then," he said with a wave of his hand.

"Pardon?"

"Over there." He pointed to the next tent.

Looking bewildered, she solemnly backed away until he nodded.

"How much?" he whispered to the Gypsy woman. When she told him, he dug out his pouch and paid her, then beckoned Emerald back over.

"You're supposed to dicker," she informed him. She tugged off the ring and took one of his hands in hers, turning it palm up as she leaned close to whisper in his ear. "She thinks you're an easy mark," she added, depositing the ring in his hand and folding his fingers firmly around it. "Did you notice she didn't even show you anything made of silver?"

He shrugged and put the ring in his pouch. He would give it back to her later.

"Come, me lady." The Gypsy woman stood. "I tell your future."

"I think not," Emerald said—but somewhat wistfully, Jason thought.

The woman held up one of his coins, her gap-toothed smile appearing again. "No charge."

"Go ahead," Jason urged.

"Have we the time? The Gothards—"

"The Gothards ought to be rolling out of bed right about now," he said dryly.

He could tell Emerald was intrigued. As he was himself—he'd never seen a fortune-telling. It ought to be entertaining. And if the brothers were already on the road, it wouldn't be such a bad thing should they get ahead.

He felt more comfortable as the pursuer than he did as the pursued.

"Are you sure?" Emerald asked, and when he nodded, she added, "Come with me, then."

He grinned. "You couldn't keep me away if you tried."

The Gypsy woman motioned for them to follow her to the edge of the encampment, near where Chiron was grazing lazily. "Milord does not believe in dukkerin'?"

"My lord," Emerald said, nearly stumbling over the two words if his ears didn't deceive him, "is a confirmed skeptic."

He swept off his hat and ducked his head to enter the woman's tent. Inside he couldn't stand straight, but the Gypsy motioned him into a beautifully carved gilt chair. Two lamps set on a low table threw glimmering light into the small space, which, in contrast to the clutter outside, appeared immaculate.

Waterproofed canvas lined the ground, and a fringed cloth, patterned with costly metallic thread, covered the table. His hat in his lap, he leaned back and stretched his legs, content to watch the show.

The woman settled Emerald on a low stool, then sat herself on the other side of the table. Emerald swept off her hat and set it on the floor.

The Gypsy reached across, took Emerald's hands, and just held them for a minute, smiling into her eyes. Then she leaned close, her gaze darting from one palm to the other. "Ah…a long life you will see." Her voice sounded different than it had outside—low and soothing.

Emerald smiled, slightly swaying to the music that drifted in from the clearing.

"And children. Four children."

Emerald stilled and shook her head. "You cannot tell that from my hands."

"The hands tell all." The woman's tone brooked no argument. She measured Emerald's white fingers against her own brown ones. "Middling," she declared. "Life is balanced." Then, "You." She swung on Jason, pointing a craggy finger with a curved, lacquered nail. "Your fingers long. Very responsible. Too responsible. You plan too much."

"Hmm." Emerald looked toward him speculatively.

He fisted his fingers to hide them, crossing his arms. He hadn't come in here to be analyzed. He'd come in here to be entertained.

And he'd kiss a ghost before he'd believe such nonsense.

The fortune-teller hitched her stool forward and made a humming sound deep in her throat. Laying Emerald's hands palm up on the table, she traced the lines with a crooked finger. "One of a kind. You go your own way." She looked closer. "Fate line is broken. A great life change."

"Oh." Jason strained to hear Emerald's whisper over the lively beat of the music. "My father recently died."

"We all lose our folks." The fortune-teller shook her head. "Something more than that."

Outside, the musicians slid into something slower and faintly sensual, the violin rising above the other instruments in long, poignant notes. With a light touch, the Gypsy indicated a spot on Emerald's hand. "A grille, like bars." Her voice shifted too, matching the rich tempo. "The bars of a gaol, where your heart hides, locked away. You must open the bars and trust." She stole a glance at Jason.

Uneasy beneath her gaze, he leaned to part the tent's opening and look outside. A whir of life bustled past the narrow slit: a woman sauntered by with a basket of laundry; a man rolled a wagon wheel along; a child chased a dog in the bright sunshine.

It seemed darker inside when he allowed the tent to close.

"Ah." The woman nodded, her bobbing earrings gleaming in the lamplight. She touched another place on Emerald's palm. "A cross. A happy marriage in this lifetime." Pausing, she looked up. "Far from home."

Emerald blinked. "Aye, I'm far from home. I live in Scotland."

An enigmatic smile creased the fortune-teller's face. She turned Emerald's hands and lightly skimmed her nails over the backs, making Emerald visibly shiver. "Sensitive. Your body begs to be touched."

Jason swallowed hard as the woman turned Emerald's hands again. "Mount of the Moon, high and full. A lover bold, creative, beguiling."

Though Emerald turned red, Jason thought that the most accurate thing the woman had said yet. Bold—last night flashed into his mind—and beguiling.

Alarmingly so.

Black Gypsy eyes fastened on his and held steady while the music pulsed in the background. "A man in love with you," she said to Emerald while still commanding his gaze, "must respect your independence…if he wishes to hold your heart."

"I'm not—" Jason started.

"Shush!" The harsh word vibrated in contrast to the sensuous violin. The woman swung back to Emerald and pointed a finger at her chest. "That green talisman…" Emerald's hand went to her amulet, and the woman nodded. "When it changes hands, a change of heart."

Emerald's fingers clenched around it. "It will never change hands, not while I live."

The Gypsy shrugged, a movement so expressive it spoke volumes without words. The music stopped. A hush of silence enveloped the tent.

Emerald rose, breaking the spell. "I thank you."

"My pleasure, me lady."

"I think we should leave," she said to Jason. Her voice was very quiet. "It was time to go almost before we arrived."

Rising, he bumped his head on the low ceiling. The woman stood as well. "I come see your pretty horse." She followed them out and watched them mount.

"My hat!" Emerald clapped a hand to her head.

"I get it, me lady."

The Gypsy disappeared into her tent and returned with the feathered hat. Moving closer, she rose to her toes and set it on Emerald's bent head, then put a gnarled hand on her arm. "You not like your fortune?"

"It was very...interesting." Jason heard the catch in Emerald's voice. "I'm afraid, though, I found it a wee bit confusing."

"All will come clear in time," the woman predicted. "Wait here, me lady." She hurried off toward the fire, returning with one of the lace handkerchiefs the women were working on there.

"It's lovely," Emerald said sincerely. "But I told you I have no money."

"We've been paid." Black eyes sparkled up at Jason. "You keep, to remember."

Emerald tucked the intricate hanky into her sleeve. "I won't forget."

"You come back?"

"Not here, I'm afraid. But I will dance with your people again. At home."

The woman reached to grasp Emerald by the hand. "Farewell, me lady." With a nod at Jason, she ducked back into her tent.

Jason steered Chiron toward the road. He remained mute until they were out of earshot. "So...you've danced with the Gypsies before."

"Aye, many times."

"You've camped with them, then. During your travels." It made perfect sense.

"My travels?" Her laughter floated back on the breeze. "Until now, I've never been farther from Leslie than Edinburgh. Twice. I told you, Jase—a group of them camps by Leslie each year."

Damn if she wasn't convincing.

He almost believed her.

FORTY-FOUR

"*I* DON'T believe it," Caithren said later when they'd stopped at the Lion in Buckden for dinner.

Jason spooned soup into his mouth, following it with a gigantic bite of bread. "But you believe in ghosts."

"What do ghosts have to do with it?"

He rolled the dice and took two markers off the backgammon board they'd set on the table between them. "Why should you believe in ghosts but not fortune-telling?"

"Dukkering," she corrected crossly. "They say what you want to hear." She poked at her Dutch pudding, using her spoon to flake off bits of the minced beef. "Or rather, what they *think* you want to hear. But the Gypsy woman misjudged me."

His compelling eyes looked speculative over the rim of his tankard. "Did she, now?"

"Aye." Avoiding his gaze, she tossed the dice and made her move. "I don't intend to have children at all, let alone four."

He stuck the dice back in their cup and rattled it, his gaze straying to the window beside them. "Do you not like children?"

"I like them fine. It's the necessary husband I'd as soon do without."

He set down the dice cup, raising a brow. "So much for the happy marriage she predicted."

"Are you going to take your turn?"

Slowly he reached across the small table and traced a fingertip across the back of her hand. A shiver ran through her. "But are you not sensitive to physical touch?" he drawled in a voice low and lazy.

She was sensitive, all right. It took everything she had not to leap across the table and kiss him. Struggling for control, she forced herself to remember last night. "Why today should you want to touch me?"

"Perhaps I've had a change of heart." He chucked her under the chin. "Like you will when your precious amulet changes hands."

She took the dice cup and firmly wrapped his fingers back around it. "The amulet will not change hands. The Gypsy was wrong."

Even with the noises of conversations and dishes rattling around them, the dice sounded loud as Jason shook them and spilled them onto the leather board. Two more of his pieces made their way into his haphazard pile. "Someday—"

"Nay. I won't ever take it off." She bit her lip, then decided to come out with it. The terrible words she'd thought to herself but never said aloud. "My mother took it off only once. To wear a pretty necklace my father had just brought her from Edinburgh. She died that day. Broke her neck when she was thrown from her horse."

"You blame your father for her death," Jason said flatly.

"I don't." She shook her head. "I never have."

He was silent for a minute, watching her drop the dice back into the cup, slowly, one by one. "You blame her," he finally said.

"Nay." Maybe she'd thought it, but she didn't believe it. "Though I won't tempt fate by making the same mistake."

"It's naught but metal and stone," he said gently.

"It's more than metal and stone," she disagreed. "It's been in my family for centuries."

"Has it?" He dipped a piece of bread into his soup. "Is there a story behind it?"

"Of course. We Scots have a story for everything." As he glanced out the window again, she touched the amulet and rolled the dice, smiling when they came up double fives. She moved her last two markers into home court and stacked another two neatly by the board. "I was made to memorize it word for word before the necklace could be mine."

He grinned. "I enjoy your stories. Tell me."

She handed him the cup. "In 1330, Sir Simon Leslie set out to accompany James, Lord Douglas, who was charged with returning the heart of King Robert the Bruce to the Holy Land. On their way through Spain, they fought with the Moors, and Douglas was killed." She paused for a sip of ale. "Leslie went on to Palestine, and there he fought the Saracens and captured one of their chiefs. When the chief's mother came to beg for his release, she dropped an emerald from her purse and hurried to scoop it up. Leslie realized it was of great importance to her, and he demanded it as part of the deal for the release of her son."

She stopped, because Jason was staring out the window again. "Go on," he said, looking back to her.

"That is it, really." Gazing down at the amulet, she traced its scrolled setting with a finger. "He had it set in this bezel and brought it home, claiming it had miraculous powers for seeing him through the journey. It's been handed down through the generations. People once came from far and wide to obtain water it had been dipped in. They would put a bottle of this water by their door, or hang it overhead, for protection against the evil eye."

His bowl empty, he set down his spoon and rolled the dice. His last two pieces clicked as he dropped them onto his pile. "But not anymore?"

She shook her head. "The old ways and beliefs are dying."

"Yet you won't take it off."

"Maybe it's nothing more than unwarranted superstition." She wrapped her fingers around the emerald. "But there will be no change of hands."

Nor, she thought fiercely, would there be the change of heart the Gypsy had predicted.

His gaze had returned to the window yet again. "You won," she said, and he nodded without looking at her. Idly she started making his pile of markers into two tall stacks. "Are you seeing something?"

"Not exactly." He lifted his tankard of ale. "I'm just getting that feeling I had last night..."

One of the stacks toppled over. "You mean that strange feeling that gives you an excuse to kiss me?"

His tankard hit the table with a thud. "I mean the feeling that we might be followed."

Cait looked out the window at the red-brick walls of the George

Inn across Buckden's busy High Street. People rode or strolled by. Ordinary people. No one appeared suspicious or familiar. "I see nothing."

He shrugged.

"Here," she said, pushing the rest of her Dutch pudding toward him. "I'm not finding myself very hungry."

He dug into the remains of her dinner. "Still worried about your fortune and future?"

"Of course not. It was naught but a lark. I've forgotten it already."

In truth, she hadn't, not really. But she was more intrigued than anything, and not by the fortune-teller's meaningless predictions. More by the fact that the woman had assumed she and Jason were a couple.

For a moment she stared unblinking at the creamy plastered walls of the Lion's common room. Jason's attitude had changed in the encampment as well. When she'd told the story of her amulet, he hadn't interrupted her to insist the fellow was a MacCallum, not a Leslie.

Gypsy magic? Would it wear off? Or might he be feeling more kindly toward her?

"Ready?" He shot another glance out the window. "We should be going."

They quickly packed up the backgammon set and slipped it into its burlap bag. She followed him toward the back door to the courtyard and stables. Once there, she stopped him with a hand on his arm. "My hat." She touched her bare head. "I've forgotten it."

"There it is." He gestured to where it sat on the wide window ledge, right where she'd left it. "I'll get it," he volunteered, handing her the backgammon set.

She pushed through the door.

Someone lunged at her.

She saw a flash of silver and heard the shout of a stable boy before she screamed. Though the man jerked back, she felt a sharp sting on her upper arm.

The backgammon set fell with a *bang!* and markers rolled out of the bag, bumping across the cobblestones as she curled a hand into a fist and propelled it into the short man's face. He yowled and grabbed his jaw, dropping his sword. A metallic twang rang out as it clattered to the stones.

Wat Gothard.

"You murdering cur!" She planted her feet, aiming to follow up with a deadly knee.

"Dunderhead!" a man shouted, thundering into the courtyard on a horse. He scooped up Wat, wheeled around, and rode out the gateway and out of sight.

The stable boy rushed forward as Jason burst out the door, rapier at the ready.

"Go!" Caithren yelled, gesturing out the gateway. The stable boy took off running. She turned on Jason. "Go! It was the Gothards, and he'll never catch them on foot. Get Chiron and go!"

His eyes frantically searched her. "You're bleeding." He dropped the rapier and reached to make a ginger exploration.

"I'm fine!" Bending to sweep his sword off the ground, she shoved it into his hands. "Just go, will you?"

A torn look in his eyes, he backed away a few stumbling steps, then turned and raced for the stables. Moments later, he galloped bareback out of the courtyard.

Reeling with both relief and disbelief, Cait sank to the cobblestones. She gripped her upper arm. It didn't hurt too badly, considering.

The stable boy limped back into the courtyard, puffing from exertion. "They're gone," he said. "No one out front saw what happened, so they were able to flee unscathed." He knelt to collect all the backgammon pieces, then looked up at her, shoving blond hair from his face. "Are you quite all right, milady?"

She waved aside his concern. "My...friend"—how was she to describe Jason, anyway?—"went after them on a horse. Maybe he will catch them."

She hoped so. If they got away, he'd likely blame her once again.

At the sound of hooves on the cobblestones, her heart sank.

"They disappeared," Jason said. "Just disappeared." He slid off Chiron, and Cait scrambled to her feet as he came close. "Besides this"—one finger skimmed her upper arm, making her wince—"are you hurt?"

"Go back!" With her good arm, she gestured sharply. "You cannot have looked well enough. You cannot give up so soon."

"What I cannot do is leave you bleeding while I play hide-and-seek. I never did make a very good 'It.'" He tugged at the neckline of her bodice and swore when it wouldn't budge. His fingers went to loosen the laces. "What the hell happened?"

"Wat," she said. "He sliced me, but I think he was going for you. He pulled back when he saw who I was." Frantically she pushed at his hands. "Oh, will you not just leave? Go after them! I can tell you the story later!"

Stuffing the backgammon pieces into the bag, the stable boy glanced up. "She punched the bastard but good," he told Jason.

"You what?" Jason's gaze shot from her arm to her face. "You hit him?"

"You want I should stand there and let him kill me?"

Tossing the hair from his eyes, the boy stood straight and snorted in approval. "She was fixing to unman him as well, I believe."

Jason stared at her a moment, then reached for her laces again.

"Jason!" Her gaze flickered toward the stable boy.

Jason's green eyes flashed with impatience. "Come inside, then." He leaned to retrieve Wat's sword. The stable boy thrust the burlap sack into his hands and moved to take Chiron.

The innkeeper stood gaping in the doorway.

"If I may see to the lady's wound," Jason prompted him.

"Of course." He ushered them indoors, alternately gasping with horror and clucking with sympathy. "Buckden is a quiet town."

"I will require a room for the lady."

The lady? Since when did Jason refer to her so? And in such an authoritative tone?

The innkeeper showed them up a flight of wooden stairs to a small chamber. "Shall I bring water and towels?"

"Please do."

"As you wish, my lord." The man bowed and backed away.

My lord. Jason didn't seem wont to correct the mistaken form of address. He simply shut the door, turned, and met Cait's eyes.

Her head swam. From the pain, the shock, the intensity of Jason's gaze locked on her own? She couldn't tell. It all seemed muddled in her brain.

She stood silent and limp while his fingers went to unlace her bodice. He eased it off and dropped it to the bed. She shivered in only her shift, like last night—except this time, instead of turning away, he reached to loosen the neckline and draw it down to expose the cut on her arm.

His breath hissed in, then fanned warm over her bare shoulder. "Sliced you good, didn't he?"

Her heart racing, she held the shift to her chest and glanced down. "Not too bad, I'm hoping."

A knock came at the door, and Jason went to answer, returning with a bowl of warm water, towels, and bandages. As he set everything on the bedside table, the door closed with a quiet *snick,* and they were alone again.

With a doleful shake of his head, he sat her on the bed. She listened to the innkeeper's heavy footfalls retreating as Jason dipped a towel in the bowl of water and dabbed at the bloody wound.

"It's clean, but deep."

She hadn't known a man's hands could be so gentle. "I'll make a poultice for it when we stop tonight."

He dabbed some more, for all the world looking helpless. "Would it be better to do it now?"

"My herbs are outside, in the portmanteau." She swallowed hard. "I'll be fine."

Nodding, he wound a clean cloth around her upper arm. Used to blood she was, but not necessarily her own. She felt dizzy, from that or from Jason's proximity—she wasn't sure which.

He looked very businesslike as he tied the bandage. Apparently he didn't notice she was about to expire from wishing he would kiss her.

"Why didn't you go after the Gothards?" she asked.

"Geoffrey Gothard will get his due." His eyes bore into hers. "But I won't see you hurt in the interim. Never that. Never again."

His voice wasn't loud, but she detected a tremor beneath the control. She was finding it hard to breathe. His hand went to the neckline of her shift, and she released her hold on it, watching his long fingers draw it up to cover her shoulder.

Suddenly she saw that her nipples stood out dark against the shift's delicate fabric. Her breath hitched in shock. Grabbing her bodice from the bed, she stood and shoved her arms into it, sending a surge of fresh pain up her shoulder and down to her hand.

"Hush," Jason soothed, helping her ease into the garment. Trembling, she stared at his chest as he slowly threaded the laces and tied a crooked bow. When he was finished, his fingers trailed up her neck, leaving shivers in their wake, until his hands came to rest on her cheeks.

He cradled her face, tilted it up, drew her closer. He was going to kiss her again, Caithren realized with a heady rush of anticipation. For real, this time, with no excuse of being followed.

She released a shuddering breath. Her heart pounded so loudly she was certain he could hear it in the still, dim room.

He lowered his mouth to hers.

His lips were soft, gentle, tender, his hands caressing. Her heart fluttered in her chest, her blood sluiced through her veins, and she pressed closer, wanting to feel him. Her arms went around him, wanting more. Wanting, wanting…

Wanting.

With a sudden clarity she knew she wanted Jason more than she'd wanted anything in her life. His hands, his mouth…all of him. Just this once, to know what it was to give herself to a man. To *this* man.

Astounding herself with her daring, she parted her mouth, darting her tongue out to trace his bottom lip. His kiss turned wild and demanding, making her pulse race. When he eased her down to the bed, she felt no pain. She felt nothing but his welcome weight, his warmth, his strength—and a strange and marvelous exhilaration inside her.

As his mouth plundered hers, one hand inched around to the back of her neck to pull her closer and deepen the kiss. She sank into it, into him.

Another knock came at the door, and he bolted upright.

"Is the lady all right?" the innkeeper called. "Will you be needing aught else?"

As Cait sat up more slowly, Jason ran a ragged hand through his hair. He rose and went to open the door. "She's fine," he said. "We were just leaving."

When the man's footsteps faded once more, Jason turned to her. "We have to leave," he said, his voice husky and…apologetic? She couldn't be sure. "Are you all right to ride?"

The door was still open. She stood and took a steadying breath. "I'll survive."

Her arm throbbed, but she wouldn't have admitted to the pain were she like to faint from it. She wouldn't be a burden on his journey, and she had to get to London herself.

There would be time to tend to the injury later. When she wasn't reeling from his kiss. And its abrupt ending.

"Let me know if you start hurting, all right?" He looked shaken. "Emerald—" He broke off.

She wouldn't answer to that name. Not after what had just happened between them.

"I'm sorry," he said, looking like he meant it. "For...for letting things get out of hand." Somehow she was sure he'd intended to say something else, but he barreled on. "It was wrong of me to—"

"I've forgotten it. Like you forgot last night. We're even now." She pushed past him out the door. "And my name is Caithren, whether you believe it or not."

FORTY-FIVE

*H*E DID BELIEVE it. Now.

And he cursed himself for not believing it sooner.

She was shorter than Emerald MacCallum was rumored to be, not to mention completely unsuited for Emerald's profession. She didn't know north from south or right from left. She cried far too easily, and she had no business carrying a pistol. Why, she wouldn't hit an outlaw from arm's length.

None of that had convinced him.

Neither had her ongoing protests.

But seeing her reaction to the Gothard brothers had exploded his entire view of the woman he'd thought was Emerald.

Though she'd defended herself, she'd urged him to go after them. She hadn't even tried to do so herself. Bleeding or not, Emerald MacCallum would have been hot on their trail before Jason even stepped into the courtyard.

She was Caithren, as she'd said all along.

He didn't like that at times like this his father came to mind. A father who had never made mistakes. Certainly not a mistake on the order of this one.

He swore at himself for two solid miles.

If he hadn't already been certain he was ill-suited for this quest of justice, he had the proof riding in front of him. First he'd taken the life of an innocent man, then he'd endangered that of an innocent woman by mistakenly dragging her into this mess.

If only he could turn back time and leave Caithren on that public coach. He would—honestly, he would—even though that would mean he'd never have held her in his arms. An almost unthinkable thought.

His arms tightened around her waist at the mere notion.

Unfortunately, going back in time was naught but wishful thinking. The hard truth was, now that the Gothards had seen them together, protecting her was more important than ever. Their wild attraction only complicated matters.

He needed a clear head to see this through. Distance, both emotional and physical. He'd proven that to himself back at the Lion in Buckden. Only by thinking of her as Emerald had he been able to check his emotions.

And only by continuing to call her Emerald aloud could he ensure she kept her distance as well.

They rode through Southoe, a sleepy village with three moated manor houses and a single old brick inn. "Are you hungry?" Caithren asked as they passed it, jarring him out of his thoughts.

"Hardly." He pushed back his hat. "I've been thinking—"

"I cannot say I'm surprised. You seem to do that a lot. Did the Gypsy not say you plan too much?"

"Hush." He tugged on one of her plaits. "And listen to what I have to say. We've no need to rush anymore. We don't have to worry about the brothers reaching London before us."

"What makes you think that?"

"They've been following me. They tried today to kill me."

"Not a very competent attempt," she said doubtfully.

"Walter isn't known for his brains. Still, they obviously had a plan, with Walter doing the deed and Geoffrey then spiriting him away. Geoffrey wouldn't want another death on his hands, and Walter is a malleable sort."

"So…"

"So they won't be racing off to London the way they planned when they thought I was dead. It seems they've decided to do away with me first. Alive, I can bear witness to their deeds, and well they know it. They're desperate. If either of them ever had a decent bone in his body, it's disappeared now that they're backed into a corner."

She was silent as she took that in.

He drew a deep breath. "Another change in appearance would be prudent. And they'll recognize Chiron as well. I'll have to board him and buy another horse." Another thought occurred to him. "Two. They won't expect us to be riding two."

"I won't try to escape you," she said, reading his mind.

"I'm glad to hear that."

He would miss holding her before him, though. The feel of her warm body, the scent of her hair, the tantalizing nape of her neck. Without thought, he pulled her closer.

Then reminded himself he had to maintain distance.

"We'll stop in the next town and stay the night," he said. "You can rest and tend to your wound while I gather what we need."

"We?"

"You'll have to change your appearance as well. They've seen you with me now—they'll assume you could bear witness too." His voice dropped. "I'm sorry. It's for your own good."

"Whatever you say, Jase," she said softly. Her hands closed over his where he held the reins.

When she squeezed his fingers, his heart squeezed in reaction.

He felt a maddening concern and tenderness for this infuriating woman. But the gentle, nurturing emotions did nothing to calm the shakes that assaulted him at the thought of Gothard following them. Caithren had been hurt and might have been killed. And it would have been his fault for making her part of this.

He was caught in a trap of his own making, and he felt the jaws closing—teeth of steel that he'd sharpened himself.

FORTY-SIX

"*H*OW IS YOUR arm?" Jason asked the next morning as he tied back his hair. He swept something long and shaggy off a table and took it over to the mirror.

Caithren sat up in bed and flexed her arm, perusing the breakfast tray he'd just brought her. "Not too bad. I used up everything I collected in the woods, though. I hope to find more today." She watched him shake out the shaggy thing and hold it high in the air. "What *is* that?"

"A periwig," he said, settling it on his head. "What do you think?"

Popping a radish into her mouth, she stared at the reddish wig. Crimped and curly, it draped far down his chest, longer than his own hair had been before she cut it. She chewed and swallowed before answering him. "You look different," she said diplomatically.

He smiled as he dug through his portmanteau, scattering clothing all over the other bed as he worked his way to the bottom. A dark blue velvet suit with gold braid trim came out, then a fine lawn shirt with lace at the cuffs, and finally a snowy cravat.

None of it was at all similar to any of the other garments he'd worn. Had the clothes been there all along? Or had he brought them back last night? She'd fallen asleep hours before he returned.

"You don't like it, then." Turning back to the mirror, he adjusted the wig's crown and flipped a hank of curls over his shoulder.

Giggling, she hid her face in her cup of chocolate.

"Many men wear periwigs, you know."

"But not such long ones." She chewed slowly on a bite of bread, studying him in the mirror. "It looks like you're trying to pass as a nobleman."

He raised a brow at that.

"And—it's red!"

"You're hurting my feelings." Though he pouted, the eyes in the looking glass were a sparkling green. "Does it look so out of place, then? My sister is a redhead, and my mother was as well. Myself, I was a skinny, freckled lad—I expect red hair would have been more fitting than the black."

She reconsidered. "The red isn't too bad. But I cannot picture you skinny and freckled."

"It's no lie. I was awkward, too. Gangly." As he fussed with the wig, Cait watched the muscles move beneath his shirt. He wasn't gangly now. "Took me years to grow into my looks."

"Ah," she said with a teasing smile. "And here I thought it was the mustache that transformed you."

"That as well." He leaned closer to the mirror and stroked his bare upper lip. "But I think I'm getting used to its loss." Turning, he reached to steal a cube of cheese off her tray.

"I thought you had breakfast downstairs."

"That was an hour ago." He filched another cube and chewed thoughtfully. "Do you like me better with or without?"

"Without. Both the mustache and the wig." She set the tray aside. "Supposing I like you at all, that is."

"Supposing." Moving to the other bed, he lifted the velvet surcoat and shook out the creases. "Your new clothing is waiting behind the screen."

"Is it?" Curious, she climbed from the bed and made her way over to have a look.

She blinked and looked again.

"By all the saints," she breathed. "It's worse than the red dress."

Draped across a chair lay a bright turquoise brocade gown trimmed with a gaudy wide edging of embroidered silver ribbon. A purple underskirt and stomacher were tossed on top. Even without trying it on, she could tell the dress's scooped neckline would reveal a lot more skin than she was comfortable displaying.

After she'd made such a fuss over the red dress, she couldn't believe he'd brought her this. She stepped out into the room to give him a piece of her mind, then dashed back behind the screen.

"Crivvens! You're in the scud!"

"Translate?" he called.

"You...you're naked!"

"One does have to undress to change clothes." He sounded amused, not cross. "Are you donning the gown?"

Touching her hands to her cheeks in an effort to cool them, she dragged her mind from its vivid picture of a bare Jason. "You expect me to wear this?"

"Hell, yes. I spent a fortune for it."

"Just who am I supposed to be posing as in this monstrosity?" She grabbed the gown and held it up to her body, gazing down at herself in horror. "Queen Catharine?" She kicked at the hem.

"No." He laughed. "My mistress."

The gown slipped from her fingers. "Your *what*?"

"My mistress. Are you undressed?"

His mistress.

"Nay. Not yet." Self-conscious, she fluffed Mrs. Twentyman's nightgown. "Are you?"

"Not anymore. Come out and have a look."

Cautiously she stepped from behind the screen—and burst out laughing.

He glanced in the mirror critically, then back to her. "What's so funny?"

"You—as an aristocrat." Tears ran from the corners of her eyes. "Y-you expect people to f-fall for that disguise?"

A small smile quirked at his lips. "As a matter of fact, I do."

"Just because one innkeeper called you *my lord* yesterday—"

"And don't forget the Gypsy."

She laughed even harder. "O-oh, aye. The Gypsy called you milord as well!"

He took her by the shoulders and turned her toward the screen, giving her a little push in that direction. She yelped, looking back over her shoulder to giggle at him again.

He pulled on her single nighttime plait. "Go get changed," he said with mock sternness.

"Very well." She hiccuped and went behind the screen.

She was thankful the long puffed sleeves didn't rub her injured arm, but the gown hugged her upper body like a second skin. Small though they might be, her breasts welled over the top. The stomacher was stiff and uncomfortable.

No surprise there.

"Don't forget the shoes," Jason called.

The shoes. Embroidered silver brocade with pointed toes. And high heels. The only positive thing she could find to say about them was that they fit.

A pity. She would have liked an excuse not to wear them.

"Very practical for riding around the countryside," she said sarcastically. She took a deep breath. "I'm coming out."

"Thank you for the warning."

His smile died and a low whistle sounded as she stepped from behind the screen. His eyes widened. "Whoa."

She teetered to the mirror and pulled her plait forward to unravel it, stilling when he came up behind her and slowly ran his hands down her sides. His palms felt hot, even through the fabric, skimming a tingling path on her skin beneath the turquoise brocade.

Cait swallowed hard. "Could I be cast as your servant instead?"

"Hmm." He blinked and jerked his hands away, as though they'd just been burned. "I think not."

She took the Gypsy-lace handkerchief and started stuffing it into her neckline.

"Uh-uh." Reaching over her shoulder, he plucked it out of her hands. "My mistress wouldn't wear that."

Her exposed bosom broke out in goose bumps. "Maybe I could pose as your little sister, then?"

"Wouldn't help. Kendra doesn't dress all that differently from this, sweetheart."

Sweetheart. Her gaze met his in the looking glass.

"And you don't look like my little sister," he added huskily.

"I don't feel like your little sister, either."

He flexed his hands. "No, you most certainly do not."

Her fingers fumbled with the ribbon on her plait. Clumsily untying it, she watched his reflection back away to sit on one of the beds.

He didn't take his gaze off her.

She'd never before had difficulty unraveling her nighttime plait.

It might help if her hands would stop shaking. She grabbed her ivory comb and reached to part her hair in the back.

"No." Jason's voice came from behind her. Confused, she met his eyes in the mirror. "Leave it loose. My mistress doesn't wear plaits."

Slowly she ran the comb through her hair. Crimped from the plaiting, it hung in shimmering waves to her waist. "Wouldn't a nobleman's mistress wear her hair in curls?" Her stomach fluttered. "And pulled up on the sides, with a bun at the back, like I've seen—"

"Not *my* mistress." He got up and began stuffing clothes into the portmanteau.

She turned from the mirror and walked over to pull a shirt back out and fold it. "Clearly you're used to having someone look after you," she said softly. "Do you have a mistress, my lord?"

Beneath the blue velvet, his shoulders tensed. "I do now."

For a long minute, neither of them said anything. Then he looked away.

It meant nothing, she decided. Nobleman and mistress. A game —just a game.

She finished folding his clothes and tucked them into the portmanteau, then went to fetch the nightgown, wavering on the unfamiliar heels. "I cannot walk in these."

"You'll learn," he said, tossing the comb into one of the leather bags. As he took the folded nightgown from her hands, his gaze swept her again from head to toe. Turning to face the mirror, she put her hands back under her hair and fanned it forward to cover her cleavage.

His eyes locked on hers in the mirror, keeping her captive. He seemed to be holding his breath. His jaw tightened.

Was he cross? With her? Why?

He backed away, his expression becoming a mask of stone. "I've arranged for two horses," he said. "We'd best go, Emerald."

FORTY-SEVEN

*R*IDING BESIDE Jason in brooding silence, Caithren sneaked glances in his direction. Encased in the dark velvet suit, his lean, hard body moved with the big black horse as though they were one. Wind whipped the long red hair around the planes of his clean-shaven face.

She had to admit she might have thought he was a nobleman if she didn't know him. Her stomach felt fluttery just looking at him. It might have been fun to playact lord and mistress under other circumstances.

But there weren't any other circumstances.

Always she would want him, and always he would come temptingly close and then back off.

It was better this way, she decided firmly. Better without any emotions, any entanglements. She needed to find her brother. Jason wanted to find the Gothards. Anything personal between them would only get in the way. And ultimately lead nowhere, since she lived in Scotland and he lived here in England.

But her stomach didn't feel fluttery anymore, just sick.

With a sigh, she tried to turn her mind to more pleasant thoughts. "I miss Chiron," she said conversationally as Jason waited to cross another bridge.

"I miss him, too." He seemed distracted. "And I hope he's well taken care of."

"You paid enough that he should be," Cait said. He could have bought a third horse for the coin he'd coughed up for board.

"Chiron has never been mistreated." He nodded as a man passed from the other direction, then guided his mount down the center of the bridge. "I'm hoping to keep it that way."

As they rode into the small town of Biggleswade, Caithren reached to pat her horse's red-chestnut neck. "This mare is a bonnie lass. What is she called by?"

"I didn't think to ask."

"Nay? Then I will have to name her myself."

"You do that." He twisted in the saddle, scanning the street. "Mind if we stop? There's a baker next to the Coach & Horses. We'll just run in and get some bread."

"I'll wait here."

"No." His gaze shifted to her injured arm. "I want you to come with me."

She'd lost this argument before, so she slid off her horse—whatever the creature's name might be—and tethered her beside Jason's.

Though the sun wasn't high in the sky yet, it seemed a long time since breakfast. Delicious smells of fresh bread came through the bakeshop's door. Jason tugged it open and hurried to pull her inside.

Unused to the heels, she nearly stumbled. "Jase—"

"Hush." Baskets tacked on the wall were brimming with crusty loaves. With a rigid hand on her elbow, he guided her over and turned to her expectantly. "Grain or manchet?"

"Um...manchet."

He shot a glance out the window, then grasped her round the waist and swung her to face the baker. "What did you say, sweetheart?"

"M-manchet," she stammered out. She leaned closer to whisper. "What do you think you're doing?"

"Two loaves of manchet," he told the baker loudly.

"Two pence, my lord." The flush-faced baker fetched two small loaves and began wrapping them in paper.

Jason pulled out his pouch. "Geoffrey Gothard," he muttered under his breath.

Cait's spine stiffened.

His attention on the window, Jason took his time paying the

man. At last she saw the tension ease from his shoulders. He tucked
the two breads beneath one arm and curled the other around her
waist. Casually, he drew her through the door and outside.

His fingers tightened just before he whirled her around and
urged her back against the building. "Pretend you're flirting with
me," he said, the words coming stilted through a wide, devastating
smile.

He pressed close, closer, until the warm bread was pinned
between their two bodies. It was broad daylight. All morning he'd
been acting like he wanted nothing to do with her.

Her breath caught when he touched his forehead to hers, hot and
close. "*Now*," he demanded in a harsh whisper. "Geoffrey Gothard
is walking this way—he won't look twice at a couple in a passionate
embrace."

She tried to lean and see for herself, but his free hand came up to
hold her face. "Put your arms around me."

She shakily complied.

"That's better," he murmured in her ear. His tongue flicked out
and his teeth nipped her lobe, making her feel shakier still.

Ever since she'd donned the turquoise gown, he'd been looking
at her differently. Maybe he just wanted to kiss her. She tried again
to see Gothard, but Jason's fingers tightened on her chin. His gaze
bore into hers, so intense her knees nearly buckled.

"You're m-making this up as an excuse to kiss me."

"If you value your life, you'll play along." His mouth brushed
her cheek and trailed down her neck, leaving a quivery path of
dampness. "You're my mistress," he murmured into the sensitive
hollow beneath her chin. "Try to look like you're enjoying this, will
you?"

Aye, she was enjoying it.

When she arched against him, he claimed her lips in a soul-
searing kiss. The heat from the bread seemed to seep into her
stomach and spread. Her head felt woozy. Her entire body felt limp.
Only the wall and Jason's arms kept her standing.

His tongue traced her lips, then swept inside, kindling a hot rush
of excitement. And, somehow, that changed everything.

Her fingers tangled in the coarse hair of the wig. The now-
familiar pleasure stole through her, and she wondered vaguely how
she could have thought she was better off without this. She clung to

his lips, molding herself against his body, wishing she could flow right into him.

Were they really being watched? Either way, she felt safe with him here, as she always had, though it made no more sense now than it had in the beginning. The melting intimacy felt genuine, not staged, and despite herself—despite the real danger—she found herself savoring every second.

Surely he felt the connection, too. She couldn't let him deny these feelings again.

He raised his head and looked both ways, then said, "He's gone."

Feeling a loss, she held him captive with a hand behind his neck and the other splayed against his back. "What else can you tell me about your mistress?" Her voice shook, betraying her emotions. "I-if I'm to act the part, then—"

He groaned, a heart-wrenching sound of capitulation. "My mistress...there's no one I'd rather kiss." The green of his eyes turned dark and unfathomable as he clasped her tightly against him. His mouth brushed hers, once, twice, caressing her lips more than kissing them, wordlessly begging her to open and let him in. When she parted her lips, he devoured her mouth with an urgent hunger.

She was stunned at the possessiveness of his embrace. He wanted her, she was sure of it...

Now that she was dressed like an Englishwoman.

But it wasn't right. She'd wanted him all along, mustached or not, long hair or short, dressed like a peasant or a nobleman. It was the man she wanted, not the package in which he was presented.

She pulled away, struggling to regain her senses. "Now you look at me differently," she accused. "Ever since I put on these clothes."

"No." He captured her gaze with his. "Ever since I saw you dance with the Gypsies."

Since then? Her heart leapt. Dancing with the Gypsies, she'd been herself, Caithren Leslie, more than at any other time since she'd stepped foot in England.

He backed away, catching the bread from between them before it could fall to the ground.

Cait blinked and put her palms to her cheeks. She focused on the loaves in his hands. "They're squished," she said stupidly.

"Gothard is gone." He handed her a loaf. "I think we fooled him."

"I hope so," she said.

But maybe not. Maybe she'd like to try to fool him again. She wasn't completely convinced this was the only way to keep from being seen, but it could be the only way Jason would allow himself the pleasure of kissing her.

That sort of bloody-mindedness she was determined to change.

The bread didn't feel as hot as it had between their bodies. Though she wasn't hungry, she unwrapped the loaf, tore off a hunk, and stuck it in her mouth. Before she could say something else stupid.

"Shall we go?" he asked her.

"Aye." Swallowing, she wrapped her bread back up. "Let's go."

They untied their horses and headed out.

The road out of Biggleswade was narrow, with a few small houses scattered alongside. As scattered as Cait's thoughts. Jason was the most confusing man she'd ever met. Exasperating. Authoritative. Protective.

But he certainly knew how to kiss.

Although it was clouding up and cooling off, the brocade gown was heavy enough to keep her warm. The gown and the hot blood pumping through her veins...

What would she have done without Jason? It felt like a lifetime since he'd kept her off the coach. She'd still be on it, wouldn't she? Slowly making her way toward London, listening to Mrs. Dochart day in and day out.

She'd have her money and her clothes—clothes that didn't leave half her bosom exposed for the world to ogle. But she wouldn't have attended a country fair, tasted syllabub, or danced with the Gypsies.

Or learned what it felt like to really be kissed.

He'd swept her plans out from under her. The trouble was, she feared he'd swept her heart out from under her as well.

FORTY-EIGHT

My dearest Malcolm and Alison,

I did not have to travel all the way South, as evidence proves the Gothards to be following the Great North Road towards London. They are not good at covering their tracks. So I hope to be home sooner than planned, which is a very happy thing, because I miss you both more than words can say.

All the day, as I ride the road, I think about my two bairns and what you might be doing. Every day that passes without you is a day I've missed forever, and I cannot wait to see your two bonnie faces and hold you in my arms again.

From what I have learned, these men are very, very bad people. I know I will be doing the world a good deed to see them gone. All the same, I would rather be with you, and I count the days until it will be so. I cannot wait to hug and kiss you, and my dearest prayer is that when I come home to you this time, it will be forever.

Your very loving Mama

~

*D*URING THE TEN long miles from Biggleswade to Baldock, the weather failed to cooperate. As the long blowing grasses gave way to Baldock's neat clipped gardens, the clouds grew darker and the wind picked up, whipping beneath Caithren's heavy skirts.

They rode past the Church of St. Mary, a pleasing amalgam of several centuries of architecture. Jason slowed before the Old White Horse. "You hungry?"

She held up her half-eaten loaf of bread. "I can wait if you can."

With a glance at the menacing clouds, he nodded. They continued on toward Stevenage, with Cait trying her best to keep the conversation flowing over the hours, so as not to think too much.

Because, truly, she didn't know *what* to think anymore.

When the temperature dropped, they donned their working-class hats even though they didn't match their upper-class disguises. Jason dug in the portmanteau and jostled his horse closer to settle his cloak over her shoulders.

"Thank you," she said, snuggling into the woolen warmth. She fastened the clasp beneath her chin. "Maid-of-the-Wave."

"Pardon?"

"I'm naming my horse Maid-of-the-Wave. Her coat is glittery like a mermaid, don't you think? And sort of reddish, like a salmon?"

He shrugged. "If you say so."

"What will you be naming yours?"

"Nothing." He shot a glance over his shoulder. "I'll be riding him only through tomorrow. He won't have time to learn a name."

She shook her head mournfully. "All creatures need names. If you won't name him, then I shall. Hmm..." Chilled, she gathered the edges of the cloak more closely around her. "Hamish," she decided.

"Hamish?" Jason slanted her a puzzled glance. "After who?"

"The young farmer who married the Maid-of-the-Wave."

His lips quirked. "You never said his name was Hamish."

"Well, I don't actually know the farmer's name. But it seems to me that about one out of four men in Scotland is named Hamish, so I figure it's a bonnie good bet."

She was blethering again.

Since Jason appeared to be choking back laughter, she looked away and caught sight of a flutter in the sky. An excuse to change the subject. "Magpies," she said, watching one of the black-and-white birds land in a tree. "Do you see their dome-shaped nest? I hope there are at least two in it."

Frowning, he glanced over his shoulder again. "Why?"

"Less than two are supposed to be unlucky, aye? And doubly so if you see one alone before breakfast." He was still looking behind them. "Are you counting the magpies?

"Pardon? No. No, I'm not."

"I don't believe the superstition, but I do know a verse." She began quoting. "One for sorrow, two for luck, three for a wedding—"

"Bloody hell!"

She gasped when he reached across and grabbed her reins. Kicking his horse into a gallop, he drove them both off the side of the road. His hat flew off.

"What are you doing?" she yelled, holding on for dear life, one hand on her head to keep her own hat from flying away.

"Just hold on!" His jaw set, he pressed on, and Cait wondered wildly what they could be running from. Six strange little round hills sat off the road a wee distance. Drawing close, he reined in and dragged both horses to a halt.

He dismounted in a flash and reached both hands to help her down. He tugged her toward one of the mounds.

"Will they stay?" she asked. "Maid-of-the-Wave and Hamish?"

He shrugged, hurrying her along. "The horses are the least of our worries."

"Don't tell me you think those brothers are after us again."

He shot a glance around the hill, back toward the road. "All right, I won't tell you."

She followed his gaze. Her heart seized when she spotted Walter and Geoffrey Gothard astride two horses.

"Damnation! Get down!" With two hands on her shoulders, Jason pushed her to her knees.

She shrieked, her hand going to her hurt arm.

"Sorry," he hissed. Her hat tumbled off as they scrambled behind the mound and out of sight. But there was no way to hide the beasts they'd been riding on. And Jason's instincts had been right. The brothers were following them. She'd seen them with her own eyes.

Quite suddenly she recalled a vivid memory of standing outside Scarborough's house and overhearing their wicked plans. As then, she shivered. But her heart was pounding a good deal harder than that day, knowing the Gothards were now bent on killing not just Scarborough, but her and Jason, too.

"Cooperate this time, will you?" Jason's eyes burned with an intense green fire. "There's nothing for it. I hope they'll stay on the road, but if they ride round this hill and get a good look at our faces—"

He broke off, and his mouth covered hers.

The caress was more than a simple kiss this time—his body covered hers, warm and heavy, pinning her to the cushiony grass. Her blood raced in both passion and fear. She felt boneless and aflame all at once, the conflicting emotions all-consuming.

Was it grass-muted hoofbeats she heard drawing near, or her own heartbeat in her ears? Whichever, stark panic overcame the softer feelings, and her heart pumped even faster as she imagined Gothard stabbing Jason in the back as she lay under him, or shooting him, or—

"Pardon my impudence," he murmured, "but I've got to make this look good." The next thing she knew, his hand was venturing under her skirt—

And the hoofbeats came yet closer—

"Damn me, Caroline," a man's voice drawled. "Someone's found our favorite spot."

FORTY-NINE

ASON OPENED one eye to get a look at the intruders, then sat up, muttering a curse. Caithren lay limp in the grass, a hand pressed to her heart while he adjusted the tangled cloak and tugged down on her skirts.

He glanced up at the young man and woman, both on horseback. Country folk, likely stealing away to court on the sly.

Horror widened the girl's round gray eyes. "Let's go! Can't you see they're quality? Let's go!" Her cheeks stained bright red, she dug in her heels and took off.

The young man wheeled and rode after her, shouting, "Caroline!"

Releasing a slow breath, Jason crawled around the mound to have a look, then returned to Caithren. "The Gothards...I guess they rode past." He raked a rather shaky hand through his hair, only to realize it was the periwig, which he nearly dislodged. "We scared off those lovers but good," he said with a smile, offering a hand to help Caithren sit.

She smiled back. "We did, didn't we?" She burst into giggles, hugging her sides. The giddiness of relief, he guessed. "My mam always said, 'guid claes and keys let you in.'"

"Good what?"

"Clothes. Dressing well can open doors for you the same as a key, aye? We've dressed the part, and they believed it, just like that."

She snapped her fingers and stood up, evidently not an easy task in the silver shoes. Her legs looked wobbly. "What are these wee hills? They look too regular to be natural."

"They're Roman barrows." Jason rose as well, brushing off his velvet breeches. "Burial mounds."

"Oh," she said, making a face. "Faugh."

"Faugh? That's it?" He leaned to pick up her hat. "No quote of your mother's for this one?"

"I'll tell you, Jase. I don't think Mam ever kissed anyone while lying on top of dead Romans."

He threw back his head and laughed.

"I wouldn't mind trying it again, though," she added.

That sobered him. "What?"

"The kissing." She shook out her skirts and pulled up on the hated stomacher. "You seem to enjoy the kissing enough, but you need to have an excuse." She squared her shoulders and faced him daringly. "You're attracted to me, aye?"

"I am." He'd be lying to deny it. "But God knows why." Maybe because she made him laugh. He'd been far too serious the past weeks—the past years, truth be told. Ever since his parents had died and left him with all the responsibilities. "And God also knows I've no business acting on that attraction."

"Why not, I ask you?" She moved closer. "I wouldn't tell a soul, and I wouldn't try to trap you, either. I have every intention of going home to Scotland, and I won't be expecting you to come with me. Before I leave, though, I'd just like to know…"

Both her proximity and her earnestness made him uncomfortable. Turning her hat in his hands, he started walking back to the horses. "Know what?"

"What it would feel like, is all." She hurried to keep up with him, stumbling in the new shoes. "What it would feel like to—"

When she broke off, he risked looking over at her. Her breath came unevenly. Her cheeks had turned a becoming shade of pink.

"You know," she said, as though he knew what she was talking about.

Which, of course, he did.

He halted mid-step. A Scottish woman propositioning him. He needed a moment to digest that.

No matter how much his hands burned to run riot all over her body, the mere idea was absurd. And it was wrong as well. Even more so now that he knew she was a provincial baronet's daughter, not some bold, widowed reward-hunter.

He'd already compromised her by traveling alone with her. There was nothing he could do about that now, but he sure as hell wasn't going to take things any further.

He turned to her and stuck the hat on her head.

"With you," she added in a whisper. "I've never wanted to before. Before I met you, I mean." Her hand went to her amulet, and her lower lip trembled. "But you won't do anything about it, will you?"

"No, I won't be doing anything about it." Her eyes were a gorgeous hazy blue. Holy heaven. "You should be grateful for that. It's wrong to take a woman and—just leave her," he said, striding over to the horses.

Teetering in his wake, she called after him. "If you believe that, have you never, then? With a woman, since you've said you're not wanting to marry. I mean..." She rushed in front of him and stood blocking his way, looking up at him. "Are you a virgin, Jason Chase?"

Her words seemed to echo across the open fields. At first he was horrified, but then he laughed. "No, I'm no virgin. But it's different in my circle of acquaintances." King Charles's court was licentious as hell. Barring his sister—he hoped—he doubted there was a courtier over the age of fourteen who could call him or herself virgin. "We have different expectations. With you, there's a matter of responsibility."

"I have no expectations. For once, could you listen to the Gypsy? Could you forget about responsibilities and just let yourself feel?"

"I think not."

He felt all too much, and that was the problem. If he thought he could simply love her and leave her, he might consider it. He hadn't been so tempted in a good, long while. Maybe in all his life.

But with Caithren it would be all or nothing—he knew that in his bones.

"Look, we've been tied at the hip for days now. All you really want from me is to get to London. And I'll get you there, I promise. A Chase promise is not given lightly."

Her eyes cleared and turned a disappointed, indistinct color.

"You have no idea what I want from you, Jason. And I don't believe you ever will." She wrapped her arms around herself and shivered.

"You're cold," he said. "And the weather looks to be getting colder. Come along. We're nearly to Stevenage, where I can buy you a cloak."

FIFTY

*T*HE CLOUDS HAD grown dark and menacing, and Jason found the interior of The Grange even darker. Brushing off the drizzle that had beaded on his cloak, he stepped into the taproom and blinked in the dimness.

Caithren wasn't at the table where he'd left her.

Panic sprinted along his nerves before he got himself under control. He tossed the new wool cloak he'd bought over her chair and walked around the tavern, checking every corner of the oddly shaped room. Then back to the table, his heart beginning to beat unevenly. He'd left her with his portmanteau and the burlap bag with the backgammon set.

All was gone.

Geoffrey's and Walter's faces flashed in his mind. But no one in the taproom looked at all concerned, and it was inconceivable that Caithren would go with the brothers without a fight. While it was true she couldn't shoot, he'd seen her in action: punching, kicking, wielding a knife. And there was no sign of a confrontation.

Still, his pulse raced, his head felt woozy. What if they'd managed to take her? How would he find them? What would he do? He couldn't think clearly when he kept seeing her standing in that courtyard with blood running down her arm. Blood from a Gothard's blade.

If anything more happened to her, he would never forgive himself.

He paced around the tavern, stopping at tables, querying one patron after another. "A woman was sitting there. Short, blond. Did she leave with anyone?"

No one had seen a thing.

When she came down the stairs, stepping gingerly on the heeled shoes, he spun around. His long legs ate up the distance between them.

"Where the hell were you?"

"Hold your tongue. Everyone is looking at us." She walked to their table, set down the burlap bag, shrugged the portmanteau off her shoulder. "I took everything with me so nothing would go missing. I was gone but a minute."

"You have a damn odd idea of a minute. Where did you go? How dare you disappear on me! I thought the Gothards had—"

"I had to...you know. Use the privy." Frowning, she peered into his eyes, and then, unbelievably, her lips turned up in a hint of a smile. "I've never seen you really angry before. I didn't think you had it in you."

"I've never thought you were missing before," he snapped out.

She crossed her arms and leveled him with a stare. "How about when I tried to escape you? Or when I fell asleep in the kirk?"

"Things were different then. Then I didn't—oh, bloody hell."

"Then you didn't *care*?" she supplied. "You cannot say it, can you? That you care."

"I care," he said. "I care about making things right. I care about replacing what you lost on my account. I care that you get to London in one piece, not carved up by a Gothard's blade."

The sound of raucous laughter came from another table. Pewter tankards clanked on wood. "I don't want anything to happen to you, either," Caithren said softly.

"Why?" he asked, though he wasn't sure he wanted to hear the answer.

"Because *I* care." Her gaze dropped to her crossed arms. "And I don't mean about getting to London or the money you owe me."

With a finger he lifted her chin. "Emerald—"

"And no matter what you call me, I care because of this—" She went up on her toes and pressed her mouth to his.

Bloody hell. Calling her Emerald wasn't working. With a groan of surrender, he closed his eyes to return the kiss.

His arms went around her, and the sounds of the tavern receded as she arched herself so close he felt her damned amulet between them. Her lips were warm velvet; her flowery scent assaulted his senses.

How could such an exasperating woman be so sweet?

At the sound of a whistle, he pulled away to much applause.

"We see you found her," someone yelled.

Caithren's cheeks went from the pink of passion to the red of embarrassment.

"Shall we go?" he asked with a laugh. He drew the new cloak from her chair and settled it over her shoulders. "It's seven miles to Welwyn and starting to rain already."

FIFTY-ONE

"WE'RE NOT going to make it, Jase," Caithren yelled through the storm. She hadn't known it was possible to feel so wet. Her new cloak was all but useless against the downpour. "If this gown soaks up any more water, poor Maid-of-the-Wave will be driven to her knees."

A huge crash of thunder made both horses shy. The sky opened up and spewed twice as much water, a feat Cait hadn't thought possible. Rain came down in blinding sheets. She couldn't see as much as two feet ahead.

She felt Jason's leg bump up against hers before his hand came through the downpour to grab her reins. "Shelter!" he hollered over the next crack of lightning. "Come with me!"

He led them off the road along a barely visible trail. Hidden in the trees sat an old thatched cottage. How he'd found the place she'd never know, but the mere sight of it lifted her heart.

She held both horses while Jason pounded on the door. No one came to answer. The shutters were all latched from the interior, and the door was locked. Water streaming into her eyes, Cait waited while he walked all the way around the one-room building.

"Closed up!" he called through the pounding rain.

She wanted to cry.

He stood stock-still for a spell, then disappeared behind the cottage and returned with a hefty log. Bracing it against his good shoulder, he stepped back and ran at the door.

It didn't give, and she winced at his anguished yell. "You're going to kill yourself," she called. "You're in no shape for this!"

But he tried it twice more, until the door crashed in. He nearly fell on his face after it, and, miserable as she was, Cait had to bite her lip to keep from laughing.

"Go inside," he told her, and she did, gratefully. After tethering the horses beneath some trees, he took their things and followed her, propping the door into its space behind them.

They stood there, dripping, for a long minute. Rain pounded on the roof. The cottage looked clean enough and boasted a bed with a thick quilt, a small table, two wooden chairs, and a brick fireplace. No wood, no candles, no oil lamps. The warped shutters let in a little light and a lot of rain that puddled near the glassless windows. But it was shelter, and Caithren couldn't remember being more appreciative in her life.

"Thank you," she whispered.

Jason gestured helplessly. "It will be cold come night. And dark. All the wood outside is soaking wet." He looked at the table and chairs.

Her gaze followed his. "You're not thinking of burning them?" When he shrugged, she shook her head. "They're not yours to burn. Besides, where would we continue our backgammon tournament?"

"That's right." Grinning, he pulled off his hat. Water poured from the wide brim. "I'm ahead."

"You are not." She set her own drenched hat on the table. "We're dead even. Seventeen matches each."

He dragged off the wet wig. His own hair underneath was just as soaked, sleekly black and plastered to his head.

"You look like a selkie," Cait said.

He unfastened his cloak and let it drop to the floor in a sodden heap. "A what?"

"A selkie. A mythical creature that takes on the form of a seal in the sea and a man on the land."

"How flattering." Amusement lit his eyes as they raked her from head to toe. "You on the other hand, look the picture of perfection."

"Aye?" Laughing, she shrugged free of her cloak. "I wouldn't be surprised if this gown weighs more than I do." Bending at the waist, she gathered her hair and twisted it. Water streamed out onto the wooden floor.

As she straightened, her hair still bunched in one hand, Jason's arms came around her from behind. She hadn't even heard him move close. He pressed his lips to the nape of her neck.

Warm and soft. Her breath caught, and she stood stone still. She hadn't imagined it the first time, she realized, a little thrill running through her at the thought. "What was that for?"

"I've been wanting to do that since the day I met you," he said huskily.

Quite unsure about this side of Jason Chase and where it had come from, she turned to face him. His penetrating gaze was entrancing. "Well, I wouldn't have stopped you," she said.

"I don't expect you would have." He took a deep breath and looked away, the Jason she knew slipping back into place. "Let me fetch some dry clothes."

Still stunned, she stood and shivered while he went through the portmanteau. One after another, their clothes came out, every piece soaking wet.

She draped the garments on the floor around the room. "I hope they'll dry," she said on a sigh.

Finally, from the very bottom, he unearthed a pair of buff breeches and one of his shirts and held them both up triumphantly. "Dry. Almost. Which do you want?" He waved the breeches, a distinct leer in his eye.

Surprised and a bit unnerved by his playfulness, she snatched the shirt from his other hand. "This will do, thank you. Turn around."

With a grin, he obeyed. One of his feet impatiently tapped on the wooden floor, the wet boot leather squeaking with each motion.

"No peeking," she admonished. Quite adept at removing stomachers now, she did so in all haste.

"Are you finished yet?"

"Nay. Stay put."

His foot kept tapping while she wiggled the gown and chemise to her waist and slipped his shirt over her head. Unexpectedly soft, it smelled warm and spicy, like he did. Reaching beneath the hem, she pushed everything down and off, leaving her shoes in the wet pile when she stepped out of it.

"Now your turn." She faced away to wait.

A hand came down on her shoulder and slowly swung her around. His gaze traced a lazy path down her body. She blushed, aware that the shirt reached only to her knees.

He raised a brow. "Much better than Mrs. Twentyman's night-gown. I think we ought to burn that thing."

"You haven't got a fire," she said crisply. "Are you going to change or not?"

"In due time."

Mindful of his eyes on her, she yanked up on the sleeves, which fell well past her hands, and tightened the shirt's laces. "Aren't you freezing?"

"Are you?"

Her skin erupted in goose bumps, though it really wasn't too cold now that she was out of the wet gown. "Not since I changed. I'll just take these clothes"—she bent to retrieve them—"and lay them out while you dress." She turned her back and started spreading the garments over what little floor space was left. "Don't worry—I promise not to look."

"It wouldn't bother me if you did, sweetheart," he drawled.

If past experience was any indicator, she had no cause to doubt him. Blushing furiously, she made long work of squeezing the water from the brocade gown and wringing out its chemise. Her shoes were alarmingly soggy, but she sat them on the floor and hoped for the best.

The stomacher was soaked, yet still just as stiff. Apparently Jason hadn't been fooling when he said there was bone inside.

"Ready," he called.

She turned, then whirled back away. "You're still half-naked!"

"If you'll hand over my only dry shirt, I can finish dressing," he said drolly.

She hugged the shirt in question around her middle. "Oh, never mind."

Averting her eyes from his bare chest, she fetched the backgammon set and removed it from the burlap bag.

"Sit," she said, plopping the drenched board onto the table. "It's wet, but I reckon it'll survive, seeing as it's made from a cow that likely got drenched in its day." She lined up the markers on their respective pips.

"I reckon it will," he said, his voice tinged with amusement. Taking the dice cup, he rolled two sixes.

She sat across from him, trying not to notice the way his muscles rippled when he leaned across the board to make his moves. Though still a livid pink, his wound looked all but healed. Rain beat down on the roof, and thunder and lightning disturbed her concentration.

Damn if she didn't lose three matches in a row.

"I'm hungry," Jason complained as she reset the board.

"There's some bread left in the pocket of my cloak."

He rose to fetch it, treating her to a view of his broad shoulders and back. He returned with a handful of white mush. "I don't think so." With a groan, he tossed it into the empty fireplace.

"Maybe it will stop raining so we can continue on to Welwyn before you waste away of starvation."

He snorted.

But the weather didn't let up.

By the time Cait had lost two more matches, the rumbling was directly overhead and nearly constant. Dark was falling. Brilliant flashes of lightning lit the room through the ill-fitting shutters, but the sporadic brightness wasn't adequate to play by.

Caithren squinted at the dice, trying to see what numbers she'd rolled. With a sigh, she rose and headed for the entrance, picking her way around the clothes that littered the floor. She pried the door free from where Jason had propped it within its frame, just enough to see outside.

The rain pounded down, assaulting her ears. "I don't think we'll be going anywhere," she yelled over the noise.

"I expect not," Jason said softly, right beside her. When she jumped, one of his arms came around to steady her. The other hand reached to shove the door back into place, blocking most of the sound.

She could still hear the rain on the roof and through the shutters, but the room seemed suddenly and immeasurably quieter. It seemed she could hear her own heartbeat over the soft sigh of Jason's breath by her ear.

Surely that wasn't possible. Just as it wasn't possible that he was sweeping aside her hair and kissing that spot on the nape of her neck again.

She shivered.

"Are you cold?" he whispered.

She wasn't sure. Was she cold or just unbearably aware of his lips on her skin? Regardless, she nodded.

"Come to bed, then. I'll keep you warm."

Hope blossoming, she spun in his arms. But when a flash of lightning illuminated his eyes, she could see they were guileless.

"I'll just keep you warm," he repeated. "I promise. A Chase promise is—"

"—not given lightly," she finished on a sigh.

She wanted so much more than to be kept warm. But she couldn't face yet another rejection. She wouldn't ask with words, ever again.

Instead, she asked with her body.

She pressed against him, ran her hands over the hard planes of his bare shoulders, pulled the tie out of his hair, meshed her fingers in its silky softness.

Her reward was hearing his sharp intake of breath.

"To bed. To keep warm," he said firmly and turned her around, guiding her across the darkened room with a hand clamped on her shoulder.

She clenched her teeth, but a groan slipped out anyway.

"Have I hurt you?" he asked. "Oh, damn, it's your arm, isn't it?"

She began to nod, then realized he couldn't see her. Turning to face him, she flattened her hands against his chest. "Aye," she whispered, her palms tingling. "I never found time to gather plants today."

"Is it getting any better?"

"Nay." She wouldn't lie. But she didn't want to alarm him, either. She didn't want to be thinking about her arm now—she wanted to be thinking about his body, warm and tucked beside hers. "It's been but a day. These things take time."

"I wish I could have a look."

"Well, it's dark. You can look in the morning, if it pleases you. For now..." She snuggled close.

Though she felt him hesitate, she also felt his heart pounding beneath her hands. With a muttered oath, he swung her into his arms and carried her to the bed, probably scattering all their care-fully laid out clothes as he went.

Not that she cared. She knew she had won.

The bed ropes creaked as he set her down, and another flash of lightning revealed his features in stark relief. Enough so she could find his lips with hers by the time the responding thunder rumbled through the sky, shaking the cottage, the floorboards, the bed.

Or maybe she was shaking. Nay, for sure she was shaking. His hands moved to cup her face, and he eased her back, coming down on top of her. His shirt rode up her thighs, and it was scandalous, but she couldn't find it in herself to care.

How could she care when her dreams were coming true?

His bare chest felt wonderfully warm through the thin cambric shirt. His lips were gentle and giving, but she could feel his reti-cence, a sweet reticence that teased her. She grabbed at his hair and fitted her mouth to his, reveling in his groan. Her world was reduced to his hands and his mouth and his body, the heat and the glory, the pure pleasure of him touching her at last.

His shoulders tensed above her as he shifted onto his elbows, sparing her his full weight. His fingers worked at the shirt's laces while his mouth trailed down, lingering in the hollow of her neck. She arched in shivery delight, gasping when she felt the lacing drawn out of its eyelets, gasping again when the same lacing dropped to the floor.

His mouth teased in the open vee of the shirt's placket, licking, biting, kissing. And lower, his lips playing over her aching breasts and grazing her sensitive nipples. It was wicked, but wickedly marvelous. It was—

He moved to draw the chain with her amulet over her head.

"Nay," she whispered, wedging a hand between them to settle the necklace back into place.

"Nay," he echoed, the word sounding foreign from his lips. His knuckles brushed her face, hesitated, halted. He stilled. "Nay," he repeated, closing his eyes and pulling away.

He sat up, breathing in slow, loud puffs.

"I said I wouldn't do this," he ground out from between gritted teeth. "It's not responsible, and—"

Reaching up, she grasped his shoulders. "For once in your life, would you forget about being responsible? I want you, Jason."

Another flash of lightning, and his answer was in his eyes.

No.

Despite her resolve, she had asked with words again—and, no, he wouldn't have the likes of her.

A sob tore from her throat—a sob born of frustration and embarrassment, endless rejection and unfulfilled passion. She leapt up and made for the door, clawing at it with frantic fingers, throwing it to the floor behind her. A mighty crash resounded from the cottage as she raced out into the storm.

He was behind her within seconds, but she kept running, darting around the shadows of the trees, until finally he caught her by the hem of the shirt and pulled her to her knees in the wet grass. She threw herself forward, shutting her eyes against the sight of him, though she couldn't really have seen him anyway in the darkness and the driving rain.

"Leave me alone!" she screamed over the deluge. Never had she realized water could be so loud. But that was good—it drowned out her harsh breathing and the staccato beat of her heart. It pounded on her skin, cold needles that drove away all her anguished thoughts as she concentrated on the chilled wetness. It caressed her body with the icy fingers she needed to cool her ardor and bring her back to her senses.

Then warmer fingers were on her, rolling her onto her back. Jason was kneeling over her. "What the hell are you doing?" he demanded over a rumble of thunder. "You'll catch your death out here."

"Leave me alone!" Angrily she pushed at his hands and struggled to her feet. "Always, since I met you, you will never leave me alone," she hollered as he came up after her.

A bolt of lightning illuminated his face for a second, just a second. But long enough for Cait to see his tortured face, his anguished eyes. And in that flash she saw that the rejection she'd seen in the cottage had been something else. She'd seen what she'd expected to see, rather than the truth.

The naked hunger.

"I don't want to leave you alone," he bellowed over the wind and the rain and another hard crack of thunder. "Damn it to bloody hell—I never wanted to leave you alone!"

And he was on her in an instant, his bare torso hot on her chilled, wet body, his mouth searching for hers.

Their lips met, and a jolt of desire shot straight through to her heart. The kiss wasn't gentle, but devouring, demanding a response she was only too ready to give. His tongue swept her mouth as his hands swept down to the hem of the shirt, dragging it up her body until he broke contact to pull it over her head.

Lightning flashed as he crushed her to him, skin against skin, fusing his mouth to hers again. Rain pounded down all around them, but they were close, so close not a drop could shimmy between their straining bodies. His lips traveled her cheeks, her nose, her hairline, leaving a burning path no cold water could erase. Unshaven roughness grazed her skin, a man's texture that gave rise to a thrill as wild as the storm.

He lowered her to the grass, his hands roaming her body and leaving a riot of sensation in their wake. Her own hands skimmed his back, his shoulders, wherever she could reach. Thunder rumbled —in the distance, then closer—matching the uneven beat of her pulse. The rain smelled chilly and fresh, but Jason smelled warm and male and unbearably exciting.

When his hand raced down her side and his fingers explored between her legs, she cried out, feeling herself wetter than the rain somehow and straining for more. More of his body, more of his mouth, more of his fingers where they teased. More, more. She pressed her lips where his neck met his shoulder and tasted him, her teeth nipping his heated skin.

He reared up, and suddenly all four of their hands were fumbling on the laces to his breeches. In moments he had peeled them off, and his mouth closed over hers as he plunged into her.

A wee bit surprised at the intrusion, Cait stiffened and gasped. He hesitated above her.

She couldn't see his face through the dark and the rain. She knew only that he couldn't stop now. She wouldn't let him. Like the rain and the thunder and the lightning, nothing would stop them.

Nothing.

She arched up against him, taking him deeper, her heart soaring when she felt him respond. Her hands clawed at his back as he rocked against her, the water sluicing over them in a relentless rhythm that matched their own.

Relentless, like the feeling building inside her, a feeling so urgent and wondrous it could come only from nature. Relentless. A jagged bolt ripped from the sky as Caithren hurtled to a point of no return.

Then she did return, only to feel Jason pull out of her as the answering thunder rumbled the earth beneath them. Shuddering, he buried his face in her shoulder. "Caithren," he choked out.

She'd thought she couldn't feel any more wonderful, but hearing him utter her name—her real name, for the first time—made her heart constrict with an unsurpassable pleasure. Her feelings weren't entirely unreciprocated...and, even more significant, he finally believed she was Caithren.

Finally.

He struggled to his elbows, hovering above her. "Caithren, sweet Cait." The words came in ragged pants. "I'm—so sorry."

She moved under him, feeling entirely too drained to respond to his distress. "I told you I was Cait—"

"Not about that."

He rolled off her, onto his back, putting a hand over his eyes. One knee was raised, and her greedy gaze roamed his body as another flash of lightning revealed it.

"Bloody hell," he said, "I lost my head, and I've"—his face constricted in anguish—"ruined you. Let you down, your family, myself...I'm so damned sorry."

"Don't you dare be sorry," Cait yelled over the crack of thunder. "Be sorry you didn't believe me, if you will—you haven't believed a word I've said since the day we met. But don't you dare be sorry for this. I am *not* ruined. A man's contrivance, that."

By all the saints, he looked wretched enough to do himself damage.

"It was good, wasn't it?" She sat up and leaned over him, shoving his hand from his eyes. "Wasn't it?" she demanded.

"It was." He sat too and clutched her close, covering her mouth with wee kisses, with all the tenderness they'd abandoned during their heated encounter. "It was good." Another kiss, and his tongue flicked out to trace her lips. "But it was wrong, and for your first time—"

"It was good," she interrupted. It had been more than good—it had been unbelievable. The sheer force and power of it, of the two of them together. "I would never have known how good it could be, and I can only be better for the knowing. I didn't have a clue, Jase. Not a glimmer—"

He groaned. "All right. It was good. My sweet, independent Cait. What is it the Gypsy said? You go your own way." He kissed the dripping rain off her nose. "Good heavens, have you ever in your life been so damned wet?"

FIFTY-TWO

*S*HE WAS STILL laughing when they made it to the cottage and he shoved the door back into place.

Except for when lightning lit the sky and seeped through the shutters, the room was pitch-black, but he managed to find some of the less-wet clothes and rub her down with them, then tuck her into the bed before seeing to himself.

Thankful that she couldn't see him in the darkness, he scrubbed mercilessly at his skin, as though he could scour away the guilt. Oh, she was right—it had been good. Damned good. Better than he'd ever had; better than he'd ever imagined. Even now, his blood ran hot wanting her again…wanting to give it to her nice and slow, the way a virgin should be treated.

Damn him for being so weak and irresponsible, for allowing his body to rule his head. He should never have taken her—it had been selfish and wrong. Wrong beyond description.

But it was done, and like everything else, he would make this up to her.

Somehow. After this was all over.

Now, he would have to work hard to put the distance back between them—the distance they both needed in order to make sure Gothard was dealt with and no harm came to Caithren.

His precious Cait.

When he crawled into the bed, she reached for him. Her lips

searched blindly for his in the darkness, fumbled, then found their target.

A sweet, sleepy kiss.

He wrapped his arms around her, settled himself against her welcoming body, and listened to the patter of rain on the roof. Distance, he thought as he felt her drifting into sleep.

He had meant to put distance between them, yet here they were, almost as close as two bodies could be. But she felt too good against him to be thinking of distance now.

The morning would be soon enough.

~

*C*RIVVENS, SHE was in the scud.

Sunlight streamed through open shutters to where Caithren lay alone in bed, naked beneath the quilt. Last night came rushing back, mad images of rain and passion she knew must have really happened, because she couldn't possibly have imagined anything so perfectly glorious.

Heat rushed to her cheeks just thinking of it.

She rubbed her aching arm. The wound felt hot beneath the bandage. She should have unwrapped it last night and allowed it some air, rather than keeping it swathed in damp cloth. But she hadn't been thinking of anything practical then—she'd thought about nothing but how Jason was making her feel.

How would she live the rest of her life without a man? Without Jason?

Every fiber in her body reacting to that thought, she sat abruptly, pulling the quilt about her shoulders. It was time to talk sense into herself. Last night had been wonderful beyond words, but she'd never feel like that again. Even should she spend the rest of her life with Jason—an idea so absurd it didn't bear considering—she'd never again experience the depth of emotion brought on by that wild combination of attraction, frustration, and weather.

Maybe it *was* her imagination. Could touching him, loving him, really feel that all-encompassing? In the time she had left with him, she would do her best to find out. But she already knew what the answer would be.

Jason had said they'd be in London by tonight. Friday—two days from now—she'd find Adam at Lord Darnley's wedding.

Then she'd go home to Scotland, where she belonged.

The door lay flat on the floor, and their clothes, save for her mistress outfit, were all gone. Crammed unfolded into the portmanteau, no doubt.

A smile tugged at her lips as she wrapped the quilt around her body and walked to the gaping hole where the door belonged. The sky was cloudless, and the last remnants of the rain glittered like diamonds in the sun's rays. Songbirds chirped in the trees. A beautiful, lovely morning.

The best morning of her life.

Jason was outside by the horses, already dressed in his nobleman disguise, securing their belongings. Her gaze skimmed his gleaming black hair and the masculine planes of his face. He had shaved while she slept, making her fingers itch to feel the smooth skin and compare it to the roughness of last night.

The very thought of that roughness brought a rush of urgent heat that weakened her knees and made her stomach flutter. She drank in his muscular physique, imagining what was underneath the fancy blue velvet suit. Nay, not imagining...remembering.

She blushed. "Good morn," she called.

He looked up, favoring her with one of those white grins that made her heart turn over. But as she watched, it faded. His eyes looked hooded, wary. "Good morn," he returned, then glanced away.

Her heart floundered in confusion. The pleasant flutter in her stomach turned to an uneasy jumble of nerves. After all they'd shared, still he was holding back.

Her face must have betrayed her disappointment, because he came toward her with concern in his eyes. She turned her back, leaning against the empty door frame. But when he laid his hands on her shoulders, her traitorous body responded immediately, and she felt a hot stab of desire.

He tried to swivel her to face him, but she stayed stubbornly facing away. She wouldn't let him see the tears that glazed her eyes.

She pulled from his grasp, and he followed her into the cottage.

"The horses did fine," he said from behind in a matter-of-fact tone. "Get dressed, and we'll make for Welwyn. I'm starving."

Then he wasn't going to mention last night. Wasn't going to reassure her. Nothing.

When she heard the clink of coins hitting the table, she turned. "For the damage," he explained, indicating the door and the mess of congealed bread in the fireplace. "The owners will have to pay someone to fix it up, wash the bedclothes and all."

Pay someone? What kind of a man hired people to do his work for him? When something needed doing at Leslie, she or Da or Cameron did it themselves.

Still, leaving the money was so like Jason. He was a good man. Despite her uncertain feelings, she felt compelled to try to reach him one more time.

"I want to thank you," she started.

"For what?"

"Last night." She clutched the quilt tighter. "I'll never forget it."

"I won't forget it, either," he said. "But that doesn't make it right. It shouldn't have happened."

He regretted last night.

Robbed of breath, she turned toward her still-damp clothes, feeling his gaze on her naked back where it was revealed by the drape of the quilt. Bare skin she'd never thought a man would see. But she'd exposed more than skin to him—more than her back and her breasts and the rest of her body. She'd exposed her entire soul.

And he'd wrenched it right out of her.

FIFTY-THREE

*H*OURS LATER, somewhere between Highgate and Hampstead, Jason admitted to himself what he'd known for days and hadn't wanted to face: He'd fallen in love with Caithren Leslie.

He wasn't ready for this. He'd tried so hard to resist. Because he'd known all along that, with Cait, it would be all or nothing.

He'd wanted the distance he needed to keep his head clear and do what needed to be done. He had responsibilities. Urgent responsibilities: little Mary, her mother, the innocent man he'd killed. Gothard. Less urgent but nonetheless important responsibilities, such as seeing his sister settled.

Distance. Until last night—until he'd lost his head—he'd maintained it. This morning he'd attempted to recover it. A hopeless, disastrous attempt. But how could he share his feelings when so many responsibilities stood between him and the woman he wanted?

He wasn't ready.

But he knew he'd hurt her. His heart sinking, he took refuge beneath the shady cover of the trees overhead, thankful Cait couldn't see his face. Silently they rode past small houses with their shutters closed against the wind, like his mind had been closed to the truth. Cows and sheep in the fields turned as they passed, pinning him with liquid, accusing eyes. Two magpies mocked him from a tree.

He sneaked a glance in Caithren's direction. She looked pale, tired, on the edge of tears, her fingers white-knuckled on the reins. His fault.

Tonight he would leave her safe at his London town house while he took care of Geoffrey and Walter Gothard. Another responsibility —keeping Cait safe.

When the Gothards were behind bars, he'd help her find her brother. He'd tell her he believed everything she'd told him, and...

He'd ask her to marry him.

Though the mere thought pulled the breath from his body, quite suddenly he knew that nothing else would do but to keep her by his side forever. Never had he met anyone who could make him laugh and live like she did. His life before her seemed bleak in comparison.

Leslie was a baronetcy—Scottish or no, the match would be considered suitable. Not that he really cared; the Chases didn't go out of their way to placate society. His own brother had, with his blessing, wed a commoner.

Another glance at Cait tore at his heart. He didn't deserve her. He'd put her very life in danger, then compounded his sins by taking her, callously, with no thought to her pleasure or the words of commitment she had every right to expect from him. No wonder she was mired in gloom.

Soon he would give her everything she wanted, if only she'd give him the chance. He'd spend the rest of his life making it up to her—making her the happiest woman on earth.

In the aftermath of the storm, the road was disastrous, a muddy mess. The day's progress had been slow and aggravating. It seemed a lifetime before they made it to the tollhouse. A lifetime of torture. He would rather have submitted to the rack.

"We're in Hampstead," he told Caithren, hoping to cheer her up. "London is in reach."

"That's good." Her voice sounded weak.

He handed a coin to the tollkeeper and motioned Cait down the hill toward the heath. "Soon I'll be able to warn Scarborough," he said. "That will be a weight off both our minds, won't it?"

Though she nodded and forced a smile, he could see her jaw was tight.

The heath was wild land punctuated by weedy ponds—even slower going than the Great North Road. Narrow trodden paths wound through sprawling acres of wooded dells and fields of heather. Since they couldn't ride side by side, Jason took the lead.

"Could that be a real tree?" Wonder in her voice, Caithren uttered her first unsolicited words since they'd left the cottage that morning. "An elm, is it not? It's amazing."

The gigantic elm was perhaps ten yards around, with steps inside leading to a wooden platform that rose above the topmost leaves. He turned to see a smile on her face—a smile he'd been afraid he might never see again. His heart warmed. "Would you like to go up?"

For a moment she looked like she was seriously considering saying no. Then her eyes lit with determination. "Aye. I would like that very much. Will you come with me?"

He eyed the platform apprehensively. It looked sturdy, and the steps didn't look too daunting, housed as they were in the trunk of the tree.

"It's not so very far up," she coaxed. "Not nearly as high as that tower outside Stamford."

There was nothing he wouldn't do at this point to make her resent him a little less. "Very well," he said. "I'll be up in a moment." At her doubtful look, he added, "I mean it this time. Just let me secure the horses."

He tethered the animals to a nearby tree that was large yet dwarfed by the elm. Then he gritted his teeth and started up, mentally groaning when he saw the stairs were slatted instead of solid.

The first few steps weren't too bad, but then the staircase started spiraling inside the trunk, getting more and more narrow. *Look up,* he told himself, *look up.* Eyes on the goal, not the drop. His pulse skittered, his head whirled, the blood roared in his ears.

Halfway up, he paused to lean against the hollowed interior and close his eyes. When he opened them, his vision was blurry, and he shook his head to clear it. One foot in front of the other, one step at a time, and if he felt as though his dinner might come up, well, he'd just have to ignore that.

Given her head start, he was surprised when he caught up to her. She seemed to be expending quite an effort in the climb. Last night must have taken its toll on her. Another blade of guilt stabbed at his heart.

What kind of man took a woman in a thunderstorm?

She glanced back at him. "You look pale."

He blew out a breath and shrugged. His gaze on her back, he ordered his legs to stop shaking, and at last they made it to the platform.

"Forty-two steps," she announced. "By all the saints, will you look at that view!" She rushed to the rail, her gaze scanning from right to left and back again.

"Beautiful, isn't it?" he said. The platform looked as though it might hold about twenty people. Wiping sweaty palms on his breeches, he stayed in the exact center. "We're lucky to have a clear day. London's often mired in fog." His stomach did a flip-flop when she leaned over the rail. "Keep back, will you?"

"London is incredible. It's enormous! I've never seen so many buildings in one place."

The view stretched for miles and miles. From his spot behind her, he pointed out the ruins of St. Paul's Cathedral, destroyed in last year's Great Fire, and the hills of Kent south of the Thames.

"And what could that be?" Cait asked, indicating something much closer, in the shrubby area at the far end of the heath. She turned to him. "A reservoir? With horses and carriages driving right through it?"

"Whitestone Pond." Jason nodded at a large marker that sat near it. "Named for that old white milestone. King Henry the Eighth designed it to keep the City free of the countryside's mud. All horses and wheels pass through it on the way in from Hampstead." He laughed at her expression of disbelief. "We'll be doing so ourselves in a short while."

"It still looks a long way to London," she said quietly.

He frowned at her tight features. "Just an hour or so."

"I-I'm hurting, Jason." She dropped her gaze, plainly uncomfortable at the admission. "My arm," she explained. "I thought I could make it through the day, but..."

"Damn, and I didn't take you foraging for plants." Forgetting his dizziness, he moved closer and slung an arm around her shoulders.

He remembered her clenched hands and the stoic set of her jaw as they rode. "Was that why you were so quiet?"

She nodded miserably.

Though he'd thought her silence had meant she resented him, he was too guilty to feel relieved. "You cannot make it another hour?"

Clouded with pain, her eyes met his. "I don't know," she whispered. "All the day I've been—"

"London can wait," he decided, alarmed. Caithren was nothing if not strong and steady. "We'll ride back up the hill, to Spaniards Inn. You saw it, by the tollgate?"

She nodded again.

"It's not far at all." He swung her up into his arms, as one would carry a small child. "You're going to be fine."

"Jason!" Despite her distress, she giggled, making his heart lift a bit. "Put me down!"

"I'll hear none of it," he told her with mock sternness, starting down the steps and forcing himself to ignore the rush of vertigo. "We'll have you in a room in no time. Can you sit your own horse?"

"Of course I can. I rode all the day, did I not?" Warm laughter rang through the hollowed trunk, bringing him waves of relief.

But the feeling was short-lived once he looked down the steep, winding stairs.

There was nothing for it, he told himself sternly. One step after another, he ordered his feet to comply. With the drop looming before him, the way down was always worse than the way up. And doubly worse carrying Caithren, leaving no hand free to balance against the wall.

His breath came in embarrassingly short pants, and the arms that cradled her were shaking. Mercifully, she didn't comment on any of that or his lack of speed. "Put me down," she repeated quietly instead. "I'm not an invalid. I only wish to rest."

He didn't put her down, and somehow he made it to the bottom. He didn't have the luxury to let his knees buckle or to sit a spell and recover his composure. Silently congratulating himself, he perched her on her reddish mare and mounted his own black steed.

Afraid to jar her, he led her slowly back over the heath and up the hill to the white, weatherboarded inn. Securing a room seemed a process that took forever. And he knew that forever to him must have seemed forever and an eternity to her.

At last he closed the door of their oak-paneled room, and she dropped into a chair, white-faced.

"That bad?" he asked.

She put on a brave smile. "It hurts. But mostly because I'm so tired, I'm sure. I didn't sleep much last night." Color sprang to her cheeks as she doubtless remembered why. "We should have gone on to London. I'm sorry I made you stop."

He wasn't falling for her false bravado. "Let me have a look."

Without waiting for her agreement, he crouched before her and detached the tabs of her stomacher. As he began loosening the gown's laces, a flush came to her skin. Her heart sped up beneath his fingers, as clear an indicator of her desire as if she had told him outright. Despite his worry, answering need rushed through him.

Damnable, unconscionable need.

He clenched his teeth and forged ahead, carefully lowering the dress's bodice and the chemise underneath, helping her pull her arms from the sleeves. She pressed the gown to her chest with a hand and held out her injured limb.

All lust fled when he lifted the edge of the linen bandage and glimpsed what lay beneath. A soft moan escaped her lips.

"Holy heaven." Jason unwound the fabric as gently as he could. "I'm sorry."

"It's all right," Cait whispered. "I know you don't mean to hurt me."

He smiled a little, then grimaced as the wound was revealed. Not long, but deep. Deeper than he remembered and surrounded by angry, dark pink flesh. A drop of red blood seeped out when the bandage fell away, and he could see a sickening taint of white inside.

"I should have been checking on this." Yet another failure on his part.

"You wanted to last night—"

"It's getting infected."

She glanced down, then averted her gaze. "It looks very bad." He watched her jaw tighten with determination. "I'll be fine, Jason. Don't worry for me. It will heal. I'll make a poultice." Her face brightened. "So close to London, there might even be a shop. I can tell you what I need—"

"I imagine it hurts like hell." He rose and paced away, then turned back. "I'd best fetch a surgeon. I believe it should be stitched."

"Stitched?" Her pretty forehead wrinkled, making his gut twist with sympathy.

"It's getting worse rather than better." He stared at her colorless face. "The doctor will know for sure. Bloody hell, I'm sorry."

Cursing himself for messing up yet again, he went downstairs to send a man to find a surgeon.

FIFTY-FOUR

*J*ASON RETURNED a few minutes later with a goblet and handed it to Caithren. She sniffed at the contents suspiciously.

"What is it?"

"Whiskey."

"I thought as much." She handed it back. "Nay, but I thank you for the thought."

He frowned. "You don't like whiskey?"

"Have you seen me drink whiskey before now?"

"No, but…you're Scottish."

"And…?"

"It's whiskey, which the Scots invented if my—"

Caithren burst out laughing—until the movement pained her arm. "We don't all fancy whiskey, Jase. It's not a law. And here you accuse me of painting all the English with one brush." She watched him slowly turn red. "Some ale wouldn't be amiss—"

A sharp knock came at the door, and Jason went to answer it.

Cait felt the blood drain from her face as the surgeon marched in, a burly man clutching a bag of implements. But she told herself to be brave. She didn't want to embarrass herself before Jason.

He thought little enough of her as it was.

"I'm told of an injury," the surgeon said. "A slash wound, is it?"

"Aye." Clutching her bodice to her chest, she held forth her bare arm.

The surgeon came closer, yet gave it but a cursory glance. He looked to the goblet in Jason's hand. "What've you got there?"

"Whiskey." Jason's voice sounded weak to Cait's ears. Or maybe the blood pounding in her head was muffling the sound. "Here," he said more clearly and offered the goblet to the doctor.

The man took it and downed a healthy gulp. "Decent stuff," he declared, then poured a thick stream over Caithren's wound.

Her breath hissed in, but she wouldn't cry. She'd shed the last tears she would in front of Jason.

"Wh-what did you do that for?" she managed to stutter.

"To cleanse it. Stop infection."

"What?" It stung like blazes. "My cousin Cam would skin you alive if he saw you wasting good whiskey like that. Give it here." She snatched the goblet from the surgeon's hand and gulped greedily, feeling the liquor burn a hot path down her gullet and into her empty stomach.

Jason appeared to be holding back a laugh. A dark glare took care of that. "I have always practiced gentle healing," she told him. "I cannot believe he did that."

She sipped again. The stuff wasn't nearly as nasty as she'd thought.

"It's not unheard of, sweet. Ford did the same for my bullet wound, and he's no surgeon, though he does fancy himself a scientist."

"Ford?" She drank again. The warmth in her stomach was spreading, and her arm seemed to hurt less. Her head was beginning to feel as though it might detach itself and float away.

"My youngest brother, Ford." Jason crouched down and gazed into her eyes. A tiny smile emerged on his face. "Never mind."

He stood and motioned the surgeon closer.

She sipped once more, then set her jaw and angled her arm out. "Have at it," she declared.

The man rummaged in his bag and came out with a needle and black thread.

Caithren winced and looked up at Jason. "Are you sure he has to do this?"

"I'm sure. Drink." He shoved the goblet closer to her lips, and she complied. "It won't take long."

She nodded and steeled herself for the pain. When it came, a sharp prick and a scraping sting as the raw edges of flesh were bound together, it wasn't as bad as she'd anticipated. Not nearly as hurtful as when the surgeon had doused her arm with the whiskey. Or maybe the whiskey had numbed it some.

Jason put a hand on her good shoulder. "You're doing fine." His voice sounded proud, or maybe impressed. It made the whiskey curl warmer in her belly. It seemed all she wanted was his trust, his approval.

Nay, not all, not if she were to be honest with herself. She also craved his arms around her, his lips on hers.

His love.

Everything—her whole world—seemed so confused. When had her goals changed? Where had this yearning come from, and why was it so overwhelming?

She didn't know. She knew only that it was wrong—wrong for her, for her plans, for her life. She belonged at home with Cameron, tending their land, their heritage. Not far away in England with this exasperating man.

Her thoughts turned to Jason more every day...her thoughts and her heart. But staying with him was impossible. Even if Jason wanted her, it would be impossible. And he didn't want her, which should have made it easier. But it didn't make it easier; it made it worse.

Much, much worse.

The hated tears flooded her eyes, and one rolled warm down her cheek. She dashed it away with her good hand.

"Nearly there," Jason soothed, stroking her hair. "He's almost finished."

She felt another jab and tug on her arm, and the tears flowed faster. Not from the pain, though...

Oh, aye, from the pain. The pain that weighed heavy as a brick in her chest. The pain in her heart.

It wasn't long at all before the surgeon knotted the thread and cut it with a knife. He tied a bandage around her arm to protect his handiwork. Then, mindful of his patient's distress, he collected his things quietly and went to Jason. "Go to Hampstead Wells and ask to see Dorothy Pippen. She sells medicinal water."

"My thanks." Jason pressed a few coins into the surgeon's hand and followed him to the door, closing it softly behind him. Cait put her arms back in her sleeves and tightened her laces.

"There." Jason came close and patted her shoulder. "It wasn't so bad, after all, was it? And now it's done."

She shook off his hand. She couldn't bear his touch. Not when she knew they'd reach London tomorrow and go their separate ways, with no regret on his part. Only pride, she imagined, that he'd kept her where he wanted her, ensuring his successful, unimpeded capture and murder of Geoffrey Gothard.

Oh, it was not to be borne! Despite a heroic effort to rein in her emotions, she rose and wandered away in tears. Her hand went into her pocket and found the miniature of her brother.

She pulled it out and stared at it, drifting to the window, where she could see the picture better in the failing light. Her thumb caressed the glass that protected Adam's familiar face.

Adam. Where was he? Though Lord Darnley's wedding wasn't until Friday, Adam might well be in London by now. Maybe she would find him tomorrow, and when she saw him, her world would be set to rights. Her plans would be back on track, and she wouldn't feel as though her life were so out of control.

Adam. Dear, familiar Adam. She gazed at his oval face, his wheaten hair, his hazel eyes. All just like hers. The foppish outfit he'd posed in, all velvet and ribbons and snowy linen, brought a smile through the tears. So unlike herself and Da, but typical Adam.

"Adam," she said softly.

"Who is that?" Jason asked from behind her.

"Adam," she said louder, feeling better just saying her brother's name. She had a goal—a worthy goal—and at last it was within reach. So close. "Adam. My brother."

When she turned to look at Jason, his face was whiter than the lace on Adam's cravat.

"What is it, Jase?" She'd never known a man to faint, but he looked as though he might keel over at any second. "Is something amiss?"

"Yes." He blinked and shook his head. "No. No." He drew a long breath, and his lips curved in a forced smile. "You're tired. Let me go downstairs and fetch some supper. Then I'll pay Dorothy Pippen a visit and get you the water."

Cait's hand went to her amulet. "I don't need special water. And I'm not hungry. Just stay with me, all right?"

His gaze skittered away. "I must at least make some inquiries and see if I can find out where we need to go tomorrow. Where Scarborough lives, I mean." He made as though to reach for her, then pulled back. "Sleep well. I'll be up later." With a distracted kiss to her forehead, he left her to go to bed.

Alone and reeling.

FIFTY-FIVE

*G*ASPING, HE *checked his momentum, but not in time. His silver blade flashed, sliced in, sending a shiver up his arm. The man before him crumpled to the ground, his lifeblood pumping into the dirt. His eyes stared unseeing at Jason... hazel eyes... Emerald's hazel eyes... Caithren's hazel eyes...*

Caithren's brother's hazel eyes.

His heart racing, Jason let out an anguished yell as he awakened. He curled up on the bed. His breath heaved. He couldn't recall what he'd eaten for supper, but it felt like it were about to come back up.

"Jason?" Caithren leaned over him, patting his shoulder uncertainly.

He moaned. His head pounded from overdrinking last night—something he *never* did—and a frustrated dampness squeezed from beneath his clenched eyelids.

Dear God in heaven, he'd killed her brother.

She would never accept him, never love him, never stay with him, never marry him. As though killing an innocent man hadn't tainted him enough, the man had been *her brother*.

With all his might, he wished she'd really been Emerald. He would still love every stubborn inch of her, and he might have a chance with Emerald. Emerald would understand the driving need for justice that had turned him into another man. Emerald would understand the way killing, even unintentional killing, changed a person.

But Caithren...sweet, unspoiled Caithren...

She wouldn't.

And he'd killed her brother. *Her brother.* How could he expect her to forgive him, when he couldn't even forgive himself?

He couldn't tell her the truth.

He *had* to tell her the truth.

"Jason?" Her hand jiggled his shoulder, spiking the pain in his head. Not that he didn't deserve it. Slowly he rolled over and gazed up at her.

"Was it the nightmare again?"

He nodded.

Her lovely eyes filled with compassion. "It will go away when you know who he was."

"I—"

He broke off. Words simply failed him. He needed to tell her...

But how?

Unaware of his anguish, she leaned closer. Her sweet breath felt heavenly, washing over him through parted lips. Clearly concerned, she leaned closer still. Her mouth was close, so close.

Resolve melted, and he closed the distance and met her lips with his, kissing her desperately. She flung herself against him. A low moan vibrated in her throat as she deepened the kiss, inviting him in to explore her velvet warmth.

Sweet Mary, she wanted him—he could feel her need pumping into him. His arms moved to enclose her, to crush her against him—

No, he couldn't do this. Not this time, not this way.

His hands fisted against her back. If he was going to accept the comfort of her body, the least he could do was slow down, show her the tenderness he'd failed to the first time. Keep his head. Protect her injured arm.

Protect his injured heart.

That heart pounding, he pulled back.

He needed to tell her.

He couldn't tell her.

Not telling her was a lie.

Though he knew he'd be damned to hell for the lie, not to

mention for taking her—*again*, when he knew the truth—he couldn't seem to help himself. Just this once, before she discovered what he'd done—what kind of man he was—he would worship her. With his hands, his mouth, his body, he would make her his, make her happy, if only for tonight.

FIFTY-SIX

*C*AIT KNEW THE moment he gave in.

His hands relaxed and pulled her close, bringing her mouth to his again. His kiss wasn't frenzied or hesitant—instead it was sweetly cherishing. It seemed as though the whole of his attention was focused on that kiss, as if, for that moment, nothing else existed in his world.

The sheer intensity frightened her. She'd wanted the chance to see if the passion of that stormy night was repeatable, but now she was afraid to learn the answer.

If it were *yes*...how would she ever find it in herself to leave him?

Not that he would ask her to stay.

The truth brought a pang to her heart. But then he rolled and took her with him, and she ended up on her back with him gazing down at her, his eyes deep green in the hazy dawn light.

She wrapped her arms around him, and he kissed her again, his tongue sweeping her mouth. She found herself a melting mass of sensation, a puddle on the mattress for him to do with as he would. But still he only kissed her, a kiss that drugged, a kiss that precluded all thought.

When he came up for air, that frisson of fear returned. She wasn't having second thoughts—never that—but intentionally loving him in a bed in the morning was so different than impulsively on a rain-swept night. A surrender of sorts, and a huge leap of trust, but she was willing to take it. She could only hope the cliff didn't prove to be too high.

Jason's hands went to the tie at her neck, attempting to loosen the nightgown's high ruffle. He only succeeded in knotting the bow. "I thought we were going to burn this," he complained, the words tainted with frustration.

"Here, let me do it." Her heart pounded while her fingers worked at the tangle. "I thought you were an expert at removing female clothes."

"Not nightgowns. I don't believe I've ever removed a nightgowns. Off-putting garments, nightgowns. Mrs. Twentyman's in particular."

Impatient, he moved to help, but she pushed his hands away.

"Wait," she said with a choked giggle. "You'll only make it harder."

"Harder." In the gray shadows she saw his jaw tense. "It's absolutely harder," he said, sounding husky and breathless.

"Nay, it's easy now." Her own voice shook, betraying her anxiety. "It's nearly undone."

"That's not what I meant, Cait." Taking her hand, he moved it down to the bulge in his breeches.

"Oh." She seemed unable to breathe properly. "Oh, my. It *is* hard. How very interesting." Exploring, she forgot she'd managed to untie the nightgown's ruffle until she heard his moan and felt his lips nibbling her throat. "Oh, Jase." Her fingers tightened, surrounding him.

"I think…" His muffled words tickled the hollow of her neck. "Not that it doesn't feel good, but I think…I think you'd best touch me elsewhere now." Lifting his head, he reached for her hand. "*Now.*"

His eyes looked rather frantic, so she reluctantly released him. "Interesting," she said again, arching in delight when his lips went back to her throat.

"Interesting?" The question vibrated right into her.

This sweet, melting seduction wasn't anything like last time, nor was it—or Jason—anything like the animals she'd observed around Leslie. "Well, now, I've seen a horse's, you know, but I've never felt—"

"A horse's?" On a choked laugh, Jason's head came up. "I've never been compared to a horse, but I thank you for the compliment. I think. Then you've seen horses, ah...?" His busy mouth went back to work, making a shiver run through her.

"Oh, aye. But our first time, well...it didn't work the same way, did it?" Her hands played restlessly in his hair. "Of course I knew it wouldn't, because Cam told me people do it face to face. I can see why. The kissing is nice."

"Mmm, nice." Settling his mouth on hers again, he kissed her long and deep, as though to prove it.

By the time he raised his head, her senses were spinning.

"Yes, nice," he repeated with a grin. One hand wandered down her body, leaving a fiery trail in its wake.

"H-have I told you that Cameron and I are breeding horses? Highland ponies." Breathless, she sucked in some air. "Lately we've been crossing them with Spanish stock, in an effort to—"

"Are you nervous, Cait?" He spread the nightgown's neckline wider and kissed each of her sensitive breasts.

She was going to die. She was going to die right there. "Maybe." An understatement. "A wee bit." A bigger understatement.

His head came up again. "Has anyone ever told you that you babble when you're nervous?"

"Cameron." Through the nightgown, his fingers lazily traced the line where her legs met, inciting a tingling current of desire. Trailing her hands down his back, she found the bottom edge of his untucked shirt and worked her way underneath it. The skin on his back felt hot. "But I don't think I've ever been quite this, um... nervous with Cam."

"I'm glad to hear it," he said dryly. "Let's get rid of this, shall we?"

He sat and tugged on the hem of the nightgown, but the yards and yards of it only got hopelessly tangled. With a shaky giggle, she rose to her knees to help him struggle her out of it.

"You're supposed to take this seriously," he said, pulling handfuls of the fabric up to blind her.

"Am I?" She gasped when cold air hit her middle, her face completely swathed in white wool. "This entire act is rather absurd, if you think on it."

"Then don't think."

As though she could. Her breasts were bared now, and she still couldn't see a thing.

But she heard his sharp intake of breath. "Good heavens. You're perfect."

She shoved the nightgown off her head, blinking in the brightening morning light. The hunger in his eyes made her blush. "Am I not scrawny?" she asked, tugging the quilt up to cover her body. "You keep telling me I don't eat enough."

"You're perfect," he repeated, sweeping the quilt right off the bed.

Speechless, she could only gasp again.

"I was wrong," he added with a wicked grin. "Besides, I so enjoy your leftovers." While she was still tongue-tied, his hands reached out and fitted themselves to her breasts, which she'd always thought were too small. "Perfect," he breathed, closing his eyes momentarily.

She fell back to the pillows, weak with shock. Or something. "This isn't fair."

"No?" His eyes opened and ravenously roamed her body.

She blushed and folded her arms across her breasts. "You should be in the scud, too."

"In due time," he said, moving closer.

"Now."

"Has anyone ever told you you're demanding?"

"Aye." Her hands went to loosen the laces on his shirt. "I'm demanding, and I blether when I'm nervous, and I'm impulsive."

"And you talk too much."

When he kissed her, her fingers faltered. "But I'm perfect," she reminded him.

He nodded solemnly. "Yes, you're perfect."

With a single lithe motion, he stood and pulled the shirt over his head, then made short work of divesting himself of his breeches. Cait swallowed hard, thinking he was perfect, too. Like the drawing she'd seen of Michelangelo's *David* in one of Adam's schoolbooks. She'd spent hours studying that picture, but she never thought she'd see it come to life.

When he came down on top of her, skin to skin, she sighed loudly in contentment.

Supporting himself on his elbows, he hovered over her. "Now, will you just hush up?"

"Oh, aye," she breathed as his mouth closed over hers. Slow and deep, the kiss left her dizzy when he broke contact. His dark head bent, and his clever mouth moved over a breast, wet and warm and tingling.

"Oh, Jase. I never knew...do all men do this?"

She felt his chuckle. "I cannot speak for all men."

"This is t-taking much longer than horses." She sucked in a breath. "Generally, the male horse bites the female on the neck—"

"Like this?" His mouth trailed up and demonstrated.

She arched in shock and pleasure. "Aye. But...go back to the other."

A low laugh filled the dim room as he lightly bit a nipple. "You like this, do you?"

"Aye, very much." Excitement surged through her when he began suckling away the bite. "But horses accomplish this much faster, aye? It's all over in a matter of minutes, like the first time we—"

When his mouth left her, she wanted to smack herself for blethering.

"We aren't horses," he said low. "And this isn't the first time." A hand skimmed down her body, tracing a sensuous path. "It's another time, another place."

Aye, it was different than last time, but no less glorious. Just different.

"I see what you mean." She squirmed and bit her lip to keep from crying out her pleasure. "I-I've never been in this place before."

"Did I not ask you to be quiet?" he murmured. His mouth started following his hand, trailing little wet kisses down her body. When his tongue swept into her navel, a stab of hot desire arced from there to deep inside. She clenched her teeth, her hands fisting in his hair.

She wouldn't say anything more, not even if—

"Oh, Jase!" His lips were tracing her hipbones and down to her thighs. Warm, oh so warm, and teasingly tender, making shivers ripple through her. "I think no horse has ever done this."

Apparently he was finished dignifying her inane comments with responses. His fingers and mouth roamed her body for long, intimate minutes. Her pulse raced faster and faster, until she feared that she might scream. As he coaxed her legs apart, her fingers clutched at his hair, his shoulders, the sheets.

He cupped her with a hand. And stilled.

Matched by her own, his breath sounded harsh in the suddenly quiet room.

She felt an incredible urgency beneath his fingers.

She waited, and waited, and waited...and when at last his hand started moving, she arched off the bed. Slowly he stroked, ever so slowly and for ever so long. Something was building inside her. Just when she thought she might explode from the pleasure, he slipped a finger inside her body.

"By. All. The. Saints." Astonished, she felt herself pulsing around it. "I—I think," she whispered, "I...think no horse has ever done this, either."

His finger retreated, a slide of exquisite sensation, then plunged deep. Again. Another finger joined the first, and the pleasure built unbearably. She called out his name and clutched at his head and shoulders, the only parts of him she could reach.

"Now," she whispered, begging him to move up and over her, craving his mouth on hers, wanting him inside her. "Please, now."

He answered with but a tiny shake of his head before he drifted down—not up, but down. And his mouth closed over her, impossibly hot, impossibly soft, impossibly thrilling.

"Oh, Jase!" She clutched at air, unable to reach him anywhere. She clutched at the sheets. Her eyes drifted closed as she clutched her emerald and hung on tight, trembling uncontrollably, feeling she might explode.

"I'm—quite—certain," she said in short, hard pants, "a horse—has never—done *this*." She meant also to ask what made him think of such a thing, but then she did explode, into a million wee pieces.

After what seemed an eternity, somehow the pieces all came back together. She found herself shuddering, gasping for breath.

His mouth curved in an erotic, heart-wrenching smile, he crawled up to meet her and put two fingers to her lips. "Hush now, sweet Cait."

And she did, not only because his mouth claimed hers. She

didn't think she could force another word out even if she wanted to. She had no breath left in her lungs.

Tenderly his hands stroked her, calming her...

Except it wasn't calming—the excitement was building all over again.

"Not again," she whispered.

"I said hush."

Over the next space of time, there wasn't a spot on her body he didn't kiss or touch or tease into awareness.

His spicy male scent was intoxicating. Her hands wandered all over him, learning the contours of his muscles beneath his warm skin. His low groans echoed her own mews of pleasure, but his movements remained controlled, agonizingly slow, skillfully bringing her to a fever pitch of passion.

When she reached down, he stilled her hand. "Hush, sweet Cait," he whispered. "This time is for you."

"There must be a way to make you feel—"

"Hush." The kiss he quieted her with was so exquisite, it brought tears to her eyes.

The wanting built and built, until she quivered and cried out, and at last he moved over her and slid inside. Wrapping her legs around him, she arched up, taking him deep...deeper, wishing she could hold him captive.

Wishing she could keep him forever.

He held still for a beat...two...three. Then, "Sweet Cait," he murmured, and began rocking against her, slowly at first, then faster. She'd never thought to feel so close to another, as though they were one and the same. She met each stroke in blissful harmony, her entire body pulsing, clutching him with her hands and her legs, with her arms and her heart. Emotions rose within her, overwhelming her body and soul, pushing her up, up...

"Nay." It was too much, too soon—she couldn't stand it. "Not again."

He lifted his head. "Again," he said, his rhythm below punctuating his words. "Fall for me, sweet Cait."

And she did.

"Oh, Jase!" She plunged over the edge, falling faster when she felt him go with her. The cliff was high, but her landing was soft, cushioned by the man she loved.

They lay still for a long, satisfying minute before he rolled to his side, taking her with him. She cuddled close as she fought to catch her breath.

Like the last time, he'd pulled out at the critical moment. Responsible Jason. It made her a wee bit sad, although she knew she ought to be grateful. Being impulsive and independent was one thing, going home with a bairn in her womb quite another.

But she didn't want to think about going home.

He kissed her on the forehead. "Your arm?"

"It's fine. I forgot all about it." She drew back enough to smile into his clear green eyes. "You made me lose my head."

"Not only that, I almost got you to stop talking." He grinned, then groaned as his gaze wandered to the now-bright window. "We'd best grab some breakfast and ride into London to warn Scarborough."

"Aye," she agreed on a sigh. "I hope I can walk. I feel weak as a day-old bairn."

"Before you try to stand, say it again." Smoothing the hair off her face, he kissed her softly. "My name."

She frowned. "Jason?"

"The other."

"Oh." Feeling her heart swell, she raised herself to meet his lips. "Jase."

"It sounds right from you, sweet Cait," he said before his mouth covered hers.

FIFTY-SEVEN

"NUMBER TWELVE. Is that it?" Two hours later Caithren indicated a brand new three-story house at the edge of St. James's Fields. "Crivvens, but Scarborough lives well. No wonder Adam aims to be his friend."

Adam. The man's name made Jason's gut twist. Swallowing hard, he helped Cait down—mindful of her arm—and tethered their horses.

"Someone else is here," she said as they started up the gravel drive. "Or rather, leaving."

A fat-bellied gentleman with an unfashionable brown beard turned from the town house's front door and headed down the steps. Jason nodded at him, but the man didn't acknowledge the gesture, avoiding his gaze as they passed.

"Who do you suppose that was?" Jason muttered as the man hurried away.

Cait shrugged. "Why does it matter?"

"I don't know. Just a feeling." The same niggling feeling he'd had when the Gothards were close by. Shaking it off, he led Cait up to the tall, imposing door.

Their knock brought an aging maidservant to answer. She bobbed a curtsy, her gray curls bouncing beneath a dainty white lace cap. "My lord?"

"I've a matter to discuss with Lord Scarborough. Of some

urgency."

"Cuds bobs, you're the second in as many minutes. As I told the other gentleman, Lord Scarborough has left town. He's expected back just in time to attend Lord Darnley's wedding tomorrow."

"That's where Adam will be!" Caithren said excitedly.

Frowning, Jason waved her off. "Who was the other man?"

"I don't rightly know," the maid said. "He didn't introduce himself."

The niggle returned. "Could he have been Geoffrey Gothard?"

Caithren made a sound suspiciously like a snort, and the maid-servant let out a short bark of a laugh before composing herself. "Not hardly. You wouldn't be asking that if you'd seen him." She brushed at her apron. "Mr. Gothard won't be showing his face around here, in any case. Not if Lord Scarborough has any say in the matter."

"He won't be showing his face," Jason repeated under his breath. The man hadn't looked *him* in the face, either. "Have you an address to reach Lord Scarborough?"

"No, my lord, we do not. Lord Scarborough will be here tomorrow. That is all I have to tell you."

"I sent him a very important letter last week." His arm stole around Cait's waist. Had it been but a week since he'd met her? Eight or nine days, if he was remembering right, but it felt like a lifetime had passed. "Might you know if Lord Scarborough received it?"

The older woman's expression was implacable. "I'm not privy to Lord Scarborough's personal matters. And his secretary went with him."

Knowing he'd get no more out of her, he sighed. "I thank you."

"My lord." With a curtsy, she shut the door in their faces.

Dejected, he stood there a minute, then turned with Cait to head back to their borrowed horses.

"I wonder if the other man learned more," she said.

"He could hardly have learned less. But I cannot shed the feeling that man might have been Gothard, or maybe Wat, or—"

"Have you eyes in your head?" A giggle burst out of her. "It wasn't Geoffrey or Wat."

"It could have been someone they hired."

"It could have been anyone. Do you know many of Lord Scarborough's acquaintances?"

"None," he admitted.

"Then it could have been a friend. Or a merchant. Or a solicitor. And even if it were someone the Gothards hired, you just said the man didn't learn any more than we did."

He nodded thoughtfully. "Judging from that maidservant's attitude, neither will anyone else."

"True enough. Which means no one will learn where to find Scarborough today, any more than we have a clue where to find Geoffrey Gothard."

Maybe she was right. Sometimes a niggle was only a niggle. "Well, I hope Scarborough got my letter, in which case he's already been warned. But on the chance he didn't, I'll come by here again tomorrow."

"We can do it on the way to the wedding." Toward the end of the gravel drive, her feet slowed, then stopped. "If you're willing to take me, that is? Of course, I could go on my own, but..."

A wave of guilt washed over him. "I'm willing to take you anywhere," he said quietly, coming around to face her.

She had no reason to attend the wedding, and he needed to tell her that. His moment of reckoning couldn't be postponed much longer.

Scarborough's red-brick town house loomed behind her, reminding him that he'd be taking her to his own town house next —and then she'd discover the truth. How much longer could he hold her heart? Before she could see the trepidation in his eyes, he gathered her close and lowered his lips to meet hers.

An adorable little sound escaped her throat. Her mouth opened beneath his, and they kissed for a long, melting minute. A kiss of desperation, a kiss of unguarded lust. A kiss so sweet it made him ache, knowing it might be their last kiss ever. Knowing he had to hurt her.

Their time was at an end. He had to explain that her beloved brother was dead and why—shattering all her new and tentative feelings for him. It would break her heart.

It would break them both.

One more night. Despair made him grasp at the thought—he could shield her heart for one last night. A day remained, a night, before her brother was expected in town.

It would be the most bittersweet night of his life, but for her it would be the most magical. He would make it so, no matter the cost to his soul. Before he confessed the truth and broke her heart, he would give her one night to remember him by.

He broke the kiss. "Cait, I..."

"Hmm?" Her eyes were a glazey blue. What shone from their depths was such loving trust...

A weight settled in his chest.

The time had arrived to come clean with it all. Part of the truth she would learn today, and the rest—the painful part—in the morning.

With effort, he mustered a grin. "As I said, sweet, I'd love to take you anywhere. Would you like to attend a ball tonight?"

Her face brightened with a spark of excitement. "A ball? A London ball? I never thought..." Her eyes narrowed. "How do you know there's a ball tonight?"

"There's a ball in London every night," he said dryly.

"And you can gain entrance?"

Her skepticism prompted a smile. "I think I can manage to get us in."

"Aye," she said so slowly he could almost see the gears turning in her head. Her gaze swept over what she doubtless considered his nobleman's costume. "That maidservant assumed you were a lord. You're a master of disguises," she proclaimed with a grin. "It would be a grand adventure. An *impulsive*, grand adventure. Am I making you impulsive, Jase?" Her eyes sparkled turquoise, the shade he'd decided meant she was happy.

If only he could keep her so.

"And Adam might be at a ball. He must be in town already." Glancing down at her now-bedraggled gown, she lost some of the sparkle. "I've nothing clean enough to wear."

"My sister keeps gowns at our town house. One of them should fit you well enough."

"You have a town house?" Her eyes clouded with confusion. "But—"

He distracted her with a big, smacking kiss, then took her by the hand. "Yes, I have a house here in town. Come along, and I'll show you."

FIFTY-EIGHT

"I'VE NEVER seen so many people!" As Caithren and Jason jostled their horses through the teeming streets, she found herself astonished at the city called London. It seemed to sprawl forever, building after building crammed together. The streets were clogged with animals, vehicles, and pedestrians. Gaudy signboards hung overhead from heavy wrought-iron brackets, appearing to block the air and the sun.

"London stinks," she added. "And it's so noisy!"

Street vendors cried their wares from every corner and in between, making mundane goods like matches, rat poison, and razors sound colorful and exciting. Customers clustered to purchase eatables and drinkables of every sort from the criers' laden barrows. In a span of less than a minute, Cait's ears were assaulted with invitations to buy hot eels, pickled whelks, asses' milk, and a singing bird. In the midst of the deafening hubbub, performers danced on stilts to the beat of tambourines.

Above it all, she heard a man singing lustily to a gathering. Dazed, she stopped to listen. "What is he doing?" she asked when Jason noticed she was missing and rode back to her.

"Teaching them new tunes. He's a ballad seller." A carriage squeezed by, nudging his horse up against hers. "When he's finished, they'll buy sheets with the words for half a pence."

Caithren was amazed. Songs were old, passed down through the generations. She couldn't remember ever hearing a *new* song. "What if they cannot read?"

"Then they'll memorize the words. Running patterers sing news ballads to report murders and executions. But this fellow is selling the latest popular songs."

A flower girl strolled by with a basket over one arm, reciting a list of her posies in singsong rhyme. Bewildered, Cait shook her head. "How can anyone think in this city, with this din? Does anyone get anything done?"

Jason laughed, and they rode on, weaving through the tumult. She followed him around a corner and onto a street bordering a busy parkland. When he stopped before a large, four-story brick house, she was confused. "Is he tired?"

"Who?"

"Hamish. Your horse. Why are we stopping?" Looking around, she glimpsed a vendor hawking fat brown sausages in the grassy square across the street. "Oh, of course. You're hungry."

Jason laughed again. "We had breakfast not two hours ago." He slid off his horse and lifted his arms to help Caithren down from hers. "No, I'm not hungry." His hands still resting lightly at her waist, he took a deep breath. "I...have something to explain to you."

She stared up at him. "Aye?"

Releasing her, he swept the red wig off his head and finger-combed his hair. "I've been less than completely honest with you, and—"

At the same time a liveried stableman rounded the corner to take their horses, one of the brick home's double front doors swung open. A tall, thin butler poked his nose out. "Lord Cainewood—what a surprise."

He couldn't possibly be as surprised as Caithren was when Jason answered to the name. "Yes, Goodwin, I've found myself in town for a few days. I apologize for failing to send word."

"No problem a'tall, my lord." The butler eyed Cait with interest. "And the lady—"

"The lady will be lodging here as well."

"Jason?" she whispered.

Jason was...a *lord*?

And *this* was his town house?

She'd fully expected his "town house" would turn out to be a garret in a questionable neighborhood. This house had several garrets of its own. Both tall and wide, its face was divided by columns and studded with big rectangular windows, each crowned with a triangular pediment.

Her mind reeled.

Goodwin held the door open wide, and Jason ushered her inside. She stopped dead on the threshold, staring at the home's interior. The enormous windows made it lighter inside than any house she'd ever seen. Carved flowers and ribbons festooned the pale painted plaster walls. A wide staircase curved gracefully up to the next floor.

She turned to Jason. "What kind of a lord are you? A prince?"

"Nothing so exalted." He offered her an apologetic smile. "A marquess."

She blinked, trying to absorb it all. Her legs felt shaky. "You'll excuse me if I need to sit for a moment." Spotting a pair of brocade chairs in the entry, she made her way over and lowered herself to one of them.

A marquess. Her head spun at the mere thought. She certainly couldn't picture her very-Scottish self the object of an English marquess's love. Not that Jason—Lord Whoever—would ever really love her. The blasted man didn't believe a word she said.

She looked over at him, struggling to focus her eyes. The room seemed too bright. "Who are you? The Marquess of What?"

"Cainewood. A castle and lands down south." He set the wig on a small gilt and marble table. "I told you about it, remember?"

The butler discreetly disappeared while Caithren digested the information. And here she'd made fun of Jason *pretending* to be an aristocrat. Well, he'd deserved it then, didn't he?

"I live in a castle as well," she said, lifting her chin. "And my father was a baronet."

"I know. You've told me."

"You believe me, then?"

He shrugged, a telltale red staining his face.

She wasn't going to feel sympathy for his predicament. To the contrary, she felt like lashing out with her claws bared. "Well, I've always told you the truth. Which is more than I can say for you."

"I never told you anything that wasn't true." He moved close and put a hand on her shoulder, his green eyes begging her to understand. "I just—left out some details."

"Details?" She pinned him with her best disdainful look. "That's got to be the most glaring understatement I've ever heard." She closed her eyes, put her fingers to her forehead, then opened them again and looked up at him. "My mam always said that credit lost is akin to broken glass."

"Pardon?" His jaw tense, he stared at the toes of his black boots. "I understand the words, for once, but the meaning eludes—"

"Broken trust can never be restored."

"Cait..." He went down on a knee before her, and she almost —*almost*—felt sorry for him.

But she felt too betrayed. "With all the deception we've had between us—"

Glimpsing something over her shoulder, he stood and pulled away. She looked up and back to see a man and a woman trooping down the stairs.

"Jason!" the female exclaimed. She ran down the last few steps and threw herself into his arms, hugging and kissing him enthusiastically. "Are you healing well, then? Any news on the Gothards? My heavens"—she touched his face—"what happened to your hair and your mustache?"

"Let me guess," Caithren said dryly, rising from the chair. "Your wife."

She wouldn't put it past him, no matter he'd taken her to his bed. The woman was petite and prettier than she was, with dark red hair and a fine complexion.

"Not my wife," Jason said. "Rather my sister, Kendra. And my brother, Ford." He gestured toward the tall gentleman. Ford had long, wavy brown hair and the bluest eyes she'd ever seen. "Ford, Kendra, this is Caithren Leslie."

"Caithren, is it?" Kendra said with a wide smile. "Familiar, aren't we?"

Cait curtsied, but Kendra rushed forward and kissed her on both cheeks. "Welcome to our home. Where did you find her, Jason? Are you two in love?"

"Kendra—"

"You misunderstand, Lady Kendra," Cait broke in. "I'm only traveling with your brother due to...unfortunate circumstances."

"You're Scottish," Kendra said. "I can hear it in your voice."

"Aye, and—"

"Scottish?" Ford interrupted. He examined her with keen interest, his gaze settling on her amulet. "Might you go by the nickname of Emerald?"

"Nay," Cait said firmly. "My name is Caithren." She turned to glare at Jason, half-expecting him to defend his brother. "Not Emerald."

"Emerald?" Kendra scoffed. "As in Emerald MacCallum? Look at her, will you? Does she *look* like she chases outlaws?" She put a hand on Cait's arm. "Men can be so thick-headed at times. I apologize for my twin. He is more thick-headed than most."

Cait's lips thinned. "No more than Jase."

"Jase?" Kendra looked to him. "You allow her to call you Jase? Now I *know* you're in love."

Cait blushed so wildly, she could only hope the color would wear off by evening.

But Jason ignored Kendra's cheeky comment. "What are you doing here?" he asked her.

Ford sighed. "I'm sorry to say I've yet to discover the name of the man you...er..."

"Killed," Jason supplied succinctly.

"Um, yes. But I turned Chichester upside down and found a tavern the man had frequented along with two companions. A serving maid overheard the men saying they were going to Lord Darnley's wedding. Tomorrow, is it not? So we ought to be able to find them there and—say, are you all right?"

"I'm fine," Jason said woodenly, though nothing could be further from the truth. Tomorrow Cait would learn he'd killed her brother, whether he told her or not.

He should have confessed the minute he'd realized the truth—surely his soul would be the better for it now. But he'd promised her a night to remember, and he wouldn't ruin it for her just to ease his own anguish.

She'd have her evening of happiness before their world collapsed.

"I thank you for making the inquires," he told Ford. "Excellent work."

"And what of Gothard?" Ford asked.

"Still unresolved. It's a long tale, best discussed over dinner." He turned to his sister. "How fares Mary? Is she..."

"Dead? No." Kendra grinned. "The doctor says it's a miracle. She's getting better."

"Better?" A rush of hope coursed through him. "She awakened?"

"Yes. Her speech is slow, and she couldn't walk at first; she has trouble walking still. But every day she improves a little. We don't know if she'll ever—"

"She's alive." Jason made his way to the chair Cait had vacated and dropped onto it. "That's all that matters."

Kendra walked over and took his limp hands from his lap. "You feel a responsibility for her, I know. But it wasn't your fault."

"He feels a responsibility for everything." Cait crossed her arms. "I've been trying to cure him of that, to no avail."

"A worthy project." Kendra dropped Jason's hands and went to Cait, a conspiratorial gleam in her eye. "Have you managed to get him to do anything just for the hell of it? Rather than to accomplish some specific goal?"

"Well, we did chase a ghost. And—"

"Cait," Jason groaned.

"We went to a fair, but that was to buy me some things. And—oh!" She grinned. "He danced with the Gypsies, though not for long."

"He danced with the Gypsies?" A flash of curiosity crossed Kendra's face. "I will need to hear more of this."

Jason rose. "Cait doesn't have time to gossip with you. We have plans. Kendra, there must be a ball this evening?"

"Lady Carsington's annual affair." She regarded him with puzzled light green eyes. "But why would you want to know that?"

"Lady Carsington's balls are boring," Ford put in.

"They are not," Kendra argued. "And I've heard Charles will be in attendance this eve. But why?" she repeated.

"I've promised Cait an evening of London entertainment. She's never been here before. And no," he added, forestalling her question, "you may not come along." He frowned at her pout, then realized it would be hours until evening and the ball. Too many hours—too much time for his sister to question Cait. "Perhaps we shall attend the theater first. What is playing at Lincoln's Inn Fields?"

Kendra brightened. "Dryden's *The Feign'd Innocence*. It's hilarious. Ford and I saw it yesterday, but I'd love to see it again."

He smiled benignly, deliberately misunderstanding her. "Maybe Ford will take you again tomorrow."

"I've nothing to wear," Caithren reminded him.

"Oh!" Kendra's eyes sparkled. "I can take care of that."

"Choose quickly," he said, wishing his siblings had stayed tucked away at Cainewood. "We need time for dinner, too."

"It isn't even noon yet." His sister's smile was all too knowing. "We'll eat first and hear your long tale. Your Cait will have plenty of time to dress after that."

FIFTY-NINE

*K*ENDRA'S CHAMBER upstairs was a confection of mint green decor. She strode to her carved-oak clothes press, threw the doors open wide, and perused the gowns hung inside on pegs. "Green, blue, purple?" She turned to Caithren. "Which do you fancy?"

"I-I don't know," Cait stuttered. "I've never been to a ball."

"No?" Kendra riffled through a few more, then pulled out a gown in a deep, rich rose and held it up to Caithren's cheek. "Lovely," she declared, dragging Cait over to a gilt-framed pier glass. "Look."

Caithren had to admit the hue flattered her complexion, but it was the most elaborate gown she'd ever seen. Gold threads were woven into the fabric in a diamond pattern, and the underskirt was shimmering gold tissue. "I couldn't possibly wear this," she breathed, wishing all the while that she could.

Even though it was English.

"Don't be a goose." Kendra tossed the gown on her curtained four-poster bed. "Not only can you wear it, you can keep it. I cannot imagine what possessed me to order it. It looks hideous on me with this red hair." She reached to lift a hank of Caithren's straight mane. "What beautiful colors. I'd wager you could wear anything with this."

When she let go, Cait watched in the mirror as the wheaten

strands cascaded back to her shoulders. Maybe her hair *was* pretty, down loose like this. She'd never paid it much attention other than to bind it out of the way.

Kendra smiled at her in the mirror. "I'll have Jane in to curl it."

"Jane?" Cait's voice sounded feeble to her own ears. Too much had happened in the past couple of hours—too much had changed.

Her world was off-kilter.

"Jane is my maidservant." Leading Cait to a marble-topped dressing table, Kendra sat her down. She pulled open a drawer filled with little boxes and bottles. "But I won't call her in until after we've finished with the cosmetics."

"Cosmetics?"

"Do you not wear cosmetics in Scotland?"

"Crivvens, nay." Cait felt as though she'd been spirited to a country even more foreign than England. France, perchance. "I've got nowhere to wear cosmetics *to*."

"What a shame." Kendra clucked her tongue. "I think you'll be happier here with Jason."

"With Jason?" Caithren jumped from the chair. "Whyever would you think I'd be with Jason—I mean, Lord Cainewood?"

"Caithren..." Kendra pushed her back onto the embroidered velvet seat. "May I call you Caithren?"

"Aye," she said weakly. "Or Cait."

"Cait, then. I like that better. Jason calls you Cait, doesn't he?" She plucked a small box from the drawer. "Anyway, as I was about to say, you can protest all you wish, but I've got two good eyes in my head."

"Two eyes?" Cait's own eyes bugged out in the mirror as she watched Kendra fluff white powder onto her face.

She couldn't believe she was allowing this, but she felt too shocked and overwhelmed to protest. Jason was a marquess.

A *marquess*.

"Two eyes," Kendra said firmly. "And I'd need only one to see the two of you belong together." Setting down the powder, she took up a stick of kohl. "Why, I haven't seen Jason squire a woman to a ball since—since forever. Or at least since we were exiled on the Continent." She leaned closer. "Look up."

"So he doesn't have a..." Cait couldn't think how to put it, and besides, it was difficult to concentrate when someone was drawing under your eye. It tickled. "What I mean is—"

"Heavens, no." Kendra laughed and stood up straight. "Of course he's been known to go home with ladies—he's a man, after all—but he never bothers to take a special one anywhere. Most especially not to a ball. I have to beg him on my knees to chaperone me as it is. He hates the things."

Now, *this* was interesting information. But Cait found her hopes rising, which wasn't a good idea. Not with all the half-truths and deceit.

She wasn't sure what to think of Jason anymore. "He just feels sorry for all he put me through."

"And what was that?" Kendra smudged color onto Cait's cheeks. "Do tell."

Caithren had never had a female friend close to her age, and though she barely knew her, she reckoned Kendra could be a good one. "He saw me confronting the Gothard brothers," she found herself explaining, "and decided I was some woman named Emerald MacCallum."

"Him, too?" Kendra opened a wee pot. "Is he daft?"

"Exactly what I said. Then, under this preposterous misconception, he tricked me into missing the public coach, to keep me from getting to Gothard first and ruining his chance at revenge."

"Revenge? As in murder?" Kendra bit her lip and swirled her finger in the pot. "He wants to see Gothard put to trial; he has no intention of killing the man."

Caithren shook her head. "You're wrong about that. He wants the reward."

Her fingertip coated with shiny balm, Kendra paused. "Cait, he *posted* the reward."

"Oh."

Of course.

Cait figured she ought to have been bright enough to put two and two together upon learning his identity, but her brain was still reeling. And Kendra didn't know the whole story. Jason's dinnertime tale had been abbreviated, to say the least.

"Nevertheless," she said, "he intends to see the cur dead."

"Jason? Nary a chance." With a decisive finger, Kendra slicked the gloss onto Cait's slack lips. "Jason would do anything to avoid murder. It's not in his nature to do harm." She capped the pot. "He's out for justice, no more. And to see that no one else suffers at the man's hands…" A small smile emerged on her expressive face. "Like you."

"Like me?" Caithren glimpsed herself in the mirror, then quickly looked away. She seemed a stranger. A mysterious stranger.

And at this moment, her feelings were as strange as her appearance.

She swallowed hard. "I'll admit he claimed as much, but do you truly think Jason took me along to *protect* me?"

"I'd bet my life on it. It's a very Jason thing to do." Kendra rummaged in the drawer again and came out with a burnt cork. "Sit still. I'm going to use this to darken your lashes. It might feel funny."

Nothing could feel as funny as Cait's stomach did now. Could Kendra possibly be right? That would mean she'd been wrong all along. And about more than just his identity. Those qualities she'd glimpsed shining through—

"Look," Kendra said, pressing a hand mirror into Caithren's limp fingers.

She raised it to her face. "By all the saints," she whispered. She hardly recognized herself. Or rather, she did, but she never thought she'd look so…

"Beautiful," Kendra said, though Cait had been thinking *English*. Kendra flicked through a small box with a fingertip. "Hold still." While Caithren watched in the mirror, Kendra stuck a tiny black heart on her cheek. "There," she said. "You're perfect."

"What is it?" Cait lowered the mirror and felt for the little heart.

With an indulgent smile, Kendra pulled away Cait's hand. "Careful, or you'll dislodge it. It's a beauty patch." She shook the patch box. "Would you like another?"

Cait felt foreign enough as it was. English. "Nay, though I thank you."

When her hand went to her amulet, Kendra's gaze followed. "My, that looks old."

"It is."

"It won't match the gown." She lifted the lid of a lovely enameled box on the dressing table. "Would you like to borrow some rubies?" Jewels flashed as she delved inside.

Cait reached to shut it. "I appreciate the offer, but nay. This belonged to my mother, and I never take it off."

"Are you certain?" A frown creased Kendra's forehead, then she smiled. "I can see that you are. I'll just get Jane, then. I've no talent with hair." She walked from the room, leaving Cait alone.

Again she took up the mirror. English. She looked very, very English. She put a hand to her quaking stomach.

Jason was a marquess. Jason had been trying to protect her.

Kendra rushed back in with a plain-faced woman at her heels that Caithren assumed was Jane. "It's past two o'clock already. The play will start in less than an hour, and we must dress you before Jane does your hair." She swept the gown off the bed while Jane put curling tongs to heat at the edge of the banked fire.

Cait's fingers shook as she detached her purple stomacher and loosened the laces beneath. What was she doing in London, dressing in English clothes, planning an evening out with an English marquess? Who would have thought, less than a month ago in Da's study—

Her thoughts were interrupted by Kendra's impatient hands drawing the turquoise gown down and off. She touched the bandage on Cait's arm. "What happened here?"

"I was cut. And then I failed to care for it properly, so it festered and had to be stitched."

"Ouch." Kendra's face scrunched up in sympathy, then turned speculative. "And I've a feeling there's more to the story. But it will have to wait for tomorrow. You won't want to be late."

Jane came to help, and together they lifted the rose gown and dropped it over Cait's head, settling it carefully to avoid damaging the artfully applied cosmetics. The top was a wee bit loose, but the cloth-of-gold stomacher took care of that, pushing her breasts up to fill it. She could only wonder what Kendra's more generous bosom looked like in the low, square neckline. Scandalous, she imagined.

The gown was stiff and heavy. Very English.

By the time Jane was done with the curling tongs, Caithren's hair looked English as well. Long curls draped to her shoulders in front and gathered in back, entwined with rose-colored ribbons.

With Kendra standing behind her, she stared at herself in the pier glass. "I look English," she whispered, watching her glossed lips form the words.

"Is that bad?" In the mirror, Kendra looked worried.

"I don't know," Caithren said. "Last month I would have thought so, but now...I'm only confused."

Kendra stepped around to face her. Familiar eyes, the same shape as Jason's, but lighter, searched Cait's. "We're not evil," she said. "The English."

"Not all of you, anyway." Cait looked down and straightened her overskirt until Kendra, with one strong finger, lifted her chin.

A gesture that smacked of Jason.

"Not most of us," she said. "And certainly not my brother." She pulled Cait into a hard embrace that took her by surprise. "Give him a chance," she whispered in her ear. "He needs you."

SIXTY

"YOU LOOK stunning, Cait," Jason said as they walked diagonally through the square toward the Lincoln's Inn Fields Theatre. "I expect you'll be the talk of the ball."

Cait saw him shoot her a sidewise glance, perhaps the hundredth since she'd come down the stairs wearing Kendra's clothes and cosmetics. When she finally met his gaze, his green eyes smoldered. "Though I must say," he added, "I think I prefer you barefoot with your hair loose and a daisy chain about your neck."

She nearly tripped, even though Kendra's gown was a couple of inches too short, and she'd thought she was becoming rather competent walking in the absurd English high heels.

He took her arm to escort her across the busy street. "You're quiet," he said, his gaze safely fastened on the traffic. "If it's because I deceived you, I'm very sorry. But I had my reasons. Though damned if I can remember what they were."

"My head is awhirl," she admitted as they dodged a sedan chair. "I never thought to find myself in London at all, let alone attending a play and a ball. I mean to enjoy it. Though I fully intend to be cross with you tomorrow."

"I don't doubt it," he said dryly. He headed toward a flat-fronted brick building with tall, rectangular windows that looked similar to the ones on his house and most of the others around the square.

"The windows are enormous." Cait looked up in awe. "The building must hold a thousand people."

"About right," he said, although she'd been fooling. A *thousand* people in one building. The concept was mind-boggling. "I don't suppose you see Palladian windows in Scotland. As for the size of the theater, it used to be a tennis court."

"A tennis court, really?" A wooden sign leaned against the wall, advertising the day's performance. Caithren read aloud. "'Sir William D'Avenant presents The Duke's Company in *Sir Martin Mar-All, or The Feign'd Innocence*, by John Dryden, adapted from Molière's *L'étourdi*, as translated by William Cavendish, Duke of Newcastle.' Whew. I am suitably impressed."

"Nothing like London pretension." Jason laughed as he ushered her toward the entrance. "Word is the play was conceived by Newcastle, but *corrected* by Dryden." He counted out eight shillings and handed them to the doorkeeper. "A side box, if you please."

Inside, the large windows allowed plenty of afternoon light to illuminate both the stage and the patrons. "We must make haste." Jason sought out their box. "The play will begin momentarily. They have to finish before dark."

A symphony played onstage, but Cait could barely hear the tune over the theater's noisy assemblage. People in the middle gallery were seated for the most part, but those in the pit were milling around, talking and laughing, some of them even fighting. Scantily dressed orange girls circulated among the crowd, offering their sweet, juicy treats in a singsong chant. Caithren suspected some of the young bucks were buying more than fruit.

The upper tier had no seats—it was crammed with people leaning over the rails. Jason led her up a flight of stairs and into a quite-civilized private box that sat off to one side, equipped with four chairs. No one else had been seated there yet, so they took the two in front.

"Never did I think to see so many people in one place," Cait said as she adjusted her skirts. "And so many sorts of people as well. I imagined only the wealthy would attend the theater in London."

"At the price of one shilling"—Jason gestured toward the top— "many can afford to be entertained. Footmen and coachmen are admitted free near the end."

298 | LAUREN ROYAL

"Who would want to come at the end?" she wondered. "You wouldn't know what was happening."

He took her hand. "Most folk don't seem to pay attention anyway."

He was right. Despite a lot of hush-hushing that rippled through the crowd when the curtains opened, no one seemed to quiet down much when the play began. The patrons in the pit scrambled to take seats on the backless benches, and Cait was distracted by more than one brawl before everyone was settled.

The play was a piece of humor, a complete farce from one end to the other. Caithren found herself laughing not only at the actors, but also at the comments and suggestions shouted to them from the audience. "Look behind you!" someone yelled, and she dissolved in mirth when the performer did just that. The spectators' robust criticism was entertaining as well.

A few minutes into the performance, a couple entered their box and sat behind them. When Jason and Cait both turned around and smiled, Cait's jaw dropped open at the sight of the haughty lady's gown. Fashioned of screaming yellow satin, the gown's train was so long it trailed into the corridor, and the neckline was so low, Cait half-expected the woman's ample bosom to pop out. Jason saw the look on her face and began to laugh, but she squeezed his hand until he settled down.

The stage was unlike any she'd ever seen. The first time the painted background moved, she gasped.

"I take it there's no moving scenery back home," Jason whispered.

"There's no scenery at all. Traveling players come to Insch sometimes and perform in whatever place is handy. I've never been in a real theater."

She watched, fascinated, while stagehands manipulated the scene. The curtains weren't closed for this, and actresses sang and danced at the front of the stage to entertain the audience during the change. Many people whistled and cheered, apparently enjoying the between-scenes acts more than the play itself.

Though she laughed at all the buffoonery, Caithren's attention wandered between the play and Jason's hand in hers. After a while, he moved his chair closer, and the press of his thigh against her skirts was distracting. She could feel his warmth. When he draped his arm across the back of her chair, she laid her head on his shoulder and sighed, wondering if she'd ever see him again.

Tomorrow she'd find Adam, and then it would be time to head back home. Adam might even attend tonight's ball, in which case she could start for home immediately.

A tiny part of her almost hoped he wouldn't be there, after all.

All too soon the play was over, and they rose to depart. "I've never laughed so much in all my life," she told Jason. "I thank you for bringing me."

He flashed a smile that sent her pulse to racing. "Nothing could make me happier than seeing you enjoy yourself."

A throat cleared behind them. He swung her around and introduced her to their box companions, Lord and Lady Martindale, who said they were going to the ball as well. Lady Martindale leaned close, her sausagelike fingers reaching for Caithren's amulet. "A lovely, large emerald," she said with a sniff, "but my heavens, the mounting looks like it's been around since the Crusades."

Cait snatched it from her hand and held it possessively. "It has."

The woman pulled back in surprise, her blond curls seeming to shudder along with her. "You're young, so perhaps you don't know that fashionable people have their jewels reset every few years."

"I'm not fashionable. I'm Scottish."

Jason stifled a laugh while Lord Martindale took his wife by the arm. "That will do, my dear," he said, making Cait a small bow. Lady Martindale looked at her curiously as they said their goodbyes and left.

Jason took Cait's hand again and drew her to the stairs. "Lady Martindale is wondering what you're doing with a provincial Scot," she commented.

"Bosh." He paused to let his gaze wander her figure-hugging gown. "You look damned English tonight."

"Not when I open my mouth."

He grinned at that and kissed her smack on the lips.

As she laughed and pulled him out of the theater, she couldn't help thinking he was acting mighty strange this eve—as though he were determined to show her a good time even if it killed him.

SIXTY-ONE

"*H*MM." AS A footman ushered them into Lady Carsington's home, Jason glanced around at the many curious faces. "I suspect Lady Martindale has arrived before us."

Before Cait could comment, their hostess rushed up to greet them. "Lord Cainewood? Why, I hardly recognized you without the mustache. You look like your brother." She smoothed her lavender lace skirt. "Do come in. Your attendance is a delightful surprise. And this is Lady…?"

When Jason blinked, Cait wondered if he felt put on the spot. "Lady Carsington," he said, "may I introduce—"

"Caithren Leslie," she piped up for herself. "Of Leslie Manor in Leslie by Insch, Scotland." Though she'd made up the manor part, her father *had* been a baronet.

"Lady Leslie," Lady Carsington gushed. "It's a pleasure to make your acquaintance."

"Lady Caithren." Jason corrected the name, but not, Cait noticed, the unwarranted title. "My companion is yet unmarried."

"Ah, I see."

Cait thought Lady Carsington saw all too much. "I'm glad of your acquaintance," she told her, her gaze wandering the crowded entrance hall. Many people were looking their way, the ladies rather obviously gossiping behind fancy upheld fans. She wondered if they were discussing Jason's new look, or her, his mysterious companion.

She was certain she'd find Adam here. He must be in London by now, and he'd never miss a social occasion like this.

"Lady Carsington," she ventured. "I am wondering if my brother is on your guest list. Adam Leslie?"

"Adam Leslie? Not that I'm aware of. Though my balls are often attended by many uninvited." Her tone said she was proud of that fact. And she seemed thrilled to have a new face at her party, because the next thing she said was, "Come, let me introduce you to some of my guests."

Cait could only gawk as the tall, elegant woman led them through an enormous entry hall and past a few other large, well-lit chambers, one set aside for card playing, another for the ladies to freshen up. In yet another room, long tables groaned with food and drink. If Cait had thought Jason's house was impressive, she was positively bowled over by Lady Carsington's abode. It could only be described as a mansion.

They were ushered into a chamber that Caithren thought looked out of a fairy tale, where the ball was in full swing. Illuminated by hundreds of candles in chandeliers overhead, masses of glittering guests danced, ate, and conversed. The ballroom's glass-paned doors opened onto a vast garden that Cait was shocked to find in the middle of London.

"Ah, Lady Haversham." Lady Carsington snagged a pale, elfin woman by the arm. "May I present a guest of Lord Cainewood's, Lady Caithren. From Scotland," she added in a conspiratorial voice, as though that fact alone should be of significant interest.

"I'm glad of your acquaintance," Cait said again with a little curtsy. "I'm wondering if you've seen my brother, Adam—"

"If you'll excuse us," Jason interjected smoothly, "I've someone I need to see. Ladies." He nodded politely, took Caithren's arm, and dragged her all the way back to the entry hall, which was all but deserted now that the most-anticipated guests—Jason and Caithren, apparently—had arrived.

Pulling her into the shadows behind a large column, he gathered her into his arms. Before she could voice a protest, his mouth came down on hers, and anything she might have said was smothered by his lips.

Caithren's heart raced as his tongue plundered her mouth. She kissed him back with wild abandon. He truly was a changed man tonight, and she wasn't sure she wanted to know why.

She'd rather just enjoy it for now.

When he finally drew back, she stared at him, dumbfounded. Her knees felt like pudding, but his strong arms held her up when she would have slumped against the tapestried wall. "I've been wanting to do that since we got to London," he said.

"Oh, aye?" She blinked at him, confused. "You had ample opportunity in your carriage on the way across town. It took forever to negotiate the traffic."

"I had other things on my mind." His fingers traced her jaw, then he tapped the little black heart on her cheek and leaned to kiss her forehead. "Come, let's dance."

As quickly as he'd dragged her away from the ballroom, he pulled her back in. The musicians were playing a sedate tune, the melody accompanied by scrapes and taps of dancers' shoes and the soft swish of ladies' gowns as they traversed the polished-wood floor in an elegant configuration.

Caithren licked her lips and cast a worried glance at Jason. "I-I cannot dance."

He smiled down at her, prodding her closer to the dance floor with a hand at her back. "I seem to remember you dancing with the Gypsies."

"But not like this!" she exclaimed, tripping over the blasted high heels.

He caught her. "It's a simple pattern. I'll give you two minutes to watch. Two," he warned with mock severity.

The music was eight beats, and the dancers balanced on their toes. Short gliding steps, a change of balance, a pause every third and seventh beat. Cait thought she had it figured out—until suddenly the women ran around the men and they all did a little hop.

"I cannot tell what they're doing," she complained. Just then the dancers bowed and curtsied. "Anyway, it's over," she said with more than a little relief.

"Ah, but there will be another."

Following some discordant re-tuning, the musicians launched into a country dance, not so different from those Cait was used to at her village dances in Leslie. "This one I can do," she declared and let Jason swirl her into the crowd.

All her reservations melted away. It was heaven being in his arms, and it didn't even seem to bother him in front of all of society.

Though the dance was energetic, she couldn't keep her eyes from his clean-shaven face. "You don't look like Ford."

"Ford?" They crossed arms and switched sides. "You have the most disconcerting habit of starting a conversation midstream. Where did that come from?"

"Lady Carsington. She said you look like your brother."

"Ah." He twirled her around. "She referred to my other brother, Colin. And yes, I expect with my hair cut and without my mustache, we do look somewhat alike. Green eyes and black hair. He's always kept his shorter. Prefers convenience over fashion, in all things."

"I like him already." The music came to a close, and she curtsied. "What other siblings are you hiding?"

"Only a sister-in-law. Colin is married." He led her from the dance floor. "Her name is Amethyst, but we call her Amy."

"The woman who gave you the watch."

"That's right." Another country dance followed the first, and he swept her back out and into the double line, leaving her with the women while he stood across from her with the men. "Amy used to be a jeweler. Or rather, she still is a jeweler, but without a shop. Colin is building her a workshop at Greystone, their home."

"Greystone," she murmured, clapping her hands and then touching them to the women's on either side of her. She remembered him chuckling at seeing that name on an inn. "Your brother married a commoner?"

Coming closer, he smiled down at her. "We Chases don't play by the rules."

"I've noticed." The dance separated them for a moment before they came back together. "You certainly don't play backgammon by the rules."

"I'm not a cheater. If I'm ahead five matches, that's only proof of my skill."

"Ha!" Linking arms, they skipped in a circle. "You distracted me with your bare chest. That is hardly playing fair."

She was getting breathless by the time a portly gentleman tapped Jason on the shoulder. "May I claim the pleasure?" he asked.

Jason didn't look very happy. But he pulled Caithren from the dance and introduced her to the man, a Lord Berkeley.

"It's glad I am to make your acquaintance," Cait said. "And by any chance, have you seen my bro—"

"Beg pardon," Jason interrupted. "We must be off." And he propelled her back to the entry and the shadow of the post.

"Wait." With two hands on his chest, she stopped him when he would have kissed her again. "Why don't you want me to ask after my brother?"

"I only want to kiss you," he protested, drawing her close. His warm breath washed over her face, and she felt dizzy. "I don't know what's come over me, but I cannot keep my hands off you." To demonstrate, he ran them down her back, all the way to her bottom.

Her pulse sped up, but she wasn't going to fall for this seduction. "Do you think my head laces up the back?"

His hands froze on her. "Pardon?"

"Don't take me for a fool. You're trying to keep me from Adam, and I want to know why."

He caught her gaze with his. "I want only to be with you tonight. Besides, do you really think you'd fail to notice your brother were he here?"

He had a point. And when his lips captured hers, she was afraid he made that point completely. So much so that she was tempted to drag him down to the floor and make him follow through.

Oh, how she wanted that. One more time before she found Adam and headed back home.

The footman opened and closed the front door, admitting a new guest, but Caithren barely noticed the footsteps or low murmur of the servants' awed acknowledgments. Jason's tongue was tracing her mouth, his teeth were nibbling her lower lip. She wound her arms around his neck and twined her fingers in his thick hair.

"Cainewood, is that you?" The voice was deep, the words drawled and amused. "Od's fish, I cannot wait to see the lady who's taken your fancy."

Caithren pulled away and stared up at a tall, dark stranger. Heat flooded her cheeks, and arousal and embarrassment made her feel weak as a newborn bairn.

Jason turned her to face the man square on.

"Egads," the man said. "What happened to your hair and face?"

"A long story, best told another time. Sire, this is Caithren Leslie." The fact that he hadn't called her by the invented Lady title was not lost on Cait, even in her confused state. "Caithren, King Charles."

King Charles? She felt the blood drain from her face. Jason supported her with one steady arm. "It-it's pleased I am to make your acquaintance," she said by rote. She caught herself before reciting the "have you seen my brother" part. "Your Majesty," she added instead with a tremulous smile.

The king reached down to take her hand and raise it to his lips for a kiss. His eyes burned into hers, a sensual, compelling black. "A pleasure to meet you, my dear. The lady who captures Cainewood's heart is a special one, indeed."

He was still holding her hand. Her heart was beating like it wished to escape her chest. She wanted to drop into the intricate parquet floor. Which was ridiculous. He was but a man.

"Love's wan e'e and ower deef," she blethered.

The king dropped her hand. "Pardon?"

"Caithren likes to quote her mother's favorite sayings," Jason explained. "Scottish wisdom."

"I'm of Scottish descent, but sorely lacking in wisdom." In a gesture that reminded her of Jason, Charles stroked his thin mustache. "And this saying means...?"

"Love is almost blind and a bit deaf," Cait interpreted.

With that, he threw back his head and laughed, a great roar that all but rattled the enormous chandelier overhead.

"She's a gem," he told Jason. Peering over their shoulders, he frowned. "Od's fish, Barbara and Frances are at it again. I'd best be off." And he made his way toward the ballroom, a commanding figure in dark red velvet trimmed with some sort of fur instead of ribbons.

Cait all but collapsed against Jason's chest. "Barbara and Frances?" she asked weakly.

"His two mistresses of the moment." When she looked up at him in shock, he just laughed. "Come along, I think you could do with some wine." He guided her down the hall toward the refreshment room.

"I didn't mean to imply there was love—I mean, that you—that line just popped into my head, and—"

"Think nothing of it."

She halted in her tracks and turned to confront him. "And why didn't you tell me the *king* might be here? He must've thought I was sodie-heid"—at the look on his face, she translated—"feather-brained, aye?"

"Kendra did say Charles would be in attendance." He led her to a table and picked up a cup. "If you'll remember."

Caithren wracked her brain while he handed her the cup and lifted a gigantic, solid silver ladle that must have weighed ten pounds if it were an ounce. "Aye, that is exactly what she said. *Charles* would be in attendance. As though he were a personal friend of the family or some such—"

"He is."

She dropped the cup, jumping back as it splashed and rolled under the table.

"We spent years together with him in exile, after the Civil War. In abject poverty, I might add. The Restoration restored more than Charles's throne—he saw our property restored as well. And he settled titles on my two younger brothers, who otherwise would have—"

"How was I supposed to know such a thing, you daftie? The longer I'm around you, the more confused I get." She looked down. "And now I've gone and ruined Lady Kendra's fancy gold shoes."

Jason only smiled. "So I'll buy her another pair or three." He filled a second cup and curled her fingers around it. "Here. Drink."

Served from an enormous silver punch bowl shaped like a swan, the wine was spiced and delicious. She drank two cups of it, danced with Jason, then drank another. Her gaze never strayed too far from King Charles. But he didn't stay long. When he left, she sagged against Jason in something akin to relief, tempered with a healthy dose of awe.

She had actually attended the same ball as King Charles. Cameron wasn't going to believe it.

Jason introduced her to Lady Castlemaine and Lord Arlington and the Duke of Buckingham. Everyone she'd ever heard of seemed to be here.

Everyone but Adam.

She couldn't bring herself to be too sorry, though. Much as she wanted to see Adam and ask him to deed her Leslie, this night was too magical to really wish such mundane matters would intrude.

Jason followed her when she staggered off the dance floor and over to a wall, leaning against the mantel of one of the immense fireplaces that flanked either end of the ballroom. They weren't lit tonight, which was a good thing, because the chamber was overly warm as it was.

A giddy little giggle bubbled out as she looked up at Jason. Surely no one in the room was as handsome as he. He wore a dark green velvet suit that brought out his eyes, and his own glossy black hair skimmed his shoulders. The hair that she'd cut. She'd cut the hair of a marquess.

She giggled again at the memory. "Will you fetch me another cup of wine?"

"I think you're tipsy enough as it is," he responded with a good-natured grin.

Now that he mentioned it, her head *was* reeling a wee bit—not that she'd admit it. "It's only this glorious night. I will remember it forever, my lord."

"I won't have you start 'my lording' me now. Not after what we've shared between us."

The thought of what they'd shared made her blush. "The wine? Please?"

He heaved an exaggerated sigh. "As you wish. But we'll get you something to eat as well."

SIXTY-TWO

*J*ASON GUIDED Cait back to the refreshment room and handed her a knot biscuit. She nibbled on the braided, anise-flavored bread while he wandered down the buffet table, loading a plate with light fare: asparagus, cubed cheese, an assortment of luscious fruits. Handing her the plate, he filled two more cups with the heady spiced wine.

Cait looked around for two open seats.

"I've another idea." Jason inclined his head toward the door. "Come along." Munching a cube of cheese, he led her back through the ballroom and out into the formal garden.

Burning torches were set about. Cait breathed deep of the night air, refreshingly cool compared to inside. Here and there a couple strolled the garden paths, but mostly it was quiet and serene.

She followed him out beyond the bright light of the torches, where he sat himself on a low brick wall. Handing her a cup, he took the plate from her and set it down.

"We cannot see out here," she complained, seating herself on the other side of the plate.

"Ah, but we cannot be seen, either." He plucked a raspberry from a small pile and popped it into his mouth. "Your eyes will adjust."

"They're adjusting already," she said, feeling lightheaded. The hand holding her cup was trembling a little, but she raised it and took a sip.

He selected another raspberry and brought it to her lips, running it back and forth across her mouth before he slipped it inside. Sweetness burst on her tongue as she bit into it. He watched her swallow, then leaned across the plate to take her lips in a gentle kiss.

He pulled away an inch. "Shall we move back near the torches?"

"Nay. I find I like not being seen." She leaned closer, meeting his mouth with hers again. With a satisfied chuckle, he brushed her lips, and his tongue flicked out to taste them.

He sat back and sipped from his cup.

An asparagus spear made its way toward her mouth. She opened, and he fed it to her slowly. "Lovely night, is it not?"

"Mmm." Anything more intelligible was beyond her at the moment.

"Are you sure you wouldn't rather go back inside?"

She shook her head. "Mmm-mmm."

When the asparagus was gone, he leaned to kiss her again, taking her chin in one hand, plundering her mouth till she was breathless. He tasted of fruit and spiced wine, lust and man. A most heady combination.

"I cannot go back inside," she whispered. "I don't think my legs would carry me."

"Are you cold?"

"Nay." But she was shivering. "Aye. I don't know."

He took her hand and drew her off the wall. "Come here, then. I'll keep you warm." And spreading his knees, he eased her to stand between them.

With him still seated, their mouths were on a level. It wasn't surprising when they met, hot and urgent. His hands wandered to her back, pressing her closer between his legs. She could feel the hardness of him beneath his breeches and her layers of skirts, and also an ache, a throbbing, low in her own belly.

"I'm not cold now," she murmured against his mouth.

He drew back and sipped from his cup, then tilted it to her lips so she could sip, too. Reaching for the plate, he selected a ripe strawberry, bit into it, and fed her the rest. Then another one, but this time he bit off a piece and covered her mouth with his, transferring it to her with a flick of his supple tongue.

Never had a strawberry tasted so delicious.

"Hmm…" He watched her, holding up the half-eaten berry. Though his eyes looked gray in the half-light, she didn't miss the speculative gleam.

He set down the berry, and his fingers moved to her stomacher, detaching the tabs at the top.

She licked her lips, tasting strawberry and Jason. "What are you—"

"Hush." He bent down on the stiff stomacher, and something snapped.

"Jase!" It hung drunkenly away from her chest, folded in half and dangling.

"Kendra's seamstress can make another." Working to loosen the laces beneath, he bent to kiss the swell of her breasts.

His mouth, warm and damp, made her heart lurch—she was certain he could feel it pounding. Something melted inside her. Her hands tangled in his hair.

He pulled away, lowering the delicate chemise that shielded her breasts from his view. "Holy heaven," he bit out, watching her chest heave. A tense moment passed, the only sounds those of their harsh breathing.

Then he lifted the half-eaten berry and rubbed it over one taut nipple.

Immediately his mouth moved to cover it, suckling off the sticky sweetness with a low groan that made heat curl in Caithren's middle. Lest her other nipple feel neglected, he doused it and fed off it, too, his teeth nipping the hard bud until a little moan escaped her lips. Then his mouth was on hers, wild and demanding, and his arms went around her, tugging her against his hard body.

The blood rushed through her veins and straight to her head, and she was dizzy, but he was holding her up. One hand groped back to find the berry, and it was in their mouths, first hers, then his, until the pulp was gone and only a tart-sweetness was left on their fencing tongues.

A woman's high-pitched laugh startled Cait as a couple meandered close. She jerked away and held the stomacher up to her chest, panting.

Jason sat straight and calmly fed her another spear of asparagus. She didn't think she could chew and swallow, but somehow she managed, and he handed her a cup of wine to wash it down. Hers, his...it didn't matter. He drained the other cup himself.

Music tinkled from a distance then abruptly ceased, telling them a door had opened and closed, and the couple had reentered the ballroom. Jason unbuttoned his surcoat and spread the sides to envelop her, and Caithren dropped the stomacher and leaned in, pressing her breasts against his chest. She wedged her hands between them to loosen his cravat and work at the laces it hid, frantic to get to the warm skin beneath.

The slap and scrape of shoes told them more people were approaching.

"Bloody hell." Jason pulled away and hopped down from the wall. Straightening his disheveled clothing, he took the plate in one hand and Caithren's hand in the other. Holding the stomacher up to cover her bosom, she teetered on Kendra's high shoes while he drew her through two small formal gardens and into a long, arched arbor, the lattice entwined with flowers and climbing vines.

Halfway through, he stopped and fed her a raspberry. And another. Laughing, holding the dress up with both hands, she chewed and swallowed. Some juice ran down her chin, and he leaned to lick it off. The plate between them, he nuzzled her neck, and a warm shiver rippled through her body. He ran his tongue up to her ear. "You're delicious," he whispered there.

"You're very sleekit," she returned.

"I'm what?" His lips grazed her forehead.

"Very...charming."

He pulled back and fed her another raspberry. "I thought I was exasperating and unimaginative. Black and white."

"Exasperating, aye. But unimaginative..." She leaned forward to tongue one more raspberry from his hand. "You're causing me to reevaluate. You seem to be changing. Or perhaps I was wrong."

"You? Wrong?" His laughter rang through the fragrant tunnel. He selected a few raspberries for himself and tossed them into his mouth. "Besides," he said around them, "the Gypsy woman said that *you* were supposed to be the creative lover. And beguiling, if I recall aright." He waggled his eyebrows at her.

"It was my lover she was talking of, not me. And will you never let that go? I told you, she misjudged me."

"I think not." Before she could disagree, he pushed the last raspberry between her lips. "You're beguiling as hell, Caithren Leslie."

Her hands and the plate were all caught between them when he yanked her against him and sealed his mouth to hers. He was a new man tonight, she thought blissfully. Something had changed him. And if that something was her...could he love her? Because she knew in her heart she loved him, no matter that he'd deceived her, and although she'd been unable to admit it, even to herself.

Until now.

Her senses careened at the thought, and his kiss, and the intoxicating fragrance of the flowers overhead blended with his distinctive scent. Just when she thought her knees would give out, yet another couple came sauntering down the arbor.

Jason pulled back with a muttered oath. "What are all these people doing out here?"

"I imagine they're wondering the same thing." Clutching the stomacher with one hand, Cait used the other to rub the spot where the plate had pushed into her abdomen. "Why don't you put that down?"

"This?" An astonished look on his face, he held up the plate. "There are still three strawberries left."

"You can get more inside."

"Ah, but I want them outside." His eyes glittered suggestively while a fingertip lightly traced her lips.

"Please, Jase." She shivered, but not from the cold. "I don't think I can stand up any longer. Not...not when you do that."

"Hmm." Looking over her head, he craned his neck to see the back of the garden. "I spy a solution. Come along." And once more she found herself hurrying after him, holding both his hand and the top of her disheveled dress.

Through the arbor, a white wooden summerhouse shone in the moonlight. The only opening was in the back, so he walked her around, pulled her inside, and they were alone. Crickets chirped beyond the latticed walls, but other than that, the only sounds they heard were their own uneven breaths.

"Sit," Jason said, waving her to the bench that ran along the circular structure's walls. "Better?"

"Much. I was...feeling weak there, for a minute."

"Good." He set the plate aside and sat close by her. "I hope to have you feeling weaker still in a minute more." And he lifted her and sat her straddling his legs, facing him.

She gave a little start of surprise, then looked around, although she knew they were alone. "This feels wicked."

"Mmm." He gave her one slow kiss. "That's the idea."

It was wicked but good. It gave her access to his face, which she covered with little kisses. And her hands were free to roam his body, although he was entirely too clothed to make her happy.

He laughed at her frustration, then tilted her head back. His mouth played in the sensitive hollows beneath her chin and along her throat. She reached under his surcoat to pull the shirt from his breeches. His skin beneath felt warm and taut, his back smooth and muscled.

When his hand sneaked below her skirts and played along one thigh, her own hands stilled on his body. "Is something wrong?" he asked, bending his head to draw the tip of his tongue along her bared breasts.

"I—not here—you cannot…oooh," she said when he lifted her skirts and rearranged them, drawing her closer so she could feel him straining against his breeches. "This is very wicked."

"You think so?" He eased his hand from beneath her skirts and started loosening his laces.

"Jason, you cannot—"

"Watch me." His hands moved to her waist, lifted her, brought her back down slowly, slowly…and she felt him sliding inside her.

At the same time he pierced her with his body, he pierced her eyes with his, holding her gaze as tightly as his hands held her steady. With a moan she couldn't quite believe came from her own throat, she felt herself opening, welcoming his warmth into hers.

She licked her lips, closed her eyes, threw back her head. "Oooh, this is very, very wicked."

Laughing low, he licked a shivery line up her throat to her mouth, then settled a soft kiss on her lips. Pulling away, she looked down. He'd arranged her skirts carefully around them.

"No one can see," he whispered. "Even should they stumble upon us. Can you move?"

She did, slowly, feeling him slip out and then back in. "By all the saints." Had anything ever felt so good?

"Excellent. Now stop." He held her hips in place with his hands. "I've a craving for a strawberry."

"What?" She tried to wiggle, but he wouldn't permit it.

"Hold still."

"I cannot!"

"Yes, you can." He lifted a berry, licked it slowly, bit off half. When he offered her the other half, she shook her head. With a shrug, he finished it, then brought his mouth to hers, kissing her long and deep until all the strawberry flavor was gone and her whole world tasted like Jason.

Involuntarily she shifted her hips, but he stopped her and deprived her of his mouth.

"Not yet. Two left."

Feeling an incredible urgency where his body met hers, she let out a wee bleat of frustration. He took up the second strawberry.

She lurched forward and took it in one bite.

"Tsk, sweet." He eased her back down on him, grinning when she moaned at the forbidden friction—a grin so lethal, she wondered it wasn't illegal. "Now we'll have to make the final one last that much longer."

He drew the scratchy tip of the berry over her cheeks, her chin. Down into the valley of her cleavage. Around her bared shoulders to her back, where he traced a tickly pattern.

"What am I writing?" When she whimpered her impatience, his face hardened in a mock frown. "Concentrate."

Around, up, down…"Caithren!" she breathed with relief.

"Um-hmm."

A curve, up, down, a squiggle…"Jason?"

"Excellent. Now…"

A big, swooping line that enclosed all he'd written. Could it be…"A heart?"

"Brilliant. I shall have to reward you."

But their names in a heart were reward enough. Could it mean—

He bit into the berry then and smeared its juice across her chest and up her neck, his tongue following the sweet path all the way to her mouth. "Now," he murmured against her lips. His hands tightened on her hips and lifted—

And another couple stumbled into the summerhouse, mouth to mouth, locked in a torrid embrace.

With a groan Caithren's head dropped to Jason's shoulder. It was all she could do to keep tears from springing to her eyes. Jason stifled a strangled laugh. The couple didn't notice. They fell to the grass in the center and started tearing at each other's clothing.

"How could they?" Cait whispered. "Don't they see us?"

"I suspect they're in no condition to care." A pained look came over his face. "I expect you don't feel the same?"

Doubtless her shocked look told him all he needed to know. "I was afraid of that," he whispered dryly, lifting her with a mighty heave and setting her on her feet.

She smoothed down her skirts and spread them wide, doing her best to hide his efforts to lace his breeches, though the other couple was half-undressed now and completely oblivious. Their panting moans filled the air, striking Caithren as sounding rather comical. Surely she and Jason didn't sound like that when they made love.

Did they?

Giggling, she followed him out of the summerhouse.

"This isn't funny," he muttered, buttoning his surcoat in a partially effective attempt to hide the bulge in his breeches. When she giggled again, he looked up and grabbed her by the shoulders, hushing her with his lips.

That move, at least, was very effective.

"Shall we make for home?" he asked against her mouth, the words teasingly warm. "I believe I've had quite enough of this ball for tonight."

With a mastery that made her pulse pound, he deepened the kiss. For a long exciting minute, she was caught in his spell. When at last he pulled away, a soft sigh escaped her.

"I've a bed at home," he said low in her ear, nibbling on her lobe. "And..." He looked up and raised a brow. "Privacy."

SIXTY-THREE

HEY RAN through the gardens, laughing all the way, Caithren struggling to keep her clothes on as they went.

A few feet from the door, Jason pulled her behind a hedge and turned her to face him. Together they got her chemise into place, her bodice laced, the stomacher attached—although it had an odd crease in the middle. She crossed her arms over it.

"There." Jason adjusted the curls on her shoulders and kissed her on the lips. "You look perfect."

"So do you." Her gaze wandered down his body and back up. He pulled the surcoat tighter around his middle. "Almost." She giggled.

He loved the way she could go from hot passion to laughter in a split second. Though that meant she could be as quick to anger as well, it was worth it. It was what made her Caithren. It was what made him want her. If only she could still love him after this night.

He knew he was hoping for the impossible.

"But that other couple," she said, "they will have grass in their hair. They're not nearly as creative as you are—as the Gypsy foretold you would be." Her teasing grin caught at his heart. "That other couple won't look perfect."

"And Charles's courtiers will think nothing of it. So long as they're not man and wife." He drew her from behind the hedge, toward the glittering ballroom. "In these circles, men expect only their mistresses to be faithful."

"Is that so?" she said, a challenge in her voice. The look in her eyes said she wouldn't put up with that sort of marriage.

If only it mattered.

Well, there was nothing for it. All he could do was make the rest of this evening as perfect as it had been so far, and then hope against hope...

He took a deep breath and opened the door to the music and the dancing and all the people who'd done their best—albeit innocently —to keep him from loving Caithren this night.

Grabbing her hand, he strolled through the crowd, a single purpose in mind: to get her into his arms again and finish what they'd started.

"Cainewood! Haven't seen you in ages! Will you introduce me—"

"Later."

Later. Later. Later. Always one more interruption, one more excuse. It seemed an hour before they escaped out the front door and stood waiting for his coachman to bring the carriage around.

Jason drew Cait near and wrapped her in his arms.

She snuggled closer. "Crivvens, it was hot in there."

"Hot?" He took her lips in a deep kiss, his hands wandering down to squeeze her bottom. "Right now it's hotter out here."

She giggled. A sweet, sweet—bittersweet for him—giggle.

When the carriage arrived, they hurried inside, and he pulled her to straddle his lap. "Can we do it in a carriage?" she asked as the door slammed shut.

"I mean to find out." His hand went beneath her skirt and wandered up her shapely legs to find her slick and ready. With a little gasp, she moved to unlace his breeches, a seductive, impatient gesture that made him bite his lip. The carriage started with a lurch, hampering her fumbling efforts. When he finally burst free, he couldn't remember ever being so relieved.

She wiggled close, wound her arms around his neck, fastened her lips on his, her tongue a warm promise in his greedy mouth. Then—*bump!*—the wheels hit a rut, and their noses mashed together.

"Sorry," he whispered, adjusting her on his lap.

"Mmm," she murmured, going again for his lips, but missing and grazing his cheek instead. "It's all right. I think." A little giggle sounded by his ear.

Steadying her head in his hands, he tried once more, managing naught but a couple of fleeting baby kisses. The carriage bucked over the cobblestones as though it had no springs, never mind how much he'd paid to outfit the damned contraption.

They jounced in and out of a pothole with a bone-rattling jolt that brought their mouths colliding together with enough force to nearly crack their teeth. "I don't think this will work," she whimpered.

Ruefully he rubbed at his lips. "I'll make it work."

Nuzzling her neck, he concentrated below instead, moving his hands to her hips in a feverish effort to guide their two bodies together. But the bench seat was hellishly narrow, and she shifted and swayed on his lap.

No matter how hard they tried, they couldn't connect. Rounding a corner, Cait bounced right to the floor and stayed there, convulsed in laughter.

"It's not going to work." Coming up on her knees, she steadied herself with her hands on his waist. Her skirts were twisted around her legs, the bent stomacher was skewed, and her tangled curls bounced on her shoulders in the same uneven rhythm as the carriage. "How long to your house?"

This late, traffic was negligible. With the exception of aristocratic carousers, Londoners kept inside at night. "Five more minutes."

"Five minutes." She sighed as though it were hours and hours. Then she reached to lace him back up, weaving on her knees while she tried to keep her balance.

He pushed her hands away, knowing he couldn't take her fingers on him now. Quickly he did it himself, loosely, then pulled her up and across his lap.

"It's sorry I am, Jase." She burrowed into his neck, her breath warm there, her mouth moist. "Do you think you can wait?"

"I reckon I'll have to."

Her only response was another sweet sigh.

"You know," he said with a self-deprecating chuckle, "my

brother brought a woman to this house last year and took her to his bed. And I was terribly righteous and told him he'd have to marry her."

She sat upright, steadying herself with an arm across the seat-back. "You mean Colin and Amy?"

"Yes." He grunted when she bounced on his lap. "Last month they had a beautiful baby daughter."

"That's very nice. But you don't have to marry me, Jason. In fact, I wouldn't countenance it." Her voice dropped until he could hardly hear it over the wheels rattling on the cobblestones. "My home is in Scotland."

With a hand on her chin, he brought her gaze to his. "Caithren?"

"Hmm?" In the soft glow from the sidelight, her eyes looked hazy blue.

"Are you enjoying yourself this night?"

She nodded seriously. "More than I ever thought possible."

"Even though you're in England?"

"Even though." Managing to guide her lips to his, she kissed him softly. "Maybe especially so." Her words were almost shy, surprising him. His Cait was never shy. "Because you're here. In England."

A heaviness weighted his chest. "Will you remember that tomorrow? No matter what happens?"

Her gaze was steadfast—and perhaps a bit curious. "I'll remember it forever."

"Good. I'm counting on it."

He was praying for it as the carriage drew to a halt. Because when the sun rose in the morning, what he had to tell her would surely break her heart.

The house was dark and still when they entered. He eased the door shut and found her lips with his as he felt for the candle that was kept on the nearby table. Pulling away, he went to light it, fumbling when her hands streaked under his surcoat. He cursed softly, and Caithren giggled.

"Hush," he whispered. "We cannot wake Kendra. I'm half-surprised she didn't wait up to hear all about our evening."

With a soft hiss, the flame came to life, and she snuggled against him, her eyes a deep blue in the sudden light. Beneath the coat, her arms tightened around him. A choked sound escaped his throat, and he fused his mouth to hers. His breath quickened at her indescribable flavor, the way her soft curves molded themselves to his harder body.

She angled her head, deepening the kiss, then suddenly broke contact. "Where is your room?" Her eyes blazed, full of impatient promise. "Hurry."

The candle in one hand, he slung an arm around her, and they scrambled up the stairs, both of them stumbling in the mad rush.

The minute his bedchamber door closed behind them, Caithren was on him, her mouth pressed to his. "Now," she demanded. "No food. No teasing. Here. Now."

He reached blindly to set the candle on a table, teasing the farthest thing from his mind. It was all he could do not to rip her clothes or his in their haste.

They tumbled onto the bed, all arms and legs and hot, wet mouths. "Now," she said again, and he drove into her, groaning at the sheer perfection of her body taking his. She climaxed with a sharp cry that met his own deep moan. He felt her tighten around him, and gusts of pleasure overcame him, stunning his senses.

In seconds it was over. This time. There would be more time before the morning, time to be slow and caring, time to taste and touch.

Time to savor the last hours before the truth destroyed everything between them.

At the thought, an ache overwhelmed him. He nuzzled her ear, then words spilled out in a whisper. "I love you, Cait."

Beneath him, she seemed to stop breathing. "I—"

"Hush." He didn't want to hear it, not from her. Not when she wouldn't be able to say it again on the morrow. "I love you, and I want you to remember that. No matter what happens tomorrow."

"Why do you keep speaking of tomorrow?" she asked in a voice soft and sated. "What is happening tomorrow? Besides the wedding and finding Adam? And hopefully apprehending Gothard?"

He pulled back and captured her gaze with his. "We will wake to the morning sun, wrapped in each other's arms. I will bring you breakfast in bed." The candlelight seemed to flicker in her passionate, hazel eyes. "And then—then I have something to tell you. And I want your promise that you'll remember I love you."

She struggled up on an elbow. "That is something," she whispered, "that I will never, ever forget."

"Then show me," he said, and she melted into his arms once again.

SIXTY-FOUR

*I*N THE GRAY light of dawn, Jason jerked awake.

He'd forgotten his head last night.

Bloody hell, what if he'd got Cait with child?

He lay stone still, a fist pressed to his heart. A few hours of mindless passion might have ruined both their lives.

If the worst came to pass, what would she do? What would *he* do? He wasn't a man to force a woman to the altar, nor was he one to want his child raised in another country, far from his love and influence. But the decision wasn't his, that he knew. If she carried his babe, Caithren wouldn't even know until after she'd returned back home. She wouldn't have to tell him. He might never find out he had a son or daughter living in Scotland.

How would she cope, a never-married woman with a child? Here she would be shunned. He was admittedly ignorant of the social pressures where she lived, but he'd wager it was the same. For the rest of her life, she might suffer for his lack of responsibility.

He could only pray his seed hadn't taken. And though he was not a religious man, he did pray, fervently.

Beside him Caithren slept, looking happy and peaceful. Though he ached to touch her beloved face, he wouldn't risk startling her awake. She would waken soon enough, and then it would be over... because then he would tell her the truth. Any feelings she had for him would die. And now she might be carrying his child—the child of their precious, fleeting love.

Could things get any worse?

Beneath his window, Jason heard the bellman call the hour of six, followed by muffled conversation. His skin prickled with a sudden, foreboding awareness. He slid from the bed and over to the window, parting the drapes just enough to see between.

Through the morning fog, he could barely make out the bellman, his lamp held high, casting a yellowish glow. Beside him, talking to him, sat a man on a horse.

A man with a squarish head.

Apparently things *could* get worse.

Letting the drapes drop closed, he dashed for the stables, pulling on his clothes as he ran.

SIXTY-FIVE

W *E WILL WAKE to the morning sun, wrapped in each other's arms. I will bring you breakfast in bed…*

Caithren woke to the morning sun, but Jason wasn't wrapped in her arms. Her heart plummeted. Then she decided he must be off getting her breakfast in bed.

Until two hours later, when he still hadn't appeared with it.

Tears stinging her eyes, she finally gave up and rose to get dressed. Everything in Jason's chamber reminded her of him. His personal style was evident in the solid, masculine furnishings. His scent clung to the bedclothes, the very walls. She cleaned up at his washstand, rinsing away the traces of his body on hers. But not the impression he'd made on her heart.

After a night of blissful loving, she'd fallen peacefully to sleep, certain he was going to ask her to wed him this morning. She'd been sure that was what he'd meant—that she should remember he loved her when he asked her to be his wife. And he hoped that his declaration of love would persuade her to agree, even though she'd already told him she belonged home in Scotland.

She had yet to decide what her answer would be. But she'd been sure of the question.

But now she realized she'd been wrong. He'd only meant she should remember he loved her when he told her they couldn't stay together. That he loved her, but it wasn't enough. There were too many obstacles, too many differences. Her family was too low-ranked. Something.

She could live with that, if she had to—it wasn't as though she hadn't been expecting it all along. But after promising the morning together to straighten things out, he'd gone off somewhere and left her alone to wrestle with all her wrenching doubts.

So much for his promises not being given lightly.

The pain and uncertainty were crushing. But Caithren Leslie could bear it.

She should have known not to take an Englishman at his word.

∼

*J*ASON HELD HIS nose as he rode past a ditch that had been used as a communal grave for more than a thousand bodies during London's last great plague. Though the remains had been covered with dirt, after two years it still seemed to reek.

Everything in his life seemed to be reeking right now.

Damnation, he'd lost Geoffrey Gothard's trail.

As he turned the corner into the secondhand-clothing market on Houndsditch, Jason found himself wishing again that Caithren really were Emerald. Emerald MacCallum knew how to track a man. Emerald MacCallum would have captured her quarry.

It had cost him precious minutes to saddle a horse and take off, but Gothard hadn't ridden away until he'd glimpsed Jason rounding the corner of the town house. Yet he'd never managed to catch up. And now the man had seemingly disappeared into the maze that was known as London.

Once again they were playing hide-and-seek, but Jason couldn't figure out the rules of the game. Gothard had chased him all the way to London—why didn't he come after him now instead of running off? It couldn't be that Gothard feared confronting him on a public street, because Jason had followed him halfway across town. The man had had ample opportunity to lead him somewhere more private.

Cursing his ineptitude, Jason kept one hand on his pocket watch as he jostled his mount between two unkempt riders. If Cait were Emerald instead, he wouldn't have panicked and left her, terrified for her safety. Not to mention he might have done a better job of following the man if he hadn't been swamped with guilt. Guilt that muddled his mind. For more than thirty-six hours he'd known the truth, known that Caithren was searching for a brother she'd never find. Every one of those hours had taken its toll on his soul.

Piles of garments cluttered the street, guarded by watchful owners. Barking madly, a dog skirted the mounds and darted under Jason's horse, making him shy. A wagon splashed mud as it careened on by, its driver ignoring several vendors who angrily brushed off their soiled goods, yelling obscenities after him.

Once again Jason had proven himself a failure, unworthy of his father's name.

He'd failed to catch Gothard. He'd failed to tell Caithren the truth yesterday, he'd failed to keep her safe from pregnancy, and he'd failed to be there for her this morning. She had no reason to attend the wedding, yet by now she was probably getting ready, excited to see her brother. He pictured her choosing a gown from Kendra's clothes press, carefully painting her face, sticking on another adorable heart-shaped patch. All for nothing.

He craned his neck. Was that Gothard's sandy head he glimpsed through the mass of haggling customers? Thinking it just might be, his hopes lifted. He dug in his heels, racing after the man, then caught up to find himself disappointed yet again.

It wasn't Gothard, after all. But the man had to be nearby...somewhere.

He would give it one more hour. Then, if he were unsuccessful, he would go home. And—no matter that it would be the hardest thing he'd ever done in his life—he'd tell Caithren the whole truth.

SIXTY-SIX

"*H*E'LL BE BACK, Cait."

Caithren looked up from her feet, which were trodding a path through Lincoln's Inn Fields, and over to her new friend Kendra. "I know he'll be back. He lives here." With a sigh, she made her way over to a stone bench. "You just don't understand. He *promised* me we would be together this morning. He said he had something to tell me."

Kendra sat beside her, her features lit with intrigue. "Any idea what?"

Slowly Cait drew her hat off and set it on the bench. Raking the long hair from her face, she watched a dove flutter from the sky and peck around in the grass, foraging for food. A fresh scent in the air hinted at coming rain, reminding her of home, but the thought did nothing to raise her spirits.

"You're hiding something," Kendra insisted. "I can tell."

"Are you always so observant?"

"Always," Kendra said smugly. "So what is it?"

"This is going to sound daft." Cait licked her lips and smoothed the skirts of the blue day dress she'd borrowed from Kendra. Until the Gothards were caught, she felt safer disguised as an Englishwoman. "I realize we've known each other less than two weeks, your brother and I, but I thought...well, I thought maybe he'd be asking me to marry him."

Kendra clapped her hands. "I knew it!"

"Nay, you don't understand." Tears sprang to Caithren's eyes—oh, how she hated that. She brushed at them angrily. "He made such a point of saying we'd talk in the morning. Then he disappeared." She turned on the bench to face Kendra. "I was wrong. He only wanted to tell me we cannot be together. But he lost his nerve, or just decided something else was more important."

Her new friend reached to take her hands. "Maybe you misunderstood about this morning."

Cait shook her head. "Impossible."

"Then something unexpected came up." Kendra's fingers squeezed tight. "I'm sure of it. Didn't you say you needed some papers for your brother? I'll wager he wanted to take care of that before he talked to you. And when he does, it won't be to say you cannot be together."

"It doesn't matter what he went to do or what he's going to say." Caithren pulled her hands from Kendra's and hugged herself. "I hadn't made up my mind, anyway."

Jason's sister fixed her with a penetrating stare. "Oh, yes, you had." She smoothed her own apple-green skirts. "Whether you know it or not."

Uncomfortable under that gaze, Caithren rose and resumed walking.

Kendra jumped up to follow. "How is your arm today?"

"It's healing." Cait shook her head in disbelief. "After English doctoring. I never would have thought it."

"They say never trust an English surgeon. Quacks, one and all." Kendra grinned. "How was it cut? You said you would tell me."

A small smile threatened to burst through Cait's melancholy. "I never said anything of the sort. You said you would ask." She took a deep breath. "Wat Gothard nicked me with his sword. We think he was going after your brother."

"He was?" Kendra stopped dead on the path, her face a mask of concern. "Maybe Jason went after Gothard. What if he's not here because he's hurt?"

"Hurt?" Cait echoed numbly. "He was going to warn Scarborough today, but he said nothing about chasing down Gothard. He doesn't know where to find him. We don't know if he's even in London."

She couldn't bear to think of Jason hurt. He didn't want her, and he didn't want to tell her, either. That was all there was to it. He would have said something were he planning to go after Gothard.

Kendra was still watching her, as though waiting to be reassured. Suppressing her own unease, Cait touched her friend's arm. "Your brother didn't go chasing after Gothard this morning." When Kendra still looked wary, Cait forced a smile. Surely there was nothing to be worried about. "I'm certain of it. You yourself said he wasn't after revenge."

Kendra nodded, apparently placated. "Still, I cannot believe you were injured. It sounds so romantic, being saved by the man you love." She leaned against the rail that edged the path, her eyes lit with envy. "My life is so boring. What sort of adventures have you two been up to?"

So much had happened, Cait didn't know where to begin. And she couldn't bear retelling all the events that had brought her to admire and love Jason in such a short time. It hurt too much. "Your brother brought me from up north to here. A long, tiring journey. Things happened."

"Things." Kendra's voice sounded speculative, but she let the matter drop. "At least tell me what you meant last night when you said you hadn't cared properly for your cut. What could you have done that the doctor didn't?"

"There are healing plants, but—"

"You've knowledge of healing?" When Cait nodded, Kendra looked excited. "Could you teach me, then? I visit the sick at Cainewood, but sometimes I don't know what to do for them, and—"

"It takes years to learn." Cait reached to pluck a leaf off a low-hanging branch overhead. "I cannot teach you in an afternoon."

"When you come to live at Cainewood—"

"I don't think that will be happening." Walking again, she shredded the leaf and avoided her friend's eyes. "Your brother doesn't love me, Kendra. Or at least not enough. I'm naught but an annoyance to him."

She knew that wasn't precisely true, but she didn't know how to put it. She only knew that if Jason wanted her, he would have been with her this morning as he'd promised.

A Chase promise is not given lightly. If he'd ever considered marrying her, he must have had serious second thoughts. Now, even should he return and ask her to wed him, she couldn't say aye. Not knowing as she did that he had doubts.

Maybe this "adventure" had changed her mind about what she wanted from life. But for her, it was all or nothing. She knew he bore guilt for taking her outside of marriage, but that was no reason to wed. A half-commitment would never do. Even should she be pregnant—a possibility after last night—she wouldn't marry him unless she was positive she had his love.

She adored children, and she'd feel blessed to have one, in or out of wedlock. Cameron could stand in as a father figure. People would whisper, but she'd never been conventional anyway.

It was a gray day, to match her mood, even darker along the paths where the trees met overhead and cast their shadows. She walked beside Kendra, listening to her own thoughts and snatches of conversation from passersby. When they scooted to the side to let a wizened old vendor pass with his barrow, he nodded to them and recited a little verse.

> *Buy marking stones, marking stones buy,*
> *Much profit in their use doth lie;*
> *I've marking stones of color red,*
> *Passing good, or else black lead.*

"Thank you, no." Kendra smiled, and the aged peddler went on. "Marking stones," she mused. "That man will be scrambling for business soon, if Jason has his way."

"Aye?" Caithren could barely muster interest, but she couldn't be rude.

"He's set some cottagers at Cainewood to making pencils from the graphite mined on the property."

"What's a pencil?"

"A long strip of graphite encased in wood. You write with it, like a quill, but you don't have to dip it. You just sharpen it, instead. Jason heard they were being made in Cumberland and traveled there to see. There is nothing he won't do to make Cainewood profitable. The Roundheads ran it into the ground while it was in their hands—when Charles restored the title and lands, Jason had to start from scratch." Her heels clicked on the hard dirt path. "My brother is an admirable sort, don't you think?"

"All this new knowledge of Jason is a wee bit much," Cait admitted. "I spent our whole journey trying to puzzle him out, and then when I finally reckoned I understood him…yesterday I discovered he's a completely different man than I thought."

"No, he's not." As they walked, Kendra ran a hand along the low fence beside her. "You may be surprised to find him titled and a man of means, but inside, he's exactly the man you saw. Or what you've made him to be." She stopped and leaned against the rail. "You've changed him, Cait. In good ways."

"I don't know…"

"Come, they sell lemonade on the other side of the square. I'll treat you." Kendra linked her arm through Cait's. "With or without brandy?"

"Definitely with," Cait said dryly.

The lemonade was cool and bracing. They walked around the fields for a spell, drinking and chatting, and after a while Cait started to feel better. Children ran circles around them, their harried mothers not far behind. Street balladers were there to entertain, as well as violinists and one lone bagpiper that made Caithren's heart swell.

She touched her amulet, rubbing her fingers over the smooth rectangular emerald. Tonight was the wedding. She'd best head back to the house to ready herself.

"May I borrow another gown for tonight?"

"Of course." Kendra eyed her assessingly. "I've a lovely one in yellow that I think will just fit."

"I'm sure it will do. Whether Jason returns or nay, I must go to Lord Darnley's wedding to meet up with Adam." By force of habit her hand went into her pocket, to feel for his portrait and pull it out.

"Ford and I can take you. We're invited and were planning to go anyway, in order to find out who Jason killed." She squinted at the miniature. "What is that?"

"Adam's picture." When Kendra reached, Caithren handed it over. "Do you see a resemblance?"

"Oh, yes." Kendra grinned, looking from the wee painting back to Cait. "You've the same eyes and chin and hair."

"That's all we share," Cait said. "We couldn't be more different." She sighed. "I'd best get back and prepare to leave."

One more night dressed as an Englishwoman to find Adam, then she would head back home where she belonged. Her hair would go back into plaits, and she would be herself again. Hopefully without these devastating pangs of unrequited love.

Her hand went up to stroke the foreign English curls—and she felt something missing. "My hat! I forgot my hat! I must've left it on that bench." She started running.

"Wait!"

At Kendra's shout, Cait turned back.

"Have you no sense of direction?"

"Nay." She laughed at herself. "Where was it, then?"

"There. Behind that big tree, and back along the path a bit."

"Aye. Bide a wee. I mean, wait here. I shall be right back."

She hurried along the shady path, relieved when she spotted the bench and saw that no one had taken her hat. Running the last few steps, she grabbed it and jammed it on her head.

Just then, a horse came thundering through the park. Someone scooped her off her feet. Her heart hammering, she found herself facedown across a man's lap, his hand tangled in the chain around her neck in an effort to wrestle her upright.

She kicked and twisted, trying to find freedom, but his grasp tightened and the chain bit into her throat. Finally it snapped, and her amulet fell to the grass, her heart plummeting along with it.

Her protection, gone. Her hope, gone.

"Let me go!" she wailed, her eyes filling. The emerald looked smaller and smaller as they rode away, her last glimpse of it blurry through her tears.

Something cold and thin pressed into the back of her neck.

"It's the dull edge of a knife," Geoffrey Gothard growled, "but one more move, and it'll be the sharp side instead."

SIXTY-SEVEN

"WHAT DO YOU mean, she never came back?" Jason paced the drawing room, then came to stand beside Kendra, staring down at her. "Where could she have gone?"

"I looked all over, then I figured she must have come back here." Her gaze kept straying to the window, as though she expected to see Cait emerge from the park across the street. "Lincoln's Inn Fields is not that big. How could anyone possibly disappear in it?"

"You don't know Caithren." He tried to steady his erratic pulse, reminding himself how easily she tended to get lost. "She has a terrible sense of direction."

"So she told me. But I thought she was fooling." At Jason's glare, she flinched. "I looked, Jason. Everywhere. I'm sorry. It's not as though I lost her on purpose. Come, I'll show you where we were. Perhaps she's waiting there now."

Calm. As he followed Kendra out the door, he struggled for calm. Geoffrey Gothard couldn't have taken her. He'd spotted him less than an hour ago.

He hoped.

Suddenly he wasn't sure. He pulled out his watch, but his hand was shaking, so he shoved it back into his pocket. Dodging the traffic that always surrounded the square, he trailed his sister across the street and into the park. Together they hurried along a path.

The gray day was his enemy, its shadows tricking him into thinking he saw Cait everywhere. "What color is she wearing?"

"Blue. The gown with the puffy sleeves that I wore to Lady Stanhope's house party."

"I haven't memorized your wardrobe, Kendra."

Wisely saying nothing, she slanted him a glance. "Here." She stopped before a stone bench. "She left her hat here. It's gone. So she must have found it."

"I've eyes in my head," he snapped.

"Your face is turning red. You never get upset. Or you never used to, until this whole thing with Gothard started. Even then, you weren't this short-tempered."

Until he'd fallen in love. "You two had no business walking here alone."

"Everyone walks here alone." The sweep of her arm encompassed plenty of unescorted women.

"Not everyone has a deviant after them." When her pale green eyes filled, he drew a deep breath. Patience. "Show me the path you were on when she left you."

Once again he followed her, scanning the square while he tried to reassure himself it wasn't possible Gothard had Cait. Or could he have his timing skewed? How long had he wandered the streets of London, berating himself for not coming clean with Caithren yesterday or the night before? He pulled out his pocket watch again and flipped it open, but for the life of him he couldn't remember what time it had been when he last saw the man.

"Wait." When Kendra stopped, he snapped the watch closed and whirled to face her. Her brow knitted, she motioned off the path. "Is that Cait's?"

A white feather fluttered near the ground. He ran closer and saw it was attached to the hat he'd bought in Wansford. "Holy heaven. Yes." He plucked it up and clutched it to his chest.

"Look, there was a horse here." Hampered by her high heels, Kendra came along more slowly. "The grass is torn up. By hooves, I think." She bent down and scooped up a glint of gold. "And what is this?" She handed it to him. "It's Cait's as well, isn't it?"

As his fist closed around the emerald pendant, his heart plunged to somewhere in the vicinity of his knees. "I've lost her," he whispered, staring at his clenched hand.

"She's lost, yes. But that doesn't mean you've lost her."

"You don't understand. This amulet is ancient—it's been in her family for centuries. She believed something bad would befall her if ever she was without it."

A sudden wind whipped Kendra's skirts. "Don't tell me *you* believe that nonsense."

Stricken, he slowly looked up at his sister. "I don't know what to believe anymore."

SIXTY-EIGHT

"*I*'LL EXPLAIN this one more time, numbskull. Now, pay attention."

Listening to the Gothard brothers argue, Caithren nervously wandered the small chamber they were in, the back half of a two-room suite at an inn that had seen better days. Besides the sagging bed, a table and two plain chairs were the only furniture. Evidently the brothers were as short of funds as Jason had guessed.

"Thanks to Cainewood doing just as I expected of him, things are right on schedule."

"What *things*, Geoffrey?"

Geoffrey's gaze flickered to Cait. A lascivious gaze. Swallowing bile in her throat, she moved around to the other side of the table and feigned unconcern, running a finger across the bare wood.

"Things." Geoffrey blew out a perturbed puff of air. "I'll be going to the wedding alone."

As he talked, he donned padding to bulk up his body. He'd also worn it to inquire at Scarborough's house, Cait realized. Jason had been right.

Still speaking to Wat, he jerked his squarish head in her direction. "You will wait here and guard the chit."

In reflex she backed up and sat on the bed. The ropes creaked, and a musty smell wafted from the mattress.

Geoffrey glared at his brother. "Think you can handle that?"

Wat shrugged.

A heavy sigh escaped Geoffrey's whitish lips. "I'll lock the two of you in, then. She won't be going anywhere unless Cainewood breaks down the door. If that should happen, you know what to do?"

Wat just looked at him questioningly.

With a huff, Geoffrey marched over to Cait and pulled her off the bed.

"Ouch!" She yanked free. "I will thank you to keep your hands off my arm. It hurts where your brother cut me."

Without answering her, he prodded her in the middle of the back and sent her sailing into the small anteroom, shutting the door behind her.

She stumbled over to sit on an unpadded wooden settle. This room was even more austere than the first. Fuming, she got back up and pressed her ear to the door, but try as she might, all she heard was unintelligible murmurs.

What was he saying? What was he planning? Her mind raced with possibilities. Was he telling Wat to detain Jason? Kill him? Kill them both? No, somehow she thought not. The way Geoffrey had been looking at her, she suspected he had plans for her before doing away with her.

She shuddered.

At the sound of footsteps approaching, she raced back to the settle. Geoffrey opened the door between the rooms, and she watched through the frame. He returned to the table and pulled a cracked mirror from a bag, along with a fake beard and some adhesive. Then he set to work, turning himself into the man she'd seen yesterday morn.

Rising again, she positioned herself on the threshold. "Why would Cainewood be breaking down the door?"

Her words came out a challenge, maybe not the wisest thing to do. But she'd never been good at controlling her emotions.

A nasty grin appeared in the bushy brown beard. "Cainewood will receive a note explaining your whereabouts. Any minute now, I expect."

"What makes you think he cares for me?" she asked, almost hoping Jason *didn't* care, so he wouldn't walk into a trap.

"Cainewood hasn't let you out of his sight." He settled the wig on his head. "Nor far from his lips, I might add."

Had he seen them, then, those times they'd kissed to hide their faces?

As though reading her mind, Geoffrey let loose a sinister chuckle. "He'll be coming after you. Conveniently keeping him from the wedding."

"I wouldn't be so sure." She wished she could put more conviction into that statement. Jason had said over and over he felt responsible for her, and he'd charged in on his silver horse to save her more than once. Just because that particular horse was stabled miles away didn't mean he wouldn't be arriving this time.

Still, she couldn't count on it. She walked to the window and looked out. Four stories down. Her first thought had been to open the window and jump. But even when Geoffrey left and she had only to deal with thickheaded Wat, it would still be four stories down.

She wouldn't be jumping.

Pressing her forehead to the cold pane, she strained to see the wall below. Vines. Old, gnarled vines, the stalks as thick as her forearm. She could climb down the vines.

But only if she incapacitated Wat somehow.

Her gaze darted around the room and into the next one. There must be something here that could help her. Whatever it took, she had to get to the wedding. It was her best—maybe her only—chance to find Adam.

And if she could save Jason from risking his life as well, so much the better.

~

SOMEHOW JASON managed to dress for the wedding, though he didn't know how it happened. His heart pounded so hard his fingers shook. He was torn in three directions at once.

One, find Cait—absolutely his first priority, but the least likely to be successful. London was the biggest city in England, a veritable rabbit warren of streets and buildings. She could be anywhere. *Anywhere.*

Two, get to Scarborough's house and warn him.

Three, go to Lord Darnley's wedding, where he might capture Gothard once and for all.

Since Scarborough was expected at the wedding, he had a strong hunch Gothard would be there, too. For the bride and groom and wedding guests, he hoped he was wrong, but at least it would be done.

Scarborough and Gothard. Those last two he could handle. He hoped.

He frowned at himself as he tied his cravat in the mirror, messing the knot for the fourth time. He couldn't think about past failures. He had to pull himself together and do what needed to be done.

Save Scarborough and apprehend Gothard.

Or go after Cait—

A knock came at the door. Giving the cravat a final yank, he went to open it.

"A letter, my lord." Goodwin proffered a neatly folded square.

The note was obviously scribbled in haste. Eleven words that made up his mind. *Your woman can be found at the Bull Inn on Bishopsgate.*

A clue. A direction. Relief coursed through him, though he knew it was premature.

He nodded at Goodwin. "Have the carriage brought round immediately."

He hoped Scarborough had received his warning letter; if not, the man would have to fend for himself. Or—

"Ford!" Grabbing his velvet surcoat—black, to match his mood—he bolted from the room and down the stairs.

SIXTY-NINE

*W*AT SAT SLUMPED in a chair in the back room, his shifty brown eyes watching Caithren pace back and forth while she did her best to ignore him.

She was envisioning Lord Darnley's wedding. There they were, walking down the aisle, Lord Darnley and his bride. Her mind conjured up a bonnie image of a man in a dove-gray velvet suit and a woman in a lovely pink gown. Very English. The kirk, of course, was enormous, this being London. Dressed in every color of the rainbow, guests filled row after row of pews. On one end sat a man wearing bright blue satin bedecked with gaudy ribbons.

Adam.

She had to get to Adam. She'd come all this way, and it was her one and only chance—

"Sit down, wench. You're making me barmy."

She sat. Geoffrey had given Wat a pistol.

Congealed food sat on a pewter plate before her, making her stomach roil. There was a spoon, but no knife. No weapons at her disposal.

When she closed her eyes, a vision of Jason's smile seemed to hover behind her lids. What was it about him that made her miss him so fiercely all this day, the first day she'd spent without him since he'd kept her off the coach? Certainly not his blanket judgments, his innate stubbornness, his overdeveloped sense of responsibility. But whatever it was, he had changed her life. Changed an essential part of Caithren Leslie.

She could no longer imagine living all her life without a man. In truth, without Jason in particular.

But somehow she would have to.

Now she knew what her answer to his proposal would have been. But he wouldn't be asking. Once he captured Geoffrey Gothard, he'd be leaving for his home in the country. She'd been telling him to leave her all along, after all.

It was painful, knowing he cared but not enough. If she could even believe he'd been telling the truth when he said he loved her. Wishing the three words had never passed his lips, she reached to touch her amulet and splayed her hand across the bareness there instead.

So much ill luck had befallen her lately.

She had to get to Adam. Everything had gone wrong, but this one thing—this *one* thing—had to go right. With her emerald or without.

SEVENTY

"WHAT DOES Scarborough look like?" Kendra whispered as she and Ford quietly entered the church.

"How the hell should I know?" Scarborough had already left his house when they'd arrived there to alert him of his brothers' plans. "We'll have to ask around after the service. Surely there will be time to warn him."

The ceremony hadn't started yet, but everyone was seated. At the far end, a harpsichordist played a gentle tune. Ford drew Kendra along one wall, so they could view the assemblage. "Jason thinks Gothard won't show up until the reception—"

"Look! There's Cait's brother, Adam!"

"Silence!" a matron warned, turning in her seat to give them a cold gray glare.

Kendra ignored her, reaching into her drawstring bag for the miniature that Caithren had left in her hands in the park, when she'd run off to find her hat. She thrust the little painting at Ford. "He looks taller than I expected, but of course you can't tell height from a portrait. It's him, is it not?"

He frowned at the picture. "This fellow looks oddly familiar."

"Because he's Cait's brother and looks like Cait."

"Makes sense." Ford looked back and forth between the man and the small oval portrait. Though his clothing was less flamboyant, the gentleman in question did indeed share the same wheaten hair and hazel eyes as the man in the painting. "Could be," he mused. The features weren't exactly the same, but close. Perhaps the artist wasn't very talented.

"Go back outside," Kendra said. "I'll bring him to you."

"We can't. It's about to begin—"

The music had changed to a sedate march, and the groom was taking his place, but Ford's protest was futile. Kendra was already down the aisle and tapping the man on the shoulder.

When he looked over, startled, she leaned close to whisper. "May I speak with you a moment?"

Looking confused, he nodded and rose to follow the twins outdoors.

They'd barely reached the steps when Kendra turned to him and began babbling. "I realize you don't know who we are, but your sister is—"

"I don't have a sister," the man interrupted.

Kendra and Ford looked at each other. Ford handed him the miniature. "Are you not Adam Leslie?"

"Nay." The man stared at it, then looked up. "Where did you get this? Adam is dead."

Kendra gasped. "Adam is *dead*?"

"I'm his cousin, Cameron Leslie." Cameron stuck out a hand. "And you are...?"

Ford grasped and shook it. "Ford and Kendra Chase. We got the portrait from Adam's sister, Caithren. Our brother has gone after her. She meant to come here to find Adam, but she was—"

"—delayed," Kendra finished for him. No sense alarming the man right off.

"I received word of Adam's death and came to fetch my cousin back home." Cameron's hazel eyes filled with concern. "Wore out four horses getting here, because she said he would be at this wedding today, and it's the only place in England I knew for certain I could find her."

"If she doesn't make it here for the ceremony, she'll be at the reception." Kendra reached to touch him on the arm. "My brother will make sure of it."

SEVENTY-ONE

$\mathcal{C}$AITHREN ROSE again and walked slowly around the chamber, pacing off her nervous energy.

How could she get to Adam?

"Sit down, wench," Wat growled from the front room.

She sat back at the table.

Jason hadn't arrived. Maybe he'd never gone home to get the note Gothard sent—assuming Gothard had told her the truth about that. Or maybe she'd been wrong about Jason altogether.

He'd ridden halfway across the country chasing after Gothard, and he was determined to find him. Saving Scarborough's life also figured into the equation. Maybe those goals were more important to him than she was. She wouldn't have thought so, but she didn't know what to think anymore.

Well, if he didn't show up, at least he couldn't be detained—or worse, shot—by Wat. And if he did show up, he could probably defend himself. Especially against Wat. Geoffrey's attitude toward his brother might be exaggerated, but it had base in fact. Wat was definitely missing something upstairs.

That weakness of Wat's should be a boon to her as well. He was still in the other room and didn't seem to be watching. Slowly she stood, sliding the pewter plate off the table as quietly as possible.

Hiding it behind her skirts, she drifted to the window, reached out and turned the latch, pushed it partway open—

"What the hell do you think you're doing?" In a flash of fury, Wat came up behind her. She whirled and raised the heavy pewter plate, smashing him atop the head with all the strength she could dredge from her body. The spoon went flying, along with putrid bits of dried meat and gravy that rained down on them both.

Wat yowled, but he didn't go down. Evidently he was stupid *and* hard-headed.

Red with rage, he came after her. She scooped the spoon from the floor and aimed its handle for his face, hoping to get him in the eye. She missed, grazing his sunburned cheek. Bright blood beaded up in a ragged line.

With a growl, he wrested the pistol from his waistband.

Dim-witted or not, he could kill her. She was already braced to bring up her knee when she heard the click of the flintlock being cocked. Icy fear gripped her heart. She shifted, thrusting both hands to force Wat's arm toward the ceiling.

As she tried to wrestle the gun from him and slam it butt-down on top of his hard skull, a blast tore through the air. Her ears ringing, she felt his body go limp and slump to the floor.

Panic rose in her throat as she stood there, the pistol in her hands, watching blood well from a neat round hole in Walter Gothard's head.

SEVENTY-TWO

"THEY'VE GOT to be here," Ford said. "Hell, there are just too damn many people."

The wedding celebration was in full swing. Lord Darnley's house was lit with hundreds of candles. Wine and other spirits flowed freely, and the resulting raucous laughter rang through the halls, the ballroom, and into his garden beyond.

"They?" Cameron asked. "I thought we came here to find Cait."

"We also need to find the Earl of Scarborough." Kendra's gaze scanned the glittering room before she turned back to Cameron and frowned. "But we don't know what he looks like."

"And two other men," Ford added, his words directed into the milling throng. "My brother accidentally killed someone, and we don't know who he was. These two men were witnesses. I've seen them and think I remember what they look like, but I've yet to spot them here. A serving maid in a tavern told me one of them might be named Balmforth."

"Balmforth?" The blood drained from Cameron's face.

"Yes." Ford craned his neck, still looking.

Kendra's gaze was riveted to Caithren's cousin. "Whatever is wrong?" she asked.

"Balmforth—"

"There they are!" Ford took off, threading his way through the crowd of revelers.

"Are you all right?" Kendra stared at Cameron. "You look like you've seen a ghost."

"Nay. It's only—" His mouth opened, but no more words came out.

She gestured toward the silk-upholstered chairs lined up against the tapestried wall. "Would you like to sit down?"

"Nay." He shook his head as though to clear it. "Lady Kendra, I don't know how to..." He blew out a breath. "Here they come."

Ford walked up with the two men, his face as white as Cameron's. Whiter, even. Kendra clutched his arm. "What is it?"

Her whispered words failed to carry through the din that surrounded them, but it didn't matter. Ford knew what she was asking. "The man Jason killed..." he started, then just looked helplessly at the other men.

"He was Adam Leslie," Cameron said. "Cait's brother."

~

CAITHREN HEARD the door latch rattle in the other room. Geoffrey was back. Somehow he realized his brother was dead.

While she waited for him to burst in and murder her, she knelt for the tenth time in as many minutes to feel Wat's neck for a pulse. Nothing.

The rattling stopped, but she felt little relief. Tears flooded her eyes. Trembling, she sat back on the floor and hugged her knees to her chest. For long minutes she stayed that way, rocking herself, a human ball of misery.

Her head jerked up when the window moved, a disembodied hand shoving it open the rest of the way. Through a blur of tears, she watched a second hand clench the ledge. A head and shoulders appeared—wide shoulders and unruly red hair beneath a man's hat. A woman hoisted herself up and through the window, landing on the floor with the grace of a cat.

Her heart pounding in fear and confusion, Caithren rose. The woman topped her by a good foot—she was taller than Jason or any man Cait knew. A sword hung from her belt, and a pistol peeked from the top of one boot. She was dressed like a man, but no one would have taken her for one. Ever.

Cait dashed her tears away and blinked. She heard another rattle of the door latch, but she was too stunned to react. "You...you're..."

"Emerald MacCallum." The woman stared pointedly at Wat. "I take it he's dead?"

"I-I reckon so."

Emerald reached to touch Cait's hand. "Don't fash yourself, dear. I don't normally hold with killing my quarry, but these brothers... well, the world is better off without them."

"B-but I've never killed a man! And I didn't mean to, even though he was such a bad one. I swear on"—she reached for her missing amulet, then let out a sob—"on my mam's grave." She searched Emerald's golden eyes, tears falling from her own. "Will I ever get over it?"

"Nay." The single word was blunt, yet kind. Emerald patted her on the back. "But others will thank you for it, and some day, you'll realize it wasn't really wrong. You'll never get over it completely, but you will learn to live with it." She backed away toward the window. "It will, however, change you, maybe even for the better."

Her hand on the sill, Emerald stilled. "A wee keek back keeps you on the right path."

For a moment, Caithren could only stare. One of Mam's sayings. Let life's experiences guide you forwards.

"You came for the reward," she said softly, remembering Jason accusing her of the same.

The other woman nodded, then shrugged and turned to duck out. Their gazes both flew to the ledge when another hand appeared beside hers, larger and squarer, with a light sprinkling of black hair across the back. Caithren gasped. A second hand settled next to it, then a face rose into the frame.

Jason's face, though so colorless Cait feared for his life.

Emerald reached down a hand and pulled him up and into the room.

He stood there, visibly shaking, looking back and forth between Caithren and the woman he'd once thought her to be. Before he could say anything, Emerald climbed out the window and was gone.

He looked back to Cait, his face still pale, his eyes wide. "Was that Emerald MacCallum?"

"Aye."

He shook his head, then pierced her with an intense green gaze. "Are you all right?"

Tears threatening, she bit her lip and nodded.

"*Caithren.*" Her name was a harsh whisper in the air. He held out his arms, and Cait rushed into them, fresh tears flowing at the feel of him crushed against her. She drew deep of his familiar, comforting scent, underlaid with a trace of the sharp smell of fear. He was warm and solid in her arms, his body still shuddering with residual tremors.

With a long sniff, she pulled back. "I...I cannot believe you climbed up the wall. Four stories, with your fear of heights."

"What do you take me for?" For a split second he looked irate or hurt; she wasn't sure which. Then his eyes softened. "I love you, Cait. I would move heaven and earth to see to your safety. Climbing that wall was nothing." At her look of disbelief, he released a shaky laugh. "Well, not nothing, but I would do it again. For you. But give me a few days first, will you? I need some time to recover."

She laughed through her tears, reaching forward to clutch his hands in hers. "Geoffrey went to the wedding to find Scarborough. You were right, Jase—he was wearing the fat man disguise, with the beard—"

She broke off at his gasp. His gaze was riveted over her shoulder.

"It's Wat." Her lids slid closed, but the tears leaked through them anyway. "I didn't mean to kill him, I swear it." She opened her eyes, willing Jason to believe she hadn't done such a terrible thing deliberately. "I hit him over the head, but he didn't fall, and then he pulled a pistol, and it went off, but it was pointing up in the air. I don't know what happened!"

Jason looked up at the ceiling. "It ricocheted, Cait."

She followed his gaze and saw the molded Elizabethan pattern was damaged. "I only meant to knock him out so I could go find Adam—"

At her brother's name, she froze. With a mighty effort, she pulled herself together. She had no time to feel this wrenching regret; not right now. She'd allow herself that luxury later.

"Adam. I have to find Adam. I must get to the wedding. It's sorry I am to leave you now, but I've come all this way, and—well, you'll be wanting to go, too, will you not? Gothard is there."

"Cait. There's something I need to tell you. I meant to this morning, but Gothard—"

"I know. There are reasons you don't want to stay with me. We'll talk of it on the way."

He took her by the shoulders. "That's not it, Cait." His eyes and voice were frantic. "Not at all. You mustn't think such a thing—"

She pressed her mouth to his, to silence his proposal. He'd scaled the wall for her. She'd been wrong, and he loved her enough, after all. Her heart sang with joy, but she hadn't time for such things now.

She put her answer into her kiss, a caress of such fiery possession that he had to know how she felt. Regretfully she pulled away, her lips clinging to his for a last moment, savoring the sweetness of his love. A love she would be sure of the rest of her life.

He'd climbed four stories for her. The equivalent of a mountain for other men.

"I love you, Jase. We'll talk of it later. I must get to the wedding."

"You don't understand—"

At the sound of pounding she tore her gaze from his and hurried into the front room, Jason at her heels. He yanked her back just as the door slammed in, barely staying on its hinges.

Beyond its frame, Kendra and Ford stood in the half-dark of the corridor. And behind them, rubbing the shoulder he must have used to break down the door—

"Cameron?" Confused, she stared at him in disbelief. He looked pale. As Jason moved behind her to shut the door to the bedroom, she took a wooden step forward.

"Cait." Her cousin pushed his way between the twins and wrapped her into a hug. Smelling of home, he rubbed her back in a familiar, comforting rhythm. "Cait—I'm..." Laced with sympathy, his voice faltered. "I'm so sorry."

"Why?" Her gaze flickered to the door shielding the other room. Could the news of Wat's death be spreading already? "It was an accident, Cam."

He pulled away, searching her eyes with his. "You knew it before now, then?"

She only looked at him, baffled.

Jason peeled away Cameron's arms and took her by the shoulders. "Caithren. The thing I've been trying to tell you..."

He looked down at his boots, then back up and straight at her. His eyes held such pain, she was taken aback.

A cold knot formed in her stomach.

He drew a strangled breath. "Adam is dead. At my hands."

She was speechless. Adam was dead? It didn't seem possible.

Jason's green gaze implored her, but she couldn't get past the shocking news to figure out what he was asking of her.

"There was a duel. Geoffrey Gothard pulled your brother from the crowd and used him as a shield. I wasn't fast enough—or skilled enough—to control my blade. And Adam died for it."

"Adam is dead?" Her words were barely a whisper. "And you knew it and didn't tell me?"

Jason just looked at her for a long, silent moment. Then he turned and walked out through the empty doorway, into the emptier world beyond.

 ~

*F*ORD CHASED Jason down the corridor. "You cannot just leave!" He plucked him by the sleeve. "How long have you known?"

"Nearly two days. And every minute I didn't tell her was agony. But I knew it would be like this." He wrenched from Ford's grasp and continued walking.

Ford ran after him. "You knew it would be like what?"

"Whatever feelings she had for me died. Couldn't you see it her eyes?"

It had been even worse than he'd thought it would be. Much, much worse.

"I couldn't stay and watch that. I love her. Damn it, Gothard's ruined my life." He started down a narrow flight of stairs.

"You never would have met her without Gothard." Ford's voice came from behind him. "She's in shock. She might need some time to absorb it all, but if she loved you before, she still will. It was an accident."

At the bottom of the steps, Jason whirled. "I killed her brother. Her *brother*. Do you reckon I'd find forgiveness for the man who killed you, or Kendra, or Colin? It was bad enough when the man was nameless. This isn't easy to live with, Ford."

The pain was excruciating, but he had to put it aside for now. He had other responsibilities.

"Just leave me alone," he said. "Go back to Kendra and Cait. And—her cousin, is he?" Ford nodded. "She loves him—he will comfort her much better than I could. She killed Wat, you know."

"What?"

"Wat's in the back room. You'll need to send for the authorities. I take it you warned Scarborough?"

"Bloody hell." Ford's eyes widened. "No. We ran into her cousin and learned the truth and—damn, I forgot. We came straight here to tell Cait what we knew, and—"

Jason was already running for the exit.

SEVENTY-THREE

*J*ASON STRODE through Lord Darnley's front door, past the gaping footman and into a swarm of glittering guests. Scarborough. Where was Scarborough? What the hell did the man look like? He'd seen him once or twice at court, but, damn it, he'd never paid much attention, and—

With a jolt of relief he spotted him. Sandy-haired, like Gothard, but taller and sporting a broad mustache. Dressed in deep blue velvet and apparently unconcerned, Scarborough stood in a circle of men, discussing the shocking news that Clarendon, the Lord Chancellor, had resigned earlier in the day.

"Barbara was leaning from her window, cheering at his departure," Scarborough said as Jason walked up. Barbara, Countess of Castlemaine and the king's longtime mistress, had always hated Clarendon. "So do you know what he said to her?"

The men leaned closer into the circle. "What?"

"'Pray remember, my lady, that if you live, you will grow old.'"

Amid their laughter, Jason touched Scarborough on the arm. "I apologize for interrupting, but there's a matter of some urgency."

Scarborough turned, a look of confusion on his face. "Yes?"

Just as Jason was about to respond, a flash of silver caught his eye.

He spun around, shoving Scarborough from harm's way as he drew his rapier from its scabbard. "I arrest you in the name of the king," he said in a booming voice, startled to hear how it carried. "You will put down your weapons and wait here for the magistrate."

The music stopped, and as one, the wedding guests turned to watch. Jason's grip tightened on the hilt of his sword. "Now, Gothard."

The disguised man's gaze held hard and unwavering. "We meet again," he drawled through the bushy brown beard. "My nearest and dearest enemy."

Words familiar to Jason. Familiar and enraging. "Once and for all, why should you call me your enemy?"

Gothard's sunburned features went tight with resentment. His blue eyes narrowed. "You have what should rightfully be mine."

"Rightfully yours?" Again Jason had the feeling he'd seen those eyes. Befuddled, his head swam. "I have nothing that is yours. And because of this misconception, you've been chasing me, trying to kill me?"

"I never wanted to kill you," Gothard said with a smile—a cold one. "Only to enjoy some of your riches. They should have been mine. Including your woman." The familiar eyes turned as cold as the smile. "I'd have had her long before now if you'd ever left her alone."

Jason ignored the threat to Cait. She was safe. But he swiped at his missing mustache, infuriated.

All the disguises and hiding, and Gothard had never been out to kill them. Just playing hide-and-seek.

"And Scarborough?" He nodded in the man's direction.

"Him I want dead." The wild sheen in Gothard's eyes said he wasn't sane. "With him dead, Wat inherits and I get what I deserve."

What he deserved was questionable at the moment. He was well and truly mad. "What about what I deserve, Gothard? What do I owe you and why?"

"Damn you to bloody hell." Gothard moved forward, then pulled back when Jason brandished his sword. "Both you and the father we share."

Pain and confusion shooting through him, Jason advanced a step closer. "We share nothing!" He slowly circled the tip of his rapier, then sliced it hissing through the air in a swift move that brought a collective gasp from the wedding guests.

The blade's thin shadow flickered across the candlelit parquet floor. His mind whirled with thoughts of little Mary, her mother Clarice, Cait and her brother Adam...all the blood, the irrational violence.

With a roar, Gothard lunged, and the first clash of steel on steel rang through the ballroom.

"I was born first," Gothard yelled. "It should be mine, all mine!"

He slashed wildly, catching Jason's sword across the middle. The vibrations shimmied up Jason's arm. Muscles tense, he swung and thrust, and again steel bashed against steel. His heart pounded; blood pumped furiously through his veins.

What Gothard was saying couldn't be true. No way in hell was he this evil man's half brother.

They scrambled onto the dance floor, and the crowd scurried back. Gothard was cornered, but Jason was incensed. He would never believe it, *never*. He edged Gothard back against the wall. Gothard took sudden advantage, and Jason found himself retreating as their blades tangled, slid, broke free with a metallic twang.

His arm ached to the very bone. Perspiration dripped slick from his forehead, stinging his eyes. But the other man's breath came hard and ragged.

Measuring his foe, Jason put his all into one determined swipe of his sword, and Gothard's went clanging to the floor and skittered into the crowd of gaping spectators.

"I came not to kill today, Gothard, but merely to see justice done." Jason sucked in air, smelled the other man's desperation. "There are those here who will see to it you won't escape."

An affirming murmur came from the crowd, and men jostled forward.

He waved them back. "Tell me what you said isn't true."

"As God is my witness, it *is* true. And you won't live to enjoy what should have been mine!" Gothard went into an all-too-familiar crouch, coming up with a pistol in his hand.

In a flash of blue velvet, Scarborough leapt forward and knocked the gun from his brother's grasp. It went flying, barely missing a matron's head as it sailed though a window with a startling crash. "You won't live to kill again, *brother*."

Scarborough nodded at Jason, who moved closer, his sword still outstretched.

An unearthly sound escaped Gothard's throat before he shoved past Scarborough and ran through the crowd. Rainbow shades of satin and silk swirled in a colorful kaleidoscope as wedding guests darted to avoid him. He burst through the doors that led to the garden, broken glass crunching beneath his feet as he disappeared into the trees.

Within a heartbeat Jason was after him, chasing him along a graveled path. Footsteps pounded behind him; he assumed they were Scarborough's and ran faster. This time he wouldn't prove himself less than a man. Even should he have to do the unthinkable, Gothard wouldn't get away.

But first he needed answers.

His lungs burned with the effort to catch up. Damn, Gothard was fast. But not fast enough. Gothard might be running for his life, but Jason was fueled by fury and a resolve born of weeks of frustration. His muscles pumped with determination; his jaw gritted with iron will.

His quarry was nearly within reach.

He pulled up short when Gothard staggered to the ground.

He hadn't registered the sharp report of the bullet. But he turned to see the pistol that had shot it. And the woman on the other end of it.

Emerald MacCallum.

It hadn't even occurred to him that she was after the reward when he saw her at the inn. He'd thought only of Cait. Now he looked to the ground and Gothard's still, lifeless form. He dropped to his knees and felt for a pulse.

Dead. Gothard was dead. He frantically searched the limp body, for a letter, a miniature, anything. Anything that would prove or disprove what the man had claimed.

"He was telling the truth," Scarborough said quietly from behind him.

Jason sat back on his heels, feeling the unmanly sting of tears in his eyes.

A crowd was gathering again, people pouring through the doors and out into the garden. Scarborough turned and conducted a hasty, whispered conversation with Lord Darnley. Together they hustled the guests back inside. It took some minutes, and by the time Scarborough returned, Jason had composed himself.

The gray day had finally delivered on its promise, and a light drizzle fell from the sky. Silently Scarborough walked Jason down the garden path, away from the sight of the body.

Their brother.

Jason dropped onto a stone bench, his hands dangling limply between his spread knees, his eyes blindly perusing the wet gravel beneath his feet.

Scarborough sat beside him. "My mother had an affair with your father before either of them married." His voice was low, his words matter-of-fact. "When he fell in love with your mother, he left mine pregnant. Eventually she was offered to my father as a widow with a young son. She was beautiful, and her family had land that bordered his. Her dowry. He didn't know the truth at the time, but when he learned it later, he forgave her. Their marriage wasn't bad, all things considered."

Jason's father—the valiant war hero—had had an illicit affair. Had left a pregnant woman. Had left behind a child.

"Geoffrey was the oldest," Scarborough continued, "but he would never inherit. He resented it. He made my life a living hell."

"I'm sorry," Jason muttered, feeling somehow as though he were to blame.

"He never knew who his own father was until our parents died. While going through their things, we found—a letter. From your father to my mother. From that moment, Geoffrey..." Scarborough seemed at a loss for words. His fingers curled into fists. "He lost his mind. It's the only way I can put it. It was as though he finally had somewhere to channel all that hatred. I'm sorry I threw him out, though. If I'd known he would come after you, I'd have coped with him somehow. I feel a substantial burden of responsibility here, and for that I apologize."

"It's not your fault." Jason shoved the damp hair from his eyes. It was his father's fault. His not-so-perfect father. A human man after all, selfish enough to act in his own interests, a man who had made mistakes.

Mistakes that Jason had paid for. And little Mary and her mother. And Adam and Caithren, and who knew how many others?

"I thank you for being so candid." Jason rose and held out a hand.

Scarborough stood and grasped it tightly. "I'm sorry."

"And for jumping in to save me from Gothard's pistol."

"I was only evening the score. You saved me from his sword. I would never have recognized him in that disguise."

Their eyes met, man to man. Two men who both did what needed to be done.

"I'll leave you to your thoughts." With a nod, Scarborough backed away, then turned and walked toward the house.

"Pardon me, but are you the Marquess of Cainewood?"

The voice was light and musical, and Jason swiveled to see Emerald MacCallum. Good heavens, she topped him in height. How had he ever insisted that Cait was Emerald?

Taken aback, he blinked. "Where is your emerald amulet?"

Her eyes looked puzzled. "My what?"

"Your..." He shook his head to clear it. "How did you get your name?"

She grinned. "My birth name is Flora. The first time I went tracking, I recovered a large cache of stolen emeralds. The news sheets called me 'Emerald' MacCallum, and the name stuck."

Of course. It made perfect sense. Another misconception that had stubbornly lodged in his head.

"Lord Cainewood..." When she swept off her man's hat, the drizzle beaded on her bright red curls. "I believe you had offered a reward...?"

He measured her, unblinking. He sensed she was a good woman, drawn to desperate measures. Something he understood now more than ever before.

And he remembered a man saying she was a mother.

"You have children?"

"Aye." Her eyes saddened, and he knew what to do.

The pouch in his surcoat was heavy. He drew it out and handed it to her.

Frowning, she spilled the contents into her hand and slowly counted a hundred pounds, then put the rest back.

"Keep it," Jason said. "All of it."

"But...there's more than two hundred pounds here! Maybe three. The reward was a hundred." Her expression said she thought he'd lost his mind.

Perhaps he had. "Keep it," he repeated. "I didn't exactly want to see justice done this way, but perhaps it is for the best." He shrugged. "As for the money…I would just as soon not picture you chasing men all over England. Go home to your family."

She smiled, her face transforming. Her eyes brimmed with tears. And once he'd thought that a woman like her would never cry. Another thing he'd been wrong about.

"Take it and make a life for yourself," he said. "And your children."

"I will," she breathed. "God bless you, Lord Cainewood."

SEVENTY-FOUR

CAITHREN COULD barely lift her feet to mount the steps to the town house.

Her father was gone, and now her brother. And, dear heavens, she'd killed a man. And Jason was gone from her life.

It was all too much to absorb.

Ford shoved open the house's front door. "Why is it that anything the authorities are involved in seems to take forever?"

A sound of derision came from her throat. "I expect they've nothing better to do than be bothersome."

"Hush, sweet Cait." Cameron patted her arm. "The question was rhetorical. It's been a long day and night, but you can rest now." Stopping short on the threshold, he turned to Kendra and Ford. "Good Lord. You people actually live here?" Clearly aghast, he stared into the plush interior.

Kendra beckoned him inside. "Father bought it in the pre-war days, before our family's capital was depleted in defense of the king. Jason is cash poor, but he has…things."

"Jason seems to have plenty of money," Cait disagreed.

"It's all relative." With a shrug, Kendra started down the corridor. "Come, we'll sit and talk."

"I don't want to talk," Cait said to her back.

Cam lifted a brow. "She wants to wallow."

Reaching the drawing room, Kendra turned with a sympathetic

look. "Go on in. I'll stop by the kitchen and ask for some refreshments."

Cait set her jaw, but followed the men into the room and plopped onto the burgundy brocade couch. Cameron sat beside her, and Ford settled into one of two matching carved-walnut chairs.

Kendra took the other chair a minute later. "Cait. Are you all right?"

"I'm fine." Her hands tried to find her amulet, then her laces, and finally fell into her lap. "It was an accident. I didn't mean to kill him."

"I'm not speaking of Wat Gothard." Kendra's eyes mirrored everyone's concern. "I'm asking how you feel about your brother. And...about Jason."

"I'll miss Adam. We weren't close, and, truth be told, I didn't hold him in high regard. We hadn't seen much of each other in years. But he was my brother, my blood, and I loved him." She struggled to swallow the lump that had been lodged in her throat since Jason told her the truth. "As for *your* brother, he knew Adam was dead, and he didn't care enough to tell me."

Ford rose. "That isn't so." As he paced the Oriental carpet, the butler walked in with a large silver tray. "I talked to him before he left the Bull Inn. He'd known for but two days, Cait, and he failed to tell you because..." He turned, and his blue eyes sought hers. "...not because he didn't care, but because he cared too much. He was afraid you would hate him once you knew."

"Hate him?" She accepted a cup of warm chocolate from the butler, but shook her head at the proffered plate of cakes. "Whyever would I hate him?"

Ford's brow knitted. "Because he killed your brother."

"That's the most absurd thing I've ever heard." Stunned, she sipped from the cup, grateful for something to do with her hands and mouth. Other than yelling or throttling Jason. "The killing wasn't intentional, and he knew I believed that. We discussed it days ago. Before either of us knew it was...Adam." At her brother's name, her vision blurred, but she took a deep breath.

"He thought that wouldn't matter to you." Ford took a cake, then just held it, as though he wasn't sure what to do with it. "Whether it was intentional or not."

The butler set down the plate and left.

"He was your brother, Cait," Ford said softly.

"It was an accident." She sat a while, open-mouthed, then said, "Now I do hate him."

But the thought that Ford could be right brought a thread of hope.

She held on to it like a lifeline.

"If not for killing your brother, why hate him, then?" Kendra frowned into her cup. "Because he left you at the Bull Inn after telling you?"

"No. Never that." The chocolate wasn't sitting well in Cait's stomach. "I had all of you, and Gothard and Scarborough were both at that wedding. He had to go." Setting her cup on a low table, she drew an embroidered throw off the back of the couch and wrapped it around her shoulders. "He had no choice."

"Then why?" Rising, Kendra came close and knelt at Cait's feet. "I want to understand. If not because he left you, why do you hate him?"

"I don't hate him." Tears flooded her eyes. Tears she wouldn't shed for Adam—not in so public a place—flowed freely at the thought of Jason's betrayal. "I love him, and he doesn't trust me to forgive him. That hurts."

Beside her, Cam took her hand. "Do you really love him, Cait? A man you've known for but days? An...Englishman?"

She nodded, afraid what he must think, yet unable to deny it.

But he surprised her. "Then you must forgive him for thinking such of you." His hand squeezed hers. "It goes two ways, aye? Remember what your mam used to say: Gae it oot and get it back."

"Pardon?" Ford said.

Kendra shot him a lowering glance.

"What we give, we have," Cait translated quietly. She took a deep breath. "Forgiveness. And trust. Jason and I...we haven't seen a lot of either between us, but maybe it must come from me first."

Kendra reached for a cake and turned it in her hands. "Make him suffer, Cait. God knows he deserves it." She looked up, and they shared a wan smile. "But then you'll marry him, yes? Because—"

"Nay." Fresh tears leaked out. "I love your brother, but I cannot marry him."

"Why?" Kendra breathed. "I thought—"

Cait shivered, but not from the cold. "Upon marriage my property would become Jason's. The land that goes with the title is worth nothing without the larger portion, the many acres that came through my mother. To me, now that Adam is gone." Swallowing against the sadness, she tightened the wrap around her. "Cameron deserves it, and I love him too much to see him lose it."

With a gasp, Cam pulled his hand from hers. "It was never meant to be mine, Cait! Any of it!"

"Aye, it was and it is." She blinked back the tears. "You were next in line. Eldest son of my father's brother. Sir Cameron Leslie, now that Da and Adam are gone. You knew that, surely?"

"Nay." He looked stunned. "I mean…Good Lord. Of course I knew I was next in line, but I never thought about it. I thought only of you, Cait. Within an hour after hearing the news, I was on my way here to fetch you back home. Knowing you wouldn't find Adam."

"See? You thought of me first. It's always been that way between us, Cam, and that won't be changing now."

SEVENTY-FIVE

*A*FTER TELLING his story to the authorities, Jason walked the streets for hours, far past the time it was safe to be outside without linkboys to light the way. Midnight had come and gone before he mounted the steps to the town house and threw open the door.

"Jason! Where have you been?" Kendra must have been watching by the window, because she flung herself at him before swiftly pulling back. "You're soaking wet."

He hadn't noticed. "I have something to tell you and Ford. Please fetch him. Now."

"Shouldn't you dry off first?" Her gaze trailed from his face down to the marble floor, where a small puddle was collecting at his feet. "Cait's upstairs—"

"Now."

"All right. I'll go get Ford."

He strode to the drawing room, lit a fire, wrapped himself in the costly embroidered throw that was wadded in a corner of the brocade couch. And waited, pacing the dark red and blue carpet.

"Sit down," he said when the twins came in.

Obediently Kendra perched on one of the chairs, but Ford walked to a small inlaid cabinet. "I could do with a brandy. And you?"

Jason nodded his assent and took the goblet when Ford had poured. He waved him into another chair. "How is Caithren?"

"She's all right," Kendra said carefully. "Disappointed and grieving, of course, but all right. Jason, she—"

"Good." Concern etched his sister's wholesome features, but he couldn't muster the energy to comfort her or listen to this now. Cait was important—the most important thing of all. But his world had turned upside down today, and he had to work that out.

He sipped the brandy, feeling it burn a path to his empty stomach. "Geoffrey Gothard was our brother."

"He was *what*?" the twins said in unison.

"Our brother." He tugged the throw more tightly around his shoulders. "Our half brother, to be more precise. As well as Scarborough's. Our father impregnated their mother before he wed ours," he said, almost mechanically. He was still having trouble wrapping his mind around that fact. "And he left her, with child, knowing she was with child. *Our* father."

An uneasy silence reigned over the room. No one moved. Jason could hear the clock ticking on the mantel.

Ford blew out a slow breath. "You said he *was* our brother."

"He's dead." When Kendra rose as though to come to him, Jason waved her back. "At Emerald MacCallum's hands. But I do believe I was pushed to the point where I might have done it myself."

Ford nodded his understanding. "He threatened the woman you love."

"No. I mean, yes—that would have been enough. But it was more than that." Shivering, Jason moved to put his back to the fire. "All these years—"

He broke off.

The words simply wouldn't come out, wouldn't align themselves in his head.

"All these years," Kendra repeated gently, "you've tried to live up to the legend of our father—the brave, honorable man who gave up his family to fight for his king. To fight in a losing war, to die in a losing war, the ultimate sacrifice."

He drew a deep breath. "That vision of him was wrong."

"Yes, it was. But you weren't ready to see it." Kendra reached for Ford's brandy and took a fortifying sip. "You were left as the head of the family too young. Too tender an age for so many responsibilities. But our father—and our mother—left together due to love for each other and the monarchy, not lack of love for us."

"I've always known that," Jason said, his voice rough to his own ears. He cleared his throat. "Unlike Colin, I never took it as a personal affront. But now we know he left another family, too. And…"

He paused to take a sip of his brandy—a gulp, truth be told—and stared into the goblet.

"Responsibilities. It seems I've always had responsibilities. I resented the senseless deaths that left me with those responsibilities, and I avoided any violence that might remind me of those deaths." He looked up. "And I hated myself for that."

When Kendra rose and walked over to him, he didn't stop her this time. Her light green eyes burned into his. "Our father hadn't been so brave and honorable, had he? Or responsible. He'd been a man. Human."

It was the same conclusion he'd come to while walking in the rain. And it was time to give himself permission to be human as well. Free of the overwhelming shackles of his father's expectations. Free to live his life with his own set of values. In his own way.

With Caithren—if only she'd have him.

If only she'd forgive him.

At long last, he had internal peace—but he didn't have the woman he loved.

"Cait and we…" His voice cracked. "We all lost brothers today."

"But ours was not worth claiming." Ford stood up. "Go to her, Jason. She's hurting."

Kendra's mouth gaped open at her twin. "When did you get to be so compassionate?"

He shot her a scathing glare, then turned back to their brother. "Go to her. She's in your chamber." His lips turned up in a hint of a smile. "You'd better hope that tall cousin of hers doesn't have it in his mind to protect her."

Jason couldn't smile, not now. And just let Cameron Leslie try to stand in his way.

His heart ached as he climbed the stairs to his chamber. He eased the door open and slipped inside, his knees going weak just at the sight of her lying on his bed. Her cousin sat in a chair alongside, murmuring soft words of comfort.

He swallowed hard. "Caithren."

She rolled over to face him, her eyes brimming with tears.

Cameron rose and walked to the door. "Remember what I told you, Cait, I beg you. Your happiness comes before—"

"Leave us, Cam." Her voice sounded breathless, uneven, doubtless from hours of crying. "Please."

Wordlessly, Cameron slipped through the door, and it clicked shut behind him.

Jason stepped closer. His fingers loosened. The embroidered throw slid from his shoulders to the floor.

"You hate me, don't you?" he whispered.

She sat up. "You're all wet. You should dry off."

He took another hesitant step closer. "Cait—"

"You hurt me," she said.

He'd go to his knees if he thought it would make a difference, but he stood frozen in place. "I'm so sorry. More sorry than I can possibly express. If I'd known earlier it was your brother I'd killed, I'd have told you immediately, I swear. But I loved you by then, Cait —I couldn't bear to deliver the news that would make you so unhappy. That would tear you from my side forever. I wanted that last night with you more than I wanted to live."

Her eyes widened through the tears. But she hugged herself, effectively shutting him out. "You didn't trust me." She swiped miserably at the wetness on her cheeks. "And you still don't trust me. How can you say in one breath that you love me, and in the next that I would be so shallow as to hold an accidental death against you?"

"But—"

"I know Adam's killing wasn't intentional, any more than my own killing of Wat."

A trickle of relief coursed through his blood. Guilt slowly began to fade, replaced by a tremulous hope. "But would you feel the same way if you hadn't killed Wat?" he wondered. "Would you have understood regardless?"

She shook her head, looking thoroughly disgusted. "See, there you go again. I'm devastated you don't think better of me. Do you remember that night in Newark, when you had the bad dream?"

He remembered. A gruesome nightmare and an angel that

soothed him. Wearing a ridiculous white nightgown. "You said you didn't fault me. You said you understood."

"And just what do you think would ever change that?"

He was afraid to believe, but he could see she harbored no anger, no resentment. It wasn't in her.

"I shall expect more respect from you from here on out, Jason Chase."

He blinked, and his breath caught in hope. "Does that mean—"

"You've left me alone all night, with little to do but think. And I think I will marry you, Lord Cainewood. Never mind that you haven't asked. But only on two conditions."

His heart soared. "Anything."

She climbed from the bed, and he reached to pull her into an embrace. But she wrenched away. "You will hear me out."

"Very well." Though his arms ached to hold her, he crossed them instead. "I'm listening."

"One. You will not underestimate me again."

"You can wager on that." He risked a small, hopeful smile. "And two?"

Blowing out a breath, she locked her gaze on his. "Cameron must have Leslie. The part that came through my mother, I mean. With Adam's death, he's already come into the title and small entailed lands. But those lands alone cannot support a man."

"Cait—"

"Nay. You will hear me out. Cameron hasn't asked for this, and he would likely strangle me if he knew I was asking for him. According to my father's will, the vast majority of Leslie becomes my husband's should I marry. But Cam deserves all of Leslie, Jase— it should have been his in the first place. He was a better son to Da than Adam and then some. So even though Kendra told me you need money, I won't see Cam go without his due—I won't take my happiness at his expense. It wouldn't be fair."

"And Caithren Leslie is always fair," he said softly. "Now, you will hear *me* out."

She sat on the bed, apparently reserving judgment.

"I was only going to say, back when you interrupted me, that Cameron can have the property—the only part of Leslie I need is you. And I *do* need you, Cait. More than I ever thought possible."

"Oh." She looked properly chagrined, but a tiny smile tugged at her lips.

"And I have something for you." He reached into his pocket. "Hold out your hand." She did, and he gazed into her eyes as he folded her fingers around a flash of green. "When it changes hands, a change of heart," he quoted solemnly.

"My amulet?" She looked at it, then back at him. "Where—how did you get this?"

"I found it in the square. When I went looking for you. The chain was broken, so I put the amulet on this ribbon until I have time to get it repaired."

She stared down at it for a moment, fingering the narrow black satin ribbon, then slowly held it out to him. "Keep it."

"Pardon?" He didn't reach for it, just gaped at her in disbelief.

"I thought that if I wore it I'd be safe. But it brought me more luck when you had it. Then I found the strength to save myself from the Gothards. All by myself, without the emerald to depend on. And it brought me your offer of love and marriage. At least I think it did—you haven't asked me yet, and I've been waiting nearly two days already."

He dropped to one knee and took her hands in his, the emerald trapped between their fingers. "Will you marry me, Caithren Leslie?"

She pulled her hands away. "Lick your right thumb."

He was speechless for a moment. "Pardon?"

"It's a Scottish custom. Lick it."

"I cannot believe—"

"*Lick it.*" For emphasis, she licked her own.

Shaking his head, he did the same.

She took his hand and pressed their wet thumbs tightly together. "It's a bond. Now ask me again."

He captured her gaze with his. "Caithren Leslie—" His voice broke, and he sucked in a breath. "Will you marry me?"

With a look so intimate it tugged at his heart, she pulled him up and slipped the necklace over his head. When he touched it, almost as reverently as she always had, she smiled.

"Jason Chase, I thought you would never ask."

And her lips gave him his answer.

SEVENTY-SIX

"*H*URRY," KENDRA urged. "It's about to begin."

"I think not." Her sister-in-law, Amy, grinned. "They won't be starting the ceremony without the bride."

Caithren turned from the window, where she'd been watching a small cluster of people gather in the bright sun that flooded Cainewood Castle's quadrangle. Blinking in the chamber's relative dimness, she walked to Kendra's four-poster bed and slid the gold brocade robe from her shoulders.

"There's no need to rush." Amy held up a sheer chemise. "Dressing for your wedding should be a calm, soothing experience." She shot Kendra a warning glance as she slipped the garment over Cait's head.

"Like yours was?" Kendra returned with a lift of one expressive brow. "I seem to remember you shaking in your—excuse me, *my*—red-heeled shoes."

Amy's eyes sparkled. "That was different. I was terrified. A shopkeeper's daughter marrying an earl. It seemed wrong." She smiled, tossing one long black ringlet behind her plum velvet-clad shoulder. "But it was right."

Kendra smoothed her mint satin skirts. "Cait has nothing to be nervous about."

"Nay." Caithren rolled her eyes. "Daughters of provincial Scottish baronets wed English marquesses every day of the week."

The other women laughed. "But I'm not nervous. This is right, too."

She believed it, with all her heart and soul. Still, it was no small step to be taking. Cait drew a deep breath and pulled her wedding gown off the bed—the first English gown that had been specifically made for her. Fashioned of sky blue silk, it had a silver tissue under-skirt and real silver lace edging the scooped neckline. The sleeves were double-puffed with a spill of silver lace at the wrists, the stom-acher embroidered with scrolling silver designs.

She held it up. "Marry in blue, love ever true."

"Is that what they say?" Kendra helped her wiggle into it, watching appreciatively as it settled into place. "Oh, it's lovely! If ever I fall in love, I want a dress just like this, but in green."

"Oh, you wouldn't want to wear green." Cait glanced up from tightening the laces. "Green is unlucky. The choice of the fairies."

Amy handed her the stomacher. "You believe in fairies?"

"Well, nay," Cait said, working the tabs. "But it's not worth taking a chance now, is it? Not on your wedding day. Besides," she added, looking to Kendra as she sat to draw on her stockings, "Jason told me you have no wish to wed."

"Not any of the men *he* chooses." Kendra handed her a pair of blue ribbon garters trimmed with silver lace. "Stodgy old dukes, ancient rich earls, widowed marquesses with children. I'm not looking to marry a boring, acceptable man. I'm waiting for peerless passion. And not," she added, "a duke. I won't be 'your graced' for the rest of my life." Tossing her red ringlets, she held out a sky blue satin shoe.

"I need the right shoe first." The shoes were straight, not made for one foot or the other, but Cait had worn them yesterday to break them in. No sense getting blisters at her wedding.

"For luck?" Kendra frowned at both shoes, then handed her the other one.

"Aye. And that silver coin I left on your dressing table goes in the left shoe."

"I'll get it," Amy volunteered.

"Do you hear that?" Cait froze. Haunting notes floated up through the open window. "Could it be bagpipes?"

"Jason's surprise." Kendra moved to shut the window. "Don't tell him you heard."

"Please leave it open. I won't tell." Cait's heart swelled as she slipped the coin into her shoe. "Though how he thinks anyone within ten miles could fail to hear a bagpiper is beyond me."

"I have something for you." Amy slipped her hand into her pocket and came out with gleaming gold. "The first thing I made in my new workshop. May I pin it on your dress?"

Cait nodded and stood, her gaze riveted to the gorgeous oval emerald stomacher brooch as Amy pinned it in place. Surrounded by diamonds and pearls in a delicate filigree bezel, it glittered through the sudden tears that filmed her eyes.

"Jason told me you gave him your own emerald," Amy said, "so I thought it would make a perfect wedding present."

Cait's fingers moved to caress it. "It's the most beautiful thing I've ever owned," she whispered. "I will never be able to thank you."

"Marry come up!" Amy laughed. "You have just thanked me already." Stepping back to view her handiwork, she examined Cait from head to toe. "God in heaven," she breathed. "You look beautiful. Come to the mirror and see."

"Nay. I cannot see myself fully dressed for my wedding." Cait played with the ends of her long, straight hair, which Jason had requested be left free and uncurled. Self-conscious, she fanned it to cover the cleavage exposed by the gown's low neckline. Touching the wee heart patch on her cheek, she sent both women a tremulous smile.

"Another sister." When Kendra gathered them all into a group hug and they bumped foreheads, Cait giggled through her tears.

A knock came at the door.

"Are you ready?" Cameron's voice came through the sturdy oak. "Colin said you're taking so long you must be eating in here."

"Quick," Kendra said loudly. "Hide the food."

They all laughed as Cait went to open the door.

"Cait?" Dressed in a borrowed deep-blue velvet suit, Cameron looked almost as English as she did. "Good Lord," he said. "Cait, you look lovely."

"Thank you." She blushed, looking down toward large cornflower eyes and a head of bright blond curls. "And who is this?"

"Her name is Mary, and she and her mother are very special

guests." When Cam lifted his hand, Mary's little hand came up with it. "She, uh, attached herself to me." He gave a sheepish shrug, but Cait didn't miss the pleased glow in his eyes. "She may be walking down the aisle with us."

So this was the Mary that Jason had run off to avenge. Caithren knelt, her silk skirts pooling around her. "Good day," she said.

"Good day," Mary returned in a small, polite voice. "I am pleased to meet you, my lady."

"I'm not—"

"You'll be a lady within the hour," Cam interrupted with a teasing smile. "You may as well get used to it." He blew out a breath, ruffling his straight, wheaten hair. "I, on the other hand, will never get used to being a sir."

"Aye, you will." Cait rose and linked her arm though his. "Shall we go?"

Luckily the three of them fit side by side down the corridor and wide stone staircase, because Mary still clung to Cam with an iron grip. The only remaining evidence of the lassie's ordeal seemed to be a slight catch in her gait and a wee slur in her speech. Cait had taken Kendra foraging around Cainewood yesterday, showing her which plants were useful, and tomorrow she would teach her how to make an infusion to help Mary regain her strength.

The bagpipe music swelled when they reached the double front doors and stepped out into the sunshine. Kendra wandered off to find her twin. Colin was waiting outside for Amy, their infant daughter Jewel cooing in his arms. The bairn between them, he bent to give his wife a sweet, lingering kiss, and Caithren smiled at the three of them together.

A family. Although she now knew she wasn't yet pregnant, she smiled at the thought that she and Jason might be starting a family soon.

It was a glorious day to be wed, the quadrangle redolent with the scent of newly cut grass, the sky blue as her gown and dotted with wee puffy white clouds. Cait's gaze swept the castle's crenelated walls and the ancient keep built on a motte—reminding her of the one outside Stamford. Beyond it was an area where the grass grew high and untamed.

"Gudeman's croft," she murmured.

"What is that?" Mary asked.

Cameron knelt down to her. "A place allowed to grow free as a shelter for brownies and fairies."

"Oh." Mary's eyes widened. "Do you know stories of brownies and fairies?"

"Many. But they'll have to wait for later." With his free hand, Cam ruffled her golden curls, then he stood and faced Cait. "It's really the old tilting yard. Colin told me they don't groom it since it's long been in disuse."

"I knew that." Her lips curved in a soft smile as she scanned her new home. A hundred rooms, she remembered Jason telling her. "Can you believe this place, Cam?"

His hazel eyes met hers. "You always were meant to live in a castle, sweet Cait."

"Aye," she said, thinking of Da's tiny castle at home—Cameron's castle now. "But who'd have ever guessed it would be such an enormous, historic one...and in England?"

Her head reeled with the impossibility of her new life. Nothing Jason had told her could have prepared her for the sheer size and grandeur of Cainewood Castle. She could scarcely believe she would be living within its four-foot-thick stone walls. As the Marchioness of Cainewood, no less.

"You'll do fine." Cam leaned to kiss her forehead, then looked up. "There's your man now."

Her gaze flew to Jason, and suddenly what had seemed impossible was gloriously real. She was going to live here, in this castle, with the man she loved.

Clearly comfortable in this place, he walked beside the gray-haired parson, deep in conversation. He wore a forest-green velvet suit that brought out his eyes, trimmed in gold braid that matched the stiff ribbon bows on his formal heeled shoes.

When he looked over at her and smiled, her heart did a slow roll in her chest.

A pretty woman in a clean but simple pink dress came up to take Mary by the hand. "It's time," she said gently, and reluctantly the wee lass released her grip on Cameron. The girl looked over her shoulder, her blue eyes lingering on him as the woman led her away.

"Her mother?" Cait guessed.

"Aye." Cameron's gaze followed the two as they walked toward the gatehouse on their way to the family's private chapel. The woman's rich brown hair gleamed beneath a pink-ribboned straw hat. "Her name is Clarice Bradford. You'll like her." He turned to take Cait by both hands. "Are you ready?" he asked.

"More ready than I ever thought possible." Smiling at him, she squeezed his fingers. "You know, Mam always said it's better to marry over the midden than over the muir."

"I've heard that said, that it's wise to stick within your own circle." Did she only imagine it, or did his gaze flick toward Clarice? "But I'm not sure I believe it."

"I don't believe it, either." Her own gaze trailed to Jason, waiting for her by the barbican. She was sure she'd never glimpsed so romantic a vision as her husband-to-be standing with the soaring castle behind him, his blue-black hair ruffled by the slight breeze, his clear green eyes locked on hers. "I reckon even mothers are wrong sometimes."

~

*T*HE PARSON cleared his throat. "Caithren Leslie, wilt thou have this man to thy wedded husband, to live together after God's ordinance in the holy estate of matrimony? Wilt thou love him, comfort him, honor, obey, and serve him, and keep him in sickness and in health; and, forsaking all others, keep thee only unto him so long as you both shall live?"

Beneath the hammerbeam roof of Cainewood's ancient chapel, dappled by the multicolored light that filtered through the stained arched windows, Jason squeezed Caithren's hand. She looked around her at the people gathered there to see them wed.

Cameron, who'd insisted on staying for her wedding before going home to his new life in Scotland. Kendra and Ford, who'd stood by her side that wrenching night in London. Colin—like Jason, but different—and Amy and their beautiful bairn. Mary and Clarice, whose tragedy had set Jason on the path that led him to find her.

They were all looking toward her, so expectantly.

"I will," she said. "All except the obey and serve part."

Cameron snickered. Kendra smiled. The parson appeared stunned.

"I accept those conditions," Jason said loud and clear.

The parson still looked confused.

"Go on, will you?" Jason prompted. "Before she changes her mind."

SEVENTY-SEVEN

OST OF THE wedding party sat around the dining room table, waiting for Colin, who had gone to settle the baby in her cradle, and Ford, who had told them he wanted to fetch something. A stack of marzipaned wedding cakes sat in the middle of the long mahogany table, which was set with the sort of fine china and crystal that Caithren had only read about in books. She kept looking down at the wedding ring that Jason had slipped onto her finger during the ceremony.

"Do you like it?" he murmured from his seat beside her. "Father sold off most of the family jewels to help finance the war, but I could have found something, or had Amy make—"

"It's perfect." She smiled at the gold band studded with emeralds, remembering when he bought it from the Gypsy woman without dickering. "There's no other ring in this world I'd rather wear."

"Whenever I see it, I'll remember your dance," he said low. "And the moment you stole my heart."

Her own heart melting, they shared a smile.

"I'm starving," Kendra announced. She reached for a cake, then froze. "Did you hear something?" She sat up straighter, twisting her head toward the high, arched windows.

Cait turned to look, too. But the dancing flames in the fireplace reflected off the beveled glass, making it difficult to see anything.

"Hear something like what?" Cameron asked.

Kendra frowned. "Like...scratching."

"I was sipping." Jason rolled his eyes, draining his crystal goblet with a prolonged slurp. "There. Was that the sound?"

"No...wait! Listen..."

"I hear it too," Amy breathed. "It's—"

"The ghost!" Kendra's eyes widened. "The Parkinson ghost!"

"What's this about a ghost?" Clearly unshaken, Cameron swirled the wine in his goblet appreciatively.

"There's no such thing as ghosts," Jason declared.

"Well, now." Cam paused for a swallow. "You won't be finding a Scot admitting to that."

Kendra glared at her brother. "Just because you cannot explain ghosts doesn't mean they don't exist. The Parkinson ghost is hardly a new legend. And haven't you heard about all the sightings in the week since we've been back?" She turned to Caithren, apparently looking for support. "Did you know this room was once a private chapel, built by Henry II when the castle was in the hands of the Crown?"

Cait's gaze swept the stone arches overhead, fit between with a centuries-old oak barrel-section ceiling. "Tonight it feels like it still belongs to the spirits, aye?"

Cameron's goblet hit the table with a little *clink*. "Tell us about this ghost." Little Mary climbed onto his lap and wrapped an arm around his neck, sticking her other thumb into her mouth. He shifted to hold her close. "What are these stories?"

Kendra sat forward on her lattice-backed chair. "Just this week Cook saw him twice, once in the quadrangle and once walking across the drawbridge, and Haversham saw him on the drive, and Sally saw him on the roof—"

"—and Carrington saw him under the barbican," Jason interrupted, "and Mrs. Potts saw him on the wall walk. Our servants have very impressionable imaginations." He reached for the wine decanter. "Let's suppose there were such a thing as ghosts—just for argument's sake, you understand. Why would this Parkinson fellow show up *now*, after all this time?"

"Could it be *my* fault?" Cait wondered.

"No." Kendra shook her head. "He died exactly twenty years

ago this month. And he was killed by a Royalist—not that he didn't deserve it, the Roundhead cur, presuming to live in *our* castle—"

"Wheesht!" Cait whispered. "There it is again!"

Kendra moved to Colin's empty chair and grabbed Amy's hand. "It's him, I know it," she whispered.

Caithren took Jason's hand as well.

"It is *not* him." Unlike his sister's whisper, Jason's voice was loud and sure. "She's famous for jumping to conclusions," he said to no one in particular. "It's a bush being blown against the window."

"It's not windy," Clarice murmured, her cheeks turning red at having said something aloud. Her daughter let out a little whine, burrowing into Cameron's shirtfront.

"Not to mention," Kendra whispered more fiercely, "there are no bushes under those windows."

Caithren turned to see the windows and gasped. Something white floated beyond the leaded panes, dipping and bobbing eerily.

Like the monk she'd seen in the tunnel beneath Newark.

Jason turned too, and, despite himself, drew in a sharp breath.

"What? What?" Kendra whispered frantically, her eyes shut tight. "What is it?"

"It's...I'm not sure." Calmly Cameron sipped his wine. "But a ghost isn't necessarily something to be afraid of, aye?"

A sudden clatter from the chimney echoed in the high, arched chamber. Cait gripped Jason's hand harder, and Clarice grabbed for her daughter and somehow ended on Cameron's lap. They all swung around, their gazes riveted to the rattling fireplace.

"Oh, my God!" Kendra breathed. "He's up on the roof, just like Sally said! Oh, my God! Oh, my God!"

They all flinched when the dining room door swung open. A rush of wind sent the tapestries fluttering against the stone walls. Evidently forgetting he was supposed to look fearless, Jason clutched Cait, and she let out a high-pitched squeak. When Kendra screamed, the rest of the females joined her.

With an unnerving suddenness, mad laughter burst forth to accompany the rattling. Colin rushed in, whipping off a white sheet with a grand gesture.

They all stared at him, dumbstruck, as he strode to the fireplace and bent to shout up the chimney. "Ford! Come on down!"

"Bloody hell." Jason disentangled himself from Cait and sat back.

Amy extracted her fingers from Kendra's and flexed her hand, shaking her head at her husband. "I cannot credit that I fell for that."

Colin grinned wickedly, raising one black brow.

"Fell for what?" Caithren asked.

"Colin," Kendra said ruefully, "is famous—or perhaps I should say *infamous*—for his pranks."

"Oh." Cait's gaze flickered to Jason. "Well," she told Amy, "if it makes you feel any better, Jase fell for it, too."

"I did not."

"Then it was someone else's heart I felt pounding beneath my hand?"

She giggled when he sputtered.

Red-faced, Clarice slid off Cam's lap and onto her chair. "There's no ghost, then?"

"None." Colin's green eyes sparkled with mischief. "The staff was quite obliging with the mysterious sightings. I wouldn't be surprised if they're about now, waiting to see how it all turned out."

The door opened, and they all looked into the corridor expectantly, but it was only Ford returning from his chain-rattling responsibilities. He took one look at Cait's good-natured pout and burst into peals of laughter.

"On our wedding night!" she chided, but she couldn't help laughing along with him.

Cam rose and, settling Mary on her own chair, walked over to shake Colin's hand. "Well done, I must say. This is my kind of family."

"Then welcome to it." Colin looked to Caithren. "You, too."

He went to the door and signaled, whereby more servants than were necessary paraded in carrying the many dishes that comprised the wedding supper. They smiled conspiratorially as they set down platter after platter, slanting sidewise glances at Colin and each other before parading back out.

Steaming dishes of chicken cullis, fricandeau of beef, and artichoke pie wafted their scents toward Caithren's nose. She *did* feel like part of this family. Jason's hand squeezed hers beneath the table. One of his feet moved to tangle with hers, and his leg pressed against her thigh, making her face heat with thoughts of their wedding night to come. When she turned to him, she felt so warm and happy she couldn't quite believe it.

A grand sallet sat on the table, a bed of young greens with mandarin oranges, eggs, and long sprigs of rosemary standing tall, stuck into lemon halves and hung with cherries. But Kendra went for a cake.

"She always eats dessert first," Ford said at the look on Cait's face.

Kendra smiled, licking marzipan off her lips. "I might not have room for it later." She took another bite. "Would you like some?"

Cait shook her head and reached for some chicken. Toasts were drunk and good-natured teasing abounded. An hour later, when the meal was finished and everyone still sat around talking, she pushed back her chair and rose.

They all turned to look at her.

"A Scots funeral is merrier than an English wedding," she declared. "Whatever happened to that bagpiper?"

Jason shrugged. "I think he's eating in the kitchen."

"Well, would somebody fetch him already?" She moved from the table and shook out her skirts. "I'll be wanting to dance."

While Ford went off to do her bidding, she gave the others instructions. "Hold hands in a circle, lads and lassies alternating. That's it. Now, who has a handkerchief?" When Colin produced one, she handed it to her cousin. "Cameron, you take the middle since you know what to do."

When the piper arrived, Caithren surprised everyone by kicking off her shoes, then running to scoop up her lucky silver coin when it rolled across the floor. Laughing, Kendra and Amy doffed their shoes as well. Although they couldn't cajole Clarice into dancing in stockinged feet, at least her shoes were flat and sensible. Wee Mary wore flat shoes, too, but she was perfectly happy to get rid of them and her stockings, besides.

"Very well." Cait turned to the piper as Ford took his place in the circle. "We'll have a reel first, if you please."

Around and around they went in time to the rousing tune, until Cameron came from the center to Cait. The circling stopped, and he laid the lace-edged hankie in a neat square at her feet. They knelt on either side, and she bestowed him with a kiss on the lips. This met with mixed laughter and gasps until Cait snatched up the handkerchief and took her place in the middle.

Around they went again, dancing until she chose Jason. Their kiss was long and deep, causing much throat-clearing and finally applause. After Jason bowed and went into the center, the circling resumed.

Jason chose Amy, and Amy chose Colin, and Colin chose Kendra, and Kendra chose Ford, and Ford chose Mary, and no one was surprised when Mary chose Cameron. By the time Cam chose Clarice they were all worn out, and Cait signaled the piper to take a rest before Clarice had to go to her knees.

Just in time—as Clarice's cheeks had gone even pinker than her dress.

"A kissing dance!" Kendra said, breathlessly making her way to a chair. "I've never heard of such a thing!"

"There's much kissing at Scottish weddings." Cait winked at Cameron, still hovering close by Clarice. "A kiss can be claimed at the beginning and end of each and every dance. Now, get up, all you lazybones. We'll have a strathspey next, and a hornpipe after that."

The piper played those and more, and some English tunes as well, and if the familiar notes sounded a bit odd wafting from the pipes, nobody cared. It was past midnight before Cait let the poor musician go and the wedding party began stumbling off to bed with a lot of final kisses and good nights.

While Ford went off to fetch a footman to see Clarice and Mary home, Cameron kissed Cait on the cheek. "Lang may yer lum reek— an' may he huv the coal tae fill it."

Jason's brow creased. "What is that, Gaelic?"

"Nay." Cait laughed. "We don't know the Gaelic. After all this time with me, you still cannot understand plain English when you hear it, aye?" She smiled. "He was wishing we live long and well."

"I thank you, then. I think." Jason clapped Cameron on the shoulder. "And I wish you a good night."

"He wants me to leave you," Cam said to Cait.

"Aye, and I second the request." Minutes earlier she'd felt exhausted, but her body came alive at the thought of the night ahead. "I'd thank you to escort our guests to the door and then take to your bed."

"Good night to you, then, sweet Cait." A little drunkenly, she thought, her cousin lifted little Mary from the chair where she was sleeping and beckoned Clarice to follow him from the chamber.

As she turned to Jason, Cait's heart thumped in anticipation. Locking his gaze on hers in a way that set the pit of her stomach to fluttering, he waited until Cam's footsteps had faded, then grabbed her hand and pulled her running up the staircase.

When he stopped before his bedchamber door, she wound her arms around his neck and went up on her toes to press her mouth to his. "You must carry me over the threshold," she whispered against his lips. "It's bad luck if I trip."

"Well, we wouldn't want to start with bad luck." Her eyes slid closed as his tongue swept into her mouth, hot and exciting. His lips still sealed to hers, he caught her up, opened the door, and stepped inside. When her feet hit the plush carpet she reluctantly opened her eyes, then blinked.

And blinked again.

The chamber was lit by candles, seemingly hundreds of them. They marched across the dressing table and along the windowsill, their flames reflecting off the beveled diamond panes. They graced the bedside tables and the massive headboard beneath the cobalt blue canopy. They sat on stands, on the floor, atop the tall, carved clothes press. But the brightest concentration flanked both ends of a wee table with a chair on either side...and their backgammon board in the center.

He swept the hair off the back of her neck and planted his lips there, warm and cherishing. "You've pulled even," he murmured, the vibrations on her nape making her arch in pleasure, "but not for long. I intend to win this eve."

"You want to play backgammon?" With a gasp of disbelief, she turned to him. "On our wedding night?"

"Um-hmm." He nodded solemnly. "I remembered this morning that when I bought the set, we agreed to come up with something to wager. Then we never did. So I've settled on a forfeit."

Warily she backed up, not certain she liked the look in his eyes. "And what might that be?"

His smile made her skin tingle. "Our clothing."

"What?" She took another step back and sat on the bed.

"Our clothing." Coming close, he took her by the shoulders and raised her to stand. His voice turned low and silky. "Whoever loses will have to remove an item of clothing. Until we are both...how do you put it?" A trace of eroticism in his smile made her breath catch. "In the scud?"

This was not her idea of a wedding night. "Can't we just take all our clothes off now?" She molded herself against his hard body and kissed him on the chin, which was as high as she could reach without his cooperation. "I'll play backgammon with you tomorrow. I promise."

"Hmm..." He bent his head, and his mouth took hers in a kiss that was desperately intimate, but short and unsatisfying. "I think not."

"But I've got the stomacher and the gown, a chemise and stockings and garters." As well as she could in such close quarters, she eyed his velvet-clad form. "And you're wearing that much or more. This could take all night!"

"Mmm." He nodded thoughtfully, and his next kiss was long: a nibbling of the lips, a persuasive caress, and finally a fiery possession that left her mouth burning for more. "I intend it to take all night."

When she tried to pull him onto the bed, he only resisted with a husky chuckle. Weak with need, it was an effort to cross her arms. "This isn't fair."

"You think not?" He stepped back, seeming to consider it. "Very well, then, I'll give you an advantage."

She frowned, wondering whether to be relieved when he stripped off his surcoat and dropped it to the floor.

"You're terribly untidy," she scolded quite ineffectively. She couldn't seem to control the tremble in her voice.

"But I have you now." He shrugged, working on the knot in his cravat. "And you always pick up after me."

"That's a reprehensible attitude, Jase. I shall have to reform you." She bent to pick up the coat and laid it neatly over the back of a chair. He was taking off his clothes—it looked like she had won— yet his demeanor wasn't one of defeat. It was all so very confusing.

When her fingers moved to the tabs on her stomacher, he shook his head and reached out to still them. Flashing a devilish grin, he handed her the cravat, then silently unlaced his shirt and stripped it off over his head.

"There." The grin widened more. "Surely now you can win. Unless..." He raised a brow. "Unless you find yourself distracted again by my bare chest."

The lacy cravat dangled from her fingers as she stared at him. Against that very tempting bare chest, her amulet nestled, winking in the candlelight. She swallowed hard, her hands itching to touch him, her tongue wanting to taste his salty skin, her body aching to meld itself with his and convince her once and for all that he would be hers, forever.

Her exasperating Englishman.

Dark as sin, his gaze captured hers as he pushed her into a chair and handed her the shirt, still warm from his body. From the folds of fabric, his distinctive scent rose to envelop her, quickening her pulse, spreading the familiar melting weakness through every fiber of her being.

Helpless to stop staring, she slowly wadded the shirt and cravat in her lap.

"How very untidy," he chided, seating himself across the narrow table. Their knees touched, and one of his slid between hers at the same time one long arm sneaked underneath and tossed up her skirts. Warm and tormenting, a finger trailed her thigh...

And he tossed the dice.

AUTHOR'S NOTE

~

DEAR READER,

I always like to see the places I'm writing about, and I had great fun researching this story and visiting all the inns that lined the Great North Road—formerly the Roman road called Ermine Street—back in the 1660s. Which ones mentioned in the story are real? All of them! If an inn was mentioned by name, you can assume it was a real place that Jason and Cait could have stopped at during their travels. But a few of them have fascinating histories and deserve more than a mere mention.

In Newark, the Saracen's Head inn dated back to 1341 and was indeed run by the Twentyman family from 1590 until 1720. As told by my fictitious Mrs. Twentyman in the story, their name really was originally Lydell and changed when one of them pole-axed twenty men. And the true tale of the little drummer boy saving Newark from capture is still told today. A frequent visitor, Sir Walter Scott mentioned the inn in his novels and his diary, calling the landlord "a man of the most gentlemanly manners." The Saracen's Head finally closed in 1956, and the building is now used as a bank, but a "Saracen's Head" bust on the facade attests to its previous use.

As for the tunnels under Newark's marketplace, the one supposedly haunted by the ghost of a monk does not actually lead from the Saracen, but rather from the 16th century Queen's Head inn. There are no recent sightings of this ghost, but the last landlord did complain of strange noises coming from the cellar and a door that seemed to open itself in the middle of the night. Employees claim that bottles have been moved and hesitate to go into the cellar on their own. And one customer swears he saw someone "not of this world" standing on the stairs. Although the distinctive round Queen's Head sign still swings beneath the eaves of the building, it is currently operated as part of the chain of Hobgoblin pubs. A nice place to stop for lunch and—who knows?—maybe a bit of a scare!

Although it was just The Angel during the 17th century, Grantham's oldest inn is now called The Angel and Royal. The grounds originally belonged to the Knights Templar, and from 1212 until the dissolution of their order in 1312, it was a hostelry for royal travelers, merchants, and pilgrims. King John and his train of courtiers held court at The Angel in 1213, Richard III signed the death warrant of the Duke of Buckingham there in 1483, and the inn enjoyed a royal visit from Charles I in 1633. In 1866, Edward VII paid a visit to The Angel, and it was then that it became known as The Angel and Royal. One of the inn's most-told stories is that in 1707, the landlord Michael Solomon died and left a legacy of forty shillings a year to pay for a sermon to be preached against the evils of drunkenness every Michaelmas Day. To this day, the annual payment is made and the sermon preached. This handsome and historic inn is still a popular place to eat and stay.

The Bell Inn in Stilton dates back to 1500, and the current building from 1642, the year in which the Civil War began. There is still a Roman well in the courtyard, topped by a charming thatched roof. Alas, the inn's black cat was invented, but inspired by one who roamed the grounds during my visit. One popular 18th century tale has infamous highwayman Dick Turpin hiding at the Bell for nine weeks while hunted by the law. Supposedly, when surprised by a raid, he threw open the window and jumped onto Black Bess to gallop up the Great North Road. But the Bell Inn is most famous for Stilton Cheese and the man who popularized it, Cooper Thornhill, the inn's landlord during the 1700s. The cheese was first made by Thornhill's sister-in-law, a housekeeper in Leicestershire. Mites and all, he served it at the Bell and named it after the village. Soon the cheese's fame began to spread, and by the time Daniel Defoe wrote his *Tour Through The Whole Island of Great Britain* (1724-27), he could say he "passed through Stilton, a town famous for cheese." In the 1980s, the inn was restored using the original plans. Today it is a charming place to stay or take a meal while absorbing some of its history, and a frequent host to politicians, actors, and pop groups.

After Jason and Cait leave Stilton, they visit a Romani encampment and refer to the people there as Gypsies. While I'm aware that the word "Gypsy" is often considered a pejorative term these days, I chose to use it for historical accuracy, because no other words existed in the English language that my characters could call the

Romani people at that time. As the term wasn't considered derogatory in the 1660s, I hope you will consider my choice as respectful as it was intended.

Caithren's home was inspired by the real Leslie Castle in Scotland. Sadly, the charming little castle is no longer open to the public, but I was fortunate to stay there when it was still being run as a luxurious B&B. Set at the west end of the Bennachie Range, thirty miles from Aberdeen, Leslie was the original seat of Clan Leslie. The current castle, a turreted 17th century baronial house, is the third fortified building on the site since 1070. By the time of my story, the property had fallen out of Clan Leslie hands…but, fanciful as I am, I like to imagine that perhaps a minor Leslie family such as Cait's might have lived there. In 1979, the decaying roofless ruin was acquired by a member of the Leslie family and restored to its former fairy-tale beauty.

Do you suppose Cait was right when she thought a romance might be brewing between her cousin, Cameron, and little Mary's mother, Clarice? To find out, read the next book in the Chase Family Series, *If You Dared to Love a Laird*. You'll find an excerpt in the back of this book.

I hope you enjoyed *How to Undress a Marquess*!

Always,

Lauren Royal

Read on for an excerpt from

If You *Dared*
to Love a *Laird*

Book 3 of the
Chase Family Series
by Lauren Royal

Sensible Clarice Bradford is content in her widowhood. She has a pretty one-room cottage and a lovely little daughter, and the *last* thing she wants is another husband. Until one fairytale evening when she's invited to a wedding at a castle...

∾

Village of Cainewood, England
September 1667

THEY'D SENT A carriage to take her to the castle.

In all her thirty-one years, Clarice Bradford had never ridden in a carriage. Gingerly she climbed inside and perched on the leather seat, settling the pink skirts of her Sunday gown.

Dressed in blue to match her eyes, Clarice's five-year-old daughter bounced up and down on the seat opposite. "I've been in this carriage, Mama. When Lord Cainewood brought me to live with you."

In her short life, Mary had been orphaned by the plague and then abandoned during the Great Fire of London. But in the year since Lord Cainewood brought Mary to her doorstep, Clarice had come to love the girl like her own.

"I remember you climbing out of this carriage. That's one day I'm unlikely to ever forget." Clarice reached across and tweaked her daughter on the chin. "It's a fine carriage, isn't it?"

Mary shrugged, her blond ringlets bouncing on her shoulders in the same rhythm as the vehicle. "I would rather ride a horse."

"That wouldn't be a very elegant way to arrive at a nobleman's wedding."

A sigh wafted from Mary's rosy lips. "I s'pose not." She nibbled on a fingernail until Clarice pulled her hand from her mouth. "Who is Lord Cainewood marrying?"

"I haven't met her, poppet, but if she's marrying Lord Cainewood, she must be a grand lady. I've heard she's from Scotland."

"Scotland. Is that very far away?"

"Far enough." Clarice leaned across the cabin and took Mary's hands in hers. "Can you believe we're going to a wedding at the castle?"

Though Mary smiled, it was clear she wasn't overly impressed. "I lived at the castle before." Last year, after Lord Cainewood's brother had swept her from the fire and brought her to Cainewood. "For a whole month."

"Well, I've only been in the great hall for Christmas dinner once a year," Clarice said. "I've never seen any of the other rooms."

"I'll show you around," her daughter proclaimed, displaying nary a hint of the awe that made Clarice's heart beat a rapid tattoo.

The castle was grandly ancient; the very thought of entering the family's private living space was both daunting and exciting. And the carriage was clattering over the drawbridge already.

Shadows sheathed the carriage's windows as they passed beneath the barbican. Then it was bright again, and Clarice Bradford found herself inside the crenelated walls of Cainewood Castle.

The carriage door was flung open, and Mary ran down the steps into the enormous grassy quadrangle. "Who are you?" Clarice heard her ask. "And who is this?"

"You must be Miss Mary," came a masculine voice. Clarice alighted from the carriage to see a man crouched by her daughter, an infant in his arms. "And this is baby Jewel. Lord Cainewood is an uncle now, aye?"

"Lord Cainewood plays games with me sometimes. The babe is lucky to have him for an uncle." Four stories of stately living quarters looming behind her, Mary ran a small finger down the child's tiny nose. "But Jewel is an odd name. 'Specially for a boy."

"Ah, but Jewel is a lass." A grin appeared on the stranger's face, lopsided and indulgent. "Though she has little hair on her head yet, she's a girl."

"Oh. Will she have hair soon?"

"Aye. A bonnie lass she'll be. Just like you."

Mary's giggle tinkled into the summer air as the man rose to his full height and caught Clarice's gaze with his.

Something stirred inside her when she met his warm hazel eyes. Since he hadn't answered Mary, Clarice had no idea who he was. He looked to be a wedding guest, though, dressed in a fancy blue suit trimmed with bright gold braid. She'd been told this would be a small family wedding. Judging from his accent, he must belong to the bride's side.

The stranger was tall. Clarice was not a short woman, but he topped her by nearly a head. Straight wheaten hair skimmed his shoulders and fluttered in the light breeze, shimmering in the sunshine. And those eyes...she felt she could get lost in them.

She gave herself a mental shake. This magical fairytale day was sparking her imagination—that was all. She'd never thought to be inside the castle walls as an invited guest to the lord's wedding— she and Mary the only commoners invited—the only non-family invited, come to that. Lord Cainewood had said that since their misfortune had inadvertently led to his marriage, he wanted them with him to celebrate. The sheer wonder of it was going to her sensible head. Making her giddy.

"You talk funny," Mary said to the stranger.

"Mary!" Clarice exclaimed, but she couldn't seem to look at her daughter. Her gaze was still riveted to the man's. He didn't talk funny, either. To the contrary, the Scottish cadence of his words seemed to flow right into her and melt her very bones.

Lud, she was afraid her knees might give out.

"Do you think so?" He tore his gaze from Clarice's and looked down at Mary. "Ye should gae a' folk the hearin', ye ken?" he said in an accent so broad it was obviously exaggerated.

At the look on her daughter's face, Clarice laughed, then clapped a hand over her mouth. Surely laughter wasn't appropriate at a lord's wedding. She schooled her expression to be properly sober. "He means you should listen to people without passing judgment," she told Mary.

The man grinned, showing even white teeth. "I'm Cameron Leslie," he said. "Cousin of the bride." Shifting the baby to one arm, he reached for Clarice's hand. When he pressed his warm lips to the back, her breath caught and she thought she might swoon.

Clarice Bradford had never swooned.

"And you two must be the mother and daughter I've heard so much about, whose trials set Cainewood on the road to meet and woo my cousin Cait." She released her breath when he dropped her hand. "Though to hear Lord Cainewood's side of it," Mr. Leslie added with a jaunty wink, "it was Caithren who did the wooing."

Clarice couldn't help but smile. His cousin Caithren sounded like just what serious Lord Cainewood needed. "I'm Clarice Brad-ford," she said.

"It's pleased I am to meet you." He looked down when Mary tugged on one leg of his velvet breeches. "What is it, sweet?"

"Will you pick me up?"

"Mary!" Clarice frowned and set a hand on the girl's shoulder.

But the man handed the baby to Clarice, then reached down and swung her daughter into his arms. "Of course I'll hold you, princess." His eyes danced with pleasure. "She's charming," he told Clarice.

"I..." She cradled the sweet-smelling babe, at a loss for words. Mary was acting inappropriately forward, to the point of burrowing into the man's neck. And Clarice...

Clarice was *jealous*.

It was absurd. The planes of his face were clean-shaven, his skin flawless and...young. The man was incredibly young. Early twenties, she'd guess. She could see it in his complexion, the straightness of his lanky form, the angle of his head. This was not a man who had yet suffered the slings and arrows of life.

And Clarice was nearly thirty-two years old. Old enough to know she had no business lusting over a young man of any sort, let alone one dressed in the trappings of aristocracy.

She'd never lusted before, ever. It was quite a heady emotion.

Her daughter was clearly just as smitten.

Clarice startled out of her trance when the whine of bagpipes filled the quadrangle.

"That's our signal," Mr. Leslie said. "I expect I should fetch the bride."

When he set Mary on her feet, the girl reached up and firmly took his hand. "May I come with you?"

"Of course you may, princess."

"Princess," Mary breathed as they walked away. Bemused, Clarice smiled down at the cooing infant in her arms, vaguely wondering how she'd ended up holding a marquess's niece. And what she was supposed to do with her.

She glanced up to ask Mr. Leslie, but he was already too distant and Mary was happily chatting away. She wondered if perhaps she'd lost her daughter to this man.

Mary had always dreamed of being a princess.

〜

CAMERON LESLIE was known to be a wee bit quiet. A man of simple needs, he didn't want for much. But when he did find something he wanted, he generally got it.

At the moment he was wanting Clarice Bradford. Or his body was, at least. His head told him he couldn't come to that conclusion following a five-minute conversation.

Good Lord, he mused as he climbed the steps to his cousin's chamber, in all his twenty-four years he'd never found himself attracted to a woman as he was to Clarice. Her quiet dignity, her wholesome beauty, something in her large gray eyes. The way she so clearly adored her delightful daughter.

A pity his time here in England was so short. He'd like to get to know the lass, but he had less than a week before he needed to head home to Scotland.

Wondering how much persuading Clarice would take to spend some time with him, he knocked on his cousin's door and called through the sturdy oak to ask if she was ready.

When the door opened, his jaw dropped. "Cait?" Dressed for her wedding, she looked different from the girl he'd known since her birth. Unbound from its customary plaits, her dark blond hair, so much like his, hung straight and loose to her waist. She wore cosmetics and a sky-blue gown trimmed in silver lace. An English gown.

"Good Lord," he said. "Cait, you look lovely."

"Thank you." She smiled, her hazel eyes sparkling as she surveyed his own attire, a deep blue velvet suit that he'd borrowed from one of the groom's brothers. He suspected Caithren thought he looked as English as she. She aimed a curious glance at the wee lassie who still held his fingers gripped tight. "And who is this?"

"Her name is Mary, and she and her mother are special guests. She, uh, attached herself to me." Cam lifted his hand, and Mary's little hand came up with it. Though he gave a sheepish shrug, his heart swelled, warm and pleased. "She may be walking down the aisle with us."

Caithren knelt, her silk skirts pooling around her. "Good day," she said.

"Good day," Mary returned in a small, polite voice. "I am

pleased to meet you, my lady."

"I'm not—" Cait started.

"You'll be a lady within the hour," Cam interrupted with a teasing smile. "You may as well get used to it." He knew firsthand how difficult it was to adjust to a new station in life, having unexpectedly found himself to be a baronet after Caithren's brother died last month. He blew out a breath. "I, on the other hand, will never get used to being a sir."

"Aye, you will." Cait stood and linked her arm though his. "Shall we go?"

Bagpipe music swelled when they reached the double front doors and stepped out into the sunshine. It was a glorious day to be wed, the quadrangle redolent with the scent of newly-cut grass, the sky blue as Cait's gown and dotted with wee, puffy white clouds. Cameron's gaze swept the enormous castle's crenelated walls and the ancient keep while he mentally compared it to the tiny castle he'd recently inherited in Scotland. Beyond the timeworn tower, the grass grew high and untamed.

"Gudeman's croft," Caithren murmured.

"What is that?" Mary asked.

Cameron knelt down to her. "A place allowed to grow free as a shelter for brownies and fairies."

"Oh." Mary's eyes opened wide. "Do you know stories of brownies and fairies?"

"Many. But they'll have to wait for later." With his free hand, Cam ruffled her unruly curls, then he stood and faced Cait. "It's really the old tilting yard. Colin told me they don't groom it since it's long been in disuse."

"I knew that." Her lips curved in a soft smile as she scanned her new home. "Can you believe this place, Cam?"

He met her hazel eyes. "You always were meant to live in a castle, sweet Cait."

"Aye," she said, no doubt thinking of her family's tiny castle at home—Cameron's castle now. "But who'd have ever guessed it would be such an enormous, historic one...and in England?"

"You'll do fine." Though they'd always been inseparable and he would miss her terribly, Cam knew in his heart she belonged here at Cainewood with the marquess she'd come to love. He leaned to kiss her forehead, then looked up. "There's your man now."

When her gaze flew to her intended, her face lit at the sight of him. Suddenly Cameron ached for the security this tall, dark-haired man so clearly enjoyed—a woman to love and a place that truly felt like his own.

A family.

Now that Cait was staying here in England, Cameron felt very alone. A family would be comforting. With several bairns who would grow up and help him make the Leslie estate into everything he and Cait had always dreamed it could be.

Clarice walked over to take Mary by the hand. "It's time," she said gently, and reluctantly the wee lass released her grip on Cam. The girl looked over her shoulder, her blue eyes lingering on him as the woman led her away.

"Her mother?" Cait guessed.

"Aye. Her name is Clarice Bradford. You'll like her." Cameron's gaze followed the two as they walked toward the gatehouse on their way to Cainewood's private chapel. Clarice's rich brown hair gleamed beneath a pink-ribboned straw hat. Her pink dress was simple compared to those of Caithren and the other women, but it suited her perfectly.

Cameron was simple as well.

He turned to take Cait by both hands. "Are you ready?" he asked.

"More ready than I ever thought possible." Smiling at him, she squeezed his fingers. "You know, Mam always said it's better to marry over the midden than over the muir."

"I've heard that said, that it's wise to stick within your own circle." Unbidden, his gaze flicked over to Clarice. "But I'm not sure I believe it."

"I don't believe it, either." Caithren's own gaze trailed to her groom, waiting for her by the barbican. "I reckon even mothers are wrong sometimes."

∾

AVAILABLE NOW!
Learn more about *If You Dared to Love a Laird* at
www.LaurenRoyal.com

ENTER FOR A CHANCE TO WIN
a sterling silver replica of Caithren's emerald amulet!*

Visit the Contest page on Lauren's website
at www.LaurenRoyal.com
and answer a question to be
entered in the monthly drawing.

No purchase necessary. See complete rules on the site.

*Please note: Depending on when you enter, the prize may be another piece of jewelry associated with one of Lauren's books. The author reserves the right to discontinue this promotion at any time.

ABOUT LAUREN ROYAL

LAUREN ROYAL is a *New York Times* and *USA Today* bestselling author of humorous historical romance. Her "truly enchanting" novels have won many awards including *Booklist*'s "Top 10 Romance of the Year" and earned raves from reviewers including *Publishers Weekly*, who calls her "an impressive talent."

All of Lauren's books are complete, stand-alone stories, and yet they are also all connected—because they all feature her beloved "outrageously funny, loyal, compassionate, and unconventional" Chase family.

Lauren writes steamy historical romance on her own and sweet/clean historical romance with her daughter, Devon Royal. She lives in Southern California with her family, their constantly shedding cat, and a stupendous collection of fuzzy socks. When she's not busy writing, she enjoys singing along (off-key) to Hamilton, dancing (badly), and (wasting time) watching HGTV.

ACKNOWLEDGMENTS

∼

MY HEARTFELT THANKS:

To Joan Royal and Karen Nesbitt, for driving me all over England and stopping at every village and hamlet and pile of rocks without too many audible groans.

To Irm Jawor, for the book of Scottish granny sayings that inspired Cait's annoying—um, endearing—habit.

To Della Floyd, RN, for expert medical information.

To the UK contingent of the Opposite View e-mail list, for answering all my very off-topic questions.

To all the honorary Chase cousins in my Chase Family Readers Group, for their enthusiastic support.

And, last but certainly not least, to every reader who has ever written to me.

Thanks to one and all!

CONTACT INFORMATION

Lauren's Newsletter

littl.ink / LaurensNews

Facebook Readers Group

facebook.com / groups / ChaseFamilyReaders

Facebook Page

facebook.com / LaurenRoyal

Website

www.LaurenRoyal.com

CPSIA information can be obtained
at www.ICGtesting.com
Printed in the USA
LVHW112133180922
728699LV00017B/272

9 781634 691512